Melissa Murphy (signature)

THE FRESHMAN

THE FRESHMAN

MONICA MURPHY

Editor: Rebecca, Fairest Reviews Editing Services
Proofreader: Sarah at All Encompassing Books

PLAYLIST

"Pick Up Your Phone" - Hojean
"long story short" - Taylor Swift
"Futon" - Ula
"Just Friends" - Olivia O'Brien
"10 Freaky Girls" - Metro Boomin, 21 Savage
"My Favorite Part" - Mac Miller, Ariana Grande
"Dreamcatcher" - Metro Boomin, Swae Lee, Travis Scott
"Boredom" - Tyler, The Creator, Rex Orange County

Find the rest of **The Freshman's** Spotify playlist here:
https://spoti.fi/3cOjLas

ONE

THERE'S a pretty girl staring at me.

I pretend I don't notice, keeping my head down, my focus on the phone clutched in my hands. I'm absently scrolling through Instagram, bored out of my skull while stuck in the waiting area at the Range Rover dealership in San Francisco, dreading the upcoming visit with my dad. My parents divorced when I was twelve, and Dad up and disappeared, moving to San Francisco so he could be closer to his business.

And his then new mistress.

That mistress eventually turned into his second wife, she gave birth to twin girls almost two years ago, and Dad forgot all about me. Until I turned eighteen and he decided he wanted to take me under his wing and turn me into his new protégé. I've resisted as much as I can, but it's tough. He's persistent.

I haven't met my stepmom or my half-sisters yet, but that's all happening today.

Good times.

Not really looking forward to meeting the new fam, but

I was coming here anyway to get my car serviced. My father knew—I'm guessing the dealership informed him of the recall issue, and now here I am.

Yes, my father basically abandoned me, but he still gets me a new car once a year, which means this is my third car since I turned sixteen. Fucking ridiculous, right? He's a rich bastard and he spoils the hell out of me with materialistic things and plenty of cash, as if that might make up for his constant neglect over the last six years.

But anyway.

Fuck thinking about my dad. I'd rather focus on the girl.

As sly as possible, I slowly glance up, my gaze meeting hers for the quickest second before she dips her head, a tiny smile curving her lush pink lips. I look away, too, gazing through the window at the bright blue sky outside. Not a cloud in sight. It's still pretty early in the day. I rolled out of bed first thing in the morning and hopped in the car, driving straight here, cursing at the traffic the entire drive.

I'd never want to live in the Bay Area, I know that for certain. I'm used to our small town and the fresh mountain air. The complete lack of traffic. How everyone knows everyone else—

Wait. That's not such a great thing. When everyone knows each other, they're all up in your business. Like when your parents get a divorce. Or you and your girl break up seemingly out of nowhere.

That part sucks.

My gaze, once again, slides to the girl, like I can't help myself. She's sitting in an overstuffed chair across from me. Her teeth are sunk into her plump lower lip, her brows furrowed as she concentrates on whatever is happening on her phone. There's a white Chanel bag sitting by her side. Golden Goose shoes on her feet.

They're scuffed and kind of dirty, which is what they're supposed to look like, despite costing around five hundred bucks.

I don't get the appeal.

That I know these things is telling. Mom isn't around much, but when she is, she's got the jumbo Chanel, the multiple pairs of Golden Goose—she's trying to appear youthful, she says—and she's always dripping in Van Cleef jewelry. Mom is a self-proclaimed designer brand whore, and she stands out like a sore thumb in our small town during the winter months. In the summer when all the tourists descend, she fits right in. Mostly.

I check the pretty girl's wrist and yep, she's got a Van Cleef bracelet clasped around it. Of course she does.

This girl is from money. My mother would probably love her.

I check her out in bits and pieces. Long, tanned legs. Black shorts that ride up, showing off her sleek thighs. A plain white T-shirt that probably costs hundreds of dollars. A bunch of delicate gold chains around her neck, some unadorned, others with tiny charms and pendants. One is a string of scattered stars.

This girl is trendy AF.

I can tell she's still staring at her phone, occasionally tapping at it as if she's sending an urgent text, and I keep my gaze away from her face on purpose. I'm not ready to look at it again. Not yet. What if I'm wrong? What if she's not as hot as I first thought? Not like anything's going to happen anyway. She's some rich girl who probably lives in Pacific Heights or Nob Hill. For all I know she could be my dad's neighbor. She's probably a spoiled brat who'll make my life a living hell just for trying to talk to her.

Forget it.

I shift in my seat, holding back the sigh that wants to escape as I return my attention to Instagram.

"Car trouble?"

Her sweet voice makes my head jerk up to find she's already watching me, her blue eyes wide and questioning. I wasn't mistaken in my first assessment of her.

She's hot AF. I can't even tell you which feature of hers is the most prominent or is the prettiest. She's just flat-out gorgeous everywhere I look. I stare at her for a moment, caught up in the shape of her lips before I realize I need to stop looking like a dumb shit and actually say something.

"No. Brought it in to fix a recall issue and get my back windows tinted," I tell her, tilting my head to the side as I contemplate her. She watches me just as boldly, not backing down, not looking away or giggling or being overly coy and flirtatious. Seemingly nothing manufactured or phony about her, which I appreciate. I figured she *would* be phony, with her trendy clothes and expensive accessories.

Girls can't be trusted. They'll stomp all over your heart if you give it to them, and then walk away like you never mattered. Happened to me before. It's happened to me practically my entire life, and not just with girls. My ex-girlfriend left me because dance was more important to her than me. I try to show interest in other girls, but they all blow me off.

Then there's my family. Dad left me because new pussy was more important. Mom left me every week when I was in high school, out looking for someone new. Something better.

Better than her old life and her son.

"How about you?" I ask when she hasn't responded.

"The recall issue." She shifts her legs, uncrossing and then recrossing them, and my gaze drops, taking them in yet again. They're long and slender and conjure up all sorts of dirty thoughts. I wonder how tall she is. "My father wanted to buy me a new one but I've only had this one for six months. I thought that was a bit—excessive."

"Sounds like we might share the same father." Mine had mentioned something similar to me when I let him know about the recall notice. I told him that was ridiculous. I've only had the car for a couple of months.

Her brows shoot up. "I certainly hope not."

Huh. Is she flirting with me? I've been off girls since midway through senior year in high school so maybe I'm out of touch. Well, not *totally* off girls. I hooked up with a couple of Italian hotties when I went to Europe over the summer. I accompanied my mom to visit her family who still lives over there. My cousin Sergio would take me out every night, and we'd get blindingly drunk. I'd kissed a pretty Italian girl. I kissed quite a few. Felt them up. On the rare occasion, I'd even get a blow job.

I had a good time in Europe. The best part? No expectations, no strings attached. Plus, I'd never see them again.

"I don't have any long-lost siblings," she continues. "Though I wouldn't put it past my father if some turned up."

She smiles. I smile too.

"What's your name?" I ask her, because fuck it. If I can flirt with a girl at the Range Rover dealership to pass the time, I may as well go all in.

"Hayden." She tucks a strand of blonde hair behind her ear. I'm a sucker for a blonde. Always have been. "What's yours?"

"Tony." I offer up a closed-lipped smile.

She does the same.

"Well, Tony, are you in college?"

I nod. Squirm in my seat a little. This girl will lose interest when she finds out where I go. She probably attends Stanford. Or Berkeley. She's probably smart as hell and a complete overachiever. "Yeah. You?"

A little laugh escapes her, and it's a sweet, tinkling sound. "Yes. Where do you go?"

May as well be upfront. Again, this is all happening at a dealership in a city I don't live in. I've got nothing to lose. "Fresno State."

Her mouth pops open. "No way," she breathes, sitting up straighter, her hand going to her chest. "I do too!"

"You do not." I chuckle, shaking my head. She has to be playing me.

"I so do! They have a great liberal arts program. I want to be a teacher, much to my father's dismay." She laughs again, a little louder this time, but I see the hurt that flashes in her eyes.

She hates that her father is disappointed in her future career choice. I feel this. I really do.

"What about you? Why are you going to Fresno State?" she asks.

"I grew up near there." I shrug. "A lot of my friends chose Fresno State, so I did too." Not the greatest answer, but it's the truth.

I knew I wanted to go to college, but I never really wanted to go somewhere far, and I had no idea what I wanted to major in. I finally found my core group of friends in high school, so why would I want to leave that? Completely immature thought process, but fuck it. I like my comfort, and currently, I find comfort in my friends.

Family dumps you. Girls do too. Friends don't. Bros stick by you no matter what.

Thankfully, a few of my friends got into Fresno State, like I did. And I've made new friends too.

"What's your major?" Hayden asks, pulling me from my thoughts.

"Business." It was the most neutral major that appealed to me, and what do you know, it made my father happy when he found out. Not that I particularly want to, but eventually, I'm sure I'll be working alongside my father, cutting ruthless business deals and buying up real estate all over the Bay Area.

That's why I need to focus on having fun in college now, because all the fun is going to evaporate from my life in approximately four years. You're only in college once. I need to make the best of it.

"Do you know what you want to be when you grow up?" Her eyes are dancing when she asks the question, and I like how direct she is. How confident she seems.

This girl seems like she has her shit together. No "poor little rich girl" vibes coming from her.

"Not sure yet," I say with another shrug, slouching in my chair. Trying for nonchalance. Like it's no big deal that I'm having a conversation with the hottest girl I've met in a long ass time.

"Are you from around here then? No, wait, you said you grew up near Fresno." She frowns. "They have a small Range Rover dealer there. Why are you here?"

"Their service department is booked out for weeks, and I didn't want to wait any longer on the tinted windows." Dad bought me the Range Rover as a belated graduation gift, bestowing it upon me right before I started college. Considering the gorgeous and very expensive vehicle ends up sitting in a parking lot most of the time, baking under the hot sun, I quickly decided I needed all the windows tinted to help keep the inside cool.

"Ah, that makes sense. And while it's here, may as well get the recall work done, right?" I nod. She smiles. "I'm visiting my dad for the weekend. He wanted family time, as he calls it. His girlfriend is only seven years older than I am."

Hayden rolls her eyes and I can't help but laugh.

"My stepmom is thirty," I tell her with a chuckle.

"I don't understand why they always trade in for a newer model," she says. "Though my mom eventually did the same thing."

"My mom swears she'll never get married again. Says my father turned her against love," I say, hating the flash of sympathy I see reflected in Hayden's gaze.

Maybe I said too much.

"Love is for pussies," she says with confidence. An older woman sitting nearby shoots her a dirty look and the smile teasing the corners of Hayden's mouth makes me smile in return. She probably enjoyed shocking that old lady. "It's true and you know it."

"It is true." My ex-girlfriend Sophie stomped all over my heart and left it a bleeding mess right before she left our high school for good and went to a performing arts school up in the mountains near San Diego. Last I heard, she was in the dance program at USC, where my best friend Jake goes. He actually ran into her recently and called to tell me all about it.

Made me feel like shit, but I had to pretend his seeing Sophie didn't bother me. It sucks when you realize people always eventually leave you. Hell, in a way Jake did too, though of course he left to go play football for USC, and I don't blame him. We got a lot closer senior year and now he's gone. I've learned a lesson from all of this, one I'll never forget.

Everyone leaves.

"So you're spending your Saturday here at the dealer, huh?" she asks.

It's a bye week at home, so no football game tonight. Not like I'd get a chance to play anyway. I rarely do. "Yeah. Hasn't been too bad though."

She grins. I grin back.

"What are you doing afterwards?"

My smile fades. "I have a get-together thing my dad wants me to attend tonight."

That is the last thing I want to do. Especially now, when I have a much more interesting prospect sitting in front of me.

Her smile disappears too, replaced with a frown. "Yeah, you know, I have something too."

This hot girl was going to ask me out. I could feel it. And that gives me the confidence to ask, "Can I get your number? Maybe we can get together sometime in Fresno."

Can't believe I never noticed her on campus before, though I guess it's not a surprise. It's a huge campus. We all sort of seem to take the same general ed classes at the same time, though, but maybe her schedule is totally different because of her major.

"Sounds good." She lifts her phone and starts tapping. "Why don't you give me your number first."

I rattle it off and she types it in her phone. "I'll text you early next week."

I smile. "I'll hold you to it."

"Oh I will." Her eyes are sparkling.

I could stare at her all damn day.

We make small talk for a few minutes more, until one of

the service advisers enters the waiting room and approaches her, letting her know her car is ready. She rises to her feet, slinging her Chanel bag over her shoulder, and she stops by my chair. The service adviser waits for her nearby, his impatience obvious.

"It was nice meeting you, Tony." She touches me on the shoulder, very lightly.

I feel that touch sink all the way to my balls.

"Nice meeting you too, Hayden," I say, my voice even. I sound normal. I bet I even look normal.

Inside, I'm anything but. This girl is hot. Interesting. Confident. For the first time in a while, I'm intrigued.

I want more.

TWO

HAYDEN

"I MET A CUTE BOY TODAY," I tell my sixteen-year-old sister, Palmer.

Yes, we come from a wealthy family and we have snobbish masculine-sounding names given to us by our snobbish parents. It's such a cliché, but I can't help who I'm born to, or what name they gave me. It's also not our fault people see our names on a roster and automatically assume we're dudes.

Thanks, Mom and Dad.

"Really?" Palmer's sitting on her bed, foot planted on the mattress and knee bent, her chin practically resting on it as she paints her toenails a lurid green color. "What did he look like?"

"Tall." I didn't see him stand, but his legs were long so I'm assuming. "Black hair. Dark brown eyes. Full lips."

Kissable lips.

"What's his name?" Palmer asks, her gaze only for her feet as she continues painting her nails.

"Tony." He was more than cute. He was drop dead

gorgeous. Beautiful. Those eyes. The hair. The cheekbones. The jaw. The lips.

Oh God, the lips.

I was fully prepared and ready to ask him out, but then he mentioned he had plans, which reminded me I also have plans, and my entire mood was ruined.

"Tony what?"

"I don't know. I didn't ask."

"Where did you meet him? Oh shit," she whispers under her breath as she hurriedly sticks the brush back into the nail polish bottle and starts dabbing at her comforter. "I got polish on it."

"Lauri is going to kill you." That's Dad's girlfriend. Since she moved in a few months ago, she's taken Palmer under her wing and bought her all sorts of new crap to get on her good side. It sort of works. Palmer will gladly allow Lauri to completely redecorate her room with all new stuff, but she's still not a huge fan of her. We don't trust her, not yet.

Well, Dad does, but he's blinded by love or lust or whatever you want to call it.

"I know," she practically wails as she jumps off the bed and heads for her connecting bathroom. I plop down in a white fur covered chair and scroll through my phone, wishing I would've gotten Tony's social media info so I could look up his photos and stare at his face for a while.

Palmer rummages around in the bathroom before she comes back into her bedroom with a bottle of polish remover and a cotton ball clutched in her hand. "Hopefully this works," she says.

I watch as she tries to take out the bright green stain on the pristine white comforter. I don't know why she'd polish her nails on a white blanket, but when you're sixteen and everything's been handed to you your entire life, you don't think about those sorts of things.

I know I didn't. Not until I left for college and was living on my own. I still had an allowance, but I had to learn how to manage my money. At first it was hard. All I wanted to do was go out and spend it because that's what I was used to.

Now, I've gotten better. I'm still a spoiled rich girl, I can't deny it. Some people hate me solely for that reason, and there's nothing I can do to change their minds. But this spoiled rich girl still wants to become a teacher, and someday make a difference. Even if her father laughs at her and tells her she's wasting her time.

I love my dad, but sometimes he can be a real asshole.

"It's not coming out," Palmer says, her panicked gaze meeting mine. "Should I get more polish remover? Just dump it all over the stain?"

"I don't know." My sister and I look a lot alike. The only difference is I'm blonder—thanks to Rafael, my hairstylist—and she's taller. Palmer is an excellent volleyball player who hopes to snag a scholarship for college. Not that she needs the money—she just wants the prestige and glory of state championships and earning that scholarship.

I can't blame her. She's really good at what she does. While I'm over here wanting to change the world by teaching first graders.

I'm my father's biggest disgrace. Well, Palmer and I both are since we weren't born with penises dangling between our legs, but that's a whole other issue. He's probably going to have more babies with Lauri. Since the moment I arrived last night, she was talking about the renovations she wants to do to the house, and how she wants a nursery.

Our dad is fifty-two. I don't know how he feels about possibly being a father again, but I'm sure if she gives him boys, he won't complain.

"Look it up on Google," I suggest to my sister. She's still frantically scrubbing at the polish. Looks to me like she's not making any difference. She might be making it worse by just smearing it into the fabric even deeper.

She yanks the comforter off her bed, clutching the giant bundle to her chest. "I need to wash it."

"I'm sure it's dry clean only," I remind her.

"I don't care. I need to get this stain out." She hurries out of her bedroom and I follow after her, pausing in the hallway while she runs down the stairs, her footsteps so heavy and loud she sounds like a herd of elephants.

I don't bother stopping her or making another suggestion. Palmer will do whatever she wants because she's just that way. Same as me. I'm stubborn. So is Palmer. So is our father. One lovely trait we got from him.

I wander into my bedroom and flop onto the bed, grateful for my old, fluffy comforter Dad got me when I turned sixteen. We didn't go live with Mom in the divorce. She went back to New York, where she's from, and Palmer and I both balked when she tried to get us to go with her. We didn't want to leave our school, our friends. Dad hired a cutthroat attorney when they were fighting over us and money, and Mom didn't stand a chance. We used to go visit her, but once I graduated high school, I stopped going. So did Palmer. She refused to go if I wouldn't go with her.

Now we get Christmas and birthday cards in the mail, but that's about it. She's too busy traveling with her various lovers, spending my dad's money.

This is why I said 'love is for pussies' to Tony. I still can't believe those words dropped from my mouth to a guy I only just met. And I sort of felt bad for offending that woman sitting in the waiting area with us, but it was also incredibly liberating. To finally admit my feelings about love. Because that's really how I feel.

Love sucks.

My best friend Gracie says this is why I can't commit to guys. We've been in college for two years together, clicking right away when we were roommates in the dorms our freshman year. Talk about getting lucky. We're also both liberal arts majors, and we have a lot of classes together. We joke how miserable we would be if we hated each other.

Because we so would be.

I know Gracie's right. I don't like serious relationships because I never believe it'll work out. Look at my parents. The last three years they were together, they despised each other. The fighting was so out of control. Mom called the cops on Dad three times. Dad put Palmer and I into therapy. It was a mess.

Life is messy. Love is even messier. I like things clean and orderly. Pretty, even. Maybe that's why I was so drawn to Tony earlier. He is flat-out pretty.

Not that he's feminine. He's just the personification of male beauty. All that unruly black hair that fell into those dark, mysterious eyes. His sculpted lips. If my memory serves, he even had a tiny dent in his chin.

I bet it's kissable, that dent.

Suddenly feeling restless, I head downstairs to talk to Dad about what we're doing tonight.

"Country club dinner, Hay," is what he tells me when I find him in his study, sitting in front of his giant iMac and nursing what looks like a scotch on the rocks. "This evening I want to show off all my girls."

I make a face behind him, and somehow, he spots me. "Don't look like that. It'll be fun."

My gaze drifts, locking on the window where I can see my own reflection. I roll my eyes at myself and Dad smiles. He's watching the window too.

"I'm twenty years old," I remind him. "You don't need to show me off to your cronies."

"I show off Lauri and Palmer all the time. Since you're never around anymore, you're the one I want to show off the most." He smiles. Rattles the ice in his glass before he takes a sip, his gaze locking on mine in the window's reflection. "Despite the fact that you want to be a teacher."

I reach over and tug on the ends of his hair, making him yelp. "Being a teacher is a noble profession."

"Being a teacher is a thankless job. Snot-nosed kids hanging all over you all day and ungrateful parents complaining to you how you just don't understand Johnny when he bullies all the other kids." Dad shakes his head, setting his glass down before he whirls around in his office chair to face me. "All for approximately fifty thousand dollars a year, and that's if you're lucky. How are you going to live on a wage like that?"

"I know I won't be living around here." The housing market in San Francisco and the Bay Area is ridiculously expensive. "Besides, I have you to help me," I say smugly.

Deep down, I don't mean it. I want to survive on my own, without Daddy's money. I want to be independent, unlike my mother, who is still on Dad's bankroll despite the fact she hasn't been married to him for years.

I refuse to live that way. Before I marry a guy—*if* I ever marry one because my views on love don't romanticize that situation whatsoever—I want to make sure I'm completely independent and can take care of myself.

I don't need a man. Not now.

Not ever.

"Looks like I'll be cutting you off at twenty-one," he says lightly, but I can tell by the darkness of his eyes that he halfway means it.

"And I'm totally kidding." I cross my arms, feeling defensive. I should've never said I have him to help me. "I can make my own way."

He barks out a laugh, shaking his head. "Sure you can. You'll find some pretty boy at the country club tonight and end up marrying him. He'll be rich as hell thanks to his father, and you'll both be set for life. That's my prediction."

Anger makes my blood run hot and I drop my arms, clenching my hands into fists. "Absolutely not. I don't want to marry some rich, sexist asshole, especially because I don't plan on ever getting married."

"Uh huh." Dad's smug expression sort of makes me want to sock him in the face. "Just watch. I know how this goes."

"What's that supposed to mean?" I'm starting to get offended.

"Look at you, Hayden. I know plenty of men who have sons around your age. They'll take one look at you and ask me how we can hook you up with junior," he says.

"That's so gross." I wrinkle my nose. "I'm not an animal you can barter with for a deal."

"You'd be surprised how many mergers are made through marriage, still to this day." He raises a brow. "I've already got my sights set on someone for Palmer."

Yikes. That sounds awful. "Does Palmer know this?"

"She's aware."

That's all he says. *She's aware.*

Aware that our father has set her up with someone he

hopes she'll eventually marry? I wonder if he paid off the guy's dad? So freaking disgusting.

"I'm not going," I say firmly. "I'll head back to Fresno tonight."

I turn on my heel, ready to make my escape from his suddenly stifling office when I hear him speak.

"I wouldn't do that if I were you. I meant what I said about cutting you off."

His voice is sharp. A tone I haven't heard him use on me in a long time. Not since I was sixteen and snuck out of the house to go over to a boy's house for a party, where I got drunk. Oh, my dad was so pissed at me. I was grounded for weeks.

Totally worth it, though. I made out with Chad Radwell that night. He was eighteen and on the varsity baseball team.

I glance over my shoulder, hating how neutral my father's expression is. Innocent, despite the implied threat in his voice. I'm sure my emotions are written all over my face, because his softens, and his tone changes, turning almost cajoling.

"Come on, Hay. Do this for your dad. I'm not asking you to accept anyone's engagement offer tonight. Just—see if any of these boys you meet could have...potential."

"I don't live here."

"It doesn't matter. We live in a modern world. You could have Zoom dates," he suggests, a chuckle escaping him. "You could come home for the weekend. Lots of sons don't live here either. They're scattered all over the country, attending college. Working."

"I'm not interested in an old fart," I warn him, and now he flat out laughs.

"Of course you're not. I wouldn't pair you up with

anyone older than...thirty."

"Oh. So someone around Lauri's age then." That was probably a shitty thing to say, but come on.

It's the truth.

"Yes, exactly." His expression is now warm and inviting, and I feel myself start to soften as well. He does this sort of thing sometimes. Emotional blackmail. Bargaining chips to get what he wants.

It's frustrating.

"I don't have anything to wear," I say, which is the truth. I haven't been to the country club in a long time. It's something I avoid as much as possible.

"Go shopping. Take Palmer," he suggests, checking his Rolex. "You still have time. We won't leave for the club until six-thirty. Seven at the latest."

I'm not about to turn down a shopping trip. He knows me far too well. "You don't mind?"

He rises to his feet and stops directly in front of me, reaching out to gently clasp my upper arms and stare into my eyes. Sincere, warm Dad is replacing mean, cold Dad of a few minutes ago. "Of course, I don't mind. Get whatever you want. Dress. Shoes. New makeup. Jewelry. Whatever."

My mind races at the possibilities. I like to think I want to change the world as a teacher, one six-year-old at a time, but I also know the truth: sometimes, I'm a materialistic bitch who likes shopping at Chanel and Gucci.

I can't help it.

"I'll go get Palmer then," I say. He pulls me into a brief hug, and just before I break away, I rise up on my tiptoes and drop a kiss on his cheek. "Thank you, Daddy."

"You're welcome, pumpkin." He smiles, looking pleased. He just got his way.

But then again, so did I.

THREE

TONY

WE'RE at some fancy country club that is definitely not my scene, but Dad and his wife Helena seem to think this is the place to be on a Saturday night. Somehow they got my sizes right and someone went shopping for me before I arrived. Meaning, I'm entering the clubhouse with them wearing brand new black pants, a white button-down shirt and a black jacket, with a black tie currently strangling my neck.

"Gucci," Helena said when I walked out into the living room to meet them before we left the house. Her assessing gaze lingered, making me vaguely uncomfortable. "I picked it out myself."

I have the distinct feeling my new stepmom was checking me out.

I wait as my father talks to someone he knows, lots of fake laughter and hearty back slaps abound between them. Helena stands next to my father clad in a pale pink, sequined gown that seemed a bit over the top to me, but now looks perfectly in place once we got here. She's beautiful, I'll give her that.

But definitely not my type.

I realize quickly that this is a social event to show off how much money you have. It's like one giant flex. Women are dripping in diamonds and various other jewels, their perfectly made-up faces making me wonder what they look like when all the makeup's scrubbed off. The air is clogged with expensive cologne and perfume, practically suffocating me. Everyone is dressed perfectly, and oddly enough— everyone also looks the same.

It's kind of boring.

As we make our way through the room, I let my father introduce me to one guy after the other, and I forget their names as soon as Dad says them, only because there's so many of them that I can't keep up. I smile and nod, shake their hands and say repeatedly, "Nice to meet you, sir," with all the earnestness I can muster.

Ever the dutiful son to my neglectful dad.

Many of them ask if I'm going to follow in my father's footsteps and eventually work for him. He tells every one of them I'm a business major, his voice filled with pride, which seems to appease them. He never mentions where I go to school.

I suppose that's his one dirty secret in regards to me. I'm attending a public state university that has no prestige attached to it—at least in his eyes. Even though I play for a D1 football team, he doesn't mention that either. I suppose it opens him up to too many questions, ones he doesn't want to answer.

Like the fact that he doesn't come to watch the games.

So I remain quiet and nod and smile, bored out of my skull. The corners of my mouth actually ache from smiling too much, and my stomach is starting to growl. When I can finally escape, I make an attempt to order a beer from the bar and the bartender hands it over without hesitation.

I leave him a ten-dollar tip.

It's like some sort of meet and greet on steroids before we sit down to dinner and I don't know a soul in this place, so I find a dark corner to stand in and lean against the wall, checking my phone while I down the beer, finishing it off way too soon.

I'm going to need a lot of those to get through tonight.

"Here you go."

I glance up to find Helena standing in front of me, a fresh beer clutched in her hand and a smile on her face. She had to be spying on me to know what I was drinking, which is creepy, but I ignore the unease I feel and swipe the beer from her hand, careful not to graze her fingers with mine. "Thank you."

Her smile grows, and she shifts closer, her overpowering scent surrounding me. I cannot deny that when I first met Helena, I thought she was pretty. She's also only in her very early thirties, which probably makes her closer to my age than she is to my dad.

"Having fun?" She raises her brows, bringing her chilled glass of wine to her lips, carefully sipping it so she doesn't smear her lipstick.

I shrug, glancing around, uneasy. I don't want to make small talk with Helena. I barely know her. "Not really."

Her lips curve into a mock frown. "Aw. Why not?"

"I don't know anyone."

Her face brightens. "You know me."

"I guess. Shouldn't you be with your friends or whatever?" I'm not interested in a conversation with this woman. She's making me uncomfortable.

And I don't need any trouble.

"Every single one of the women in this room is a calculating bitch, including me." She takes another step closer, the skirt of her dress brushing against my legs. I'm trapped, the wall directly behind me. I can't move, and I'm pretty sure she knows it. "Besides, I'd rather try and get to know you better. I still can't believe we've never met until today."

"This is what happens when your husband abandons his oldest child," I tell her, taking another fortifying gulp of beer.

She scowls. "He didn't abandon you. Your mother kept you from him."

"Keep believing that." My tone is cryptic. We watch each other, yet she doesn't say a word. Neither do I.

Seems like Helena uses silence as a weapon, just like me.

After a couple sips of wine, her scowl slowly eases away. "You look exactly like your father, you know that?"

"Yeah. I guess."

She moves so her upper arm rubs against mine, the light glinting off the many sequins on the front of her dress nearly blinding me. She's like a walking pink disco ball. "You don't say much, do you?"

I slowly shake my head. Most of the time I keep quiet so I don't say anything stupid that could come back to haunt me. With this woman, I'm guessing she has a mind like a trap and would use my own words against me someday, if they worked in her favor.

Fuck that. I'd rather keep quiet and pretend she doesn't exist.

Her contemplative gaze locks with mine, a smile teasing at the corners of her lips. "I like you. Maybe someday we could—"

"Helena! There you are!" A platinum blonde woman rushes toward us in a cloud of sky blue ruffles, taking hold of Helena's arm before she turns her attention toward me. Her perfectly arched brows shoot up practically to her hairline. "Well, well, well, what do we have here? Already trading Anthony in for a younger model?"

I tense up, hating how this woman is regarding me like I'm a piece of meat.

Helena laughs, sounding uncomfortable. "Of course not, Lauri. This is my stepson, Tony."

"Your *stepson?* Oh my goodness." Lauri rests her hand against her chest, batting her eyelashes at me. "I'm so sorry. I totally put my foot in my mouth just now."

"It's cool. Nice to meet you." I raise my beer bottle in her direction, like I'm toasting her, just before I take a swig.

"We probably shouldn't be seen with each other," Helena says to Lauri, which makes me frown. What the hell is she talking about?

"You're right. So silly. Their rivalry is completely over the top." The women air kiss before Lauri returns her attention to me, wagging her fingers at me. "Nice meeting you, Tony. Call me next week and let's do lunch, love!" she says to Helena before she disappears as fast as she came.

"What was that all about?" I ask Helena once Lauri's gone.

"Oh, your father is making enemies as usual, including Lauri's fiancé." Helena's smile is mischievous. "Lauri and I have remained friends through it all thankfully, despite their hatred toward each other."

Huh. I know my dad has had some dirty dealings in the past. When I was younger, everyone figured we were mob, only because we're Italian. I always thought that was bullshit. But as I've gotten older and started to understand the way the world works, I've long suspected dear old dad has made some less than legal business transactions. He's in real estate—he buys large businesses for cheap and breaks them up, selling each individual piece of the business for far more than what he originally purchased it for.

In his type of business, he pisses people off. He underbids. Overbids. He's sneaky. I've done some research recently. Google is my friend, and there is all sorts of information out there in regards to my father. I've barely scratched the surface. Should I even contemplate working with him at all?

I don't know.

Helena goes on about her friendships with the various women in this place, and how my father has messed them up thanks to pissing off all their husbands. I'm only half listening to her, my gaze searching the crowd. Does it make me a shit human that I don't care about Helena's problems? They feel really trivial compared to the kind of lifestyle she leads. She doesn't have to worry about a thing. My dad is taking care of her financially, and she's locked him down for a while, thanks to having his children.

I'm sure she's pissed she didn't give him a boy.

A blonde girl in white suddenly enters the room, and she's swept up in someone's arms, her face averted, though I can hear her tinkling laugh from where I'm standing. Awareness settles over me, prickling my skin. She moves in a way that's familiar. I shift to the right, trying to catch sight of her face, and when she pulls away from the woman hugging her, I realize who it is.

Hayden from the Range Rover dealership.

Well, holy shit. Tonight just got a hell of a lot more interesting.

"I'll see you later," I tell Helena absently as I push past her, ignoring her when she calls after me.

I weave my way through the crowd, ignoring the smiles and the nodding heads as I pass them, these fake, plastic people acting like they know me when I'm a complete stranger. It's not until I'm standing directly behind her, breathing in her delicate scent, fascinated with the elegant tilt of her neck, the way her hair slides across her shoulder as she speaks animatedly to the woman standing in front of her, that I finally jolt myself out of my trance and say something.

"Hayden."

She glances over her shoulder, doing a double take. "Tony from the dealership? Is that you?"

I can't help but smile. Her voice is soft and lilting. Sweet sounding. Her eyes are wide and she's grinning at me like I'm the best thing she's seen in a long time.

I can't help but return her smile. "It's me." I hold my arms out. "In the flesh."

"And what pretty flesh you are," she murmurs.

I rear back a little, surprised at what she said. And she doesn't back down from it either. She just watches me, completely forgetting about the woman she was speaking to only a second ago. We stare at each other for a moment before I realize this is the perfect opportunity for me to check her out completely.

The white dress she's wearing should be criminal. It covers up a lot, yet reveals plenty too. It's short, showing off those killer legs. The ruffled skirt hem flirts with her slender thighs, and while the dress is long sleeved, it has this deep V-neck that shows off her cleavage perfectly.

I'm a leg man. I always have been. But Hayden's tits are absolute perfection.

"I didn't expect to see you here tonight," she says to me while I stand there gawking at her like an idiot.

"I didn't expect to see you either." I slip my hands in my pants' pockets, trying for casual. My blood is buzzing, racing through my veins at just having her this close. "Guess we both had the same plans."

"Guess so." She turns away from me, grabbing the hand of a girl wearing a dark blue dress and yanking her to her side. "This is my sister. Palmer."

"Nice to meet you." I shake her little sister's hand. She watches me with narrowed eyes, her lips parting, revealing the braces on her teeth. Definitely younger. She's blonde too, and her features are similar to Hayden's.

"Who are you again?" she asks me.

"Oh sorry. This is *Tony*." Hayden puts extra emphasis on my name, sending her sister a knowing look.

Hmm.

"Wait a minute. Range Rover Tony?" Palmer studies me carefully and I can't help but chuckle. "Hayden told me she thought you were cute."

"Palmer!" Hayden nudges her sister with her elbow.

"What? It's true! You're always telling me I should be truthful and never hold anything back." Palmer rubs at her side where her sister jabbed her. "It's no big deal that you think he's cute. From the way he's staring at you, I'm sure he thinks you're cute too."

Hayden glances over at me, her eyes lighting up when she catches me staring, just as her sister said.

"So you're talking about me to your sister, huh?" I ask Hayden, taking a step closer to her. I think of Helena and how she invaded my space only moments ago, and I hope like hell Hayden doesn't think I'm doing the same thing to her right now.

Clearly, she doesn't, thanks to her taking another step closer to me too. So close, our chests are almost brushing. I can smell her delectable scent even stronger now, and unlike all the other cloying fragrances filling the room, I can't help but inhale her like I'm some sort of junkie.

"I told my sister I thought you were cute," she says, her expression like a dare. "That's all."

"You think I'm cute."

"Cute is too common of a word for you, but yes. It'll suffice for now." Hayden smiles, showing off her straight, white teeth.

Damn. Everything about this girl is pretty. Perfect. She doesn't have nearly as much makeup on her face as all the other women who are here, and she definitely doesn't need it. That sexy white dress showcases her banging body to perfection. The scattered star necklace from earlier lays against her throat, a delicate spray of gold upon her smooth skin. I'm intrigued by that necklace.

I want to touch it. Trace it with my fingertips. See if I can make goosebumps rise.

The whine of a mic being turned on sounds over invisible loudspeakers, and the majority of the room gasps in response. It's followed by the tinkling of silverware against glass, and I turn to see a man standing on the stage in front of a podium, a fork in one hand and a wineglass in another. He taps the edge of the glass again with the fork, just before he announces into the mic, "Welcome everyone. Please do find your seats. Dinner will be served momentarily."

It's a free for all after that, and I watch Hayden be helplessly dragged away by her sister, still smiling while we continue to stare at each other. I'm tempted to go after her, but she turns away at the last second and follows after Palmer. I watch Hayden walk toward the other side of the room, my gaze dropping to the sway of her hips, the way the skirt flutters around the back of her thighs.

One wrong move and I could see her ass. That skirt is fuckin' short.

I like it.

"Tony! There you are." I turn to find my father striding toward me, a grim expression on his face. "Let's go sit down."

I follow him, grateful he's not trying to introduce me to anyone else. He's too determined to find our table. I don't even understand how anyone actually knows where they're supposed to be seated in this place, but I'm sure it's some country club secret I'm not privy to.

Whatever. This isn't my scene. And it probably never will be.

Once we find our table, I settle into the chair to the right of my Dad's. Helena appears soon after us, her cheeks flushed, clutching a full glass of wine. I'd guess she's had a few of those already, and Dad sends her a disapproving look. She ignores him, plopping into her seat and flipping her hair over her shoulder before she sets the glass down on the table.

"I saw you speaking to Lauri." The irritation in my father's voice is obvious.

Anger flashes in Helena's eyes. "I can still be friends with her. It's not my fault her boyfriend got the Kaminsky deal."

Guess she's not one to back down.

Dad glares. "I told you not to associate with their family."

"You cannot control who I talk to, Anthony. I'm not a child," Helena huffs, sounding exactly like a little kid. "Lauri is my friend. Can't really say that about any of the other women in this room, so I'm going to keep talking to her whenever I can get the chance."

"I don't trust her boyfriend."

"You shouldn't." Helena smiles. "I'm sure he'd love to get me alone and drill me about all of your secrets."

It's the way she says *get me alone and drill me* that has me raising my brows. Helena notices too. "Don't give me that look. I saw you openly flirting with Hayden Channing," she tosses out.

Dad whirls on me, anger flaring in his gaze. "You know Hayden?"

"I just met her at the dealership earlier—" I start, but he thrusts his finger in my face, his furious gaze meeting mine.

"Do *not* talk to her. You're not allowed to even *look* at her, do you hear me?"

I lean back to get away from his shaking finger. "What's the big deal? I don't even know her."

"Keep it that way." Dad growls, reaching for his drink and slamming it back until there's nothing left in the glass but ice.

I watch him, remaining quiet, wondering what the hell the Channing family did to him to make him so angry. Helena won't even look up from her phone. Dad suddenly stands and leaves the table, and I watch him make his way toward the nearest bar.

"Don't mind him."

I glance over at Helena. "He's pissed."

"He's always angry lately." She shrugs.

"What did Channing do to him?"

"According to your father, Brian Channing has stolen three deals from him, all within the last couple of months." Helena rolls her eyes. "I think he might be exaggerating though."

"Bad blood then?"

"Terrible blood. I've been friends with Brian Channing's girlfriend for a long time. Longer than I've been married to your father." She gestures at me with her wineglass in hand. "You met her. She's my friend, Lauri."

Wait a minute. Lauri, the platinum blonde, is with Hayden's dad? That's her father's girlfriend she was telling me about at the dealership?

"Got it." I try not to react, but this is wild.

I'm connected to Range Rover Hayden and I didn't even know it.

"You should probably avoid her. Hayden," she clarifies when I look at her strangely, "spending time with her will set your dad off."

"Not like he ever spends any time with me," I say with a little shrug. "What does it matter to him who I'm with or what I'm doing?"

"I'm being serious, Tony. Like your father said, Hayden is off-limits. I won't have you ruining my friendship with Lauri because you want to fuck Brian's whorish daughter," Helena retorts.

"Whorish? And who said I wanted to fuck her?"

The people sitting on the other side of the table are watching us with obvious interest. I have no idea who they are, but when I turn to glare at them, they look away quickly.

"You didn't have to say anything. I saw the way you looked at her." Helena smirks. "From what Lauri says, Hayden spreads her legs for pretty much anyone."

I seriously cannot believe what Helena is saying to me. Why is she being so crude? So damn disrespectful? "Do you have a grudge against her or something?"

"I'm just letting you know the truth. It's the least I can do for you, since you're my stepson." Her smile is brittle. "Just watching out for you, that's all."

Dad comes back with two glasses clutched in his hands, settling in his seat before he turns to Helena and starts whispering ferociously.

I ignore them, wishing I didn't have to deal with them.

But thanks to Hayden, this night keeps getting more and more interesting.

FOUR

HAYDEN

"WHAT WERE you doing talking to Tony Sorrento?" Dad asks me once he has me out on the dance floor.

Dinner was a painful affair of eating dry chicken and pretending to enjoy my father's friends' stories. They all talk about themselves and their successes and how much money they have. I know pretty much everyone at this country club tonight is rich and successful, but aren't we more than that? Shouldn't we be discussing world problems and what we can do about them, especially considering how much damn money everyone has?

But no. It's one big *my bank account is bigger than yours* bragfest at this table.

Some of them have sons who accompanied them tonight. They're all mildly attractive, I can't lie. One in particular is extraordinarily good looking. He's seated across from me and flashes a cocky smile in my direction every few minutes, as if he expects me to melt in my chair because he's looking at me. His father lists his stats as if he's a stud horse we might be interested in purchasing.

From the near salivating expression on my father's face when they were talking, I'm thinking I wasn't too far off the mark in my thoughts.

The stud in question is a lacrosse player. A senior at Harvard, pre-med. Wants to be a plastic surgeon like his father. Considering Lauri knows his father so well, I'm gathering he's the one who gave her the recently purchased fake boobs that are practically spilling out of her blue dress.

I glance down at my own chest, feeling flat compared to Lauri. I have nothing against breast implants. I get why a lot of women want or have them. But I don't think I want boobs so big they'll bust out of everything I wear if I'm not careful.

"Who is Tony Sorrento?" I ask my father. I am playing innocent, and assuming Range Rover Tony is who he's talking about.

And why *wouldn't* I talk to him? He's the hottest guy in this place, hands down.

Dad takes a deep breath, exhaling slowly as he whirls me around the dance floor. They actually have a live band playing, and the singer is crooning some ballad from the nineties, I think.

It's kind of awful.

"He's no good."

That's a very blanket statement, and it doesn't say much. Meaning he's probably never had a conversation with Tony before in his life. "You know him?"

"I know enough."

"So you know him personally? You two hang out? Golf buddies, maybe? At the very least, drinking buddies?" I prod further.

Irritation flits across his face. "No, I've never personally spoken to him."

Just what I thought. "Then how do you know he's no good? Making assumptions about people you don't know isn't fair," I tell him.

Anger makes the color rise in his cheeks. And my father is usually such a cool customer. Nothing rattles him—with the exception of my mother. And sometimes me. "His father is a complete asshole."

"Maybe he's nothing like his father."

"The apple never falls far from the tree," Dad points out, and I laugh.

"I'm nothing like you."

"You're more like me than you'd ever want to admit." He grins, his hand tightening around mine. Talking about himself always seems to please him. "Just—leave that kid alone. I didn't even know Sorrento had a son, let alone one that's about your age."

"Then how do you know who I was talking to?" My tone is innocent, but I'm trying to dig. I want to know exactly why my father feels this way toward the Sorrento family.

"I saw you speaking with him earlier and I asked who he was." Dad sends me a stern look. "Stay away from him."

Silly man. This makes me only want to talk to Tony more. Don't parents realize that? If the one you're interested in suddenly becomes forbidden, all you want is what you can't have.

My gaze starts scanning the room as I continue to dance with my father, but I don't spot Tony anywhere. It's also kind of dark since they dimmed the lights once the music started, so it's difficult to see.

"May I cut in?" asks a smooth, male voice.

I glance up to find it's the plastic surgeon's son, Joseph.

My father gets a huge smile on his face as he releases my hand, steering me toward him.

"Please do." Dad winks at me before he quickly exits the dance floor, leaving me with Joseph and no other choice but to dance with him.

He pulls me into his arms, holding me at a respectable distance before we start to move. He's smooth, I'll give him that. Wonder if he had cotillion lessons—I did. I was supposed to be a debutante, but I convinced my parents it wasn't for me. Both of them pushed hard, though. All that money spent on cotillion lessons for nothing? They were pissed. I'm sure they'll do the same to Palmer.

"I'm glad we finally get to meet," Joseph says after a few seconds of silently dancing.

"Me too," I say, a weak smile curving my lips.

"Your stepmom has told me a lot about you," he continues.

"She's not my stepmom," I correct.

"Oh. Well, your dad's girlfriend then. She's really sweet."

"Sure. Yes. She's okay, I suppose." I send him a curious look, not wanting to discuss Lauri with him. "Why aren't you at school right now?"

"Oh. I came home for the weekend. It's my father's birthday tomorrow." His hand shifts on my back, dropping lower. If he keeps going, it'll eventually be on my butt, and I won't stand for that. I barely know this dude.

"How nice. Is there a party?"

"Yes, tomorrow afternoon at our house." His face brightens. "You should come. Lauri and your father are both invited."

"Maybe I will, though I have to head back home tomorrow."

"Where do you live?"

"Fresno."

He makes a face. Everyone is so snobbish about Fresno. "Why?"

"I go to Fresno State."

"What's your major?"

"Liberal arts." He frowns at my response. "I want to be a teacher," I explain.

Joseph laughs. "Let me guess. For first graders?"

I don't know why his accurate guess irritates me, but it does. Maybe it's his mocking tone. The amusement in his gaze makes me think he's making fun of me.

"Sorry. I need to use the restroom." I withdraw from his arms before the song even ends and flee the dance floor, exiting the room as fast as I can. I find the hallway where the restrooms are and push my way into the ladies' room, hiding away in a stall so I don't have to look at anyone while I cool down.

Joseph seriously infuriated me. Why can't rich people have simple dreams? I could be anything I want, that's what my father always told me, ever since I was a little girl. So why does he balk at me being an elementary school teacher? And why does everyone else think it's a big joke?

I don't get it.

The bathroom door opens and I hear two females talking, their voices low, as if they're trying to keep it down.

"No one's in here," one of them says. Her voice is familiar.

"Are you sure?"

Oh shit. That voice is definitely familiar.

"Positive," the other woman says firmly. "Now hurry and tell me what's going on before someone comes in here and interrupts us."

"It's Joseph," says the more familiar voice. "He wants me to go to his father's party tomorrow."

"And why wouldn't you? They always throw the *best* parties."

"Because he'll try and make a move on me again. I know he will."

I cover my mouth with my hand, shock coursing through me. That's Lauri who's speaking. And she's claiming that Joseph—the guy I just danced with, Mr. Future Plastic Surgeon, is trying to make a move on her. When she's already with my father.

Ew.

"What's wrong with that? I mean, I know we're both with older men, but sometimes I really miss young dick." The other woman laughs.

"I know, though Brian doesn't lack, if you know what I mean."

Oh God, she's talking about my father. I do not want to hear this conversation. Not like I can reveal myself though, because then they'll know I heard it all.

"Anthony is so tired all the time, and when he drinks too much, he deflates."

"Can't get it up?"

"Yes, and then he passes out and snores so loudly, I go sleep in one of the guest bedrooms." A sigh escapes her. "What did you think of my new stepson?"

"A hottie," Lauri says firmly. "Tall, dark and mysterious."

"Right? Oh my God. He's *gorgeous*. And full of resentment toward Anthony. I wonder if he'd be willing to get back at his father by fucking his dad's wife behind his back."

The two women burst into laughter, and I realize the other woman is Tony's stepmom.

Double ew.

The door suddenly bangs open and a slew of chattering women enter. I wait it out a few more minutes, praying Laurie and Tony's stepmom have left, and by the time I exit the stall, I see the coast is clear. I hurriedly wash my hands and leave the bathroom, practically running down the corridor in hopes I can find my father and warn him that Lauri might be having an affair with someone my age when I come to a complete stop.

Joseph is closer to Lauri in age than my dad is. And she didn't flat out say she was involved with Joseph. More that he's always making moves on her. That's two very different things. Do I really want to open up this can of worms when I have no proof that anything's actually going on?

Not really.

Sighing, I turn and head for the outside patio to get some fresh air. There are other people out there too, most of them couples who are probably seeking privacy, but I won't stay long.

I just need to collect my thoughts first.

I'm heading toward the farthest right corner of the terrace when I spot him. Sitting on a chair all by himself, a cigarette dangling from his mouth. It's rare to see someone my age actually smoke a cigarette. Everyone I know vapes. And I'm not one to find smokers attractive. Smoking kills. It's the worst. A nasty habit.

But Tony Sorrento slouched in a chair in a full suit and a loosened tie around his neck with a cigarette between his full lips is something I cannot resist.

"Tony Sorrento."

He glances up when he hears his name, a faint smile curling his lips as he plucks the unlit cigarette from his lips. "Hayden Channing."

Hmm, someone mentioned me to him. "You know my last name."

He tips his head. "You know mine."

"My father told me," I admit.

"Same." He hesitates for only a moment. "My father hates your father."

"Mine hates yours too. I think they're mortal enemies." I take a few steps closer, so I'm standing directly in front of him. A breeze picks up, catching my skirt so the hem grazes his knees.

"Did yours forbid you from talking to me?" He raises a single dark brow, his expression questioning.

I burst out laughing. "No. Though he did call you, and I quote, 'bad news'."

"I've never met your father before in my life. He doesn't even know me," he says with a grimace.

"That's what I told him! How could he know you're bad news if he's never even met you?" I shake my head.

"Exactly. People are so judgmental." His gaze rakes over me, lingering on my chest for a little too long and making my skin warm. Guess he's not put off by my natural breasts. "Can I confess something to you?"

If he confesses he's attracted to me and wants to sneak away into a secret closet somewhere, I'm going to readily agree, no questions asked. "Sure," I say, my voice cool. Like he doesn't affect me whatsoever.

"Today is the first time I've seen my father in years," he admits. "We talk on the phone, or we text, but that's about it."

Oh. That's not even close to what I expected him to confess. Though he did mention he was seeing his father for the first time when we were at the dealership. "How long has it been?"

"Give or take six years," he says with a shrug.

"Really?" I practically squeak. When he nods, I continue, "If you haven't seen him, how did he get your cars to you?"

"He had them sent. He has everything sent. He sends me gifts in the mail. Deposits money in my account. Makes sure my mom and I have everything we need. When I moved out for college, he took care of my tuition, my living expenses, everything." He looks off in the distance, the breeze ruffling his dark hair. "He gives me everything but his time."

My heart pangs for him. I know what that feels like. "I assume he's busy."

"Yeah, with his new family," he mutters with seeming disgust. "Today is the first time I've met my stepmom too. Though she's not that much older than me."

Interesting. No wonder she acted like he was a brand-new toy for her to play with. "Guess it's been a big day for you then."

"Yeah. Sure." He shifts, digging through his front pocket before he pulls a lighter out, settling the cigarette between his lips before he brings the lighter to the end and lights it. He immediately blows out a hazy string of smoke and I can't help but frown. "I'm guessing you hate smoking."

"It's a dirty habit," I say without hesitation.

"I'm sure you've got a few." He sends me a knowing look.

Ooh. That was kind of hot.

"Wouldn't you like to know," I tease, hoping I sound sultry, though maybe my response is silly. I don't know.

He smiles, but says nothing, and his lack of response is unnerving. Look, men don't scare me. They never really have. I've always been a flirt. I can admit I like a guy's attention, but I don't need it twenty-four/seven. Yes, I had the typical relationships in high school, but once I got into college, I became selfish.

Who needs a relationship? Not me. I'm too young. I'd rather be free. Look what happens when people fall in love and get married?

They lie. They cheat on each other. They fight. They get divorced.

No thanks.

That's why I always keep it light. I don't let men intimidate me or push me into something I'm not interested in.

This guy, though? He leaves me on edge. Worse, he makes me curious, and I don't quite understand why. Maybe it's the intense way he's watching me right now. Smoking is gross. I've never understood the appeal, but I'm kind of attracted to the way he keeps putting that cigarette in his mouth, his lips pursed the slightest bit before he pulls it away and exhales.

It's—oh God, I can't believe I'm thinking this—sexy.

"Why do you smoke anyway?" I ask, sounding annoyed. I clear my throat, hoping he didn't notice.

"I only do it when I'm stressed," he answers.

I'm frowning. "You're stressed out right now?"

"Fuck yeah I am." He grimaces. Scrubs a hand along his jaw. "Sorry. It's a lot, having to deal with my dad and his new family and being at this stupid party or whatever the hell you want to call it. Wearing a Gucci suit and acting like a man for my father's sake, when I feel like a kid playing dress up."

Aw. This is an incredibly honest moment we're sharing, and that was such a vulnerable thing to admit. Unable to stop myself, I go to the chair next to his and sit on the edge of the cushion, turning my body toward his.

"Would it make you feel any better if I told you that you look good in the Gucci suit?" I ask him, my voice light. A little flirty.

I'm trying to shift the mood. We don't need to get serious right now. I don't do serious. Not really. Serious means something, and right now I'm looking for...

Nothing. Just a little fun.

He smooths his long fingers along the jacket's lapel, and I get the sudden image of him trailing those fingers on my skin. "I guess the Gucci suit paid off then."

I laugh. He chuckles.

We stare.

And it doesn't even feel uncomfortable. Not one freakin' bit.

"I'm not supposed to like you," I admit softly.

"Back at you." His eyes crinkle at the corners when he faintly smiles, and I exhale softly at his confession.

"But I do," I whisper.

He slowly leans forward, stubbing the cigarette out in the ashtray on the table in front of us. I didn't even notice it, I'm so hyperfocused on him. He's so close, he could touch my thigh. My hip.

Tony Sorrento could touch me wherever he wanted to.

"Want to get out of here?" he asks, his gravelly low voice twisting me up inside.

I'm startled by his question. "And go where?"

"I don't know. Did you drive your car?"

I slowly shake my head.

"Me either." His expression is pure frustration.

"We can get an Uber," I suggest.

His lips curl into this beautiful smile that takes my breath away. "I like the way you think."

"Your father won't be mad if you leave early?" I ask.

"Like I care. He hasn't seen me for years. He has no room to talk," Tony says, his voice filled with disdain.

I can't blame him for feeling that way. It must hurt, not having his father around, though I can also relate since I rarely see my mother anymore. Why do wealthy, busy parents think it's okay to buy our love with materialistic things, and believe that's going to be a good enough replacement for them?

It's not. I don't refuse my father's gifts, but sometimes, I wish he would just show up. Especially when I was younger. I played volleyball in high school too, though I was never as good as Palmer, and I begged for him to come to my games. Just one during the season, that's all I wanted. So many dedicated parents came to every single game, cheering their children on, forming a bond that was cool to see. One I appreciated more than any of the other girls on my team because, to them, their parents just showed up. To them, their parents becoming friends with the other parents was normal.

For me? I was lucky my dad showed up to two games the entirety of my high school career. Two out of what felt like a billion. That's it. And he spent the majority of the time during both games on his phone and rarely watched me play.

Once I graduated, it felt like a breath of fresh air, getting away from my father. Distance helped the resentment I was feeling toward him lessen.

Earlier this afternoon, though, it all came back. I know the real reason he wanted me to go to this dinner. To show me off. To pair me up with someone. As if I'm for sale.

"Will your father be mad if you bailed out?" Tony asks.

I slowly shake my head, though I'm really not so sure. "He'll understand."

If he knew I was about to hop into an Uber with Tony Sorrento, son of his supposed mortal enemy, he wouldn't understand whatsoever. He'd be freaking livid.

Guess that's the chance I'm going to have to take.

FIVE

TONY

WE'RE in the back seat of a black Mercedes SUV. Bougie Hayden wouldn't settle for less, despite me saying we'd get to where we wanted to go whether we were in the back of a Prius or a Mercedes. We didn't need an Uber X.

She claimed it made her feel safe, so I went along with her decision. Besides, I'm not the one paying, not that money matters. Not to me. I don't think it matters much to Hayden either.

Two rich kids not really giving a shit about anything, that's who we are.

I have to admit though, this car is sleek as fuck. The driver barely looks at us and murmurs only a couple of words to Hayden when she speaks with him after he arrives at the front of the country club where we're waiting for him. When we slip into the vehicle, we sink into soft, comfortable leather seats. Chilled bottles of water sit in the center console between us, and there are even a couple of chocolate mints left for us as well.

"Nice," I say to Hayden when the car pulls away from the curb, the engine purring.

She smiles at me and grabs the bottle of water closest to her, undoing the top and taking a sip. I watch her, entranced with the elegant length of her neck as she tips her head back, the string of stars that lies at the base of her throat. Her skin is smooth, all the way down to the center of the V-neckline of her dress, and I wonder if she has a bra on.

I'm going to guess no.

"I'm not usually so impulsive," Hayden says, swiveling her head in my direction. I meet her gaze, see the excitement sparkling in her eyes. "This is a total moment for me."

Not sure if I believe her. She seems like the impulsive type. Up for anything. "You going to tell me where we're going yet?"

A smile spreads across her face as she slowly shakes her head. "No. It's a surprise."

"I don't really like surprises." The ones I've dealt with through most of my life have all been bad news.

"You'll like this one. Promise."

We make our way out of the city, taking the Bay Bridge over into Oakland, but I don't say anything about it. I'm just along for the ride, though my curiosity grows. We make small talk, chatting about everything and nothing, and when we go silent, we both stare out our windows. The silence doesn't feel awkward or uncomfortable though, especially since we don't know each other very well. I sneak glances at her when I can, amazed at how pretty she is. Amazed that she chose to leave with me, when she doesn't even know me.

I still don't understand exactly what came over me earlier, making the suggestion to her that we leave, but I don't regret it. That dinner was a nightmare. Dad showing me off to his friends. Helena and her disturbingly hungry gaze when I'd catch her watching me. I know she was talking about me with her friend, like she thinks I'm hot or something, and that's just beyond strange.

I have zero interest in fucking my dad's wife.

Must admit, knowing that Hayden's dad doesn't approve of me makes me want to spend even more time with her. Is that why I suggested we leave together?

Nah, it's more than that. I'm attracted to this girl. I don't know much about her, but I like her. Guess she likes me too.

The car finally stops on top of a hill, right in the middle of a residential area, and Hayden jumps out of the car with a cheery thank you for the driver. I exit the car as well, glancing around, a strong breeze hitting me hard and blowing my jacket open. I press my arm against it, shivering against the coolness that accompanies the wind and Hayden laughs as she approaches me.

"Colder than I thought it would be out here," she says.

My gaze drops to the front of her dress, her nipples poking against the fabric. Yep, just as I suspected.

No bra.

"Where the hell are we?" I ask her.

She stops directly in front of me, ignoring my question. "Come on."

I let her take my hand and I follow behind her, just enough distance between us that I can watch the sway of her hips as she walks. The way she moves hypnotizes me, and I'm hit with the temptation to slip my hand beneath her skirt and touch the top of her silky smooth thigh. To slide my fingers into the front of her dress and see what I encounter. To kiss those smirking lips.

But it probably wouldn't be too smart to make a move on her when we're the only two people outside this time of night. She'd probably scream bloody murder and call 9-1-1.

If she's smart, she would. She doesn't know me. I could be anyone.

"Here we go," she sing-songs as a church looms ahead of us, the parking lot surrounding it completely empty. She tugs on my hand. "It's around back."

"What's around back?" I ask, picking up my pace so I can walk beside her.

"You'll see," she says mysteriously.

We make our way around the giant parking lot to the back of the building, coming upon a kiddie park. As in, it's a fenced-off area filled with all those plastic houses and slides we used to play on when we were little. There's also a tall, faded yellow and blue plastic jungle gym with slides coming out on either side and a fake rock wall in the front. Hayden stops in front of it, drops my hand and calls, "Follow me!"

Then she proceeds to scramble her way up the slide, her sandaled feet scrambling, her skirt flapping up and showing off a fair amount of her perfect ass.

I just stare and laugh. "What the hell are you doing?"

"Come up here with me!" She's standing in the fort part in the center of the structure, a domed blue roof over her head.

I cup my hands around my mouth and yell, "I'm too tall."

She rests her hands on her hips and rolls her eyes. "No, you're not. Get up here."

Giving in, I climb up the other slide that isn't as steep, my brand-new Gucci shoes slipping on the surface. I send myself sprawling, almost faceplanting into the slide as Hayden just laughs.

"You can do it!" she encourages.

I glare at her and, with all my strength, shoot myself up

the kiddie slide, duck through the tunnel and find myself in the fort with Hayden. I rise to my feet slowly, worried I'll hurt myself, but the roof clears my head.

"See? Not so tall." She grins up at me, reaching out to touch my cheek. Her fingers burn my skin, rendering my mouth dry. "Look that way." She curls her fingers around my chin, gently turning my head and my breath catches in my throat at the view.

The entire city of San Francisco is spread out before us, a twinkling, glittery cityscape view from behind an unassuming old church in a neighborhood in Oakland. "I would charge money for this view," I breathe as I take it all in.

"Right? We used to come to this church when I was really small, when we lived nearby," she explains.

I glance over at her. "You used to live in Oakland?"

"Berkeley. A long, long time ago, when I was little, before my dad made all his money." Her smile is small. Even a little sad. "He told us he used to go to this church when he was a kid, so he brought us all here a lot. Said it made him feel young again, going to church here. I found out later this was right around the time my mom caught him cheating with his assistant. She told me he went to repent, though it's not a Catholic church, so whatever. I was so young, I didn't understand. I had no idea what she was talking about. I only figured it all out when I got older." A sigh leaves her and she takes a step forward, her hands gripping the waist-high wall in front of her, her gaze for the view only. "My parents' marriage was really fucked-up."

I go to stand next to her, my arm brushing hers. Sparks catch at first touch, warming my skin, but I try to play it cool. "My parents' marriage was fucked-up too. They fought a lot."

"Same with mine. A couple of years ago, I had a flash of

a memory of this church and Palmer and I drove all over this neighborhood, searching for it. We got so lost." She laughs, and shakes her head. "I found it by accident."

"Why didn't you ask Siri?" I'm teasing her, and she smiles.

"I didn't even know what the church was called. Plus, it was kind of fun, driving aimlessly, no one telling us where to go or what to do. Getting lost together. Palmer and I laughed and laughed the entire time. She got so mad at me, because she had to pee, and there was nowhere she could go. No bathrooms anywhere, no stores to go into, or open fast-food places around. She ended up squatting behind that tree over there." She points to a giant oak nearby. "And she admitted to me later that seeing the view was worth her nearly peeing her pants."

I rest my hands on the wall in front of us, my right hand close to her left one. I could hear the warm affection Hayden has for her sister, and I'm a little jealous. There's no one I care about like that beyond my friends, and if I were ever to admit that to any one of those assholes, they'd probably make fun of me. I mean, I took my mom's cat with me when I moved out of the house, and I love that little fucker too, but come on. It's a cat.

"You really love your sister," I say.

The barest smile curves her lips. "I do."

"I have no siblings." I pause, realization dawning. "Wait. I'm lying. Helena and my dad have twin girls."

"London and Paris." Hayden glances up at me to find I'm already looking at her. I don't know how she can keep a straight face, saying those names out loud. Together. "They're adorable."

"Those are the stupidest fucking names I've ever heard in my life," I mutter.

She bursts out laughing, the tinkling sound making my gut twist, and not unpleasantly. "They really are adorable, though."

"They are pretty cute," I agree. "But their names?"

"Ridiculous."

"They're not even Italian," I say with light disgust. How did Helena convince my dad to go along with that? Because I know he didn't come up with those names. No way. That's all Helena's doing.

"Oh, so if you have kids, their names have to be Italian? Like Rocco and Lorenzo and Rosa?"

"More like Claudia and Francesca and Vincent," I say, thinking of my cousins with those exact names. "Not going to worry about it though, because I'm never having kids."

"You're not?" Funny how she doesn't sound surprised.

I shake my head. "I don't want to be a father. Don't plan on ever getting married either. Love is for pussies, remember?" I smile down at her.

She scoots a little closer, and I can feel the heat from her body emanating toward me. "You know I feel the same way about love. And I don't ever want to get married either."

"Being married is like being in prison," I say, my voice fierce because I mean it. Look at what marriage did to my parents. Now they hate each other. Dad's all in love with Helena, but that'll fall apart eventually. Look at how easily she's pursuing me when she's barely been married to my dad for two years.

Fuck love. Fuck marriage. Fuck it all.

"Being in a relationship is basically like prison too," she adds. "Friends come and go. Family is forever, even if you want to shoot most of them." I laugh at that. "Why put yourself in a long-term relationship when you know, eventually, you'll just be miserable? It's too much pressure. Too many expectations."

Damn, it's like this girl set up shop and is now residing in my brain. She's saying all of the things I feel, and I've never met a girl before who thinks like this.

Thinks like *me*.

"Totally agree. I'd rather be alone than in a relationship." I slide my hand closer to hers, settling two of my fingers over two of hers. "I like you, Channing."

"I like you too, Sorrento." She hip checks me, and I stumble like a dumbass, my hand slipping away from hers. "But we're not about to embark on anything, you know what I mean?"

I'm frowning. "No. Explain."

She turns to the side, toward me, and my gaze drops to her chest. All that exposed skin. Her nipples beaded little points beneath the thin white fabric of her dress. My mouth waters at the idea of seeing her exposed tits, and I'm about to reach for her waist when she takes a step backwards, as if she knows exactly what I was going to do next.

The disappointment that crashes through me is undeniable.

"We have chemistry." Her voice is low. Sexy. I lean in closer so I can hear her better. "I can feel it. I know you can feel it too. For one, you can't stop staring at my chest."

Busted. I lift my gaze to hers to see her eyes are full of amusement. "Sorry."

"Don't apologize. I can't stop staring at you either. You're extremely good looking," she admits.

I stand a little taller, pleased by her words, and nearly hit myself on the plastic roof. "You're fucking gorgeous."

"Thank you," she says with a laugh, shaking her head. "But I think it's best if we remain friends only."

What the hell? "Why?"

"I like you too much. I think this could be a great friendship. And sex only gets in the way." She turns to look at the view once more, but I'm too stuck on staring at her, absorbing her words.

"What do you mean, sex only gets in the way?" I sound like a dumbass, but maybe my brain is too clouded over with lust and I can't really focus on the friend part.

"It'll ruin everything. Mess with our heads, trick us into thinking we're capable of having a casual thing, when, deep down, we know our feelings will eventually take over everything else. We'll fall in love, we'll be the golden couple on campus, and then we'll slowly but surely start to resent each other. Until eventually, it'll turn into a giant nightmare and we'll get into horrific screaming matches in public. Our friends will secretly place bets on when we'll end things, and some of them will beg us to do it because they're so sick of our shit. It'll turn into this monotonous pattern of fighting and fucking, until eventually, we break up."

I gape at her, struck dumb by her explanation, her vision. All of it. What she says sounds kind of hot, but also really messed up. "How much exactly did you have to drink tonight?"

She laughs and laughs. "Not a drop. You're just shocked by what I said because, deep down, you know that's a fairly accurate assessment of what could happen."

"I have no idea what would happen between us. I can't see into the future."

"I can. I don't even need a crystal ball." She sends me an amused look.

"Look, I had zero plans to take this beyond a casual hookup." Unable to stop myself, I reach out, drifting my fingers down her arm. Goosebumps rise at my touch, pleasing me. Look at how responsive she is, and I'm barely touching her. "Possibly turning into friends with benefits."

"Is that offer supposed to flatter me?"

I drop my hand from her arm. "I don't know. Did I offend you?"

"Not really, but that's not how it's going to work for us, Sorrento. Like I said, I like you too much. We like each other too much."

"I barely know you," I practically scoff.

"You want to know more."

She's not wrong, damn it. "I can keep this casual."

"Really?" She arches a brow and takes a step back, reaching for the tie at her waist. "So if I were to strip down right now, drop to my knees and give you a blow job, you'd let me walk away after I let you come in my mouth?"

Jesus fucking Christ, hell yes, is what I'm dying to say.

Instead, something else comes out of my mouth.

"I'd worry about you. How would you get home?"

"That's *my* problem. We're strictly casual, remember?" Hayden slowly undoes the tie, her top loosening, offering me a glimpse of the swell of her breasts. "What if I told you I'm a big girl and I don't need a man to help me get home?"

I scrub a hand over my face, trying to sort through my suddenly chaotic thoughts. The top of her dress is completely loose now, that V neck open wide, the edges literally catching on her nipples. It's a complete tease of a view, showing me something, but not everything. "You'd be all alone on a Saturday night in an unfamiliar neighborhood. That's dangerous."

"Like I am right now? All alone with you? In an unfamiliar neighborhood? Are you dangerous, Tony?" She reaches beneath her skirt, hands going to her hips before she starts to tug downward. Next thing I know, her panties have fallen to her knees and she holds onto the blue wall, carefully stepping out of them, until they're nothing more but a crush of sheer nude lace crumpled in her hand. "You could take total advantage of me right now, if you wanted to. I could scream and scream, and no one would hear me. Even if they did, they'd brush it off. Believe someone else would call the cops, because no one ever wants to get involved. You could have your way with me all night out here, and I couldn't do a thing to stop you."

My body goes stiff, and not in the good way. I'm both turned on and disgusted by what she just said. "I would never do that to you."

"See? You're proving my point." She shifts closer, smacking her hand against my chest, her panties pressed against my shirt. She removes her hand, leaving the panties to fall and I catch them, clutching them in my palm. "If this was casual between us, you would readily agree to all of that. You wouldn't care what I thought about you, and you definitely wouldn't worry about me getting hurt either. You'd be too focused on the fact that my tits are practically hanging out, and I just took off my thong, and I offered to give you a free blowjob. That's all that would matter."

I blink at her, hating that she's right. I barely know her, yet I don't want to treat her like that. I respect her too damn much.

I respect women in general too damn much.

"Shit," I moan, hanging my head back, and she laughs some more. My agony must really crack her up.

"Don't feel so bad. You're one of the good guys. I knew it the moment I met you."

"Really?"

She nods, smug as hell with her confidence. "Definitely. So while I'm sure it would be *amazing* between us, and I'd probably rock your world, we can never go there. You wouldn't be able to walk away from me."

Now it's my turn to laugh. "You really think so?"

"Oh, I know so. I can see it in your big brown eyes, which are very beautiful, I might add. Everything that makes up your face is worthy of a magazine cover. Or a romance book cover. Do you read romances, Tony?"

"Fuck no," I immediately say.

"You should. You might learn a thing or two. Anyway, what was I saying? Oh, I know. You're a good guy, and you're attracted to me, and I can admit I'm attracted to you, but it would never work, because we share the same views when it comes to relationships, and it's that relationships suck. So we're just going to have to be friends. That's it. End of story." She looks toward the view one more time, her hands going to the fabric belt at the front of her dress, redoing it so the fabric covers her breasts once more. "You weren't even tempted when I had my tits out."

I was so fucking tempted. But I don't say so. Instead, I shove my hand into my pants' pocket, stashing her panties there. I'm keeping them. Maybe that makes me a perv, but I don't give a shit.

"I'm more of a leg man," I tell her, which is the truth.

Her lips curve. "Should we get out of here?"

"How are we getting home?"

"Uber, duh." She whips her phone out of the pocket of her dress and starts tapping. "They'll be here in ten minutes. Wanna make a bet it's the same car that dropped us off?"

Before I can say anything, she's gone, sliding down the slide, hands clutching her skirt since she got rid of her panties, screaming as she goes. I watch her, fascinated with the way she dances across the grass, skipping and turning as she opens the little gate of the playground and turns to look at me, waving her hand.

"Let's go, Sorrento!"

I go down the slide as well, making my way toward her. She runs ahead of me, her skirt swaying, her laughter infectious. I can't help but smile, despite the feeling that I lost something tonight.

Pretty sure I lost my chance at her.

She turns, walking backwards, pointing at me. "Swear we'll find each other on campus."

"I swear." I hold my hand up, wishing I had a stack of Bibles.

"You won't blow me off because I wouldn't blow you?" A giggle escapes her, and I wonder if she's drunk.

But she told me she didn't drink tonight so...

"I won't. Promise." And I don't promise shit to anyone.

"See? One of the good ones. You can keep my panties as a souvenir, Sorrento, so you won't ever forget this night."

Even without the lacy souvenir, I know I won't forget this night.

Ever.

SIX

HAYDEN

I WAKE UP SLOWLY, like the sun rising. Little fingers of light. A tease of color, a splash of dawn. The sky grows brighter, brighter, until finally, there is a giant ball of blinding white shining in your eyes and it hurts to look at it.

That's me. My eyes crack open into tiny slits. I can't see anything. Slowly they open, until my teenage room comes into full view, and the sun shines through the filmy curtains, casting the room in too much brightness.

My head aches and I blindly reach for my phone where it rests on my bedside table. I check the time. 11:47 a.m.

Shit.

Sitting up, I push my hair out of my face and glance around the room, my phone still clutched in my right hand. I think of what happened last night with Tony, and I inwardly groan.

What was I thinking, throwing myself at him like I did? Undoing the top of my dress like I did? My confidence bordered on stupidity.

He probably thinks I'm obnoxious. Ridiculous. Worse?

A cock tease.

I check my phone to take my mind off what I did. There are Snaps from Gracie, my roommate. She sent me multiple images from last night, where she was at some party, solo cup clutched in hand, giant smile on her face, pretty boy standing by her side, his heavy-lidded eyes trained solely on her.

I envy her ability to chase after men, to immediately fall in love with them, and pick up the pieces so quickly when they abandon her. I'm not built like her. I used to be grateful for that. She felt too much, I always told her, and she readily agreed.

I don't feel enough at all.

I'm all bravado and bullshit. Just like my father. He should've never told me to stay away from Tony Sorrento.

Now all I want to do is see him again. Talk to him again. Maybe let him actually touch me.

A shiver steals over me at the thought.

There's a rapid knock on my door and then Palmer is slipping in, fully dressed and looking ready to go somewhere.

"You're still in bed," she says accusingly.

I flop back on the pillows, my head sinking in downy softness. "So? It's Sunday."

"Dad wants to go have brunch at the Whitmore." A fancy hotel in downtown San Francisco that was once a mansion that belonged to one of the richest families on the West Coast. "He already left with Lauri. I said you'd drive us there."

"I'm not ready." I cover my face with my hands, thinking of eating quiche and French Brioche toast while sipping a mimosa, seeing people I know at the other tables. Dad preening, going on about his girls, his gaze locked on Lauri.

No thank you.

"Well get ready." Palmer swats my comforter-covered feet. "Hurry."

I leave it to my baby sister to pick out an outfit while I get ready. I took a shower last night after I got home, so that chore is thankfully eliminated. I throw on some makeup. Palmer curls my hair.

We're out of the house in less than twenty minutes. A miracle.

Traffic somehow works in our favor and by the time we breeze into the hotel restaurant, I can tell Dad and Lauri have only just begun eating. When he spots us, his eyes light up and he rises to his feet, dropping his white cloth napkin on top of the table.

"There are my girls," he says in greeting and we go to him. Palmer hugs him and kisses his cheek like an enthusiastic puppy. My greeting is cooler. More refined. I'm still a little miffed at his treatment yesterday, and I want him to know it.

Lauri watches all of this with thinly veiled disgust on her face. She doesn't understand the dog and pony show of Sunday brunch, though she's definitely caught on to the rich flaunt of Saturday night dinner at the club. If she sticks around long enough and has children with my father, she'll eventually get it.

Maybe. Sometimes I wonder about Lauri. Especially now that I know Joseph, the plastic surgeon's son is trying to get into her panties.

Gross.

Daddy sends us to the buffet and we grab our plates, walking among the many tables laden with food. This isn't your typical all-you-can-eat buffet you find in middle America. The only thing I can compare this to is the Sunday brunch at The Ritz in Paris. There are no congealed eggs in a giant vat being warmed under a heat lamp. Here, there are elegantly cut glass platters stacked with fresh, fluffy pancakes and perfectly golden, crisp French toast. A chef waits behind a partition, ready to make you a crepe with the ingredients of your choosing. A variety of fresh baked breads and cheeses. Meats of all kinds, most of them you'd never think of eating for breakfast. Sweet pastries that are like little works of art.

And champagne. Plenty of champagne. As a teen, I felt so grown up when my father would let me partake. One Sunday brunch, in particular, I remember. I was seventeen, a newly-minted senior in high school, and it was cold outside. A typical San Francisco summer day. I drank so much champagne my face turned red and I couldn't stop talking.

Basically, I was myself, amped up to a million.

Once we're settled at the table with our plates, fresh mimosas awaiting us, Daddy launches in.

"Where were you last night?"

My mouth is full of the omelet I just had the chef prepare for me. I chew and chew, hating the way he watches me, prepped to catch me in a lie. I may be only twenty, and still fresh in my adulthood, but I've been around long enough to know what he's about. His questioning ways, his suspicions.

"Oakland," I answer after I swallow, reaching for my mimosa and taking a sip. It's more champs than orange juice, and the alcohol tickles my nose.

His right brow shoots up. "Why the fuck were you in Oakland?"

Lauri reaches out, settling her hand on his arm. "Brian. Please. Someone might hear you."

He breathes heavy, his nostrils flaring. I continue eating my omelet, though inside I'm quivering. I didn't think he'd be so angry.

"Do you know what time you got home last night?" he asks, his voice tight.

I set my fork on the edge of my plate and meet his gaze. "Yes, Daddy."

"I'm assuming you weren't alone when you went to Oakland."

I shake my head, remaining silent.

"You live on your own when you're at college, but when you're here, you're still under my roof, and you must follow my rules. Do you understand me?"

I nod and bow my head, keeping my gaze downcast. This is what he wants. The obedient daughter, taking her punishment by him making a semi-public spectacle in the middle of a restaurant. One of the most elegant restaurants in the entire city. There are business associates of his in here. Men he plays golf with. Women he's probably slept with. This is his domain, and I'm just lucky enough to be allowed inside.

"Who were you with, Hayden?" This comes from Lauri, and I barely lift my head, glaring at her. This isn't part of the script, and I don't like her interfering. In the past when I've gotten in trouble like this, if I immediately agree that I was bad, my father doesn't search for the answers. He forgets all about who I could've been with, and what I might've been doing.

Is this because he doesn't want to know? Doesn't want any sort of vision of what his oldest daughter could be doing when she's out late at night? That's my assumption.

Lauri is just flat-out curious. Worse, she's probably worried I was with her precious Joseph.

When I say nothing, Lauri, the big mouth, continues. "Joseph left soon after you did."

My instincts were right. I say nothing still. I just let my lips curl into a tiny closed-mouth smile.

Her eyes shoot daggers. Jealousy is not a good look for her. At all.

When I glance in my father's direction, I see that he's visibly relaxed. The tension is completely gone from his shoulders. He's probably pleased with the assumption that I was with Joseph in Oakland. Doing God knows what. I hope Lauri envisions the two of us entwined together, naked limbs clinging like vines. She deserves it, for being tempted to cheat on my father.

If he ever catches her with Joseph, there will be hell to pay.

"You'll come with us to the party this afternoon," Dad commands, as if I have no choice in the matter.

"I need to get back home. I have school tomorrow. An early class."

"You stay up all hours of the night on a daily basis," he counters. "You're going to that party. You can return back to your apartment later."

I blink at him, letting my gaze slide in Palmer's direction. She's too busy eating, acting like whatever's happening right now isn't.

I envy her youth. The expectations are high, but not the same. He just wants her to get good grades, excel at her sport and do what he says, no questions asked. It's easier when you're young. When you haven't tasted freedom yet. Palmer doesn't know any better.

Though I was nothing like my sister when I was her age. I was rebellious. Defiant. I strained beneath my father's demands, rather than giving in to them. I never caused a public scandal, but I tended to do what I wanted, despite his protests.

I got in plenty of trouble with him. Phones and laptops and cars taken away. He broke me early on in my senior year, only because I wised up to his game and knew if I did what he asked, and behaved how he wanted, I would be granted freedom.

It's been two years since I've moved out, but my wings are still clipped. I'm only free when I'm not here. The moment I return home—and he demands I do often—I'm caged. Locked away. Reminded of my place, of my duty.

I am a different person when I'm gone, and I prefer that version of myself.

"Am I making myself clear?" he asks, interrupting my thoughts.

I meet his gaze once more. "Yes, Daddy."

Lauri smiles. She enjoys watching me squirm. This is why she aligns herself with Palmer. Getting in good with the daughter still at home is a smart move on her part, I can't deny it. Why bother trying to butter me up? I'm not the one she needs on her side. The three of them against me is a smarter move.

She doesn't know that, deep down, Palmer would never turn against me. We suffered through our parents' divorce together. In my baby sister's eyes, the only one she can really trust is me. And I feel the same way about her. Our parents betrayed us. Used us in battle during the custody proceedings. It was awful. A time in my life I'd rather forget.

Palmer feels the same way.

So Lauri can kiss my sister's ass all she wants, and Palmer will take everything Lauri gives her gladly. I would do the same if I were in my sister's shoes.

It's almost sad, how we all use each other in a way. The only person I truly love. Like, absolutely adore blindly, is Palmer. That's it.

She's all I have.

Once brunch is over, we return home and change clothes—again—for the birthday party. When we're ready, we all pile into my father's Mercedes SUV and head for Dr. Joseph Dubrow's house. As we enter the foyer with the soaring ceilings and the brightly colored art on the walls, I realize it's a monstrous, tacky palace, recently redecorated by Dubrow's new wife. At least she has the decency to be older than Lauri, but still. She's young compared to his former wife, according to gossipy Lauri, and she spends the doc's money as if it's endless. Which I suppose it is.

We're led through the house, Misti Dubrow asking us if we want a tour and my father politely declining. She flirts with him. Lauri inserts a snarky comment here and there, and I wonder if they're actually friends.

Doesn't seem like it.

The party is outside, and it's supposed to be an elegant affair. What I notice first upon coming outside are the flowers. Clusters of deep red roses everywhere. Swags of roses. Arrangements in the center of the tables, on the bars, around the pool. They must've spent thousands of dollars on red roses because they are literally all over the place, their overpowering scent making me sneeze.

"Joe loves the color of blood, that's why all the roses." I overhear his new wife, Misti, explain to a group of women, including Lauri. Misti's face is stretched taut, her blood red glossed lips plump with filler. I'd guess she was originally a patient of his, and that's how they met. He was married. She was single, younger, prettier than his wife. Time to trade in for a new model.

I'm sure when Misti first went to see him, he gave her Botox. Made her lips fuller, her eyebrows arched in perpetual surprise. I bet she was stunned silent when she first saw her face, shocked by her new youthful appearance. I'm sure she was beautiful. They always are.

Now she looks the same as they all do. In a few years, Lauri will resemble this woman. A plastic surgeon has a signature look, though I don't think they do it on purpose. But it's there, in the curve of a lower lip or the tip of a newly sculpted nose. They're artists, working in skin and bone and cartilage.

The women laugh at Misti's words, and one of them asks her to explain.

"Blood to Joe means money. He deals with blood daily, you know, and that's how he makes his living. The deep red color is his favorite. When we first started seeing each other, he'd always bring me a single red rose, so dark it was almost black," Misti explains with a wistful sigh.

I linger on the outskirts of this group of women, my father having already left to mingle, and Lauri completely ignores me. Even Palmer found someone to talk to. Dubrow has a daughter a year younger, and they're friends.

But there is no one here for me. Just this new wife and her tales of blood-colored roses. Her friends listen to her with rapt attention, and I pretend to do the same, morbidly fascinated with her tale.

"Does he love this then? The way you decorated it?" one of the women asks eagerly, seemingly desperate for more details.

Misti's gaze flickers, and I know immediately the answer is no. He doesn't like all the roses. He probably thinks they're tacky, because they are. There are roses literally covering every available surface, and the scent is cloying. If anyone has allergies, they're in serious trouble.

"He loved it. So surprised," she says, and I'm sure the last bit is true. He was definitely surprised.

But not happy about it.

I leave the group of women and wander around the back yard. It's a beautiful spot, when you banish the decorative roses from it. There's a giant pool and a garden with multi-colored flowers blooming. Lush green grass everywhere. As I draw closer to the patio, where the party guests are mingling, a server approaches me, carrying a tray laden with glasses of champagne. I take one with a murmured thank you and he smiles at me. He looks about my age, and he's cute. Not as attractive as Tony though.

"What's your name?" the server asks boldly, and I raise my brow, about to answer when a deep male voice speaks up.

"Go serve someone else."

Shocked, I glance to my left to find Joseph Dubrow Jr. standing there, brows furrowed and eyes dark.

The server scurries away without another word.

"That was rude," I accuse mildly, taking a sip from my champagne. It's crisp and cold, better than the champagne at the restaurant.

"He was flirting with you. He's just the help. Asshole needs to learn boundaries," Joseph says, edging closer to me. His thunderous expression lifts, and it's an all-sunny forecast now. "I'm glad you came."

"Are you really?" I sound bored. I *am* bored. I don't want to be here. I wish I was in my car, making the long, boring drive back to Fresno, blasting one of my favorite playlists on Spotify and singing along with the songs.

Joseph nods, his expression cool. Like I mean nothing to

him, though his pale blue eyes glitter with unmistakable interest. I look away, unnerved. "Pretty sure we're the only two people the same age at this fucking disaster of a party," he says.

I glance around, mentally noting that he's right. "Why is it a disaster?"

"The roses. Misti went overboard, as usual. She has no restraint. Not like my mother." He sips from his lowball glass, the liquid a warm, golden brown. No champagne for him. "My father hated them on sight. Told her they're tacky."

"They are," I agree.

Joseph barely cracks a smile. "Misti grew up in a small town north of here. They've been married for two years, but she's not used to this sort of thing."

"She told all of her friends your father loves the color of blood. It reminds him of money," I feel like a snitch, but I figure he'd find it amusing.

"She would say that." He rolls his eyes. "But I don't want to talk about her."

My tone immediately changes. "What do you want to talk about then?" I fall into my old habits so easily. Flirting with boys. Playing coy. I'm not interested in him. Not at all.

"I was hoping we could talk more last night at the club, but you disappeared with Sorrento." His expression is neutral, but the eyes...

They give away everything. Like he knows my leaving with Tony was a secret.

I stand up straighter, trying for nonchalance. Probably failing. His observation rattles me, just like he knew it would. "I left the party on my own."

His smile is sly as he brings the glass to his lips. "No, you didn't. I saw you."

I'm quiet, my brain scrambling for a response. An explanation.

"I was in the lobby when I caught sight of you two outside. A car pulled up, and you both got in the backseat." Joseph is now full-on grinning, and he rocks back on his heels, confident while I squirm. "I'm guessing your dad would shit a brick if he knew you left the club with his enemy's son."

"How do you know the Sorrentos are my father's enemy?" I ask, hating how in the dark I am over all of this. I suppose this is what happens when I leave for college and don't pay attention to my father's business dealings.

Really, when did I ever pay attention to them? Never. I didn't care growing up, despite him trying to explain what he did. I still don't care. The moment I could get away from my father, I fled as fast as I could.

Though I am rather curious when it comes to Tony and his family, and what they mean to my father. Why all the hate for them? I don't understand.

"Lauri told me," he says. The second the words leave him, his lips tighten, and I see something in his gaze. Something that tells me he probably shouldn't have revealed that.

"You two are *very* friendly." Now I feel like I have something on him.

"She's friends with Misti," he says as his answer, which isn't a good enough reason for me.

"How are you two so close, when you're supposed to be away at Harvard?" I ask, my tone one of pure innocence.

"I—ah—ran into a little trouble last summer, so I'm home for the semester." He stands up straighter. "I'll go back in the spring."

"What a shame." These men who are all bluster and

swagger, but beneath it all, it's bullshit. I am so over being played.

Maybe this is why I'm drawn to Tony. He didn't lie. Oh, he could've. He could've made up some bullshit about how he attends Stanford or USC. He could've said he was a famous athlete, or brilliant beyond measure and poised to be the next Steve Jobs. They all say this sort of thing, when it's so unnecessary.

I like honesty in a man.

I also like forbidden things I'm not supposed to touch.

Like Tony Sorrento.

SEVEN

TONY

I SLEPT in way too late. By the time I get out of bed, it's past ten and the house is eerily quiet. Considering there are twin toddlers in this place, you'd think I'd hear them screaming and babbling in the halls.

Climbing out of bed, I shuffle into the connecting bathroom and take a piss. Wash my hands. Splash cold water on my face to wake myself up. My hair is sticking straight up, and I try to smooth it down with my damp hands, but it's no use. I'm clad in only my black boxer briefs, and the water is icy enough to make my skin break out in goosebumps. The last time I saw goosebumps was on Hayden. Last night when we stood on the jungle gym, her hands looscning her dress, exposing gooseflesh dotted skin.

With her devilish smile and taunting words. The flirty skirt of her dress flapping in the breeze, dancing around her slender thighs. Her panties still crumpled in a lacy wad, left in the front pocket of my discarded trousers that lie crumpled on the floor where I abandoned them last night.

After everything that happened, how surreal the entire

moment was, I could almost believe last night wasn't real. Though I know it was.

Her panties in my possession are my evidence.

I walk out of the bathroom at the exact same moment my bedroom door swings open, and there stands Helena in the doorway, clad in a thin white silk nightgown with a matching robe that's open. Her eyes go wide when she sees me. "Oh! I didn't think you were awake."

"You didn't even knock." I scratch at my chest, vaguely irritated my new stepmom barged into my room when I'm practically naked.

It's like she walked in on purpose.

"Sorry." She rests a hand on her chest, drawing my attention to her tits. They are plumped up nicely, the low neckline of her nightgown offering a delectable view. Though I'm not interested. "I was checking in on you to see if you wanted breakfast."

"You're going to make me breakfast?" I ask.

She laughs, and it's a pleasant tinkling sound. Flirtatious. She's far more flirty than she was last night. "No, silly. We have a cook for that."

"Where's my father?"

Her expression falls. Guess I wasn't supposed to mention him. "Holed up in his office."

"And my sisters?"

"Taking a nap. You slept in late." She steps farther into my room, shutting the door behind her. "Did you sleep comfortably last night?"

What is this woman about? "Sure."

"Good." She stops right in front of me, and I can see there's a lot of skin on display, though I'm showing more. She's studying me with interest, and usually when an attractive woman checks me out, I feel a stir.

Nothing is stirring. Not at all. Thank fucking God for that.

"I just wanted to let you know it makes your father very happy that you're here. That everyone he loves is under one roof," she says, her voice low, her eyes glowing as she watches me.

"I'm sure he's thrilled." That's all I say. What else is there to say? He just wants to control me. That's the sense I got last night.

"I should warn you though," she starts, then clamps her lips shut, her gaze unsure.

"Warn me about what?"

"Your father wasn't happy when you left." She tilts her head to the side, her dark hair spilling over her shoulder. "We didn't know where you were."

"I had to leave. That country club shit is stifling," I say honestly.

"Who did you leave with?"

I remain quiet.

"Because I saw you get into a car with a certain blonde," she continues.

Fucking hell. "It was nothing."

"Sneaking off with Hayden Channing is a big deal to your father, Tony. He won't be pleased."

"I'm not here to please him."

"You should be. He's worth a fortune, and he wants to retire soon," she says. "And he wants to leave everything to you."

Alarm races through me. "What do you mean, everything?"

"The entire business. He wants you to take over soon. You have to know this."

"He's never mentioned it to me before."

"I suppose it's an unspoken expectation. Your father has lots of those." She crosses her arms, plumping up her breasts. "He's allowing you to go to college, so you can get it out of your system, as he says."

"Get what out of my system?"

"Partying. Football. Whatever else you do. Once you graduate, you're expected to come work for him." She steps even closer to me, her robe brushing against my bare legs, and rests her hand right at the center of my chest. "Your skin is so hot."

I take a step back and her hand drops. "What the hell are you doing?"

"Nothing." She blinks at me, her baby blues wide. "Just trying to help you understand what's going on here, and what's expected of you."

"It looks like you're trying to get with me," I say, sneering.

She throws her head back and laughs. "Why would I need to do that, when I have your father in my bed every night? You're just a baby."

"I'm closer in age to you than he is," I remind her.

Her lips form into a tight line, ignoring what I said. "Just—be smart, Tony. Align yourself with the right people."

"Or what?" I ask.

"Or you'll find yourself on the wrong side of your father, and you don't want that," she says.

"What happens if I don't want to take over the business?" I don't know why I asked her that, but she's closer to my father than I am. I haven't figured him out yet. I never really have. And it's not like he's talking business with me right now. It's all *happy reunion and let's have a good time* vibes coming from him.

Guess he was going to hit me with the heavy business stuff later.

"Then he'll sell it to someone else, I suppose. Which is the wrong move, if you ask me. He has no desire to let me help. Claims I wouldn't understand. And the girls are too young. Even if they were older, he wouldn't leave it to them. He says what he does isn't women's work." Her voice is filled with disgust.

Charming. My father is a sexist asshole. "I don't want it."

"You'd be a fucking fool to give it up. Don't be stupid. You could make the business grow. Make it bigger." She smiles, and it's this cunning curl of her lips. I wouldn't be surprised if her tongue snuck out and she licked them right now. "I could help you."

"I need to take a shower." I took one last night, but she doesn't know that. "You should leave."

She doesn't move. Just stares at me for a moment, contemplative. "Do you need assistance?" she finally asks.

As if she's offering her own personal services...

What am I even thinking? Of course, she's offering herself up as "help".

"I thought I was too young for you."

"I could teach you a few things," she offers.

"No." I tip my head toward the door. "You should leave."

She turns away, her robe fanning out like a cape. "You don't know what you're missing," she says as she makes her way for the door. "Just think about what I said, Tony. And know that your stepmother will always be here for you. Whenever you need me."

The door quietly shuts, the soft click ringing loud in the room, and I rush toward it, not subtly when I turn the lock as loud as possible. I don't need that bitch coming back in here.

I return to the bed, yanking the covers up before I grab my phone. What the fuck is going on here? I feel like I'm trapped in some sort of mystery movie, where everyone is making a move on each other, and nothing is what it seems.

It fucking sucks.

ONCE I GET my shit together, I leave my dad's house without a goodbye to any of them. Just a quick text to my father, thanking him for letting me stay for the weekend. I make it back to Fresno in record time, and I've never been more relieved to pull into my condo parking lot as I am right now. I grab my overnight bag and head for my place, grateful to find my friends doing the usual in the living room. The blinds are drawn and the room is dim, save for the flashing of the giant TV mounted on the wall. There are old, empty pizza boxes on top of the coffee table, and cans of soda and beer scattered everywhere.

Home sweet home.

"Tony! Bro! How was it?" This is from Caleb, who's slouched in a gaming chair, controller in hand, gaze fixed on the TV.

"Sucked," I say cheerfully as I let my bag drop on the floor. I go to the couch and sit on it, popping open the pizza boxes to see if there's any leftover slices inside.

I'm out of luck.

"How's dear old dad?" asks Diego. I'm surprised he's here. He's usually with Jocelyn all the time now.

"Bossy as fuck." I send him a look. "What are you doing here?"

"Jocelyn is hanging out with her friends at her apartment. I had to get out of there," he explains. "Was kind of sad you were gone for the weekend."

I rest my hand over my heart. "Aw, did you miss me?"

He reaches for the paper plate next to him, grabbing a leftover pizza crust and threatening to throw it at me. "No," he says with a laugh.

"How was your stepmom?" Caleb asks. He looked her up on Google when I told them where I was going this weekend, and he deemed her fuckable.

He deems every woman with a decent face and nice tits fuckable, so this wasn't exactly news.

"I think she wants to fuck me," I tell him. I probably would've said this even if it wasn't true just to see his reaction, but...

It is true.

Caleb turns his chair around, forgetting all about the game as he studies me. Meanwhile, he dies a glorious, gruesome death on screen. "What the actual fuck? Are you serious?"

I nod, ignoring my growling stomach. "She came into my room this morning in nothing but a sexy nightgown."

I don't mention the robe. Figured that would detract from the point I'm trying to make.

"No way," Caleb breathes, his eyes wide. This is the stuff of fantasics for him. "Did you take her up on her offer?"

"Hell no." I shake my head. "I don't trust her."

"You don't have to trust someone to fuck them," Caleb says solemnly. Always full of good advice, this guy. "You can just bang her and be done with it."

"She's married to my father, Caleb. That would make things really awkward," I remind him.

"You never see that guy much anyway. What's the big deal?" He shrugs.

I grab an empty beer can and hurl it at him. He bats it away with his hand at the last second, laughing. "No thanks. I don't need the trouble."

"Is she hot at least?" Diego asks.

"She's attractive." I keep my tone neutral. Helena is a beautiful woman. She carries herself well. As if she was born to be a rich man's wife. I'm sure her propositioning me is not the first time she's engaged in a discreet affair my father doesn't know about. I'm also fairly certain he's cheated on her too. He did the same thing to my mother.

Mom couldn't handle it though. She'd call him out every single time, and after a while, he got so obvious with it all, I wondered if he wanted to get caught. Just to get the marriage over with. But they held onto each other a lot longer than I thought they would. Probably because of money.

As in, my dad didn't want to give her any.

"What an opportunity. I'd fuck that so fast. At the very least, I'd let her give me a blowie," Caleb says with a grin.

"You're an idiot," I tell him.

"So what? Sometimes you've gotta do it for the stories, you know? Hashtag no regrets."

"I have no regrets," I tell him.

"Liar. You regret all kinds of things."

"Like what?"

"Like Sophie."

"I don't regret her." My response is immediate.

She is the last person I want to talk about.

"You regret letting her go without a fight. Don't bother denying it. You told me that right after she left," Caleb says.

The look on Diego's face is full of sympathy. There's a

guy full of regrets. But he took a chance and went after what he wanted. Who he loved. In the end, he came out on top.

At the time of my breakup with Sophie, I thought I regretted letting her go. Not like she gave me a choice. She came to me, ready to end things, her decision already made. She didn't give me a chance to fight for her. Her mind was made up.

"It's hard to keep hold of someone who doesn't want you." I think of my father. And my mom too. I could go full-blown woe is me right now, and sink into a deep depression over the fact that no one wants me. No one cares enough to stick around.

But I don't. Instead, I think of Hayden. And how glad I am I left the country club with her and went to that church. The view was stunning. The girl showing me the view even more so.

I contemplate telling Caleb about her, but in the end, I remain quiet, and I talk shit with them for the rest of the night as we play Call of Duty. Eventually, Diego leaves to go back home to his girls. Caleb gets a booty call. I'm left alone.

There was no point in telling them about Hayden anyway. Caleb would want the dirty details and if he found out she went to Fresno State, he'd immediately go in search of her. Not to snag her from me, but only because he's curious. That's how he is. Like an overeager puppy, he doesn't know when to stop.

No, it's best I keep her to myself. For now, Hayden is my secret.

EIGHT

HAYDEN

I'M in the library on campus because it's the only place I can study without anyone disturbing me. After freshman year, Gracie and I moved in together, along with two other girls, into a two-bedroom apartment off campus. We stayed in the same apartment but with two different girls the beginning of this fall semester, and while I could probably convince my father to pay my rent for an apartment all by myself, then I would miss the full college experience, as I call it.

Besides, I enjoy living with Gracie. She's fun. Sometimes, though, she's *too* much fun, like today. I need peace and quiet, and she wants to talk to me about the latest guy she's been going out with. She's the type who'll describe his dick size and tell me all the dirty things he says to her—or the lack of dirty things he's not saying to her. I'm sure she'll fall madly in love with this one.

Gracie is in love with the idea of being in love, which is the complete opposite of my feelings. I think romantic love is a crock of shit we've been groomed to believe in since coming out of the womb. Gracie respects my feelings. I respect hers. Meaning, we are the perfect balance as roommates and friends.

And while I'm always down to offer up my best friend advice about her latest guy, I really need to concentrate on this paper I have to write for my American Classics in Literature class. It's due in two days, and I think I have about two sentences written so far. That's it.

FML.

I'm tucked away into a corner of the library not many people use, sitting at a small table and tapping away on my laptop when I swear I feel someone watching me. I lift my head and look around, but see no one.

Probably just my overly vivid imagination.

One thing I can't stop thinking about is Tony Sorrento and what happened between us Saturday night. I'm still not exactly sure what gave me the courage to act so boldly, and I sort of regret it. Coming on to him like that, offering him a blow job when I really don't know him at all? What the hell was I thinking?

But my instincts were correct. He refused my offer. He's a good guy, despite what my father thinks. And now, Tony Sorrento probably thinks I'm crazy. Worse? A tease. Why would he want to hang out with me and be my friend when I told him sex would never be part of the deal?

Not that he's only looking for sex, but come on. An attractive guy like him probably doesn't need any more friends who are female. I'm sure women throw themselves at his feet. I practically did, in jest.

Sort of.

If he'd been more persuasive, more of a player, I would've melted at his words. Given in at his first kiss. I like a confident man with major moves. I also adore a confident man who respects women. Tony is firmly in the second category.

Proving my point, yet again, that he's one of the good guys.

Turning him down probably ruined my chances at keeping him as a friend. It's already Wednesday. I haven't heard from him since the Uber dropped me off at my father's house. We hugged, me withdrawing quickly for fear I might've clung to him a second too long, before I climbed out of the car and ran up to the front door of the house, never once turning back. Trying my best to act like I didn't care.

Truth? I did care. I cared a lot. He still lingers in my brain. And while I'm a modern woman who could reach out first since I have his number, I'm reluctant. What's the point? His unspoken message is clear.

He has zero interest in ever seeing me again and has already forgotten I even exist.

With a sigh, I refocus on writing my paper, putting down a bunch of nonsense because having words to work with is better than no words at all. I have no idea what I'm really trying to say so I just let myself ramble on the page and then I'll fix it later. It's become my process in college and so far, it's really working for me.

God, at least something is.

I put my AirPods in and fire up my study playlist to help my concentration even further and get to work, ignoring the text notifications that keep coming through. Every single one of them is from Gracie. I adore her, but sometimes she's a complete pain in the ass.

It's when I'm almost finished with the rough draft of my paper that I get a text from an unfamiliar number. Curiosity fills me and I check the message.

I see you.

Glancing up, I scan the area, but see no one. Another notification comes through.

You don't see me?

Unease slips down my spine when I realize just how alone I am, tucked back in this corner of the library, with no one else around. I'm near a giant wall of windows and there are so many people still wandering around campus. I can see the crowded sidewalks, people sitting at picnic tables or lingering in the quad in clusters, chatting with each other. While I'm all alone up here with my creeper texter. I can imagine him lunging for me. I run toward the windows and beat on them with my fists, screaming for someone to notice me, but no one does—

I shake myself out of the thought, mildly concerned by my overactive imagination.

Grabbing my phone, I send the anonymous someone a reply.

Who the hell is this?

I wait a few minutes, but there's no response. So frustrating. It's not like I give out my number a lot, but I do on occasion when I meet a cute boy. They're usually not so creepy though.

Giving up on the paper, I shut my laptop and start gathering my things, putting them all away in my backpack. My phone buzzes, but I ignore it, eager to get out of here and amongst people versus being back here all by myself.

I sling my backpack over my shoulder and rise to my feet, clutching the strap tightly as I make my way toward the front of the library. My phone buzzes again, a reminder that I have a text, but I'm not checking it until I get around other people.

For some weird reason, I don't feel safe.

"You're ignoring me," says a voice from behind me and I shriek.

Literally shriek.

In the middle of the Fresno State library. The place goes dead silent, and the few people I can now see swivel their heads in my direction, glaring at me.

I whirl on him, ready to give this guy hell when I find Tony Sorrento standing there, a giant grin on his beautiful face, looking very, very pleased with himself.

"Gotcha," he says softly.

"Ugh, you're the worst!" I come for him, smacking his chest and he grabs my wrist, holding my hand in place, so I can feel the warmth of his skin beneath the soft fabric of his blue T-shirt. His chest is actually very firm and muscular, and I can even feel his heart beating.

It starts to beat even faster, and I'm just arrogant enough to believe it's because we're standing so close.

"Did I scare you?" he asks, his thumb rubbing the inside of my wrist slowly.

A shiver threatens to steal over me, but I keep myself in check. "Yes, you did," I say breathlessly.

"Not my fault you forgot to put my number in your contacts." He slowly releases his hold on my wrist and it takes me a second to realize that. I drop my hand from his chest, feeling stupid.

Mr. Safe and Respectful from Saturday night is long gone, replaced by a dark-eyed devil who is purposely trying to aggravate me.

"It slipped my mind," I say, trying to sound nonchalant. I'm also trying to imply that maybe he slipped my mind too, though that isn't true. Not even close to the truth. I've been thinking about him a lot.

Too much probably.

"I didn't mean to scare you."

"You didn't." I turn away from him, lift my chin and start walking. Of course, he falls into step beside me. "When you're not terrorizing me, what are you doing in the library?"

"What are *you* doing in the library?" he throws back at me.

I send him a withering glare. "Trying to write a paper."

"How'd it go?"

"Terribly," I answer, deciding to be truthful. "I was distracted."

"By what?"

"My crazed secret stalker." I come to a stop. So does he. "Otherwise known as you."

"My texts aren't the only thing that distracted you," he says with a sly smile. "I saw the way you stared out the window. There wasn't a lot of typing going on."

"Ugh, you were totally watching me. That's creepy." I resume walking. So does he. We're in the more heavily populated part of the library, not too far from the front desk and the exit doors, and there are so many people milling about. "Why didn't you just approach my table and say hi like a normal person?"

"I didn't want to scare you."

"Really." Please. He's full of shit.

"That's why I texted you. I thought my name would be in your phone and you'd know the text was from me," he further explains.

I suppose he's right and it is my fault I forgot to punch in his information when he gave me his number. You think I would've, since I was halfway waiting for him to text me after our magical Saturday night. Though maybe it wasn't so magical for him.

He's here though, isn't he? So maybe it was.

We exit the library, the cool fall breeze washing over me and sending a chill over my skin. I shift my backpack on my shoulder, wishing the sweater I tossed on earlier this morning was thicker, and I glance around, noticing a group of guys clustered in a group not too far from where we're at, watching us with unrestrained curiosity.

"Friends of yours?" I ask when I see Tony flick his chin at them in acknowledgement. They all do the same thing in return, looking ridiculous.

Ridiculously hot, but whatever.

"Yeah. We're on the football team together," he says, his voice casual as he studies them. Like no big deal.

"Wait a minute." I turn to face him. This is a very big deal. "You're on the *football team?*"

He nods.

"You play football. For the Bulldogs." He better not be lying to me. I've met more than one liar in my time here at college.

"Well, yeah. I don't get much playing time though, since it's my first year," he explains.

Huh? "Because you're a transfer? Did you go to community college first?" I ask.

"No." He slowly shakes his head, his full lips curving upward. "I'm a freshman."

Okay, now I'm full-on gaping at him. "You're a what?"

"A freshman," he repeats slowly.

I squint up at him, fighting the panic that's rising within me. "How old are you?"

"Eighteen."

"Oh, fucking shit," I mutter under my breath, turning away from him. I press my hand against my forehead, rubbing it as the words rock through my brain on repeat.

A freshman. A freshman. A freshman.

"You have a problem with that?" he asks, sounding amused.

"I'm a junior." I whirl on him once more. "I'm almost twenty-one."

"And I'm almost nineteen." He shrugs, like *so?*

"Thank God you're not jailbait," I fling at him.

He actually laughs, the asshole. "I thought it didn't matter, since we're only going to be friends. Sex just complicates things, remember?"

I hate it when people throw your words back at you, like Tony is doing to me now. Tony, the eighteen-year-old. The freshman.

What the actual fuck?

I feel a little betrayed, but I guess I shouldn't. We never discussed what year we were in college. We just knew we went to the same one. And I'm assuming he didn't realize I was a junior, just like I didn't know he was a freshman.

"Does it really bother you that badly—that I'm younger than you?" he asks, his question interrupting my thoughts.

I don't know how to feel about it. "Did you know I was older?"

"No, but I don't care. Age is nothing but a number."

He's so nonchalant. Like no big deal. While I'm the one over here freaking out, and while I don't usually freak out about a lot of things, for some reason, this is blowing my mind. Why, I don't know. There's only a two-year difference between us, and in the scheme of life, two years isn't much.

But I can only imagine what Gracie will say to me when she finds out the mystery boy from Saturday night is only eighteen. He's a baby. Barely out of high school.

I blatantly scan him from head to toe, not really giving a

crap how I look doing it. He certainly doesn't look barely out of high school, that's for damn sure. Glancing over at his group of friends who have somehow shifted closer to us, I ask, "Did you go to high school with those guys?"

"Some of them," he answers, appearing completely unruffled by my freak out, which I can reluctantly appreciate.

"And are they all freshmen too?"

"Yeah, actually, they are. Hey, get over here," he calls to them and they quickly approach us, a bunch of swaggering, testosterone-filled man-boys with big smiles on their faces, their gazes trained on me.

Every single one of them is attractive. It's distressing how good looking they are. Girls walking past them are openly staring. One of the guys in particular pulls from the group and chases after a girl, stopping her a few feet away so they can chat, and it is obvious he's flirting with her.

"Guys, this is Hayden," Tony announces to them. I half expect him to call me his girlfriend—ugh, no—or claim I'm off-limits to them, like some sort of caveman, but thankfully, he says none of that. "Hayden, these are my friends."

I smile. Wave. "Hi," I say weakly, overwhelmed in their presence.

They all crowd around us, emanating that male confidence athletes tend to give off. You've seen them before, all throughout high school, and they're the same in college too. They strut around campus as if they own the place, nodding and smiling at everyone as they pass by. These guys are young and cocky and the world just falls at their feet, I'm sure.

"You Tony's girl?" one of them asks me, shaking back his shaggy blond hair.

"Not my girl. She's just a friend," Tony corrects, answering for me.

I glare at him, annoyed he said that. I can speak for myself.

"Well, well, well. That means she's fair game." He steps forward, straight toward me, extending his hand. "I'm Jackson."

"Nice to meet you." I shake his hand, dazzled by Jackson's smile. It's big and white and downright blinding.

"She's not interested," Tony tells Jackson, though that doesn't seem to deter him.

"Hey, don't speak for me," I accuse Tony, before I turn a smile on Jackson. "I might be interested."

Tony scowls. Jackson preens like he won a prize.

I just laugh. Boys. They're so silly.

They all start jostling for my attention after that. The guy who ran after the girl comes jogging back, introducing himself to me as Caleb with a wink and a knowing smile. Such a flirt. There's also an Eli and a Diego and Jackson, of course, plus a couple of other guys whose names I didn't catch. They're talking over each other, giving Tony endless shit, all of them sending questioning looks my way, but Tony doesn't say a thing. He doesn't really react either. He's as cool and as quiet as can be, while I'm still quietly freaking out, but for a different reason.

Being with these guys is...overwhelming. The entire situation is. There is more to Tony than I actually realized. Like the fact that he plays D1 football. And that his quiet confidence is actually really attractive, despite his only being eighteen years old.

He doesn't act eighteen. He seems so much older than his friends, who are all trying to gain my attention for a variety of reasons, each of them making me laugh and shake my head. They remind me of overeager puppies. Cute and rambunctious and always eager to please.

I'm not one to chase after jocks, but I could see wanting to insert myself into this group and hang out with them. As friends only, though. I'm not interested in any of them, despite their handsome faces and well-toned bodies and obvious confidence.

Tony intrigues me, but I can't. It just...

It wouldn't work. I'd fall for him hard and he'd disappoint me. Break my heart.

Eventually, they all do.

"I should go," I say after a few minutes of small talk. "It was nice meeting you all."

"Nice meeting you too, Tony's friend," one of them says, making all of them laugh.

Except Tony.

"See ya around." My gaze meets Tony's and he inclines his head toward me, a sort of silent goodbye I guess, and before I can say something stupid like, "call me!" I turn and walk away.

But he doesn't let me go. Nope, I can sense Tony following after me, catching up with me with ease, thanks to his long stride. "I feel like an idiot," I tell him when he's walking beside me.

"Why?"

"For not realizing your age."

"Again, is it really that big of a deal? Friends can be friends, no matter what age," he says, his expression one of pure innocence.

I come to a complete stop. So does he. People walk past us, irritated since we're standing in the middle of the sidewalk that leads to the south parking lot, but I sort of don't care.

"You know we're probably going to end up as more than friends," I say, because fuck it.

It's probably true.

He runs his hand along his jaw, contemplating me with those dark, dark eyes. "I thought you said that would mess everything up between us."

"I'm not wrong and you know it. If we fall into some sort of relationship, it's going to eventually ruin everything."

"We don't have much to ruin," he points out. "We've only just met."

I tilt my head to the side. "True."

"So how can we ruin something that isn't much of anything?" he asks.

I blink at him, trying to process what he said. "You're talking in circles."

"No, you are," he throws back at me. "Instead of trying to dictate how this is going to play out between us, why not just...let it be."

"Did you just call me a dictator?" My voice rises. I sound borderline shrill, and it reminds me of how my mother used to yell at my dad when they were still together.

God, that really sucks.

"No, I just happened to use the word dictate." He contemplates me, while I squirm where I stand. "I bet you're one of those people who overthink everything."

I am so, so grateful he didn't say one of those women, or worse—one of those *girls*.

So far he hasn't proven himself to be sexist, and I appreciate that.

"But like I just said, why can't we just...hang out? See where this takes us? We don't need to label everything, do we? We can be friends," he says easily.

"Friends who..." I prompt.

"Friends who what? Spend time together? Mess around?" He shrugs, slipping his hands into his jeans' pockets. "Maybe we will, maybe we won't."

Oh God. He is temptation personified. I can't even believe we're having this conversation on campus, on a bright and sunny Wednesday afternoon, surrounded by strangers.

Life is weird.

"We spend time together, we will," I tell him firmly.

"Maybe," he adds. "Maybe I don't want to."

"Ha! You liar. You're the one who's pushing for it," I remind him.

"If you're not interested in me, just say it." He smirks, his expression like a dare.

I cross my arms. "I'm not that interested." I sound like a thirteen-year-old denying her middle school crush.

"Uh huh," he says, his deep voice full of doubt. "Keep convincing yourself of that."

"You're too young anyway," I throw at him, feeling hostile. Why am I so heated? "What sort of moves could you have? I've got two years on you."

"So what? I've got moves you've probably never even heard of." He starts to chuckle.

"In your dreams." I start walking again.

So does he, and he follows me into the parking lot, not saying a word. Just grinning and walking. I think he's enjoying himself.

Which of course, infuriates me.

"I have moves too you know," I retort, picking up my pace.

He does too, keeping in stride with me. "I'm sure you do. Can't wait to see you execute them on me."

"Execute?" I pull out my keyless remote from my backpack and hit the button, my Range Rover chirping. "You make it sound like I'm going to kill you."

"The French do describe an orgasm as a little death," he says.

I roll my eyes. "Oh, now you know French? Are you trying to impress me?"

"No, but I know about orgasms." He grins. "And how to give them."

"To yourself?" I try to keep my expression neutral, but I've just been hit with the mental image of Tony completely naked and jerking off, his hand wrapped tightly around—

Swear to God, sweat starts to form on my hairline. And it's not even close to hot outside.

"Ouch, down woman." He rests his big hands against his chest, his gaze going to my car. "I have the same exact model, but mine's black."

"Fitting. I'm the angel, and you're the devil." I open the passenger side door of my beautiful white Range Rover and toss my backpack on the black leather seat before I shut it, rounding the front of the vehicle before I open the driver's side door. "It's been an interesting conversation with you, Tony, that's for sure."

"Hey, it's worked in my favor. Yours too, you know." He steps closer when I shut the door and roll down the window, and he leans his forearm on the window's edge. "You said love is for pussies. We can do whatever we want, we just can't fall in love, right?"

"Right." I start the car and then turn to look at him, my gaze snagging on his thick forearm, the light smattering of dark hair that covers it. He's got nice arms.

He's got nice everything.

But he's only eighteen, the angel on my shoulder says.

So what? Eighteen and primed to fuck, isn't that what they always say?

That's from the naughty devil on my other shoulder.

"Don't worry. I can see the cogs turning in your brain. I'm not going to fall in love with you, Channing," he tells me with a grin, pushing away from my car.

"I'm not going to fall in love with you either, Sorrento," I toss back at him, rolling up the window. I back out of the parking space, Tony watching me the entire time so intently, my palms start to sweat and I turn at a terrible angle. So bad, I have to drive forward before I can back out, properly this time.

His mere presence is intimidating me, and from the giant grin on his face, he knows it.

I pull up beside him and give him the finger before I gun the gas pedal so hard, my tires squeal.

As I drive home, I give myself a pep talk. I am definitely not going to fall in love with that boy. No matter how many moves Mr. Mysterious has in his arsenal. I can withstand his charm.

I know I can.

NINE

TONY

"WHAT ARE YOU UP TO, BRO?"

This comes from Jackson, a few hours after my encounter with Hayden on campus—or I guess you could say, *our* encounter with Hayden, since all my friends were there.

Acting like a bunch of dumb fucks, but yeah.

We're currently at my condo I share with Caleb and Diego. Eli and Jackson are over, hanging out with us, and Diego is with Jocelyn. They've gotten back together after a rough time apart, and they have a baby. He already told us he's moving in with her next semester, which is cool. I get it. Hell, I encouraged it. They need to be together. Those two love each other, and they want to make it work.

Since living in the dorms isn't required for freshmen at Fresno State, I fully planned on finding my own apartment near campus—Dad offered to pay, why would I turn him down? Somehow, though, I was convinced over the summer that living with a couple of assholes was a good idea.

Who am I kidding? I didn't want to live alone. I've done

enough of that to last me a lifetime, thanks to my parents never being around when I still lived at home.

Caleb is one of my closest friends, so it was a no brainer living with him. Diego has been my friend for years too, though we've gotten even closer recently. He's never around though. He spends all of his free time with Jos and their baby.

The craziest thing is I'm now friends with guys I hated the entirety of high school. Eli Bennett was the quarterback at our rival high school, and his taunting ways on social media drove us crazy. Guy called us out constantly—and then we'd play against them and beat his ass every single time.

I think he just did it for the drama. Guy loves to flap his lips.

Wasn't much of a fan of Jackson Rivers either, who played with Eli, though I didn't know him that well. Turns out they're both actually pretty cool. Even Caleb gets along with Eli, and they had a near run-in our senior year over Ava, Eli's girlfriend. Our best friend's little sister. That's how we all became friends in the first place—thanks to Ava and Eli dating, and Jake reluctantly accepting him as one of us.

Might not make sense, considering it's all twisted and a bit of a mess, but we've let the past remain where it belongs when it comes to Eli.

That's why we're currently sitting around our living room after football practice, playing Call of Duty and drinking beer while waiting for our pizza order to show up. Hanging out like we usually do. Talking a bunch of shit to each other.

Again, as we usually do.

Jackson snaps his fingers in front of my face, reminding me he asked me a question.

"Repeat yourself," I tell him, loving how easy it is to play video games and get lost in my thoughts all at the same time. And women say men can't multitask.

Jackson rolls his eyes. "I asked, what are you up to?"

His question is way too vague. "What exactly are you talking about?"

"You and the girl. The sexy blonde."

My brain immediately conjures an image of Hayden. My favorite one—standing on the jungle gym, the top of her dress loose, as she rids herself of her panties. What a moment. She kind of blew my mind that night.

Actually, she really blew my mind that night.

And she's definitely a sexy blonde. Of course, within seconds of reimagining that moment between us and me actually taking advantage of her instead of being a goddamn gentleman, I get blown to bits across enemy lines and I'm out of the game. I throw my controller onto the ground in disgust and finally answer Jackson. "We're friends."

That's all I say. My lack of response for most things drives my friends crazy.

It's my best trait.

"You tapped it yet?" Jackson asks, his focus still on the giant TV in front of us, his fingers working the game controller furiously.

"No." Haven't even kissed her yet.

He sends me a quick look. "You going to tap it?"

"Yes," I say firmly, because she can protest however much she wants, and we can go round and round like two people in strong denial, but that's all it is. Denial.

We're hot for each other. I can feel it. There's so much chemistry between us, you can practically touch it. I want her. She wants me. Yet, for whatever reason, she doesn't want to cross that line.

Whatever. I won't push. I'm not a creep. She has no idea just how patient I am.

I'm the most patient motherfucker she's ever going to meet.

"You so sure about that? She was eyeing every single one of us," Jackson says, ever the observant when it comes to attractive women.

The only reason Hayden acted interested in any of my friends is because she was trying to irritate me. And because I knew that, it didn't irritate me whatsoever. I kind of wished a really hot girl would've walked by so I could've ogled her for a few, but unfortunately that didn't happen.

Or if it did, I didn't notice.

"I'm sure she was, but don't read too much into it. I didn't want to stake my claim in front of her, but I'm staking it now," I say, glancing at everyone in the room. This includes Eli and Caleb. They act like they're not paying attention, their gazes only for the TV, but I know they can hear me. "She's mine."

"Not interested," Eli immediately says, his lips curving into a shit-eating grin. "Got my own sexy blonde."

I say nothing. I've known Ava Callahan for a long time, and while I can admit she's attractive, I don't like thinking of her in that way. She's Jake's sister. That's it.

"She's too feisty for me," Caleb says with a yawn. "I like them more agreeable."

"Oh, she's definitely not agreeable," Eli adds. "You can just tell."

This is facts.

"Agreeable is boring," Jackson adds. "I like a challenge."

"Is that why you won't just go for it and finally give Ellie what she wants?" Eli asks, his face a mask of complete innocence. This is a sensitive subject, one they've talked about before. We've all talked about it before. I stay out of it, though, because it's pointless.

Jackson is never going to get with Ellie. Mark my words.

"She's my friend. She's too young. I'm not interested in her," Jackson says, his voice edged with finality. He's gone over this what feels like a hundred times, I'm sure.

Ellie is Ava's best friend, and she's not so secretly in love with Jackson. We all know it. Ellie knows we know it. She knows Jackson knows it too, and she wishes he would do something about it. He won't take it any further than friendship though, because she's a good girl, according to him.

Good girls don't interest him. Readily available women don't interest him either.

"There are too many women on this campus to settle on just one pussy," Caleb declares. He's the player of our group, and he's always got not-so-wise words to say. "I get why Diego is with Jocelyn. They have a baby. They're a family now. He's doing the right thing, and he's always loved her. I just thank God it's not happening to me."

He bursts out laughing. Jackson joins in. Eli chuckles, but I can tell he's uncomfortable because he's madly in love with Ava and doesn't want anyone else.

I don't laugh either, because I have no opinion on one pussy or a thousand pussies. Everyone has a unique set of circumstances, and we all approach situations differently. I wasn't lying when I told Hayden I thought relationships and love and marriage was a joke. They are. I'm the biggest nonbeliever in love out there.

But I'm not adverse to spending time with her and possibly turning it into something...more. I know how to keep it casual. What's the harm in that? I'm the one who keeps suggesting friends with benefits. And she's the one who keeps turning me down.

So fuck it.

"Your hot blonde?" Jackson says to me, pointing his beer can at me. "She's a challenge. I can tell just from the look on her face."

"She can be annoying," I admit.

Jackson laughs. "The challenges usually are. Look, she's pretty, but she might be too much for you to handle. You're a pretty calm guy. Maybe turn her over to Caleb and he can give it a go."

Say the fuck what?

"She's not a toy to be passed around," I say with disgust.

"I already said I'm not interested," Caleb says, tilting his nose into the air as if he's a snobbish female connoisseur. Which I suppose he is, considering the number of girls he's been with over the years.

Guy is only eighteen and he's been with *a lot* of girls.

Speaking of eighteen...

"She's twenty and a junior. Meaning, she thinks we're all too young," I tell them.

They all start making noise, most of it dismissive.

"Has she seen me in action?" Caleb asks, pointing at his junk. "I'm fuckin' impressive."

We ignore him.

"We don't know life without smart phones," Jackson adds. "I've got years of porn watching under my belt. I know what's up."

I make a face. Watching internet porn definitely teaches us a few things, but I wouldn't consider that as part of my sexual experience.

"As if that's a life skill," Eli says, not holding back as

usual. It's his best and worst trait. "I'm sure she's watched lots of porn too. She'd call you out on any fake ass move."

"She seems like the type to suggest watching porn with you to get in the mood," Jackson says, his mood shifting to sullen. He didn't like us making fun of the porn mention, but he asked for it. "She's probably boring in bed."

Doubt it. She was pretty adventurous with me Saturday night, practically stripping in front of me, and we'd only just met.

"How about we don't talk about her behind her back, hmm?" I suggest.

"Oooh," they all say together, before they start laughing.

How they knew to say that at the same time, I don't get. I just scowl at them.

"You've got it bad," Jackson says.

"Tony has a crush," Caleb teases in a high-pitched voice.

"About damn time, after what Sophie did to you," Eli says.

We all go silent, and my good mood evaporates. I hate hearing her name. Thinking about her. It's not that I'm still madly in love with Sophie. I just hated how things ended for us. How she broke up with me and up and left right before the second semester of our senior year started. She was done with me. Done with our school and her friends. Done with the entire area, and she's already moved on. I felt abandoned, but what else was new?

I didn't like it. Vowed I wouldn't let it happen to me ever again. Who needs a relationship?

That's why I keep telling myself I don't want one with Hayden. She may think I'm a nice guy, and I'm not going to deny that I respect women, but that doesn't mean I don't know how to have a strictly casual and purely sexual arrangement with someone. I am up for it.

Game for it.

Ready for it.

I hooked up with a girl at a frat party a few weeks ago, but it was nothing serious. A lot of kissing. A little bit of touching. She was perfectly willing to give me a BJ, but at the last second, she bowed out.

Thank God because within minutes, she was in one of the bathrooms, puking her guts out, her equally drunk friend holding her hair back and sending me death glares, like it was my fault she was puking.

Whatever.

"You all need to get laid," Eli says, pointing at me and Jackson. "I know it's been a while for you two."

Jackson shoots daggers at his friend with his eyes. I say nothing, because Eli is right. It's definitely been a while.

"And maybe you shouldn't have sex with that angry blonde," Eli continues, pointing at me. "She'll chew you up and spit you out."

"I think he'd like that," Caleb says with a chuckle.

"Shut up," I practically growl, grateful when the doorbell rings.

I go to the door and grab our pizzas from the delivery guy, tipping him before I kick the door shut and bring the boxes into the kitchen. "Dinner is served."

We crowd around the counter and dig into the boxes, not bothering with plates or napkins. We don't need any of that stuff. We're all hungry savages with one thought on our minds.

Feed me.

Once we've got a few pieces of pizza in our stomachs, we slow down, eating more leisurely. After taking the time to go to the fridge and grab more beer, I settle onto one of the barstools that lines the counter, sipping on my beer and finish another slice, contemplating life. Hayden. What I should do next.

"You going to pursue her?" Caleb asks me.

I nod, setting my piece on my plate before I turn to look at him. "It's probably a mistake, but yeah."

"You're not an idiot, Sorrento," Caleb reminds me.

I smile. "Gee thanks."

"I'm being serious. You don't make rash decisions, you don't go after girls unless you're truly interested in them. I always wondered if you were some sort of robot or whatever," Caleb says. "You move through life as if nothing ever affects you."

It's a defense mechanism, cultivated through years of dealing with the abandonment of my parents. If you act like nothing bothers you, then it can never hurt you, right?

At least that's what I tell myself.

"I'm just—"

"Particular," Caleb finishes for me. "I'll stick my dick in anything, but you take your time. Get it good and juicy first."

I wince. "Gross, man."

"Whatever," he says with a chuckle. "I always thought it was the right move to try and get with as many girls as possible, because you increase your chances in eventually finding the right one, you know?"

"Are you in search of the right one?" I'm kind of shocked he's even suggesting this.

"Aren't we all? I'm not a complete heartless asshole," Caleb says, his expression turning thoughtful. "What I'm trying to say is maybe you've had the right idea all along. Instead of chasing endless tail, I should be more picky like you are. Then maybe I could find someone I really, truly love."

I send him a look. His expression is sweet and innocent, like an angel descended from heaven.

Right before he bursts out laughing and shakes his head. "You fell for it, huh?" He nudges me in the ribs.

"I know you better than that," I mutter, even though for the briefest second, I did sort of fall for it.

I should've known. Caleb isn't looking for anyone special. None of these guys are, with the exception of Eli, who I'm sure thinks he's already found her.

I might not believe in everlasting true love, but I know a good one when I see it, or in this case, her, and I know Hayden is a good one. She's full of all kinds of possibilities.

And I want to explore every single one of them.

As long as we keep it casual.

WE'RE COMING out of practice the next day when I spot a familiar blonde head in the distance. As we draw closer, I can see she's wearing navy blue leggings and a red Bulldogs T-shirt, looking like a fangirl waiting for her favorite player to walk off the field.

I can't help the grin that grows on my face when our gazes connect. Her hopeful expression transforms into a frown and I laugh. She shakes her head, mock glaring at me, and I grin the rest of the way, until I'm standing directly in front of her.

"Couldn't resist me, could you?" I tease.

She rolls her eyes. Crosses her arms. Looks away before, reluctantly, facing me once more. "I couldn't stop thinking about you, okay?"

Her brutal honesty is much appreciated. "Same."

"You couldn't stop thinking about you either?" She raises a brow.

"I couldn't stop thinking about *you*." I tap the tip of her nose, and I swear to God she blushes. "Why are you here?"

"I was waiting for you."

"How'd you figure out where we were practicing?"

"It's not hard, Sorrento. I've got a brain."

"Never said you didn't." I start walking again, heading for the parking lot, and she falls into step beside me. I'm having a déjà vu moment right about now, but I decide to switch it up a little from our last parking lot encounter. "Want to grab dinner with me?"

"Are you asking me out on a date?" Her voice is ultra-high and I catch her batting her eyelashes at me, over-exaggerating everything. Mocking me, though I'm not insulted.

I feel like the mocking thing might be *her* defense mechanism.

"No. I'm asking if you want to grab dinner as friends. That's it," I say solemnly.

"I would be delighted." She rests her hand on her chest.

"Want me to drive us there?"

"How about we take separate cars? Like friends do," she suggests. "I can follow you."

"Sure," I say easily, not about to argue.

"How was practice?" she asks as we make our way toward the parking lot.

"Tough. They're working us extra hard lately. I think we're being tested. They want to see if we'll stick." The season is winding down, and it's been a good one. I haven't gotten much field time—most of my friends haven't, with the exception of Diego—and this is when they put us to the test. See if we have what it takes for them to want to keep us next year.

It's also a great way to get rid of the slackers who can't hack it. I see the way the coaches watch me and Jackson. We both didn't take things seriously at the beginning of the year, and we're paying for it now.

I may have been distracted a couple of months ago with moving out, a new school, a new life, but I'm focused now. I want this. I've got nothing else. This bachelor's degree I'm pursuing is nothing but a piece of paper that'll make my dad proud. Once I graduate, he'll pull me into the family business and my life will no longer be my own. I need to have something that brings me joy. Something that's for me and no one else.

Football is it for me. My one outlet that no one can take away from me. It helps me forget about my troubles and focus on the game. I need that. More than I realized.

"When's your next game?" she asks.

"This Saturday. It's a home game," I answer.

"I'm going," she says firmly. "I want to watch you play."

"Good luck, I don't get on the field much." There's no point in lying.

"Why not?"

"First, I'm only a freshman, as you like to remind me."

She grins.

"Second, I kind of fucked around at the beginning of the season with Jackson, and now the coaches hate us," I explain.

"What do you mean, you fucked around with Jackson?" Her brows shoot up. "Sounds dirty."

"Ha, right. No, nothing like that." I stop at the front of my car. I almost passed right by it. "How about I explain everything over dinner."

"Okay." She nods, her expression neutral. "But I'm paying for my own meal."

"That's fine."

"And I'm sitting across the table from you, not right next to you." She waves her finger between us. "This is not a date."

"We've already established that," I say coolly.

She rolls her eyes. "Are you always this calm?"

"Not in bed." I grin.

"Who says we need a bed?"

Touché, Hayden.

Motherfuckin' touché.

WE END up at a sushi place not too far from campus, and it's packed with fellow college students. I've been here before, and while it's not the best sushi I've ever had, it's worth the price and the crowd.

We pick out a couple of rolls to share. I order an iced tea, Tony sticks with water. I watch him as he speaks with the server, noting how his hair is damp, as if he just took a shower, but his cheeks and jaw are faintly lined with stubble. I withhold the sigh that wants to escape the longer that I stare at him. He's hot.

So hot.

His gray T-shirt stretches across his wide chest, tight enough to offer me a teasing outline of his pecs. I bet he has a six pack. I've been with attractive guys before, but there is something exceptional about Tony.

"You're staring," he tells me once the server leaves our table.

"Sorry." I prop my elbow on the edge of the table and rest my chin on my fist. "You're pretty."

"Pretty?" He doesn't appear happy with my assessment.

"Yes. I'm not changing my choice of words, no matter how much you don't like it," I tell him with a faint smile.

He smiles in return. "You're pretty too. I like the Bulldog gear."

"I wore it just for you."

"I also like how you don't hold back. You tell me how you feel."

"I don't like to play games," I say with a one shoulder shrug.

"Me either."

"Plus, friends should be honest with each other."

"A friend who lies to you isn't a friend at all," he agrees.

"Right? That's why I say what I feel."

"Okay. My turn." He rests his forearms on the table, leaning forward, his voice lowering. "I think you're fucking sexy."

My stomach flutters. "Are you attracted to older women?"

He rolls his eyes. "It's only two years. It's not a big deal."

"Says the eighteen-year-old." I grin. It's fun to tease him. He gets this little line between his eyebrows when he's irritated, and it's there right now, front and center.

"Does it bother you that badly? Because if it does, maybe we can't be friends." His arms drop off the table and he leans back against the booth behind him, his expression devoid of emotion.

I wonder if anyone's told him how attractive he is when he's mad.

"It bothers me a little." Again, I'm being honest. It's the least I can do. "But I'll get over it."

"Really?"

"I'll try."

The server returns to our table with our drinks and a bowl of spicy edamame for us to snack on.

"Do you have many friends who are girls, Sorrento?" I ask once the server's gone.

He slowly shakes his head. "My friends' girlfriends, but that's about it. I had friends who were girls when I was in high school."

"A few months ago?" I need to quit prodding him about the age thing, but it's like I can't help it.

"Yeah. A few months ago, since I'm merely a baby in your eyes." He quietly owns it, which I respect. "But I haven't met a lot of girls since starting here."

I nearly scoff. "I find that hard to believe."

"Girls I'd want to be friends with," he adds. "You're the first."

Jealousy spikes. Of course, he's met girls. Pretty girls who probably throw themselves at him. Girls who chase after jocks, who want the status of being with someone on the football team. They're all over campus. I was never one of them. Yet here I am, interested in this one.

"Maybe I want to be your only friend who's a girl," I admit. "I can get jealous sometimes."

"Are you saying you don't want me to have lots of female friends?" He raises a brow.

"It would probably bother me, yes," I say with a nod.

"That's not a very friend-like thing to do."

"Sometimes...I have not-so-friendly thoughts about you." Another honest confession. Look at me go.

"Like you want to murder me in your sleep?"

"Like I want you naked in my bed," I say.

He tenses up. I watch it happen. Is that a good thing? Or a bad thing?

The server returns to check on us, and I immediately

wish he'd leave. He starts talking with Tony like he knows him, and they keep up a three-minute conversation while I'm over here squirming in my seat, absently snacking on edamame.

I just told Tony I basically want to have sex with him, and I'm dying to know his response.

The server finally leaves, but Tony says nothing. He takes another drink. Leans back in his seat, practically sprawling in that way a confident man does.

Yes, I called the eighteen-year-old a man, because he is quiet and patient and has this ease about him that is both incredibly attractive and absolutely annoying. He doesn't act like any guy I've ever met before, and he's frustrating me.

"Did you hear what I said before we were interrupted?" I finally ask.

He slowly shakes his head. "Repeat it."

Is he playing me right now? "You asked if I wanted to murder you in your sleep."

"Oh. Right."

"And I said I want you naked in my bed."

"Again, not a very friendly thing to say, Hayden."

"It's *overly* friendly," I stress.

"Nope." He shakes his head. "You've completely left the friend zone with that statement."

I see the amusement dancing in his dark eyes. I sort of want to throttle him.

"You mentioned friends with benefits." I pause. He nods. "Is that offer still on the table?"

Yes, I went there. How can I not? He's in my thoughts constantly.

"Are we negotiating a deal right now, in the middle of

Wasabi on Fire?" He glances around before returning his gaze to mine. "My dad would be proud."

"We can't negotiate public deals. Our fathers would kill us."

"My dad probably has someone tailing my ass right now, and he'll report back that I was with a certain Hayden Channing." Tony grins. "I'm sure he'll call and chew my ass out later."

"Your father actually has someone tail you?" I'm shocked.

"Sometimes." Tony shrugs, like it's no big deal. I would be so pissed if my father did that.

"That's such an invasion of privacy."

"I'm sure your dad has the Find My Phone app." He inclines his head toward my phone, which is currently sitting on the table. "He's tailing you constantly."

True. How often does he check it though?

Probably more than I think he does.

I change the subject and ask him about football, vaguely humiliated that Tony wasn't readily agreeable when I mentioned the friends with benefits scenario. I wasn't lying earlier when I told him I couldn't stop thinking about him. He was on my mind for the rest of the night. I dreamed about him. Uncomfortable dreams where he rejected me and I chased after him. I felt bad about my reaction to his age, yet here I am, reacting about it all over again. It's dumb.

I'm being kind of dumb.

Maybe I'm handling this all wrong. I've always been aggressive when it comes to guys. When I see something I want, I usually go after it. But I've been burned a couple of times. Maybe I should switch tactics and try something different.

Should I be quiet and let him make his move on me? I'm

sure he's got some moves. He said so himself. And I should definitely not judge him for whatever moves the youngster might have.

Yeah, I am a horrible human, even in my thoughts.

Finally, our sushi rolls arrive and we start eating. I'm suddenly ravenous, devouring the sushi like a woman who's been held in captivity with no food for the last week. He watches me with amusement, and I want to ask him what's so funny, but I wisely keep my mouth shut.

That, and my mouth is constantly full of sushi, so I can't really speak anyway.

"You were hungry," he says when I finally set my chopsticks on the edge of my plate, my stomach full.

"Starving."

"Me too." He points at the empty plates that held our rolls.

"It was better than I remember."

"You've been here before?"

I nod. "Lots of times. I come with friends. Been on a few dates here."

"This isn't a date, though. According to you."

"It's not." I tilt my head, contemplating what I should say next. Immediately deciding I'm going to keep up with the theme and not hold back. "Are we just going to go round and round for the rest of the night? It's silly, don't you think?"

"You're the one who's silly."

"Don't put this on me," I say, mildly offended. "You're the one who didn't answer when I asked if the friends with benefits deal was still on the table."

"Well, it is."

"Well, good."

He laughs. Shakes his head. "What the fuck, Hayden? You're kind of a trip."

"I'm not normally like this," I reassure him, though I might be telling a teeny lie. "I think you bring it out of me."

"What else could I possibly bring out of you?" he asks with a grin.

"We should test it and see." My smile is coy.

Within minutes, we're leaving the restaurant, walking toward our matching Range Rovers that are parked right next to each other. I regret not taking his offer to drive me, but then again, I didn't want to leave my car in the campus parking lot either.

"Want to come back to my place?" he asks.

"Just to hang out?" I ask him, not wanting him to think I'm going back to his place for sex.

Not yet, anyway. Ha.

He shrugs. "Sure."

"How many roommates do you have?"

"Two, but one of them is never there."

"You share a room with either of them?"

"It's a three-bedroom condo, not too far from campus," he explains. "I have my own room."

Nice. All the guys I hooked up with my freshman year either lived in dorms or shared a room in a tiny apartment filled with six other douchebags. The guys I dated back then were the absolute worst. Young and horny and not interested in any type of conversation. They were only after one thing. At first, that's all I wanted too.

But now...I'm second guessing all of my earlier decisions in life. With men. Boys. I don't know what I want anymore.

That's not true. I know what I want currently.

Tony.

"Any of them home right now?" I ask.

"They probably are. Couple of our friends are probably there too. They sit around and play Call of Duty all night."

Typical. I'm sure he plays Call of Duty as well.

"I'll follow you to your place. I can't stay long though. I have an early class tomorrow," I say.

We stop in front of our parked SUVs. "What time is your class?" he asks.

"Eight." I make a face.

"That sucks," he says easily. "But don't worry. I won't take up too much of your time."

What the hell is that supposed to mean?

I follow him back to an apartment complex that isn't too far from mine. As in, we live literally down the road from each other.

Of course we do.

He waits for me as I park, and then leads the way to his condo. It's a newer complex, filled with two-story condominiums that cater to college students, and there's a giant gym in the center of the complex that's full of people. Most of them women clad in sports bras and leggings on the various machines.

"You work out there?" I ask him as we walk past it.

"Sometimes. I get a good enough workout with football practice most of the time. We do a lot of strength conditioning," he explains.

I am dying to see his abs. Does this make me a shallow person?

Probably.

When we're finally at his place, he opens the unlocked door for me, and the first thing I see is a stairwell. Once I'm in the living room, I see it's filled with guys. Like, a lot of guys. The TV is on, but there's no sound. Music is playing, and it's really loud.

"Tony! Where the fuck you been?" yells the blond. Jackson. He approaches us, his gaze going to me, his expression sobering right up. "Oh shit. It's the sexy blonde."

Clearly, he's drunk. Or high. Maybe a combination of the two.

"You guys remember Hayden, right?" Tony asks as he stops to stand right next to me. "Be nice."

"You telling that to us or to her?" The one who winked at me says that.

"Shut the fuck up, Caleb," Tony says good-naturedly.

"Hey guys." I wave at them, glancing around the living room. They have a giant dark gray sectional couch that everyone is sprawled on, and the place is relatively clean. Impressive, considering there are at least six guys crowded around this room.

"What are you doing?" Tony asks Jackson.

"Call of Duty tournament," he says with a shrug. "We're bored."

"Sorry I'm missing it." He glances over at me. "Want to see my room?"

"Sure."

I follow him up the stairs, appreciating his ass in those black joggers. He's long and lean but muscular too. I bet he'll fill out even more over the next couple of years, especially if he sticks with football. He smells good too. Clean with a hint of salt, like the ocean.

"Ladies first," he says when he stops in front of the third door on the left and opens it, holding out his hand and inviting me in.

I enter the bedroom, relief hitting me that it doesn't look like a pit from hell. It's clean. It smells normal. There aren't any discarded empty soda cans or water bottles cluttering his bedside table. His bed is actually made. It's neat and orderly and there aren't any personal items anywhere. No photos, no trophies, no art on the walls. It's downright barren, which kind of makes me sad.

Then I notice the dark gray lump sitting just behind his pillows. I take a step toward the bed, and the animal lifts its head, contemplating me with wide golden eyes. "You have a cat."

"That's Millicent," he says.

I send him a look. "Millicent?"

He shrugs. "She was my mom's cat first, so she named her. Then when my mom was never around, she adopted me."

"Millicent adopted you?" I go to the bed, reaching my hand toward the cat. She gives my fingers a delicate sniff, deems me acceptable and then rubs her head against my knuckles. I scratch her chin, and she begins to purr.

"She had to make nice with the only person in the house who'd feed her on a regular schedule, right? I'd wake up in the middle of the night to her sleeping on top of my head. Kind of sucked at first, but we grew on each other." He smiles faintly. "I couldn't leave her in that big house all alone when I moved down here. My mom would take off and probably forget all about her. She would've died."

My heart cracks. This is the sweetest thing. "So Millicent is *your* cat."

"She is now." He stands beside me and strokes along the cat's back. "She's cool."

This guy keeps surprising me. He's not your typical eighteen-year-old asshole, that's for sure.

"Your apartment is nice," I tell him as I head for the window. The blinds are still open and I peek outside to see he has a view of the grassy area in between the buildings. "I like it."

"Yeah, we do too." I glance over at him to find he's already watching me. "Where do you live?"

"Not too far from here, actually," I answer.

"We're almost neighbors?" He lifts his brows.

"Yep. Makes sense, don't you think?"

He frowns. "What do you mean by that?"

"Our paths were bound to cross." I don't mean to sound like a mystical woo woo, but I sort of am. I believe things happen for a reason, and people are put into our life for a purpose. I'm not sure why Tony is in my life yet, but I'm sure I'll find out soon enough.

"You really think so?" he asks.

"For sure." I spot the chair that's pulled away from his desk and I go to it, sitting down. "What should we do now?"

"Participate in a Call of Duty tournament?" He smiles, and I can tell he's teasing.

"Oh yes. I love Call of Duty."

"Really?" His smile fades.

"I'm joking," I reassure him with a soft laugh. "Should we watch a movie?"

"Netflix and chill?"

"Is that still a thing?"

"It will never not be a thing," he says with confidence.

"You know, I'd love to, but I should probably go home." I check my Apple Watch. It's already close to ten. Getting up for my eight o'clock class just about kills me, but I didn't have a choice. "It's getting late."

"You're really going to leave? You just got here." He plops down on the edge of the bed, his hands braced behind him, his legs spread wide.

I immediately imagine kneeling before him. Reaching for the fly of his jeans. Undoing it slowly...

I shove the thought out of my brain, contemplating him.

He's tempting. There's something about him that's so inviting.

Too inviting, really.

"Thank you for asking me to dinner," I tell him.

"Thank you for going with me." Swear to God, he spreads his legs even further.

"I'm going to watch you play Saturday," I remind him.

"Doubtful, but I'm glad you're going to the game."

"If I put it out in the universe, Sorrento, that means it's going to happen. Quit being such a doubter." I go to him and give him a gentle swat on his thigh.

It's as hard as a rock.

"You believe in that sort of thing?" He cocks a brow as I quickly step away.

"For sure." I nod. "Can't wait to see your moves on the field."

"Wait until you see my moves in here." He sits up, smiling, and pats the mattress.

I laugh, thankful he lightened the mood. The tension was ratcheting up between us. If we were going to stay in here alone much longer, something definitely would've happened. "Thank you for the tour of your bedroom. See you Saturday."

He snags my hand before I can leave, pulling me toward him. I go to him willingly, toppling onto the bed, practically on top of him, and he rolls us both over so we're laying side by side, our legs dangling off the edge of the mattress.

"Don't go yet," he murmurs, reaching for my face. He cups my cheek, those brown eyes scanning my face, landing on my lips. "Stay a few more minutes."

I stare at him, my gaze searching. His dark eyes. The sharp nose. Cheekbones I want to kiss. Full lips I really want to kiss.

Before I can say anything, his mouth lands on mine. Soft and sweet and oh, so persuasive. I sink into the kiss, opening for him, his tongue sliding against mine almost immediately.

It's dreamy. Of course kissing Tony is dreamy. I wouldn't expect anything less. He isn't too pushy, but he's not too shy with it either. He kisses and kisses me as if he's starved and I'm the only thing that will satisfy him. His big hand still cradles my face, his other hand linked with mine. He tastes good. He knows what he's doing with his tongue. This isn't awkward.

Not at all.

The kiss goes on. Becomes hungrier. We don't stop. We barely let up for air. I roll over onto my back and he follows, hovering above me, but not really touching me.

I want him to touch me.

Eventually, I begin to feel restless. A little needy. I try and scoot closer, desperate to feel him, when something rubs against my head, startling me.

We break apart, Tony chuckling. "I think Millicent is curious."

I glance above me to find the cat watching us, just before she ducks her head and rubs her face in my hair.

"Watch out. She'll keep rubbing your head, and then she'll chew on your hair," he warns.

The cat does exactly that, making me giggle.

"Right before she sinks her teeth into your skull," he continues.

"No way," I say, giggling again when she rubs and rubs. It feels kind of nice. She's purring loudly, really getting into it.

Right before she sinks her teeth into my scalp.

"Ow!" I duck away from her, sitting up, smoothing my

hair down as I glare at the cat. She curls up beside Tony and sends me a smug look.

Yes, a cat can look smug. This one sure does, at least.

"Sorry about that. She's a little weird sometimes," he says, sitting up as well. His lips are swollen and his eyes are heavy lidded. He looks very pleased with himself.

And very, very tempting. Meaning, I need to leave, before I do something stupid.

Like get naked and fuck this guy when I told him I would never do that.

I rise to my feet. "I need to head out."

"Don't let Millicent drive you away," he says with a laugh.

"You can't get rid of me that easily." I lean in and drop a quick kiss on his lips, then exit his bedroom. I practically sprint down the stairs, calling out a quick goodbye to the guys before I exit the apartment.

I flee like a criminal leaving the scene of the crime, finally taking a deep, calming breath when I'm sitting in my car and starting the engine. No one chased after me. Not Tony, and not any of his friends, though I didn't expect them to.

Laughter bubbles up inside my chest and I let it free, shaking my head, my hands landing on the steering wheel. I have no idea what Tony and I are doing right now, but I have to admit.

It's fun.

ELEVEN

TONY

GAME DAY. Bullshit, as usual. Sitting on the sidelines. Silently begging for a chance to play. This is a different scene compared to high school. Bigger crowds. Bigger stakes. Bigger everything. It's intimidating. Some of the guys that are new on the team already thrive on this shit. Eli Bennett for one. He loves attention, and this atmosphere feeds his soul. He can't wait to be top dog on campus. He's already making plans for senior year, while I can barely wrap my head around the fact that we're actually here.

I've gotten more serious, though. I give it my all every single practice. I ask questions when we go over plays because I want them to know I'm paying attention. I want to prove it to the coaches that I want to be here.

That I deserve to be here.

We're halfway through the third quarter when our star tight end gets injured. Like carry him off on a stretcher while he grimaces in pain, injured.

Second string is out thanks to a recent knee surgery.

"Sorrento!"

I glance up to find the offensive line coach marching

toward me, his jaw moving a mile a minute as he chews on a wad of pink gum.

"Yeah?" I ask him weakly, unsure of his approach.

"Grab your helmet and get out there." He jerks his thumb toward the field. "Your time is now."

Oh. Shit. I jump to my feet and shove my helmet over my head. "My time is now for what?"

"To prove yourself to me once and for all. Get out there. Show 'em what you got!"

I jog out onto the field, wincing as I hear my name announced as the replacement. There are a few boos, accompanied by some weak applause. I don't think the boos are toward me. No one knows who the hell I am. I think the fans are just pissed and sad one of our best players just got injured.

Our quarterback Ash Davis calls a huddle and I head into it, my heart rattling around in my chest like it wants to leave my body. He says a few things about the next play, then specifically says my name.

"Yeah?"

"You good, bro? You're as white as a ghost," Davis says.

Swallowing hard, I nod. "I'm good."

"You know the plays?"

If I'm not working on classwork, I'm going over the Bulldog playbook. "Yeah."

"Good. Let's go!"

They all roar, with the exception of me. I get into position. Swear to God, I hear Bennett and Caleb yelling for me from the sidelines, and I try to tune them out.

I tune everything out, but the QB and the plays he's calling.

This is it. We launch forward, me running to the right,

on the outer edge. I glance over my shoulder as I keep running, see the ball sailing toward me.

It's also headed straight for the opposing player trying to block me.

I jag to the left, and turn, facing Davis. I see his face beneath the helmet, his eyes wide, his expression grim as the ball falls...

Right into my hands.

I grip that fucker and start running, a grunt escaping me when I'm tackled to the ground.

"And the Bulldogs get a first down thanks to freshman Anthony Sorrento!" the announcer says.

The crowd goes wild.

I rise to my feet, glaring at the asshole who took me down. He glares back.

"Lucky catch."

"Fuck off," I mutter as I rejoin my team, my smile barely contained.

"Nice play, Sorrento," Davis says to me as we get back into position.

His compliment makes me feel good, it's like I'm floating on the field for the rest of the game. I make a couple of mistakes, but nothing awful. We score a touchdown. Our defense holds the other team when they have the ball. It goes like this, back and forth, right into the fourth quarter, until there are only a few more minutes on the clock and we're leading by a touchdown and a field goal.

The other team scores. Everyone on the sideline groans. The defensive line coach looks ready to choke someone out. It's nonstop drama out here, and for once, I'm totally enjoying it. Because I'm actually living it, versus sitting on a bench and watching it.

Once we have the ball back, I make a few completions

and gain some yards, but never get the chance to run it into the end zone. But we do score again, and we cement the win. Normally I'm sitting on the bench throughout the game, so it's a totally different feeling, being on the field. We all crowd in a circle, chanting and yelling. People from the stands spill out onto the field as well, including a lot of local sports reporters, and I watch in awe as we're swarmed, treated like gods.

I remember this feeling from high school, but it's amplified out here. In this giant stadium instead of our little field, surrounded by thousands of onlookers in the stands. It's kind of insane, how many people are here tonight in support of us.

It's also pretty fucking awesome. I can't stop smiling.

Ash approaches me with a grin, clapping me on the shoulder. "Didn't think you had it in you, but good job tonight," he says before he walks away.

"Thanks," I tell him but he's already gone.

It feels like with tonight's game performance, I totally redeemed myself.

The offensive line coach joins me as we all start to walk off the field.

"You did good, son," he says. "Would like to focus on your technique this week during practice. You could still use a little work."

"Sounds good," I say, in a daze over all the congrats and compliments. Grateful as hell that he wants to work with me.

"You know you're playing for the rest of the season, right?" He squints at me.

I squint back. "Seriously?"

"Johnson's out with that ankle break. It's severe—in two places." Coach's expression is grim. "And Phillips is done for the year. His knee surgery took him out completely."

Phillips had pro aspirations, too. Sucks to hear his chances are most likely over.

I enjoy football, but it's not my everything. I don't want to go pro. I'm a decent player, but I'm not pro material. I don't think I have the discipline for it either.

"Party tonight," Caleb says to me once we're in the locker room. Our lockers are right next to each other's. "At the frat house. It's already started, so show up whenever."

"I don't know—" I start, but Caleb shakes his head, his fierce expression making me stop talking.

"Nope. You're not going to bail out like you did last time." He grabs hold of my shoulders and gives me a shake. "We're celebrating *you* tonight, asshole. You have to be there."

"I did nothing." I'm trying to play it off.

"You played," Caleb stresses.

"But I didn't score."

"Doesn't matter. You did great. You showed them that your heart is still in the game." He releases his hold on me, his expression as serious as I've ever seen it. "I was afraid you lost your love for football."

I say nothing. When you have no one loving you, it's hard to love anything else. Even football.

Sounds fucking pitiful, but it's true.

"I'm exhausted," I tell Caleb. "I just want to go home and collapse in bed."

"The only way I'll let you do that is if you've got that hot blonde waiting for you in your bed naked," Caleb says.

I think of Hayden. Waiting for me. Naked in my bed.

"Yeah. Not happening," I say.

Such a shame.

"Then you're coming to the party." Caleb grins. "Whether you like it or not."

I EVENTUALLY SHOW up at the frat house with Jackson as my date. He joined this fraternity along with Caleb, and they tried to get me to join with them, but I declined. Why go through the initiation and everything else, when I could benefit from the parties through them? That's all I care about anyway.

The house is two-story, red brick with black shutters on the windows. It has a distinctive, almost formal appearance, yet there's all sorts of revelry and debauchery going on inside.

Maybe that's the appeal.

As we approach the massive front door that's standing wide-open, I see there are people everywhere. On the front porch, inside the house, outside in the back yard. The moment I show my face, I'm greeted with plenty of "congratulations" and "good jobs!". I nod and smile in return, saying thank you, shocked they'd know me. Caleb can tell.

"You made a splash tonight," he says with a grin. "Enjoy it."

I didn't even think people knew my name, let alone could recognize my face. It's weird.

Once we're inside, girls approach us, expectant smiles on their faces, their gazes directed at me.

"You played good tonight," a bold one says, reaching out to trail her fingernails along my arm as she walks away.

She's using the 'leave them wanting trick', and I suppose any other night it would work on me.

I can't help but glance around the place, wondering if Hayden is here.

From what I can tell, she's nowhere to be found.

She sent me a simple text after the game.

Told you that you'd play tonight.

That was it. No praise. Just an *I told you so.*

My response was a smiling emoji, because I had no idea how to respond. I was sort of annoyed with her flippant attitude. This girl works really hard at keeping me at a distance, and the more I realize this, the more irritated I become.

Maybe I'm just irritated in general, I don't know. Sexually frustrated? Yeah, probably. I feel like I've been teased and taunted for days, and I'm left standing alone with my limp dick in my hand.

Metaphorically, of course.

When we finally make it into the kitchen, Caleb offers me a hit off a weed vape he's got tucked into the front pocket of his hoodie, but I decline. Now that I'm actually playing, and will continue to play, I don't want to get drug tested and kicked off the team. There's too much at stake.

Caleb always acts as if he has nothing to lose. Jackson is the same way. Booze, girls, drugs, they'll both do it all, fuck the consequences. Caleb's a little crazier than Jackson, though. And his recklessness is part of his appeal to the girls.

To us too. He's always a good time.

As time drags on, I slam back a few beers, which leaves me feeling mellow, and find a chair in the living room to sit in, like a king surveying his castle. A few girls sit near me and start bombarding me with observations and questions. The beer has loosened my tongue, and I answer all of their questions, wishing I could find at least one of them attractive.

But I don't. They're cute, don't get me wrong, but none of them are Hayden. And despite my mild annoyance with her, if she marched in here right now and demanded I leave with her, I would.

Women. They frustrate the shit out of me.

"Tony!" I glance up to find Jocelyn standing there, a wide smile on her face.

"Jos." I rise to my feet and pull her into a hug, noticing all of the girls watching her with suspicion. I'm sure they view her as competition. "Where's our boy?"

"With Jackson and Eli." She glances over at the girls sitting on the floor and offers them a little wave. "You played well tonight."

"I did all right," I say modestly with a little shrug. Jocelyn's praise means something. She's watched me play pretty much throughout my entire football career. Her opinion matters.

"You did great. Diego said you're going to start for the rest of the season," she says.

"Crazy, right?" I shake my head, trying to pretend that shit doesn't scare the crap out of me, but it does. It's a lot of pressure, something I didn't think I'd have to deal with as a freshman. "Coaches don't have a choice, though."

"Don't let them down. Prove to them how good you are," she says. "Take your opportunity and use it to your advantage."

"You sound like a mom," I say with a grin.

"That's because I am one." She swats my upper arm, laughing.

We both glance over at the same time to see the girls rising from the floor and leaving. The moment they're gone, Jocelyn sends me a knowing look. "Groupies?"

"I guess. They just sat down and started talking to me."

"Tony has a fan club."

"I leave that shit up to Caleb."

"Caleb is already pissing off his fan club base. He shouldn't move on from girl to girl so quickly."

"I guess he can't help himself." Caleb comes from a loving family with parents who've been married for over twenty years. I don't get why he acts the way he does.

"He could, he just chooses not to." She settles on the armrest of my chair. "Have you met anyone yet?"

"No."

"You sure about that?" She raises a brow.

Damn it. I'm sure Diego mentioned Hayden to her.

"It's nothing. Just a hot blonde I met at the Range Rover dealership." I try to play it off, but Hayden is so much more than that.

"In San Francisco. Yet she just so happens to go to school here. Talk about a coincidence." Her eyes dance with mischief. "Some people call that fate."

"I don't believe in that bullshit." Though if I remember correctly, Hayden actually does.

Which is surprising to me, considering how straightforward she is.

"That's too bad. I think it's sort of sweet. Diego says she gave you a lot of shit. And that she was pretty."

If we were still in high school and Diego said something like that to Jocelyn? They would've gotten into a huge fight and Jos would've been jealous. They've come a long way. They're a lot more pleasant to be around. I think baby Gigi gets some of the credit for that.

"All accurate observations," I say with a nod.

Jocelyn's expression turns pensive. "It was nice, seeing you chatting with the girls. You know at every social event, you're almost always alone, watching everyone else have fun?"

I send her a look, but say nothing.

"It's true. You're an observer of life, Tony. And you make great observations, don't get me wrong, but it's always struck me as kind of sad, how you don't put yourself out there more," she explains.

I feel seen. And it also makes me feel uncomfortable.

"You always were the one to have everyone over, hosting the parties. It didn't matter how messed up your house was. You just wanted everyone there. I always figured it was because you didn't want to be alone. That's why I was so glad to see you with Sophie. She brought you out of your shell. You were actually participating in your life, versus sitting back and watching it happen."

"Jos—" I start, but she cuts me off with a look.

"Hear me out." She rests a gentle hand on my shoulder. "You're an amazing guy, Anthony Sorrento. But you can't keep letting things just happen to you. You need to grab life by the balls and make it happen."

"Are we talking about balls now?" I lift a brow, trying to lighten the mood, but Jos won't have it.

"Just—instead of being the one who always offers advice, you need to be the one who takes it." She gives my shoulder a squeeze. "And you need to open yourself up more. Have an adventure. You should text that pretty blonde and invite her over here. Flirt with her. See where it takes you."

"Not everyone is going to find their greatest love at this young of an age, Jos. Hayden is probably just some girl I met one time, you know?"

"I know. But you don't truly know unless you give it—her—a try. Put yourself out there, bro." Now she sounds like

Diego. She's smiling, so I assume she knows this. "Have fun. Live a little."

Another squeeze of my shoulder and then she leaps to her feet, waving at me before she goes in search of Diego.

Her words linger with me. Pound in my head. Throb in my heart. Maybe Jocelyn's right. I'm not really living my life. I'm just letting shit happen to me. I'm an observer, she definitely got that right, but I'm more than that.

Right?

Pulling my phone out of my pocket, I look up Hayden's number and start typing. Before I can overthink it or erase everything I just said, I hit send.

And then I wait.

TWELVE

HAYDEN

YOU SHOULD COME HANG **out with me.**

The text comes from Tony at almost midnight. I turn my phone screen in Gracie's direction, showing the text to her.

"Feels like a booty call," I say.

Her expression is smug. She loves a booty-call text on the weekend. Or any day of the week. She calls them opportunities we shouldn't pass up. "Ooh. Take him up on it. When was the last time you got laid?"

"A long time." I roll my eyes. Stare at my phone. Contemplate sending him a response.

But what should I say? If I was in bed already, I'd hit him with a big nope.

I'm not in bed though. I'm still dressed with the day's makeup fading on my face. We're currently sitting in the living room, watching Euphoria for what feels like the fiftieth time and talking about hot guys on campus. And what do you know, a hot guy from campus sends me a booty-call text.

Fitting.

"You going to answer him?" Gracie asks.

I glance up to find her watching me expectantly. I haven't told her all the details about Tony yet. Specifically, that he's only eighteen. I kind of don't want to witness her reaction to this news.

And then again, I kind of do.

"Should I?" I ask her.

Gracie's response is an enthusiastic nod. "Hell yes! Why wouldn't you?"

"I don't know." I shrug, thinking of my father and how he wants me to have zero contact with Tony. He'd be so pissed if he knew how much time we've spent together already. "It'll go nowhere."

"Isn't that the beauty of it all?" When I send her a questioning look, Gracie continues. "You keep saying you don't want a relationship. You also told me this guy doesn't want one either. I say you grab this unicorn and ride him like a bucking bronco until you get sick of his shit."

She makes it sound so easy. Like I can just fuck him and dump him. I tell myself I can do that. I've done that with other guys before. But...

Will it be so easy with Tony? I like him. I like talking to him. I like looking at him too. Oh, and I like kissing him, that's for sure.

"Here's where I admit something to you." I grab a pillow and cradle it in front of me, my gaze never leaving Gracie's. "He's only...eighteen."

I wait for her reaction, bracing myself. The only thing she does is clap her hands together, the crack of her palms meeting so loud I visibly jump. "Is he a virgin?"

Say what? "I don't know. I didn't ask. And wouldn't you think most eighteen-year-old guys aren't virgins?"

"You never know. I encountered a few our freshman year." She grins. "And I rocked their world."

"You're not reacting like I thought you would," I mutter.

"What? Did you expect me to give you shit about robbing the cradle? If we were in high school and you were a senior dating a sophomore, I'd probably give you shit." Her expression turns pensive. "Though there were senior guys dating sophomore girls when I was in high school, and no one gave a shit. There were seniors dating freshman girls and it didn't matter. But if a girl dated a younger guy in high school? You got called out for it. Which is ridiculous."

So ridiculous. I totally agree.

A sigh of relief leaves me and I sag against the couch. "I definitely thought you'd accuse me of robbing the cradle."

"No way. Look, even if he's had sex before, he's like an unexplored gold mine. You've chipped off the gold, see if it has potential for more. So you keep working for it and eventually, you'll be rich," Gracie says, like this is a perfectly logical analogy.

"What in the world are you talking about?"

"I'm saying that he has a lot of potential. You can teach him your ways," she says.

"It's not like I've had a ton of sex." I've had five partners. I lost my virginity at seventeen to the guy I dated briefly my senior year. Very cliché. I've messed around more than I've actually had intercourse, which I think is typical. It's not like I have a ton of experience.

But I might have more experience than him, which I think is Gracie's point.

"You've got two years on him. You've probably had more sex than he has," Gracie says. "And you can teach him what you like. Make him an expert on your body. Girls will thank you later."

The idea of me teaching Tony moves so he can use them on other women in the future leaves a sour taste in my mouth. "I don't know about that."

My phone buzzes, causing it to slide toward me from where I left it on the couch. I pick it up to find another text from Tony. All it says is:

????

"Is that your young man?" Gracie cackles the moment the words leave her mouth.

I glare at her. "Yes."

"Answer him!"

I send a response.

Where are you?

Tony: **Frat party. It's boring.**

Me: **You want me to come over and spice it up? Is that what you're asking for?**

Tony: **Definitely.**

Me: **What frat?**

He sends me his location.

"He's at a frat party," I tell Gracie.

"Is he in a frat?"

"I don't know. I don't think so." But honestly, I'm not sure. I don't know much about this guy. At all.

"Come on. Let's get you dolled up for your booty call." Gracie leaps to her feet and heads for the bathroom.

I follow her, and let her curl my hair, though nothing too elaborate. I remove my old mascara with a makeup wipe and add a fresh coat to my lashes. I change into my favorite jeans and a cute cropped top.

"What do you think?" I ask Gracie once I'm back in the living room and ready to go.

She whistles low. "Hottie."

"Really?" I go to the mirror near the front door. We use it to make sure we look decent before we leave for the day— or night, like I'm about to. Maybe. "I look like I'm trying too hard."

"No, you don't. You look pretty, Hay. And since when do you care so much about looking like you're trying so hard? Usually you just go for it. You're just you." I glance over my shoulder to find her smiling at me. "Is this boy special?"

She draws out the last word.

"He's just a boy." I stare at my reflection as I keep repeating that mantra in my head.

He's just a boy. He's just a boy. He's just a boy.

So why does this feel like something that could be more?

"My expectations are too high," I say to Gracie. And to myself.

"Stop dawdling and go to this party. It's midnight."

"It'll still be in full swing." I grab my purse and send her one last look. "You want to go with?"

"Hell, no. I'm tired." She yawns, and I can tell it's real. "I'm going to bed. But I'll keep my phone right beside me. Text me if things go haywire and you need a rescue."

"It won't," I reassure her.

"You never know. I'm here for you, babe." She blows me a kiss.

In minutes, I'm in my car and driving to the frat, which is located in a neighborhood on the other side of campus. Traffic is light because it's late, and I have a mental conversation with myself the entire drive.

This is no big deal.

You're just going to hang out with him.

Maybe, if you're lucky, you'll kiss him.

But that's it! That's all he'll get from you tonight. Leave them wanting. That's what my mother used to tell me and Palmer when she talked about boys with us.

I frown. Mom was giving us advice about boys when we were really young. Advice that was probably mildly inappropriate. But what else is new? My mom and dad have never been in the running for parents of the year awards.

When I finally find the frat, I see that it's busy. Lots of people are still hanging around, and the streets are lined with cars. I park a few blocks away from the house, grateful I didn't wear shoes with heels. Though if I had, I would've berated myself because, oh yes, that looks like I'm trying too hard.

Instead, I slipped Birks on my socked covered feet. Gives me enough of a dressed down look to balance out the curled hair and crop top.

When I finally arrive at the house, I see that I'm not the only one who adopted that look. Girls in jeans and socked feet with Birks are everywhere. Maybe we all look one and the same. There's nothing distinct about me, and I'm worried that maybe he'll find me uninteresting. Though that shouldn't bother me since there are plenty of other guys on this campus. Lots of cute guys. I don't know why I'm so hung up on this one.

I stop in the middle of a crowded living room and tell myself to quit the pity party. I am not an insecure whiner. So why am I thinking like one?

Strong fingers suddenly wrap around my upper arm and I stop, turning to find the very boy I'm stressed about standing in front of me, as pretty as I remember him.

Okay, it's not fair to call him pretty, but he is truly just so flat-out gorgeous that I find myself staring at him for a moment like a starstruck fan.

"You made it," he says, his deep voice curling around me and making me warm.

"I did." I smile, secretly hoping he doesn't let me go.

"You want something to drink?"

I nod. Smile. Stare at him like a dope.

He smiles too, releasing his grip on my arm. "Come on. Let's find you something."

Tony rests his hand lightly on my lower back as he guides me through the crowd. I walk beside him, the smile still fixed on my face, and I notice more than a few girls glare at me as we pass. Like they don't like seeing me with Tony?

I don't get it.

We go into the back yard and Tony pours me a beer from the keg. I take the cup from him with a murmured thank you and sip, making a face.

It's warm. Mostly foam.

"Not good?" He asks.

"You try it." I hand him the cup.

He takes a drink and winces, then turns away from me and pours it out onto the grass. "Awful."

I laugh. "It's the thought that counts?"

He tosses the cup in a nearby trashcan. How thoughtful of these frat boys. Usually they're not so conscientious. It's red Solo cups and empty beer cans everywhere. "They're running out of everything. Maybe we could get a shot of something in the kitchen?"

His hand is on my elbow like he's ready to take me back inside, but I dig in my heels and slowly shake my head. "I don't need any alcohol. Unless you do," I add.

"I've had enough." He glances around, his hand still on my elbow, before he returns his gaze back to me. "Let's go sit over there."

"Over there" is an empty bench on the far side of the yard, underneath a giant tree. We go to it and settle in, snug next to each other since the bench is small. He slings his arm across the back of it, stretching out his legs, and I feel surrounded by him.

It's not unpleasant. Not at all.

"What did you think of tonight's game?" he asks.

"I think you played amazing." I mean, he looked amazing to me. My dad is more of a basketball fan. We didn't watch a lot of football in my house growing up.

"I was all right," he says with a modest shrug, his gaze fixed on something in the distance. "I'll be starting for the rest of the season."

"That's a big deal, right?"

"Yeah. I'm kind of freaked out, if you want the truth." His laugh is self-conscious, and he still won't really look at me.

He is unlike any other guy I've ever been with. They're usually full of bravado and brag nonstop. Overly cocky and downright flippant about anything. Everything. The world is their oyster and they'll do whatever it takes to make it theirs, no hesitation.

Tony is much more...subtle. Calm. Real.

So real.

"Why are you freaked out?" I ask.

"What if I fuck up?" He turns his head toward me and I realize we are sitting really close. Kissing close. My gaze drops to his lips. His lower lip is extra full. Bitable. "The coaching staff already watches me extra close because I fucked-up so bad early in the season."

He doesn't seem like the type to fuck-up. He seems rather methodical in everything he does. "How did you fuck-up?"

"I bailed on practice a couple of times. Wasn't feeling it. Didn't care. Had a new friend who felt the same, so we always took off together." He looks away again, his jaw tight. "When you go from being on top of the world to the very bottom rung, it's kind of difficult."

"Big fish in little pond to small fish in giant pond," I murmur.

"Exactly."

"Why did your coaches say you'll play the rest of the season if they supposedly have no faith in you?" I ask.

"They don't really have a choice. I'm third string. First and second are hurt. Both season-ending injuries. I'm all they've got left," he explains.

"I'm sure you'll rise to the challenge."

"Maybe. I don't know." His gaze returns to mine once more. "I don't want to talk about football anymore."

"You're the one who brought it up," I point out.

He smiles. "I guess you're right."

I decide to change the subject first. "Are you in this frat?" I ask him.

"No. Caleb is. So is Jackson. I don't like hanging out with so many people all the damn time." He sends me a meaningful look. "I half-expected to find you here tonight."

I arch my brow. "Do I look like the hang-out-at-a-frat-party-every-weekend type?"

"No. I think it was more wishful thinking on my part."

Aw. That was a sweet admission.

"My roommate and I went straight home after the game," I say.

"Why?"

"We don't really go to the games that much." If at all. "Once it was done and we struggled with getting out of the parking lot for so long, we were kind of over the entire evening."

"I get it," he says with a nod.

"You want me to be real with you right now?"

His dark eyes linger on mine, his expression intense. "I always want you to be real with me."

"I half-expected you to ask me to meet you somewhere when I sent you that text earlier." I'd been trying to flirt, but it came out sort of bratty and had a very 'told you so' vibe. "You sent me a smiley face. That was it."

"I was busy."

Ouch.

"With someone else?" Ugh. I sound jealous. I need to stop.

"With the team," he stresses.

Oh. I figured he found some other girl to talk to. Hook up with.

"Did you think I was with a girl?" he asks when I still haven't said anything.

"You have every right to see whoever you want. We're nothing serious," I say haughtily, immediately hating my tone. I have no claim on him.

"Because I did talk to some girls earlier," he says.

My stomach knots up and I'm grateful I didn't drink any beer. I'd probably puke it back up.

"Are you trying to make me jealous?" I raise a brow, pretending I'm not bothered.

But I am. I'm bothered.

A lot.

"No. I'm just telling you the truth."

He remains quiet, which drives me crazy. "What happened with those girls?" I try to keep my tone casual, but I'm pretty sure I'm failing.

His arm drops so it's wrapped around my shoulders. "Wait a minute. Are you actually jealous?"

I lift my chin, secretly enjoying the heavy weight of his arm pressing on me. "Of course not."

"Can I admit something?"

I turn to look at him and find he's already staring at me. "What?"

"None of them interested me."

Those knots start to loosen, and I feel instantly lighter. "Why not?"

"Because I kept thinking about you."

Oh. The knots are completely undone. I'm nothing but air.

I part my lips, breathless from his forthright admission. "Okay, bu—"

I don't even get the word out before his mouth lands on mine, silencing me. His lips are soft and warm. The kiss is tame. Honestly? It should be unmemorable. Just our mouths connecting, no tongue involved. Our lips barely parted.

This moment shouldn't be such a big deal.

But that first touch of his mouth on mine and sparks ignite all over my body. His hand cups my shoulder, gently pulling me toward him. I rest my hand on his thigh to brace myself, startled by the hard, lean muscle beneath my palm. He breaks the kiss first, his gaze lingering on my mouth, his tongue wetting his lips.

Something unfurls within me at seeing his tongue. Something warm and liquid that I want to feel again.

And again.

Leaning in, I kiss him this time. And oh God.

Oh God.

Sparks fly between our lips. The kiss is electrifying. Even better than that kiss we shared in his bedroom a few nights ago. A whimper of surprise escapes me. He groans low in his throat, cupping my cheek with his free hand, his touch firm as he parts my lips with his tongue. It goes on for long, delicious moments. Lips connecting, breaking apart, reconnecting. Tongues sliding. Circling. He licks at my upper lip teasingly. I bite his lower lip, my teeth coming together slowly, tugging.

Again, he breaks away first, his chest rising and falling rapidly with every panting breath. "That wasn't a friendly kiss."

I slowly shake my head, enjoying how rattled he appears. I wonder if I look the same. "Not at all," I agree.

"I thought that was all you wanted."

"Don't forget I was the one who asked if the friends with benefits deal was still on the table." Reaching out, I rest my hand against his firm chest, his rapidly beating heart pounding a steady rhythm beneath my palm. "You're very persuasive."

He actually grins. "You think I'm persuasive?"

"I think your lips are," I tell him truthfully.

He leans in for a brief kiss, and I feel the brush of his lips all the way down to my toes. "Wait until you meet the rest of me."

THIRTEEN

TONY

WE END up in the back seat of my Rover. The moment she shuts the door, I'm pulling her close. Until she's on top of me, straddling me, her hot body pressed to mine, our mouths locked. The longer we kiss, the steamier the interior of my car gets, until the windows are fogged and my hand is up her shirt, fingers curled around the thin lace of her bra.

She laughs against my mouth. Gasps when I press my thumb against her hard nipple. "I'm not fucking you in the back seat of your car, Sorrento."

"Didn't want to fuck you back here," I murmur against her lips, just before I dive in for another kiss. She has this way of curling her tongue around mine that makes me shiver.

Makes me pretty fucking hard too.

Or maybe I'm hard because of the way she grinds on me. Her lower body is flush against mine, and I swear I can feel the heat of her, even through her jeans and mine. I slide my hands down her back, until they rest on her ass. It's round and perfect and squeezable and I do just that, pulling her into me. As close as she can get.

She gasps into my mouth, a shuddery sigh escaping her. "What are we doing?"

I chuckle. "You haven't figured it out yet?"

She tilts her head to the right, her mouth landing on my neck. She kisses and licks me there, and fuck me, that feels good. "You are too good looking."

"Thank you?" Is she trying to insult me?

"And you smell fucking amazing." She sniffs my neck. Nips my earlobe. "Your hair is so soft."

She runs her fingers through it, making me shiver.

"And your dick is really." She shifts her hips. "Really." She presses firmly against me, whimpering. "Hard."

I tighten my grip on her ass, lifting her. Lowering her. She takes the hint, rubbing against me in earnest, her mouth on mine once more. We're going at it. Dry humping in the back seat of my car, our breaths accelerating, my heart thumping. I do not want to come in my jeans. Fuck that. But if she keeps this up.

I'm probably going to.

Her rhythm quickens and I remove a hand from her ass, slipping it up the front of her shirt, curling my fingers around her breast once more. I tug the lace down, toying with her nipple, circling it again and again. A strangled cry sounds low in her throat, her entire body going still for only a moment, just before she starts to quake.

"Oh God," she whispers against my lips and I crack open my eyes, pulling away from her slightly so I can watch.

Watch Hayden come.

Her eyes are still closed, her lips parted. Her hands grip on my shoulders and her lower body still grinds against me. I'm still grinding against her, my hand still under her shirt, cupping her. She's panting. And once the shivering subsides, her lips curl into the faintest smile as she slowly opens her eyes.

"Um." She's full-blown grinning.

"Yeah." I smile at her in return, our chests rising and falling, brushing against each other. I lean back against the seat, taking her with me, our mouths meeting in a lingering kiss. "You enjoyed that."

"A lot," she says with a laugh.

I swallow the sound, kissing her deeply, sliding my hand around her neck, up into her silky hair. This girl is twisting me up inside. Making me feel things I didn't think I could. She's fun, flirty, contrary, a challenge, yet easy to talk to. To be with. To give an orgasm to.

Or maybe she gave herself that orgasm. She was grinding pretty hard on my cock just now.

"But what about you?" she asks, her lips brushing mine. She reaches between us, her fingers trailing over the front of my jeans, making me suck in a sharp breath. "Let me."

I kiss her hungrily, starved for her. The girl doesn't even hesitate. She's undoing the front of my jeans, her hand slipping inside, stroking the front of my boxer briefs. She curls her fingers around the length of my dick, essentially feeling me up before they dive beneath the cotton, her busy fingers meeting my bare flesh.

"Ah shit," I grunt out when she gives me a squeeze.

She pauses everything she's doing. "Want me to stop?"

"Fuck no," I grit out and she laughs, just before she kisses me again.

She strokes and teases. Her pace slow. Fast. Gentle. A little rough. I lift my ass, and she tugs my jeans and briefs down so they're curled beneath my knees. I'm reaching for her too, my fingers going to the snap on her jeans but she jerks her hips away.

"This is about you," she whispers.

Just before she readjusts herself and bends down, her mouth landing on my cock.

"Fuck." The word is stuck in my throat, my hand in her hair as she bobs up and down on my dick. She licks the head. Sucks it. Her hair falls over her face, over me so I can't see what's happening and I brush it back to watch this gorgeous girl work me over with her mouth.

I am visual. What guy isn't? And seeing her hunched over me, her cheeks hollowing out as she sucks me deep, I know it's not going to take long. The sensation is building at the base of my spine. My cock. I'm gonna shoot off like a goddamn rocket here any second.

As if she knows, she strokes me with her fingers, her mouth sucking. I lift my hips, offering up a warning cry right before the orgasm takes over me.

She removes her mouth from my cock, and I come all over her fingers, watching helplessly, her hand still gripping me tight, squeezing every last drop out of me. Holy fuck.

Holy. *Fuck.*

Once the shuddering has subsided, she drops a sweet kiss on the tip of my semi-hard dick just before she moves up, her face in mine.

"Um," I tell her, at a complete loss for words.

She laughs. "I felt the same exact way."

We kiss. I can taste myself on her lips, but I don't mind. Fuck, it makes me hornier, but she pulls away, a sly smile on her face.

"Like I told you, I'm not about to have sex with you in the back seat of your Rover, like that damn song," she says with a laugh, reaching for the Kleenex package that's stashed in the pocket on the back of the driver's seat, wiping off her hands with a couple of tissues.

I frown, thinking for a moment before I finally remember the song. "Whatever happened to those guys anyway?"

"Who? The Chainsmokers?" She shrugs when I nod. "I don't know."

"Me neither." I reach for her again, needing more. Another kiss. A little tongue. Closeness. I don't want to stop looking at this girl. Or touching this girl. "This has been the best night."

"I'm sure," she says wryly, giving me a firm kiss before she pulls away completely. "I should go."

I tug up my underwear and jeans, righting myself as best I can while she's watching me, her teeth sunk into her lower lip. "When can I see you again?" I ask.

"Soon." She reaches for the door handle. "I'm sure we'll run into each other on campus."

I frown. She baffles me, but not in a bad way. Why can't she just say, let's get together tomorrow, or whatever.

"You really think so?" I ask.

She opens the car door, a rush of cool air filling the steamy interior. "Oh I know so. See you around, Tony."

I watch her go, flinching when she slams the door. Leaning my head back, I stare at the car roof, shaking my head.

How is it that I'm the one who just got a blow job, yet I feel...used?

Not in a bad way. Not at all. I just can't figure this girl out.

Yet.

FOOLING AROUND with a pretty girl in my car after being a part of a team that won an important game leaves you sitting on top of the world.

This is how I feel as I go about my Sunday. I can't stop thinking about what happened between Hayden and I last night. To the point that I've pretty much forgotten about the game win. My moment with Hayden is in the forefront of my mind. Talk about hot. The entire experience leaves me wanting more.

More time with Hayden. More kissing, touching, all of it with Hayden.

What we're doing isn't something I'm overly familiar with. Meaning, I'm not an expert at this relationship stuff. Hooking up stuff? Yes, I've hooked up with a few girls since Sophie, but never one I actually wanted to continue seeing. And Sophie was never forward with me. I made all the moves, and they were unsure and a little awkward, because I had no idea what the hell I was doing.

With Hayden, it's like a cat and mouse game. Bait and switch. Whatever. I don't feel like I'm being tricked, but it's actually...

Fun.

The flirting. The banter. The innuendo. The kissing. The everything else. She's a challenge. She plays hard to get, yet flaunts what she's got right in front of me. Like she wants me to chase. And I do.

She's a smart one, Hayden Channing. Left me sitting in my car wanting more of her. All of her. I admitted she was all I could think about before. Now?

I'm fucking obsessed.

I went home and jerked off in the shower to the memories of our encounter. Those whimpers she made when we kissed. Her taste. The sting of her teeth when she bit my lower lip. Watching her come. Watching her swallow my cock. It was hot. A moment I won't ever forget.

Now I'm desperate to make more moments with her.

Homework calls, but I don't want to do it, so I distract myself with laundry. The great thing about laundry is I can still think about Hayden while I do it. Homework would require all of my concentration, and I'm not feeling it.

When do I ever feel it? I'm not stupid. I get good grades. Even when I bailed on football practice, I was going to class. Jackson? He skipped plenty at first, but he's getting better about it. I like to think I'm helping him keep on task. Caleb and I work on homework together, though I'm the one who always has to remind him to stay on top of it. I don't know why I care so much.

Maybe it's because they're my friends, and I have no one else to focus on. No family. No girl.

Well, I feel like now I have a girl.

No one else is up yet in my house. Caleb is sleeping. Jackson stayed the night and is asleep in Diego's room. The house is a mess, and once I throw my darks into the dryer, I start picking up. Tossing out beer cans and garbage. Wiping down the kitchen counters. Loading up the dishwasher.

"Aren't you a happy homemaker this morning?"

This is how Caleb greets me. I turn to find him standing by the fridge, and he looks trashed. His eyes are bloodshot and his hair is a mess. He peeks in the fridge, makes a disgusted face as he shuts the door and goes to collapse on one of the kitchen stools behind the counter, watching me as I add detergent to the dishwasher and start it up.

"Couldn't sleep," I answer truthfully.

"Why not?" He scrubs his face.

Messed around with a girl. Can't wait to do it again.

That should be my answer, but it's not what I say out loud.

"Excited after last night's game." I shrug. Play it off.

"You did good. You'll continue to do good. I have faith." He shakes his head. Rubs his jaw. "I drank too much."

"By the looks of you, more like you smoked too much."

He smiles, but it's faint. "I hit the vape a lot. Still feel a little stoned."

"No shit." I grab a mug out of the cabinet. "Want coffee?"

I brought my expensive coffee maker with me when I moved in here. I'm one of the rare guys I know who's addicted to coffee.

"Sure."

I pour Caleb a cup and dump in some sugar and creamer before I stir it, then set the steaming mug in front of him. He grabs it and takes a sip, holding the cup in front of his mouth, his eyes narrowed into slits. "Shit's pretty good."

"I know."

"Why are you taking care of me?"

"Why wouldn't I? You're one of my best friends. You look like you need some TLC." I turn off the coffeemaker and pull the pot out, dumping the rest of it in the sink.

"Aw, you care." He sets the mug down, resting his hand against his chest. "Are you gay for me, Sorrento?"

"Shut the fuck up." I shake my head as I rinse out the coffee pot and then open the running dishwasher to set it in there before I face him once more.

"I saw you talking to the blonde last night." His mouth kicks up on one side. "She's a hottie."

I sort of want to go territorial on his ass, but I restrain myself. "The hottie's name is Hayden."

"Right." He takes another sip. "Does Hayden-the-hottie have any friends?"

"I'm sure she does, but you don't need to mess with any of them." I can only imagine if I helped hook up one of Hayden's friends with Caleb. He'd fuck her and dump her, and Hayden would end up pissed.

No thanks.

"Why the hell not? I'm offended." He grins, not looking offended whatsoever. "I'm an upstanding gentleman."

"No, you're really not." I lean against the counter, watching him. "I don't think you should chase after Hayden's friends."

Caleb's sigh is exaggerated. "You're probably right. I'm guessing they're all ball busters like her anyway."

I press my lips together so I don't say anything rude. I really hate how he calls her a ball buster.

"Being with a strong woman isn't that bad," I tell him, thinking of his mother. She's a sweet, agreeable woman who has always been kind to her son's friends. She would show up at every high school football game, screaming and encouraging us from the stands. Caleb makes her proud. I think we all kind of do.

She's nothing like my mother at all. Sometimes I wonder if the woman who gave birth to me even remembers my name.

"I'd just rather take the easy way out. You're the one who likes them complicated," Caleb says, frowning. "Actually, you all do. Every one of you, with the exception of Jackson."

"Just because we're interested in having a relationship with someone?" I ask.

Shit. The word relationship just passed my lips. And

I'm not supposed to be pursuing anything like that with Hayden. We're keeping it simple. Just friends with benefits.

"Yeah, who needs that?" He sips from his coffee. "There are so many women on this campus."

Since meeting Hayden, I haven't noticed any of them. Not really.

"Dude, you're not even listening to me," Caleb says irritably. "I bet I could bring a naked woman into the kitchen right now and you wouldn't even notice."

I blink him back into focus. "Did you just say something about naked women?"

Caleb snorts. "I'm guessing you'd only care if I brought a naked *Hayden* in the kitchen."

"You're not allowed to see Hayden naked," I say, immediately incensed at the mere idea.

What the hell? Why am I thinking like this?

"Bro, until you put that chick on lock, she is fair game." He chortles when he spots the expression on my face. "Ooh, I just pissed you right off, didn't I?"

He's harmless. Giving me shit, but it still riles me up. "I like her," I admit.

That's all I say. What more is there to say? I do like her. A lot. More than I probably should.

I told myself I wouldn't fall hard and fast for a woman once I got into college. I agreed with Caleb and Jackson over the summer that we should keep ourselves single for as long as possible. We don't need to attach ourselves to girlfriends. We'd miss out on opportunities. Hookups. Being adored by lots of girls versus just one.

And here I go, meeting a woman only a few months into school, and now she's the only one I can think about. The only one I *want* to think about.

"You only just met her," he reminds me. "What about our pact?"

"Was it really a pact?" I ask.

"Yeah. I thought it was. And I'm sticking to it. So is Jackson. You should too." He points at me.

"I'm happy where I'm at right now, thanks," I say, thinking—yet again—of Hayden. Feeling smug.

Hoping I get to see her again soon.

"Jumping on the first girl you meet," Caleb mutters under his breath. "Fuckin' ridiculous."

"What did you just say?" I ask.

"I don't get you." He sounds truly perplexed as he waves his arm around. "There are so many hot babes on this campus. And all of them are dying to get a look at your dick, especially after last night's game. You shouldn't limit yourself to just one so early in our college years. Find someone else. Better yet, find a couple of someone else's. Make out with a few of them. Cop a couple of feels. Make a move, son. The bounty is out there."

He sounds ridiculous.

"No thanks," I tell him, his words reminding me of how I definitely made some moves last night.

Not going to tell Caleb about it though. He'll just want all the dirty details and I don't feel like sharing them.

"What happened last night at the party?" Caleb asks.

"What do you mean?"

"I saw you sitting in the living room surrounded by a bunch of hot girls watching you with lust in their eyes. Groupies?" Caleb nods, his eyes gleaming. Not giving me a chance to answer. "Good job."

"They were boring. And Jocelyn drove them all away."

Caleb frowns. "The hell? Why would she do that?"

"We started talking and next thing I knew, they all

bailed." I shrug. Jocelyn's little speech is what kicked me into gear and encouraged me to text Hayden, so go Jos.

"You can't let women you're not with ruin your game play. That's exactly what Jocelyn did. No offense against her, but Diego maybe needs to keep her closer," Caleb says. "She cock-blocked your ass."

"You sound like a complete asshole. Next thing you'll suggest is she needs to be on a leash."

"Not a bad idea. Seriously, stick with your man and don't interfere with my night. That's what I would've told her," Caleb says.

Here's the deal. Caleb says terrible things. He thinks terrible things. But he says and does these things in such a way that it's completely harmless. He needs a ball buster like Hayden to put him in his place.

He just can't have my ball buster.

I shake my head. "You are something else." I remember something. "Didn't I just lay claim on Hayden to all you assholes a few days ago?"

"I didn't take you seriously," he says. "I thought maybe you two were really just friends."

Yeah. Not any longer. "Well, as I just said, I like her."

"Whatever. Forget Jocelyn. Forget that Hayden chick. What happened after Jos drove the girls away? Tell me you chased one down and let her suck your dick." He grins. "I know that's what I did last night."

I'm sure he did. So did I. But again, not going to tell Caleb that. "No, I didn't. You saw me with Hayden, remember?"

"Oh." He frowns. "Right. Last night was like a blur. I need to lay off the weed. It's fuckin' with my head." He pauses for only a moment. "A lot of things are fuckin' with it, if I'm being real right now."

"What are you talking about?"

Caleb blows out an exaggerated breath. "I might've let a girl suck me off, but she didn't finish. She got mad at me and left me high and dry," he says irritably.

"Groupies are like that," I tell him.

"That's where you're wrong, my friend. Groupies don't get mad. They gladly suck your dick and sometimes they swallow too," he explains, his expression serious.

Suspicion fills me. "Who were you with last night?"

"Nobody you know."

Caleb is a terrible liar. It's written all over his face who he might've been with. And I think I know who it is.

"Don't tell me you were with Baylee."

Guilt washes over his features. Busted. "No."

"Liar."

He sighs. "Okay, yes. I was with Baylee. She showed up, and she looked hot as fuck. Even hotter? She kept ignoring my ass every time I tried to get her attention. She was flirting with one of my new frat brothers. A freshman like us, and a complete idiot. She was hanging all over that guy."

A sigh escapes me. We have been through this before. Caleb and Baylee were an on and off thing all throughout high school. Baylee was Cami Lockhart's best friend our senior year, since Cami moves through best friends at a pretty fast clip, and we all hated that bitch. But we could tell that Baylee was miserable pretty much the entirety of senior year, being Cami's sidekick. I don't know why she put up with her.

Don't know why she puts up with Caleb either.

"You can't keep giving her false hope," I tell him.

"She tricked my ass," Caleb says. "Once I got her away from that dude, she pulled me into the bathroom, locked the door and then got on her knees. What was I supposed to do?"

"I don't know, tell her to stop?" I suggest.

"This girl..." He shakes his head, and he actually appears a little lost. "She's been in my life for so long. She knows how to push all my buttons."

"She's probably in love with you."

"She's stupid if she is. I'm going nowhere."

"Come on, Caleb." He can also be a little dramatic at times.

"No, it's true. I peaked in high school, bro, and I know it. I will take advantage of all the babes at the frat parties, and I'll do what I can to get through school, and maybe if I'm lucky, I'll play on the football team, but overall? This is it for me. Once I graduate, I'll find some boring ass job and I'll end up marrying some boring ass woman and we'll have a couple of boring ass kids. We'll go on vacation once or twice a year. Maybe I'll buy a travel trailer or some shit, I don't know. Maybe we'll go to the beach a lot. We'll get a dog. The kids will love that fucker so much and when he dies, we'll bury him in the back yard." Caleb sighs. Scrubs his hand over his face again. "I basically described my parents. I'm still pretty fuckin' upset that our dog Buddy died two years ago."

Is that what Caleb's afraid of? That he thinks he's destined for mediocrity?

"You choose your own path," I tell him. "You don't have to end up like your parents."

"It's not like I'll mean to do it. It'll just happen. This is why I'm so hell-bent on fucking every chick on this campus. Once I get married, I'll be lucky to get it once a month. Then it'll just be me, my hand and internet porn," Caleb says morosely.

At least he didn't say he'd cheat. I think of my father. He's a cheater. Mom was too, though she was a lot more discreet about it. Helena hit on me, and that is seriously messed up. No way would I cheat with my dad's wife. That's some sick and twisted shit.

"You won't end up like that," I tell him. "It's all a choice, Caleb. You can make your life however you want it to be."

I think of my life. My father's plan. The words Helena said to me. How I better live it up now because soon I'll be taking over and running my father's empire.

Just thinking of my future when it comes to my father's business freaks me out. I don't think I want that.

But maybe Caleb's right. I don't have a choice.

It'll just...

Happen.

FOURTEEN

I HANG out in the quad in front of the library on purpose, hoping for a glimpse of Tony and his football friends. Does this make me a pathetic, wannabe groupie?

Maybe.

Do I care, since it's not necessarily obvious that's what I'm doing?

Nope.

At least Gracie is with me. We're sitting at a bench table, our books spread out in front of us, enjoying the abnormally warm—well, maybe not so abnormal for around here—fall day. The sun is shining, and it's intense. Thankfully, there's also an occasional breeze, which brings relief.

"You look good," Gracie says.

I glance up to find her watching me. "Thank you?"

"Why do you say it like a question?"

"You're the one who helped pick out my outfit," I remind her.

High waisted jeans, white Nikes, tight-fitting black long-sleeved shirt that's cropped, revealing a little sliver of belly. Delicate silver rings on my fingers, big silver hoops in my ears, my hair perfectly straight and parted in the middle like the Gen Z girl I am. It's a look I'm liking a lot.

Will Tony like it too? Not sure. Will I actually get to see him today?

Also not sure. But I'm hopeful.

So hopeful.

"Yeah, and you look hot." Gracie sighs. Shakes her head. She actually seems disappointed in me. "I don't know why you can't just text this dude and ask him to meet you somewhere. We've already been out here for over an hour."

"And hasn't it been productive? We got a lot of homework done. Plus, I bought you Starbucks." I point at her mostly empty cup.

"I'd rather have Dutch Bros." She mock pouts.

"Sorry, my precious princess. Can't have it all I guess." I shrug, vaguely annoyed. Doesn't she remember all the schemes I've helped her with to get the attention of a boy she was interested in? They have been numerous over the years.

"Let's get Dutch later." Her eyes light up. Dutch Bros. is her favorite place to get coffee. She's addicted. So am I. "And then we can grab Chipotle for dinner."

"We are so basic, it's pathetic," I tell her, only half-serious.

"I revel in my basic bitchiness," Gracie says with a grin.

"I know you do. I do too. This is why we're going to be basic girls right now and hope the boy eventually shows up." I glance around the quad, of course not spotting a group of hotties anywhere. "I'll give it another hour, tops."

"Oh God. No." Gracie shakes her head. "Thirty minutes."

"Forty-five."

"Forty."

"Deal," I tell her, laughing.

"Seriously though. Why can't you just call this guy? The game playing thing is more my strategy," Gracie says.

I love her brutal honesty.

"I don't want to seem too pushy," I admit. It's like I can't explain why I'm doing this. It's more fun for us to meet up on campus like a happy coincidence, am I right?

Clearly, I'm being ridiculous.

Gracie's mouth pops open. "You're worried you'll seem too pushy? Who are you and what did you do with my best friend?" She reaches over the table to touch my face and I dodge out of her way at the last second.

"Knock it off! What's the big deal? So I don't want to seem pushy, so what?" She's making me feel weird.

"You never worry about that sort of stuff. You just—do it. Consequences be damned. That's my favorite trait about you. The one I always wished I could emulate. Now you're emulating me and I'm worried." Gracie frowns, her delicate brows drawn together.

From the expression on her face, I'd guess Gracie *is* truly worried. Which is the last thing I want her to be.

"This guy, he feels...different." I bite my lip, wishing I hadn't confessed that.

"It's because he's eighteen. Younger men feel different." She laughs.

"I'm being serious." Her laughter dies, and I continue, "He barely kisses me and I feel like I'm about to go up in flames."

"He did more than barely kiss you," she reminds me.

Yes, I told her a few things, but not everything. How hot it was in his car. How easily I came, and how much I wanted to satisfy him. I don't know what came over me, but next thing I knew I had his dick in my mouth.

And I'm not complaining. Not one bit. It was fun. It was exhilarating.

I've been missing him ever since.

"True," I say and she sends me a look. Like I'm annoying her.

I probably am.

"What is it about him that makes him so special?" Gracie asks, sounding genuinely curious.

"I can't even put my finger on it." I prop my elbow on the table and rest my chin on my fist. "He's sweet. Quiet. Thoughtful. *Extremely* attractive." He's a great kisser. He has a big dick. He's polite. Who knew polite would be such a turn on?

Well, it is.

"I can't wait to see this guy."

"I call dibs," I tell her teasingly.

She shakes her head. "Come on. I wouldn't steal a guy from you."

I sober up. "I know." We respect each other's boundaries. Even better? We have different taste in men, which makes it so much easier between us. We're not drawn to the same guy.

"I know and respect your usual anti-relationship stance, but maybe...maybe this guy could be good for you," Gracie suggests softly.

A sigh escapes me. "Maybe? I don't know."

I'm being ridiculous. I sort of know—I totally think Tony could be good for me. He could make me forget my anti-relationship status, though that's dangerous territory I'm wading into it. I need to keep my guard up. I'm sure his is still up too.

Our parents really did a number on us.

"Has he texted you?"

I shake my head. "But it's only Tuesday. And I'm sure he's busy."

Gracie's lips thin, but she says nothing. She doesn't have to. If a guy's interested, he texts. Often. This is a code she lives by. She's met lots of guys who weren't interested, aka, they didn't text her very much. And she's also met guys who've texted her constantly. Same with me. I'm not going to take Tony's lack of texting as a bad sign.

Yet.

"He's starting on the football team now. I'm sure practice is taking a lot out of him," I add.

"Stop making excuses for him, though I suppose you're right." Her expression turns thoughtful and she taps her lips with her index finger. "I've never gone out with a Bulldog football player before."

"I'm surprised."

"Right? Me too! I tend to be drawn to the more artistic types." Her expression turns dreamy as I'm sure she thinks of her latest crush.

His name is Robin. His parents named him for their favorite Bee Gee—no joke. I had to look up who the Bee Gees were when Gracie explained this fun fact. So did she, she admitted. Once I heard their music on Spotify, I knew who she was talking about.

I always thought Robin was a girl's name.

But anyway, her Robin is in a band. His hair is dyed black and hangs in his face. He paints his nails black and rims his eyes with kohl liner. He looks straight out of an emo band, circa 2011. Gracie currently thinks he's the hottest thing alive.

"Are you seeing Robin tonight?"

"Yes. I'm going to watch him perform." Her expression

lights up and she starts bouncing in her seat. "You should come with me."

"No. No way." I shake my head. I've been to a few small concerts watching her latest musician crush, including one last week, and they've always been God awful. Bad music. Sloppy performance. Lots of pissed-off teenagers clamoring for these guys' attention, wearing their best trashy outfits that they changed into the second Mom dropped them off at the front door.

I might've done this type of thing myself a time or two when I was in high school. I know the drill.

"Oh, come on. If we don't find your hottie, you have to come. It's the least you can do to pay me back for sitting out here with you."

"Is it really such a chore, sitting in the sunshine, getting your homework done and drinking your free PSL frap?" I ask, vaguely annoyed.

"Yes. Yes, it is. I could be at home, getting ready for tonight." She smiles. "You should see the outfit I have picked out."

I can only imagine.

My gaze drifts as Gracie drones on about Robin's band and how good they are. He's the lead singer, of course. Writes all the lyrics. Blah, blah, blah.

My gaze snags on a tall, dark haired and extremely handsome boy standing among a cluster of other equally tall, extremely handsome boys, and I realize my hard work has paid off.

It's Tony and his group of friends.

They're talking. Some of them animatedly, though not mine. He just stands there, listening intently. One of them smacks Tony in the shoulder, and he just laughs. My heart catches in my throat when I see that dazzling smile on his face. How relaxed and at ease he seems with his friends. I remember how he was when I saw him at the country club. Stiff. Tense. Cautious.

He doesn't like his dad. He wasn't comfortable with him at all. Such a shame.

But I get it.

"Hey." Gracie snaps her fingers and I startle to attention. "Did you hear anything I just said?"

"No." I tilt my head in the direction of the group of guys nearby. "He's here."

"Who? Your man? No way." She squints in the distance, the breeze ruffling her long, golden brown hair so strands blow across her face. "Which one is he?"

"The dark-haired one on the left." My gaze lands on him once more, and everything inside of me starts to ache.

"Ooh, he's cute." She sends me a look, and I think she's impressed. "Like, really hot."

"I know." I sound smug. I *am* smug.

Tony is a complete hottie.

"You sure he's only eighteen?" She stares at him once more.

"That's what he told me."

"Hmm. Well, he's gorgeous. The boys on campus get prettier and prettier every year, I swear. I don't remember anyone looking like him when we were eighteen. Oh God, they're headed this way. Get over here."

I frown at her. "What do you mean?"

"Come sit by me! He might not recognize you if your back is to him." She pats the empty spot beside her. "Hurry!"

I scramble so awkwardly over the bench in my attempt to move, I almost send myself sprawling on the ground. Luckily enough, I catch myself and move over to her side, sitting right next to her. Pushing my hair out of my face, I go for nonchalant.

Like no big deal. I've been sitting like this the entire time.

Gracie rearranges our books so that mine are facing me and hers are more on her side versus all sprawled out. We sit, watching expectantly, as they approach. My heart is racing. My stomach is jittery, and maybe that's from the coffee I just drank, but maybe not.

Maybe it's because Tony is finally here.

My instincts were on point.

The group is about to pass by us before one of his friends knocks him in the arm with his fist and points straight at us. They all stop and stare.

"Oh Shit," Gracie mutters, "They're looking at us."

"I know," I say out of the side of my mouth.

"Dude, they're all so good looking." She sounds shocked.

"I know," I repeat.

They turn and head up the sidewalk toward us, Tony leading the way. His gaze catches mine and he smiles at me.

I smile back, fighting the urge to jump up and tackle-hug him.

"Oooh, he's smiling at you," Gracie practically squeals, and I elbow her in the ribs so that she calms down.

Thank God, she does.

"Hayden." He stops right beside our table, his friends hovering behind him. "Look at you."

I blink at him, pleased by the tone of his voice. I can tell he's happy to run into me. "Yeah. Look at you."

He laughs. "Your hair isn't usually so straight." He reaches out and yanks on a strand and I want to giggle like I'm ten.

But I don't. I keep a straight face.

Barely.

"Who's your friend?" One of them asks. It's Caleb. The player.

Oh no.

If he flirts with her, even the slightest bit, she will fall madly in love.

"This is Gracie. She's my roommate and best friend," I say, sending a look to Caleb that says *I will cut a bitch if he tries to flirt with her.*

As in, he's the bitch I will cut, so he better back off.

"Nice to meet you," Tony says to Gracie, offering her his hand.

She takes it, sending me a quick look that I can't quite decipher. "Nice meeting you too, Tony."

Tony's smile widens when his gaze returns to mine. "You've told her about me."

"I have."

"I'm flattered."

"It's no big deal." I wave a dismissive hand. It's Gracie's turn to elbow me in the ribs.

"What are you guys up to?" Gracie asks.

"We just finished class. We always meet up here in the quad on Tuesday when we can and grab a late lunch before practice," Tony explains.

I file that information away for later. "Nice," I say casually. As if I haven't been out here waiting for him. "I'm so glad we ran into each other."

Gracie giggles. I ignore her.

"Me too." Tony shoves his hands in his pockets and we just stare at each other for a moment. Memories of our encounter in his car ping between us and the tension grows thick. I can feel it.

Can anyone else?

Gracie clears her throat. "Hey, Tony. What are you doing tonight?"

Oh no.

"Nothing. Why?" His dark brows pull together.

"Well, I'm going to a concert at Strummers, and I invited Hayden to go with me." I glare at her, silently willing her to shut up, but she just keeps talking. "And I thought it would be fun if you came with us too."

Tony's words are for me. "You cool with that?"

I shrug. Like it's no big deal, though inside I'm dying. I mean, I don't want to go to this shitty concert, but if I can go with Tony? Then, yes. Please sign me up. "Yes, I'm cool with it."

"Great." His focus is now on Gracie and he smiles at her. She appears a little dazzled by its appearance and I want to tell her, *girl, same.*

But I don't.

"Thank you for inviting me," he continues.

"You need a date?" Caleb pops out of the group and approaches Gracie, a flirtatious smile curving his lips as he saunters toward her. "Because if you do, I'm your man."

"I'm going tonight to watch the lead singer. He's my *boyfriend*," she says pointedly.

Well, Robin isn't her boyfriend yet, but I guess she doesn't need to clarify that particular fact to Caleb.

"And I'll be your bodyguard. What do you say? I'm sure your *boyfriend* would appreciate two big, strong football players watching over you in the crowd."

"I can handle the crowd. I've been there before," Gracie says tightly.

"There are some shady characters at Strummers," Caleb says.

"Caleb," Tony starts, but his friend keeps talking.

"You'll need some protection tonight, a pretty little girl like you." His gaze roams over her, as if he likes what he sees.

And, oh shit, that lights Gracie up like a Christmas tree. I seriously hate how he just called her a pretty little girl, but whatever.

"The teenaged girls that usually show up are pretty rabid," Gracie says, and I can tell she's going to cave.

"They don't bother Robin though," I add, and both Caleb and Tony swing their heads in my direction with questioning looks on their faces.

"Robin?" Caleb asks.

"Who's that?" Tony frowns.

"My boyfriend," Gracie says weakly.

Now Caleb is looking at her. "You have a boyfriend named *Robin?*"

"His parents named him after their favorite Bee Gee." Gracie sends me a murderous look. I didn't realize I wasn't supposed to say Robin's name out loud.

"What the ever-loving fuck is a Bee Gee?" Caleb scratches his head. He appears genuinely perplexed.

"What time does it start?" Tony asks me.

"I'm not sure. This is all Gracie's plan." I am highly amused. I thought it would be a bad idea to have Caleb tag along, but he's funny. And he's got Gracie all flustered, which is kind of cute.

Maybe I should feel bad for Robin, but the guy gives me strong narcissistic vibes. He's not a very good singer, though I can admit he's a decent lyricist. My theory? He's in a band for the girls. Plain and simple. Considering they're mostly teens and he's close to twenty-five, that's super creepy.

Even twenty-year-old Gracie might be too old for him.

"I'm glad I ran into you." Tony smiles, taking a step closer. I can tell he wants to touch me.

I want him to touch me too.

Should I be honest and admit this was no coincidence? Nah.

"I'm glad too." I smile at him in return. He reaches out and grabs me, pulling me in for a hug and I cling to him. He clings to me too, for a few extra seconds. My entire body lights up as if he flipped a switch inside me, and I want more.

When he pulls away, I feel bereft. As if I'm missing something. He looks a little lost too.

"Hey." We both glance over at Gracie when she yells at us. Caleb is still standing next to her, grinning. She points at Tony. "Meet us at Strummers at eight, okay? Concert starts at nine. Don't bring your friend."

She jerks her thumb in Caleb's direction.

Tony frowns. "You want us there an hour before it starts?"

"There will be a line," Gracie says.

"The Bee Gee is that in demand?" Caleb asks incredulously.

Gracie sends him a death stare. "Come on, Hayden. We need to go."

"But—" I start.

Now I'm the one getting a death stare.

"See you at Strummers?" I ask Tony.

He smiles. "Definitely." He rests his hand on my shoulder and gives it a squeeze, just before he leans in and drops a quick kiss on my lips.

I feel that touch all the way to my toes and back up, settling in my core.

"Hayden!" Gracie's voice is sharp. She's standing by the

table and gathering her books, shoving them in her backpack.

I go to join her, my gaze trained on Tony as he walks away with his friends. Caleb flips around, so he's walking backwards, that goofy grin still on his face.

Gracie lifts her hand, giving him the finger.

He just laughs.

"What the hell?" I ask her as I shove the last of my schoolwork in my backpack and jerk the zipper closed.

"That guy is a douchebag. An annoying, sexy douchebag," Gracie says, her tone laced with hostility. She slips her backpack strap over her shoulder, looking prepared to go in for battle.

"He's not so bad." I have no idea what Caleb is really like. I've barely talked to him.

"He's awful. Giving me endless shit. Over something I had nothing to do with and can't control." Gracie shakes her head. "Robin can't help it if his parents gave him a girl's name."

Huh. That is pretty awful. But Caleb looks so harmless.

We head for the parking lot, which is the opposite direction to where the boys are walking. I wonder where they're going. Has Tony been to Strummers before? I wonder if he'll like the music. It's not that great. And the place will be filled with mostly screaming females. That's how it was when we were there last week.

Yes, I went there a week ago to watch Robin, the shitty singer, perform his shitty songs with the poetic lyrics. I am such a good friend, I deserve a medal.

"Caleb is probably acting that way because he knows he's getting under your skin," I point out to her.

Which isn't that easy to do. Gracie is usually very

accepting of everyone. Especially guys. And I don't mean that as an insult either.

It's the truth.

"Be prepared for Caleb showing up tonight," I warn her.

"I really hope that doesn't happen," Gracie says, sending me a look. "He's fucking hot."

"Wait, what?" I come to a complete stop. "Are you talking about Tony?"

Gracie stops too. "No! Well, your boyfriend is hot too, but so is his friend. His annoying as fuck, rude as hell friend is utterly fuckable."

Oh no.

"Gracie. You have Robin," I remind her.

"Not really. I think he considers me a groupie like the rest of them." She sighs. "But I don't really want Caleb either. He's awful."

"They're all awful," I say in agreement, because this is what we do. Bash a little on the male species.

Well, one of them isn't awful.

At least, right now he isn't.

FIFTEEN

TONY

CALEB CLIMBS into my Range Rover and immediately takes command of the music situation. He grabs my phone and punches in my security code—that I've never given to him, he just somehow knows it—and opens up Spotify. He does a little searching, leans over and turns up the volume, and a familiar beat starts playing.

"Well you can tell by the way I use my walk..."

"The Bee Gees," Caleb tells me with a grin.

I shake my head as I navigate our way out of the condo parking lot. Strummers is in the Tower District in downtown Fresno, and since I've never been there before, I have the directions going on my phone. As in, Siri is guiding me with her soothing Siri voice.

"So the 'Stayin' Alive' guys," I say to Caleb, once the song is mostly over and we're on the freeway.

"Yeah. This song is fucking ancient. How old are his parents?" Caleb asks no one. "*Saturday Night Fever* came out in 1977. I looked it up."

The song ends and a new one starts. Melodic keyboards play. "What's *Saturday Night Fever?*"

"A movie about disco music." I glance over at Caleb to see his expression is pained. "It's kind of catchy, which I fuckin' hate to admit."

I laugh. He looks downright miserable. "Why are you listening to it then?"

"I thought it was funny." He grabs my phone again and searches for another song. "We're blasting the Bee Gees if we spot Gracie and Hayden in front of Strummers, okay? That'll piss Gracie off."

"Is that your new job in life? To piss Hayden's friend off?"

"It's fun. Girl reacts big. And she's cute as fuck." Caleb grins as he starts bopping his head to the beat of "Dream-catcher." He usually likes his music a little harder, so I'm surprised. "I can't wait to see this Robin asshole."

"The band probably sucks," I say.

"Such a doubter." Caleb shakes his head. "Though I bet you're right. I looked up who was playing tonight on the Strummers' website."

"They have a website?"

"Yeah. Well, I think it was more Google listing the acts. A band called Bat's Cave is scheduled at nine. I assume that's them. Sounds like a bunch of edgy shit. I bet they paint their fingernails black."

I say nothing, meaning I'm in silent agreement.

Caleb's got my phone again, and he switches the song to "10 Freaky Girls" by 21 Savage, which makes a lot more sense if you know Caleb.

This song slaps. Makes me think of high school. Makes me miss Jake. It was one of his favorites. It was on the playlist we listened to in the locker room to get hyped before a game.

"Love this song," Caleb says. "Wish I had ten freaky girls on a yacht."

"You would."

"Have you talked to Jake lately?" he asks me.

See, the song makes him think of Jake too.

"He texted me a few days ago," I say. "He mentioned he's coming home for Thanksgiving."

"That seems so far away."

"It's next month," I point out.

"True. I planned on staying at the condo for Thanksgiving," Caleb says.

"You're not going up to see your family?" His parents are nice, simple people who somehow created this larger-than-life perv Caleb.

"What are you doing for Thanksgiving?" he asks me.

"Staying at the condo I guess," I admit.

"I was planning on keeping you company." He won't look at me. He's picking off imaginary lint from his knee.

I feel like a sap, but Caleb wanting to stay at the condo over Thanksgiving break when he could go home and be with his family is...nice. Thoughtful. Who knew he had it in him?

Me. I did. I always did. He puts on a show, but deep down, he's a nice guy. He's just—sex-crazed. Out to conquer every girl he can before he falls into a boring, miserable life. At least that's what will happen, according to him.

And that sucks. Why does he set himself up to fail?

I think of my future, and Hayden suddenly appears in my mind. Seeing her on campus earlier had felt like a jolt to my bloodstream. She was sitting at a picnic table with her friend, and her entire face lit up when she saw me. Like she'd been waiting for me.

Totally reading too much into it, but I can't help it.

I know I smiled at her much the same. Caleb slapped my shoulder. Jackson called me pussy-whipped. I ignored him because he has no idea how I feel about Hayden, or what's happened between us so far.

I'm not pussy-whipped.

Not yet.

Ha.

When we finally arrive at Strummers, I have to circle the block because there's no parking in the front. And there's a long line in front of the building, made-up mostly of young teenage girls dressed in the ugliest clothes imaginable.

"Slow down when you make a pass this time," Caleb advises me as we head for the front of Strummers again. "I want to see if I can spot Gracie and Hayden."

I go a lot slower as we drive by, and I'm the one who spies Hayden's blonde head first. "There they are."

Caleb switches the music to the Bee Gees immediately, cranking up the volume. "Roll down the window!" he screams at me.

I do his bidding, amused. We both swivel our heads in the girls' direction and they're watching us. Hayden's smiling. Gracie's scowling.

Caleb leans over me, trying to shove his face through the open window. "The Bee Gees!"

Gracie gives him the double finger from her hips, as if she's poised to shoot him.

He falls back into his seat, laughing. "This is going to be an interesting night."

I just laugh along with him.

We finally find a parking lot and then make our way to the bar. Because that's all Strummers is. A nondescript building with a bar inside that hosts various musical acts that command a small audience. I've heard of it, but I've never been, and when we approach the line, I realize pretty much every single person standing in it is female.

And they're all watching us questioningly.

"There are *so* many girls," Caleb says. He sounds impressed.

"Maybe you can find ten and put them on your yacht," I suggest.

"Huh?" He frowns.

"The song," I remind him.

"Oh right. Yeah. Not interested in ten tonight. Only one." He makes his way toward her, pasting on a cocky grin as he zeros in on Gracie. "Did you like the song I played for you?" he asks her eagerly.

"You're an idiot," she says, turning her back on him.

I approach Hayden much more subtly. "Hey."

She smiles up at me as I lean in and drop a chaste kiss on her cheek. I want to do so much more, but I'm restraining myself. "You made it," she says when I pull away.

"Sorry we're a little late. Blame it on him." I point at Caleb. "He was primping for his date."

"So was she." Hayden gestures to Gracie. "And she wasn't getting pretty for Robin either."

I wince. "Is his name really Robin?"

Hayden laughs, the sound melodic, stirring something within me. Everything about her stirs me up. Leaves me wanting more. "Yes, it really is. She was so pissed I told you guys. She'd never admit it, but that's the only thing holding her back from this guy. His name."

"Caleb grabbed onto that little fact and hasn't let it go. He forced me to listen to the Bee Gees on the drive over here."

"The Bee Gees aren't bad," she says.

"Yeah, but they're old as hell. Like before our parents' time," I say. "I'm guessing Robin's parents are super old."

"Maybe. I don't know. I don't really care either." She grabs hold of my hand, interlocking our fingers as she pulls me closer. "Look, I'm sorry you had to come tonight. I'm sure there are about a million other things you'd rather do than go to a shitty local band's concert."

"I don't care, as long as I'm with you," I say truthfully, stepping closer to her.

She squeezes my hand, her lips curved upward. "That's an overly friendly way to feel about me."

It doesn't even bother me that she brings up the friend thing. She knows we're more than that. Especially after what happened in my car. "I have overly friendly feelings about you on a daily basis," I tell her.

"Hmm, that sounds interesting." She leans in closer. "Maybe you'll have to share a few of those *overly* friendly feelings you have for me later. Like after the concert."

"You should come back to my place," I suggest.

"How about you come back to *my* place?" she offers.

That definitely has more appeal. Less dudes. No jealous cat who might bite her. Probably cleaner. "Deal."

We turn our focus on Gracie and Caleb, who are currently arguing. The group of girls standing in front of them in line are facing them, ogling Caleb openly. It's actually pretty damn amusing.

Though neither Gracie nor Caleb appear amused.

"Please. Just—shut up. You say the worst things ever," Gracie says with a sneer.

"Aw, babe. You wound me." He rests his hands on his chest, putting on an exaggerated pained look. Bottom lip stuck out and everything. "Why you gotta be like this?"

"Why do *you* have to be like this?" She waves a hand at him.

"Like what?"

"Like an asshole!"

"Okay, okay." Hayden releases her hold on me and goes to Gracie, steering her away from Caleb. "I think we need to diffuse the situation for a bit."

"Man, she's feisty," Caleb says when I go to stand next to him. His gaze never strays from Gracie. "I bet she's wild in bed."

"Caleb." I sigh. He sends me a questioning look. "She's here tonight for *someone else*. Another guy. Not you."

"That doesn't deter me."

"You told me recently you didn't like a challenge. You want them easy." I hate the words coming from my mouth, but I'm basically quoting Caleb's words back to him, which doesn't make me feel as bad.

"That's until I met this hottie. I mean, look at her." He whistles low, scanning Gracie from head to toe. I know this, because he makes it very obvious.

"Not interested," I tell him, though I silently admit Gracie is gorgeous. The long brown hair threaded with gold, the long legs—she's tall—the flashing hazel eyes that turn golden when she's angry.

I can enjoy looking at a pretty woman. I'm not fucking dead. But Gracie does nothing for me.

"Right. You've got the blonde. Who is also a hottie. I mean, check *her* out." He obviously stares all over again, this time, his attention all for Hayden.

My Hayden.

I shove Caleb in the shoulder, sending him toppling. "Knock that shit off." He's harmless. I know he is. And I'm not worried about him making a move on Hayden, because I already staked my claim and he won't forget that. Which sounds like macho sexist shit, and that sort of sucks, but whatever.

It is what it is.

Hayden and I keep up the small talk and slowly but surely, Gracie comes back down from her Caleb anger high and starts to participate. Caleb sticks to his phone, interjecting the occasional comment that shows he's actually listening.

Eventually, the line outside starts to move. They're letting us in. Anyone underage gets a wristband, so they won't serve us at the bar, so that means we all do. The cover charge is minimal and I pay for all four of us. Not because I'm showing off, but because I don't want Caleb to have to pay since he's always running on a tight budget.

"Thanks man," he murmurs once we enter the dark building.

"Anytime," I reassure him.

The space is cramped, the ceilings low. There's a bar on the far side of the wall that runs the entire length of it. On the opposite side, there's a small black stage that's seen better days. There are a couple of guys on the stage, testing the speakers and other equipment, low music playing in the background. The teenage girls all rush to the front, crowding each other as they jockey for the spot with the best view.

"Are all these girls here for Bat's Cave?" Hayden asks Gracie. She sounds shocked. I'm guessing Bat's Cave doesn't usually command such an adoring crowd.

"Not sure. Maybe some of them? Robin told me a lot of people would be coming for the opening act. Some blond dude who croons love songs he wrote himself while he strums his guitar." Gracie rolls her eyes. "Robin hates him."

Hayden opens her mouth, looking ready to respond, but Caleb beats her to it.

"Robin hates everyone because he's named Robin and his name makes him feel emasculated," Caleb says in a high-pitched voice.

Then he starts to laugh.

Gracie whirls on him. "I'm surprised you even know what that word means."

"I'm in college. I'm not stupid." Caleb actually appears offended. "Does your precious Robin go to Fresno State?"

She sulks. "No."

"Figures," Caleb mutters.

"Give it up," I tell him. "Let her enjoy her night watching Robin."

"God, that name," Hayden says, shaking her head. "I shouldn't make fun since I've got a boy name, but holy crap. I *hate* it. I don't even like it that much for a girl. No offense to all the Robins in the world."

"Listen. All of you. Stop making fun of him. His band is the most important thing in the world to him, okay? He thinks this performance tonight is going to take him to the next level. He's played at Strummers a couple of times already, but there's a record exec here tonight. He's a scout looking for talent. At least, that's the rumor going around," Gracie explains, her expression like stone. Pretty sure we've pushed her too far. "He texted me earlier this afternoon letting me know everything, and now I'm on pins and needles, hoping he finally gets noticed. This could be life changing for him. That's why I'm here tonight, and why I wanted to bring some friends so we can show our support. But if you don't want to be here, then leave, okay? Just go."

We're all quiet as another swarm of young teen girls push past us, all of them chattering a mile a minute, their mouths open wide, the flash of their braces reflecting off the harsh fluorescent lights above. I feel bad over what's happened tonight. I can tell by the look on Hayden's face that she does too.

"I'm sure they're gonna suck big hairy balls, but if you want us to yell and cheer for them when they walk on stage, I can do that," Caleb says earnestly, his gaze shooting to mine. "Right, T?"

"Yeah," I say lightly, hoping Gracie doesn't kill Caleb before the night is over. "For sure. Whatever you want us to do."

"Thank you," she says to me, her chin tilted upward when she looks in Caleb's direction. "Stop saying they suck."

Caleb salutes her. "Yes, ma'am."

The four of us eventually decide to push forward among the sea of girls, trying to find a better position so we can see the stage. I overdressed for the occasion with my jeans, black T-shirt and favorite leather jacket that I rarely wear, which means I'm currently sweating my balls off. Don't want to take it off and carry it though, because I'm not about to lose the jacket either.

"I like the rocker look you've got going on tonight," Hayden says, running her hand down my sleeve. "This leather is soft."

"Thanks." Her compliment makes sweating my ass off worth it. "You look great too."

Understatement. She's wearing a white tank with a black bra beneath, the straps showing, the entire thing showing since the tank is extremely thin. Skintight black jeans that make her legs look endless. Red Chucks on her feet, meaning she went for comfort and I like that. Her eyes are heavily lined with black, and her lips are this deep, ruby red.

"Thank you. Gracie had this whole aesthetic she wanted to present tonight, so she's the one who dressed me. We're groupie girls." She holds up her hand, her index and pinky finger straight up along with her thumb, and sticks her tongue out. "Like we hang out at the Roxy, circa 1983."

I have no idea what she's talking about.

"I had to Google it. It's a venue in Hollywood where a lot of the eighties rock bands would perform," she further explains. "Robin is very much into that nostalgic vibe, according to Gracie."

"That's...interesting," I say.

"Right? Weird. But I'm having fun, so whatever." She laughs. Scoots closer to me so our bodies brush against each other's. "I'm glad you came."

"Yeah?" I touch her hair, push it off her shoulder, my fingers brushing against bare skin. The tank top is plain yet sexy. Especially with the black bra beneath showing through. I stare at her chest for a moment, not caring if she knows. Pretty sure the bra is lacy.

Also pretty sure if I keep staring, I might be able to see her nipples. Never did get to see them last time, which is a damn shame. Hope to rectify that soon.

"Yeah. At least I don't have to suffer alone." She laughs.

Unable to resist any longer, I kiss her.

She stops laughing, circling her arms around my neck as she clings to me.

The room goes dark for a moment, a hush settling over the crowd. I break away from Hayden, our heads turning in the same direction when the bright lights come back on, three beams of light shining upon the stage. Coming together and illuminating a lone figure in the center. He's sitting on what looks like an ornate wooden throne, a guitar resting on his lap, his face in shadow because of the lights.

The girls start hysterically screaming. It's a deafening sound and Hayden pulls away from me, her eyebrows raised in shock. She turns to face the stage and I loom behind her, my hands on her hips, both of us watching. Waiting.

Once the screams die down—somewhat—the guy leans forward, longish blond hair hanging in his face, his mouth so close to the mic, his lips brush against it as he speaks. "Good evening. My name is Jackson Rivers," he says before he starts strumming his guitar.

The girls scream even louder.

"WHAT THE FUCK!" Caleb yells over the din, glancing over at me, his eyes wide with surprise.

Yeah. That was unexpected.

I'm in shock. I had no idea *Jackson* was playing at Strummers tonight. Or that he played at all.

Well, that's not true. He'd throw parties and always sing and play his guitar, but I figured it was a way for him to get chicks. Not once when we were hanging out together over the summer or ditching practice, did he ever mention he played for actual money. I didn't think he was serious about it.

At all.

"DUDE! Did you know about this?" Caleb is hollering at me.

I slowly shake my head, my gaze going back to the stage.

He's playing a song I've never heard before, and the girls are losing their damn minds, singing along with the lyrics.

As in, they already know the lyrics. To a song I've never heard before.

"What in the hell is happening right now?" Caleb cups his hands around his mouth and screams at the top of his lungs, "JACKSON, I'M YOUR BIGGEST FAN. YOU MAKE MY PANTIES WET."

Gracie grabs my arm, glaring at me. "I hate your friend so fucking much."

I'm laughing. I can't help it.

This is the most surreal moment of my life.

SIXTEEN

HAYDEN

"WHAT'S CALEB'S PROBLEM?" I ask Tony.

Caleb won't stop haggling the guy on stage. He literally just screamed, *"Jackson, I'm your number one fan! Let me suck your dick!"*

The teens went absolutely nuts, many of them glaring at Caleb before they all started screaming they were Jackson's biggest fan and they also wanted to suck his dick.

Some of these girls don't look any older than fourteen.

It turned into an all-out yelling contest, Caleb provoking the girls every step of the way. That Jackson dude started to look uncomfortable and would ask everyone to settle down, even in the middle of a song. He kept sending looks in Caleb's direction, which only encouraged Caleb to yell even more.

"We know him. He's on our football team," Tony explains, his gaze meeting mine. "You met him at my house, remember? Jackson. He practically lives with us, and we had no clue he's been out here performing for teenagers. They know the words to his songs. I bet he has a freaking fan club. And we had no idea."

Oh. *Oh*. The guy who flirted with me the first time I met Tony's friends on campus. He was cute. Blond. Blue eyed. Tall and broad. He looks a lot grungier on stage, though. He's giving off serious Kurt Cobain vibes—another musician before my time, but at least I know who he is and what he looks like, thanks to that T-shirt I wore all the time in middle school—right down to the cardigan he's currently wearing. It's old and threadbare, a nondescript beige color over a simple white tee. His fingers gleam as he plucks on his guitar thanks to all the rings on them. His jeans are tattered and torn, and he's got dingy, used to be white Vans on his feet.

The Vans kind of ruin the vibe, but maybe he's putting his own spin on it.

"You really had no idea?" I ask once the crowd has finally settled down. Even Caleb is quiet.

"None." Tony shakes his head, his gaze never leaving the stage. "That dude is full of secrets."

Jackson sings a couple more songs, including a cover of Nirvana's "Heart Shaped Box," no surprise. Though he slows it down and makes it his own—a version I think I might prefer over the original. And then he's done. He smiles. Murmurs good night into the mic. The lights go down. Within seconds, they're back up.

And the throne sits on the stage. Empty.

Caleb shoves his way in between me and Tony. "We need to go find that asshole and ask him what's up."

"They won't let us backstage," Tony says.

"We'll tell them we know him," Caleb stresses. "Like, I beat his ass in Call of Duty on almost a nightly basis, know him."

"Not every night," I say. Both guys frown at me.

"Clearly he's performed here before. I'm guessing he goes missing sometimes?"

"It's not like we're his keeper, but yeah. What the fuck?" Caleb appears bewildered. So does Tony. "I probably took it too far saying he made my panties wet."

"And the dick sucking offer. That wasn't subtle at all," Tony says, sounding amused.

"You're an asshole." Leave it to Gracie to be completely blunt. "I swear to God, you yell something like that to Robin or anyone else in Bat's Cave while they're performing, and I'm going to kick your ass."

Caleb bops her on the nose with his index finger. "I'd like to see you try."

Without hesitation, Gracie lunges for Caleb, her arms stretched out, fingers curled into claws as she swings at him. He ducks out of the way, laughing the entire time, and I grab Gracie around the waist, pulling her away from him.

"Chill out," I tell her, noticing that a couple of big, burly dudes are watching us. "You don't want to get kicked out before Robin performs."

If looks could kill, Caleb would be dead, thanks to Gracie's glare. "Keep him away from me. I mean it."

Caleb goes to stand on the other side of Tony. I'm in between Tony and Gracie, so maybe that'll be enough space to keep them from fighting with each other?

Probably not, but I'm hopeful.

I chat with Gracie while Tony talks to Caleb. She's a bundle of nervous energy, hopping up and down, shaking out her hands, as if she's about to enter a boxing ring. She's anxious on Robin's behalf, and I think it's cute, how she always throws herself wholeheartedly into a guy and their potential relationship.

Roadies appear on stage, setting up equipment,

including a drum set. Some of the teens leave. Actually, a lot of them leave, and we're able to shift even closer to the stage. Gracie looks worried.

"I thought they would stick around for the main attraction," she says, nibbling on her lower lip.

"Looks like our friend stole the show and the crowd," Caleb crows.

Tony hits him in the chest, and he shuts up.

A sigh escapes Gracie when her gaze returns to mine. "If this doesn't go the way he expects, Robin is going to be in the worst mood ever."

"Have you witnessed his bad moods before?" I ask.

She nods. "He's very moody."

I glance over at Tony, who winks at me. On anyone else, I would think it's a cheesy move. With Tony, I can't ignore the little shiver that streaks through me. That wink is full of promise. That smile curving his lips? Also full of promise. He appears completely unruffled, even after his friend made a public spectacle of himself, and Gracie tried to start a fight. Even after tons of teenaged girls screamed their heads off for their friend and they had no clue said friend was even doing this, he's as cool as a freakin' cucumber.

I always thought that saying was stupid. Now I think it's pretty apt.

"It's going to be fine." I rise up on my tiptoes and hook my arm around Gracie's shoulders, giving her a squeeze. She's taller than me and this position is uncomfortable, so I let her go. "He's going to put on a great show and that record exec is going to scoop them up. Next thing we know, we'll be watching their music video on YouTube and they'll make millions touring the world."

I am talking big, huge dreams right here, but it's exactly

what Gracie needs to hear. The tension visibly leaves her shoulders and she nods, the smile growing on her face.

"Hell yeah! And I'll get to say I knew him back when they were nothing," she adds.

"Exactly."

Within minutes, the band comes out on stage and starts tuning their instruments. Some of the girls yell their enthusiasm, but it's low decibel compared to the pitched screams from earlier.

Hmm.

Tony snags my hand and pulls me close, ducking so he can whisper in my ear. "Tell me the truth. Do they suck?"

I pull away, so I can look into his eyes. I shake my head while saying, "Yes."

His dark brows draw together. "Yes, they suck, or no they don't?"

I tug on his hand so now I'm the one whispering in his ear. "They're awful."

"Really?" Our faces are so close, our cheeks are touching. "They're that bad?"

"Terrible. Caleb is going to have the time of his life, screaming at them," I say solemnly.

"Want me to talk to him? Tell him to keep it down?"

He is truly the sweetest. If I was smart, I would make him my boyfriend as fast as humanly possible. But the idea of having an actual boyfriend still makes me a little nervous. "Please. Gracie's a nervous wreck. And I don't want her to get arrested for murder. That'll ruin our evening."

Tony smiles. "He only does it to antagonize her."

"Thank God you're not like that."

"Why would I want to antagonize my friend?" He smiles, obviously teasing me.

I kiss him, because he's so close. "Right. And all the friend talk isn't supposed to annoy me."

"Does it? You're the one who originally wanted to keep it friendly," he reminds me.

I pull him in closer and really kiss him. With tongue and everything, right here in the middle of the crowd. He responds quickly, wrapping his arms around me so our lower bodies are nestled close together, our mouths still fused, our tongues tangling. I'd much rather do this than watch Robin and the rest of Bat's Cave perform.

"Get a room," Caleb says, his voice so close, I pull away from Tony to find him standing right beside us. Like he could lean in and kiss us too.

Tony shoves a hand in Caleb's face, pushing him away. "Get the fuck out of here."

Caleb laughs. "I'd try and make a move on someone, but I'm afraid they're all underage in here."

"I'm not," Gracie says.

I glance over my shoulder and send her a look that says, *what the hell are you doing?*

She just shrugs like she can't help herself.

"You two shouldn't speak to each other for the rest of the night." Tony readjusts himself so he's standing behind me, arms wrapped around my waist, chin resting on top of my head. Oh, this is nice. "We're keeping you guys separated."

"Whatever," Caleb mutters.

Guitars start playing, and we turn our attention to the stage. Robin and the lead guitarist are both angrily strumming, and the sound is nothing but noise. Not necessarily a song.

There was no announcement, no introduction. Robin leans into the mic and starts singing. He's slightly off-key, and I can't help but wonder if he has a frog in his throat, but Gracie is hopping up and down, screaming for him.

Cheering him on.

I do the same. I hear Tony yell his encouragement. Even Caleb joins in.

And thank God, he doesn't say anything inappropriate.

It goes on like this for a solid thirty minutes. They perform song after song, not any I'm familiar with, despite Gracie playing their music for me in the car on the way over. Actually, she's played them for me a few times. They're on Spotify, of course, or was it Sound Cloud? Probably both. As they play on, they start to sound better, but I have to admit...

Jackson Rivers is a better singer and guitar player. Not that I would ever say that to Gracie.

There was something so intimate about Jackson's performance, though. Despite the constant screaming from the audience, the way he plucked at his guitar and crooned his lyrics into the mic, it was as if he was singing to me and no one else.

Watching Robin, it seems like he's trying too hard. Maybe he's nervous, since he knows the record exec could be out here, watching them? I don't know.

But now I feel sort of bad.

I start swaying to the beat, trying to get into it. The drummer is actually pretty good. I pay attention to the lyrics, and I have to say Gracie is right. They're not bad.

Tony keeps his hold on me while I move, his hands resting lightly on my hips. People start to crowd us, trying to get closer, and Gracie becomes annoyed.

"I can't see!" she yells.

"Sit on my shoulders," Caleb leans over us to yell at Gracie.

She crosses her arms. "Over my dead body."

"Fine." Caleb shrugs. "I offered."

I keep moving to the beat. Tony laughs in my ear, his mouth so close it tickles. "They're ridiculous."

Within minutes, Gracie makes her way over to Caleb and he's hoisting her on his shoulders. She shouts with delight, a giant smile on her pretty face.

"I can see everything!"

She sings along with the songs as loud as she can, her thighs clamped tight around Caleb's head, his arms gripping around her knees so she doesn't fall off. She points at Robin when he finishes the song and the crowd goes wild, but he scowls at her. That's his only acknowledgement of the girl he's dating.

What a jerk.

The band launches into another song and Tony grabs hold of my hand, murmuring, "Come with me," before he yanks me away from the crowd gathered around the stage.

I follow him, not worried about Gracie. Despite her irritation with him, she's safe with Caleb. I think he's just trying to get a rise out of her.

But all thoughts of Caleb and Gracie and their argumentative foreplay disappear the moment we're tucked behind a wall, near the back exit. Tony wraps me up in his arms and lifts me, his big hands cradling my ass, and my legs automatically wrap around his waist. He's so strong. I should've known, considering he's an athlete who trains daily, but still.

I'm impressed.

There's no buildup, no words spoken. He's suddenly kissing me. Devouring me, really. His hot, hard mouth on mine is working its magic, breaking down my defenses, making my muscles, everything within me loosen. Public displays of affection aren't my jam, but somehow, I'm letting him grope me in the darkened hallway of a bar, and I don't care who sees.

None of those teenagers out there would care anyway.

His fingers press into my flesh and he slowly thrusts against me in time with the thrust of his tongue in my mouth, and oh God. It feels so good. I moan. I twist my fingers into his hair and tug extra hard. I push my pelvis against his, feel the hard ridge of his cock and my panties grow instantly wet.

I want him. Worse than I did last time, because now I know. His taste, how his cock feels in my mouth, what he looks like when he comes. I want all of that again, and more. I had no idea I could be so turned on while listening to Bat's Cave screeching in the background.

It's Tony who ends the kiss first. "We probably shouldn't do this here."

He's panting, pressing his forehead against mine, his chest heaving. I touch his cheek. Rest my hand against his chest, the pounding of his heart a speedy rhythm beneath my palm. He's so hot. I say that out loud.

"It's this fucking jacket. I'm burning up. Should've never worn it." He sounds so angry, I start to laugh. Eventually, he does too.

"I like it," I whisper against his lips after our laughter dies. "You look sexy."

"You're fucking sexy in this tank top." He removes one hand from my butt and I cling to him, my thighs tight around his waist. He settles that hand on my breast, his thumb streaking across my nipple in the barest caress. There's a growing ache between my legs, and my mind is suddenly filled with images of me and Tony. New ones, where we're completely naked. Rolling around in a bed.

"I like the black bra," he says, interrupting my dirty thoughts.

"I knew you would." I grin, smugly.

"Hey. I thought we were just friends here."

"Really?" I lift a single brow. "After what happened in the back seat of your car, you can still say that with a straight face?"

"I just like giving you shit." He chuckles.

"There's nothing friendly about this." I slide my hand down until it rests directly over his erection.

Damn, that thing is impressive.

"I have to disagree. It's really fucking friendly." He thrusts against my hand, making me wish I was touching bare skin.

I idly stroke him. "We should probably get back."

His eyes look ready to cross at any moment. "Really?"

"They're going to wonder where we went. Then they'll try and find us." More stroking, my fingers curling, molding the exact shape of him beneath the denim.

"Let them find us." A ragged breath leaves him when I squeeze. "You keep that up and I'm going to come in my jeans."

"We can't have that. I don't want to waste it." My hand drops and he looks disappointed. "Put me down."

He does as I ask, settling me on my feet. "What did you mean by that? You don't want to waste it?"

"When you come tonight, it'll either be in my mouth, or inside me." I smile. He groans. "That's what I meant."

"You're a fucking tease," he practically growls, his face pressed against my hair.

"You like it." Grinning, I take his hand and lead him back toward the thinning crowd. Where did all the girls go? Is it past their curfew? I mean, it is a school night.

We say nothing else as we make our way to Gracie and Caleb. She's still sitting on his shoulders, and she's swaying to the music, which is sort of forcing Caleb to do the same. The band is performing a slow song, and those left remaining in the audience are swinging their arms in the air back and forth, their lit phones in their hand. We stop right beside Caleb, who sends us a knowing look before he squeezes Gracie's thighs, making her squeal and glance down.

"They're back," he says, sending us both a knowing look.

Within minutes of our return, the performance is over. Robin shouts out a hoarse thank you. Gracie shrieks her approval. There's a smattering of applause, a couple of hoots and hollers, and then the stage goes dark.

They're done. Finally.

Gracie climbs off Caleb as if he's a tree, dropping to her feet with a thud. "Thank you," she tells him, and he nods his answer, rubbing his shoulders. "Was I too heavy?"

"Nah, you're pretty light, for being so tall," he says as he stretches out his neck.

"I need to go check on Robin," she says to me. "Do you mind waiting here?"

"Sure. They'll wait with me." I indicate to the guys.

"Good. Give me a few. I don't even know if he'll have time to talk to me right now. Hopefully he'll be talking to the record exec. Scout. Whatever they are." Gracie takes off before I can say anything else.

The moment she's out of earshot, Caleb moves in closer, his voice dropping. "They sucked absolute ass, just as I predicted."

"I know." I make a face, feeling bad. "I should've warned you."

"They weren't very good," Tony agrees. "Lead singer almost seemed...nervous?"

"You mean Robin?" Caleb keeps a straight face, but he looks ready to burst out laughing. "Maybe knowing there's a scout in the audience worked him up. We know how that feels, right?"

Tony nods in agreement. "It's the worst."

"What do you guys mean?" I'm confused.

"When we were in high school, we had college coaches come out to scout us," Tony explains. "The majority of them were looking at our friend, Jake. Teams from across the country were interested in him."

"Wait a minute." I look Tony dead in the eye. "Are you talking about Jake Callahan? Son of Drew Callahan?"

They both nod, grinning. "He was our quarterback. Drew was our team's coach."

"Oh God." My father might've not been a football fan, but everyone knows who Drew Callahan is. Former quarterback for the Forty-Niners. Took them to a couple of Super Bowls. Was a sports announcer for a short period of time. "You just—hang out with the Callahans on a regular basis?"

I'm not one to be dazzled by celebrities, but Drew Callahan was a hottie back in the day. He still is, if you're into older men. And I've seen photos of Jake Callahan.

He looks just like his father.

"Our friend Eli is going out with their daughter, Ava. Our Bulldog QB dates their oldest daughter, Autumn," Caleb says.

"No way." I don't really keep up with what our college football team does, but there's a memory niggling at me. Reminding me that yes, I did hear that tasty little fact before about our QB and his connection to the

Callahan football legacy. "I want to meet the Callahans someday."

"They're all pretty awesome," Tony says. "Jake is one of my best friends."

"He's at USC, right?"

"Yeah, and kicking ass there too," Caleb adds. "Not to change the subject, but I want to know where Jackson is."

"Text him," Tony says, waving at the phone clutched in Caleb's hand. "Ask him."

"Do you think he noticed us?" Caleb starts tapping away.

"How could he not? You were constantly screaming at him," I say drolly.

Caleb grins. "Couldn't help myself. All those girls yelling for him, singing along with his drippy romantic songs. Dude has a fucking fan club and he's been keeping it a secret from us the whole time. Little fucker. He's the new Justin Bieber!"

"I wouldn't go that far," Tony says with a laugh. He turns his attention to me. "What did you think of him?"

I don't want to say something that makes it look like I'm lusting over Jackson Rivers, which I am so not. My lips still tingle from Tony's kiss. And my fingers are itching to touch him again. But...

"He has a very—intimate way of performing. I get the appeal."

"So you'd be a screaming fangirl over him too if you saw him again?" Caleb's brows shoot up.

"He's a decent singer. Even better? He's a great performer. He made me want to pay attention," I say.

"I get it," Tony says with a nod. "He drew you in. He has a way about him. He draws everyone in."

"He only draws me in because I want to kick his ass in video games," Caleb says.

Tony rolls his eyes. I laugh. I'm really enjoying spending time with these two tonight. And Gracie. Speaking of...

"Why did you keep giving Gracie shit?" I ask Caleb.

"She's cute when she's mad." He shrugs.

"You made her really, really mad," I say slowly.

"I know, right? She's so easy to provoke. Maybe it's my charm she can't resist."

"You're so full of shit," Tony practically groans.

"What the fuck ever. Look, she's taken. It's easy to flirt with and irritate a girl who's interested in someone else. She takes the bait I throw out, but it's not like she wants to be with me," Caleb further explains, "I'm like that annoying little brother you want to punch in the face."

I don't bother saying he doesn't know Gracie very well. Because he doesn't. She could lose interest in Robin within the next few days, and move on to someone new almost immediately.

Like Caleb.

"Hey, she's coming over here right now," Caleb says, his eyes going wide. "Oh shit, she looks pissed."

Gracie is, indeed, stomping her way over to us. She grabs hold of my hand and starts walking, the guys falling into step behind us. "We're leaving," she declares. "I hope Robin chokes on his precious microphone and dies."

She drags me out of Strummers, and I am dying to ask her what happened, but maybe she doesn't want to discuss it in front of Tony and Caleb.

Once we're outside, Gracie lets me go, wrapping her arms around herself since the air is so shockingly cold. "I went backstage to congratulate him and there was a girl kneeling before him with her hand around his hard dick! Can you believe it? He's letting some gross groupie give him head that he doesn't even know! I came to watch him tonight and everything! God, what an ungrateful prick. He doesn't even appreciate my support!"

"Wait a minute. Some chick is willingly sucking his dick right now?" Caleb sounds shocked.

"Yes." Gracie blows out a harsh breath, glaring at the building.

"Did he see you when you walked in on them?" I ask her.

"Of course he did! He chased after me too, his dick flapping in the breeze as he ran down the hall, trying to talk me out of leaving. He swore to me it meant nothing." Gracie snorts. "I've heard that before."

Caleb laughs and Tony slaps him in the chest, silencing him.

"Did he say anything else?" I ask.

"When I refused to go back into his dressing room with him, he accused me of being on a date with this guy." She jerks her thumb in Caleb's direction. "Ridiculous."

Caleb grins. "I'm honored."

"You would be," Gracie mutters. Her eyes still ablaze with anger, but her lower lip is trembling. She's close to losing it. "He's such a dick."

"Yeah, he is," I agree, rubbing her upper arm. Her skin is like ice. "We should go home."

I send Tony a pleading look, noticing the disappointment on his face. I was going to suggest I ride home with Tony and Caleb, but I can't leave Gracie alone now. Not like this. She's hurting. Thanks to a dude named Robin who's in a really shitty band.

Gracie sniffs loudly. "Okay. Do we have any liquor in the house? I need to get drunk."

"I don't know," I say, my brain cataloging everything we have in the apartment. Maybe a couple of beers in the fridge? I don't remember. I'm not a huge drinker, especially at home.

"We've got liquor," Caleb says. "Come over to our place and hang out."

Gracie sniffs again. "Okay." She meets my gaze. "Let's go."

Well. I certainly didn't expect her to say that.

SEVENTEEN

TONY

TWENTY MINUTES later and all four of us are walking into the condo to find Diego, Jocelyn, their baby girl Gigi, Eli and Ava all crowded into the living room, the girls chatting away. Diego holds his baby girl above his head, baby talking to her while she coos and smiles, her lower lip shiny with drool.

He's gonna get drool on his face if he doesn't watch it.

Gracie comes to an abrupt stop, a smile breaking out across her face. "Aw, a baby."

"You get to meet a Callahan right now," I murmur close to Hayden's ear. I raise my voice. "Ava. What the hell are you doing here on a school night?"

Ava glances over her shoulder to smile at me. "Did you forget? It's October break. We don't have school this week."

I only graduated in June, yet I'm forgetting all about our October break. A break we've had since I was in kindergarten. "Oh right."

"How easy they forget," she teases before she leans in and drops a lingering kiss on her boyfriend's lips. "I've been spending as much time with this guy as possible."

Eli waves at us.

"What are you doing here?" I ask, my question for Diego. Yes, he technically lives at the condo, but he rarely comes over anymore. He's pretty much moved in with Jocelyn, which makes sense.

"We were bored. I thought you guys would be here, but when I showed up, the place was empty. Then Eli texted me saying he couldn't find Jackson anywhere, and Ava and Ellie were with him, so we all decided to hang out here," Diego says with a shrug. Jocelyn walks over to pluck the baby from his hands, snuggling her close. "But Jackson wasn't here either."

"Ha! I can tell you where Jackson was tonight." Caleb rubs his hands together, and I know he's relishing this moment.

I glance around, not spotting Ellie anywhere. Then I hear a toilet flush and water start to run. "Hold on," I tell Caleb. "Ellie should hear this too. Maybe she already knows and can give us information."

"Ellie is Ava's best friend and she's got a thing for Jackson," I explain to Hayden.

"Who are your friends?" Ava asks curiously.

"I'm Hayden." She waves at Ava, who waves in return. "And this is my best friend, Gracie."

"Nice to meet you. I'm Ava."

"Callahan?" Hayden asks.

Ava nods. "Yeah."

Hayden smiles. "Tony was just telling us about you."

"All nice things, I hope," Ava says with a laugh.

Ellie walks out of the bathroom, stopping short when she sees us standing in the living room. "Hey guys. Is, uh, Jackson with you?"

"Nope, but we saw him earlier." Caleb launches into

the story of going to Strummers. The crowd of teenage girls waiting in line outside. The guy coming out on stage. The shock we felt when we realized it was Jackson. How he performed and the girls went crazy for him the entire time.

"Where is he now?" Diego asks when Caleb finishes.

"I don't know. I texted him asking where he went, but he never responded," Caleb says. His gaze swings to Ellie. "Did you know about this?"

Ellie slowly shakes her head, obvious shock written all over her face. "No, I didn't."

That's weird. I always thought Jackson kind of led her on, considering he talks to her so much. But it's always through social media and rarely in person, especially lately. Sometimes they hang out, but in public he always treats her like a friend. It's confusing. I'm sure Ellie is confused by his behavior too. I do know this though. Ellie is truly his number one fan when it comes to his music.

So why wouldn't Jackson tell her about his performing at Strummers?

"We should go back to my place," Eli says, his gaze swinging from Ava to Ellie. "Maybe he's there."

Jackson and Eli live together.

"Good idea," Ellie says with a nod, before whipping her phone out of the back pocket of her jeans. "I'll text him."

Ava leaps to her feet and approaches us, giving me a big hug before she turns to Hayden. "So nice to meet you. Sorry we have to leave."

"It's okay." Hayden smiles and the girls hug. "We'll all have to hang out sometime."

"Sure," Ava says with a smile.

The three of them leave within seconds, Diego and Jocelyn and the baby following behind them. Until it's just the four of us.

"Let's check out our liquor stash," Caleb says to Gracie as he leads her into the kitchen.

I turn to Hayden once they're gone. "You do realize Ava is still in high school."

Hayden frowns. "Seriously? God, why are you all so young?"

I chuckle. "She's a senior. She started dating Eli last year, when we were seniors," I explain. "Ellie is a senior, too."

"They're just babies," Hayden murmurs, her gaze thoughtful. "Long distance relationship, hmm? I could never do it."

"My hometown is, like, an hour away. No big deal. They're making it work," I say.

"Still. He's a year older, away at college. And what is she doing when she graduates? Going here?" Hayden lifts her brows.

I can't imagine Ava going here, though she might, just for Eli.

"I don't know," I say with a shrug, not really caring.

All I can think about is getting this girl in my room so we can be alone.

"Age difference in a relationship when we're this young matters," she says, as if she's a wise, old person.

Compared to all of us, she sort of is.

"Says the twenty-year-old," I tease her, and she mock scowls at me.

"Whatever," she says, her voice full of attitude. "You'll see what I mean when you're twenty and I'm—"

She stops talking, a sheepish expression on her face. I think I know what she's referring to, though. She's talking like we'll still be together in two years, which is very un-Hayden like. Does that kind of talk scare me?

It probably should.

"Let's go to my room," I suggest, grabbing her hand and pulling her close to me. Her warm body fits perfectly next to mine, and my hands are itching to explore every single inch of her.

"You don't want to hang out with Gracie and Caleb? Have a couple of drinks?" she asks, sounding a little nervous.

Surprising. This girl seems to grab life by the balls and not let go. So what's up?

"Nah. Your friend will be okay with my friend, right?" I slip my arm around her waist, pulling her in even closer. She's warm. She smells fuckin' good.

Hayden nods. Rests her hand against my chest, her gaze on mine. "She's a big girl. She can handle Caleb. Hopefully."

"He's not so bad." I steal a kiss, quick and fleeting, and I immediately want more. "Though I'm more worried for Caleb."

Hayden laughs. Rolls her eyes. Rises up on tiptoe and brushes her mouth against mine. "Let's drink something and then we'll go up to your room," she murmurs.

I rest my hand on her perfectly shaped ass. "Promise?"

Her smile is naughty. "Oh yeah."

The moment we enter the kitchen, I spot Gracie with her fingers wrapped around the neck of a vodka bottle, chugging. Caleb is throwing back a beer, making a smacking noise with his lips when he's finished.

"Look at you," Caleb says to Gracie when she sets the bottle on the counter with a loud thump. She wipes any excess vodka from her lips with the back of her hand. "I hope you know how to hold your liquor."

"I can handle it. Been doing this for a while now,"

Gracie says with confidence. She holds the bottle out to Hayden. "Want some?"

"No thanks," Hayden says, shaking her head. "But I'll take a beer."

Caleb hands her one, and then gives me one as well. I crack it up open and take a sip. I plan on nursing it. I want to be relatively sober when I get Hayden Channing all alone and naked in my room.

Because that's the plan. It's happening. There will be no holding back tonight. I want it. Pretty sure she wants it too. She keeps looking at me, a secretive little smile curving her perfect lips. I'd grab her and haul her up into my room right now if I could, but I guess we have to make nice for a while.

We drink. We chat. Jackson never responds to Caleb, though he keeps texting him. Gracie's phone starts blowing up, and she ignores it at first. So do we. Until Caleb can't take it any longer.

"I'm sure it's your cheating ass boyfriend," Caleb says to her. "Check your phone."

"No." Gracie shakes her head.

Caleb glances at her butt, then whips her phone out from the back pocket, handing it to her. "Come on."

"Fine," she says with a sigh as she opens it up and checks her messages. "Oh God. He's begging." She frowns as she reads each message. "He claims he's sad and he needs me."

Hayden shakes her head. "Talk to him tomorrow. He's awful, Gracie. He doesn't deserve you."

The phone rings, and Gracie answers it immediately, her expression drawn in concern. "Yes. No, I'm sorry. I didn't hear my texts come through. What happened? The exec barely talked to you guys? Oh no..."

She walks away with the phone clutched to her ear, murmuring consoling words to the jerk who had another chick's fingers wrapped around his dick not even an hour ago.

"She's not one to tolerate a cheater normally," Hayden says to the both of us.

"He's an asshole," Caleb says vehemently, slamming back the rest of his beer before he grabs another one. "Who can't sing for shit."

Facts. All of it.

We drink quietly, all of us straining to hear Gracie talking to Robin in the other room. But her voice is too low, and she's not saying much.

I sling my arm around Hayden's shoulders, pulling her in so I can drop a sloppy kiss on her forehead. She tilts her head back, smiling up at me. "Ready to go up to my room?" I ask her.

She nods, sneaking her arms around my waist and holding me tight. "Definitely."

Gracie barges back into the kitchen, grabbing the vodka bottle and taking another long swig from it before she finally speaks.

"The record exec wasn't interested in them," she announces. "Robin's devastated."

Caleb looks ready to make a smartass remark, but I give a quick shake of my head, and he clamps his lips shut. Thank God.

"Where is he?" Hayden asks, leaning her head against my chest.

"Driving around the Tower District, crying as he talks to me. He wants to come pick me up." She bites her lower lip, and I can feel the faint shame emanating off her. "He says he needs me."

"What about the other girl?" Caleb asks.

"What other—oh." Gracie waves her hand. "That was nothing."

"Gracie..." Hayden starts.

"It's okay. He just wants comfort. I won't fuck him. Promise." The smile on her face is small. Even a little sad. "Please don't give me shit. I feel terrible about what happened. We made fun of him the entire night, and he sounded so defeated just now. I feel guilty."

I'm about to point out that she never made fun of him the entire night. Not once. That was on the rest of us, even Hayden a little bit. And the last thing Gracie should feel is guilty.

But whatever. That isn't my problem, it's Gracie's. I just don't understand people who forgive cheaters so easily. Like my parents. Why did they string each other along like that? People who can't be loyal bug the shit out of me. I'm loyal to the bitter end to my friends. Some might say I'm loyal to a fucking fault, but I will never stand for someone who cheats on me.

That is some straight-up bullshit.

Witnessing the ups and downs of Gracie and Robin is reminding me why I'm not interested in a relationship. Gracie going to that asshole right now during his supposed, 'time of need' is borderline pathetic.

Keeping it casual with Hayden is the way to go. Relationships are too messy.

"I'm going to talk to her," Hayden murmurs to me before she lets go of me and steers Gracie out of the kitchen and into the living room.

Caleb shakes his head, disgust written all over his face. "She shouldn't let him get away with it."

"I agree," I say quietly.

"He manipulated her into thinking she's the one who should feel guilty," Caleb continues.

"You're right," I say with a nod. "This is why relationships suck. You just end up hurting the one you supposedly love, or you end up getting hurt."

"What do you mean, relationships suck?" Caleb appears confused. "I always thought you were looking for the perfect girl, and it looks like you just found her."

"What are you talking about?" I ask.

"You and Hayden have been all over each other tonight. Not that I think it's a bad thing. Just don't go around saying you don't want something when you act like you do," he says with a shrug.

"Hayden and I –we're just hanging out," I say, knowing it sounds lame. "I don't need the perfect girl. I already figured out there's no such thing, thanks to Sophie."

At one point, I definitely thought she was perfect. Until our relationship turned into a complete disaster and she left.

"Uh huh. But you realized quick high school relationships are meaningless," Caleb says.

"Don't say that to Ava and Eli. Or Jake and Hannah. Asher and Autumn. Diego and Jocelyn." I frown. Damn, the list is long.

"Exceptions."

"All of our friends' relationships are exceptions?" I raise my brows. "The odds aren't in their favor. Someone from that group is going to break up. I'm calling it now."

"Who do you think will?" Caleb asks.

"Not Diego and Jos. They've been through enough, and they already broke up once. Ash and Autumn have been together a long time. They're making it work despite being long distance for the last three years, so I doubt they will either. Jake's going to cling to Hannah as his life becomes crazier and crazier..."

"Eli and Ava then," Caleb suggests, though I can tell it pains him to do so.

"Yep." I nod. "Maybe we should make a bet on it."

That is probably a terrible idea.

"No way. That's fucked up," Caleb says with a shake of his head.

"Yeah, it is fucked up. But come on. It's life, man. As a wise woman I know once said, relationships are for pussies," I say.

Caleb grins. "Who said that?"

"Hayden."

"No shit?" He rubs his jaw, looking thoughtful. "She's smart. I agree with her. I know I called her a ball buster, and I kind of still think she is one, but she's cool. So is Gracie. When she's not chasing after a loser."

"Right, but we're just keeping it casual, Hayden and me." I am completely lying to myself. When I dragged Hayden out of the crowd earlier and kissed her against the wall, I was feeling anything but casual. I want her. I want her naked in my bed tonight. Will she stay the night with me? Or will she somehow convince Gracie not to leave with that asshole and they'll both end up going back to their place, leaving me high and dry.

A shitty way for me to think, but I can't help it. Our interactions have been leading up to this moment, and I'm ready for it to happen. Beyond ready. This has the potential to be a monumental night for me. And I will be totally disappointed if she bails.

I'll get over it and move on, but still disappointed.

"Please. Like I just said, you were all over her tonight," Caleb says.

"You were all over Gracie," I point out.

"That was just for fun. It's not like I had my tongue down her throat." He shrugs one shoulder. "She's cool. I'd be down to fuck her. But she'd get hung up on me and my big dick, fall madly in love with me, and chase me all over campus. I don't want to have to file a restraining order against her."

I laugh, ready to give him grief, but someone else beats me to it.

"You're such a dick."

Oh shit.

We both turn to find Gracie is in the kitchen, and Hayden is standing right next to her. They're both glaring. At Caleb.

"I was just kidding," Caleb says with a light laugh.

Gracie's eyes are glassy, like she might've been crying. She points at Caleb. "I was ready to forgive you for how awful you were to me tonight, but forget it. Fuck you, Caleb." She offers a gentle smile in my direction. "It was nice hanging out with you tonight, Tony, but I've got to go. Robin is waiting for me in the parking lot."

"You sure you're okay, Gracie?" I follow after them toward the front door, leaving Caleb in the kitchen. "You really want to leave with that guy?"

She nods and sniffs, a watery smile on her face. "I'll be fine. Thank you. I know how to handle him."

Hayden gives her a hug before Gracie opens the door, and we both stand in the doorway, watching Gracie walk toward an older, beat-up black Toyota Tacoma. I'm surprised ol' Robin drives a truck, but then I notice there's a bunch of sound equipment in the back of it, so that makes sense.

She opens the passenger side door, climbs into the

truck, and waves before she pulls the creaky door shut. Robin revs the engine before he pulls away from the curb, his tires screeching as the truck's back end swings. As if he's losing traction.

Guy can't sing or drive. Great.

"Is she really going to be all right with him?" I ask Hayden as we watch them leave. I swear I can still hear his squealing tires.

"She will. Though I told her not to go." Hayden shakes her head. "He doesn't deserve her. He's a total prick."

"He is," I agree as I shut and lock the front door.

"She told me she feels bad for him," Hayden continues. "He was crying to her on the phone. He claims he was so nervous and that's why they had a bad set, but I don't know. I've heard them live before and it wasn't much of a difference. He's just trying to divert her from the fact that she caught him with another girl."

These manipulative tactics feel familiar. My mom did this shit to my dad all the time when they were still married. Even when they were going through their divorce. It worked most of the time too. Dad felt guilty for a lot of the shit he did to her.

Sometimes I wonder if Mom ever feels guilty.

I'm going with not really.

Caleb appears, a sulk on his face. "I'm going to bed." He stomps up the stairs without a backward glance or acknowledgement of our good nights we call out to him.

"What's his problem?" Hayden asks me once he's gone, sounding vaguely amused. "He's the one who said she'd fall in love with him and he'd have to get a restraining order."

"Caleb never knows when to quit," I explain.

Hayden turns to face me, her hand rising to rest on my chest. "Unlike you?"

"What do you mean by that?" I frown.

"You're one of the most restrained people I know, Tony Sorrento. Calm. Thoughtful." She steps closer, her head tilted back as if she's waiting for a kiss. I give her one, keeping it light. "I like that about you."

"I'm glad we're friends," I tell her in all seriousness as we slowly walk toward the stairs.

She swats my chest and then takes my hand, a smile stretching her lips. "Forget all this friend talk. Take me upstairs and ravish me, sir."

"Ravish you?" I let her drag me up the stairs, enjoying how eager she seems.

Since the heated kiss at Strummers, I've felt the same way.

"I watched Bridgerton on Netflix. I'm all about the historical romance right now. You're like one of those noble dukes with the stiff upper lip who has a hard time showing his feelings," she says.

I have no idea what she's talking about. "I'll show you something stiff."

She throws her head back and laughs. "Perfect. That's what I was hoping for."

EIGHTEEN

HAYDEN

THE MOMENT we're in Tony's room, he's closing and locking the door—a promising sign—and pulling me into his arms, our bodies flush together so that I can feel every inch of him, and he can feel every inch of me.

I shiver when he leans in and drops a kiss on my bare shoulder, his lips soft and warm, his hands shifting to grip my hips lightly. "Your skin is so smooth," he murmurs as he shifts inward, his mouth now on my neck, right at my pulse point.

I close my eyes, tilting my head back, trying to banish what I heard earlier from my mind. Yes, I was spying on Tony and Caleb's conversation, so what? I tuned out what Gracie was saying about Robin, and while I feel bad about it, I was also trying to listen to Tony and his thoughts on relationships.

They haven't changed from the first time I met him, and the dreamer in me sort of hoped they had. But he's repeating my own words, yet again. That "relationships are for pussies" remark will haunt me the entire time we're supposedly together, I know it.

He acts like he's into me. I'm not dumb. I know when a guy wants to be with me. And it's not just a sex thing. We've messed around. We definitely have a connection. I'm pretty sure tonight is the night we actually have sex, and I actually like this guy. I think he feels the same way.

I don't want to be just friends with him. I know that much.

Am I setting myself up to fail? Maybe. Am I willing to take that chance?

I don't know.

Tony is young. And he's not a believer in high school relationships—God, who is? I'm not a believer in them either. He's barely out of high school. I'm two years older than he is. Just *thinking* about a long-term relationship happening between us is probably doomed to fail. When does love ever prevail? Not in any relationship I've ever seen.

"Hayden." Tony's rumbly voice against my throat pulls me from my thoughts and I take a deep breath. "Where'd you go?"

"I was thinking," I admit truthfully.

"I must be doing a shit job then," he says, chuckling into my skin.

"You're definitely not doing a shit job." I pull away slightly so I can stare into his deep brown eyes. They're dark and mysterious, and I wish I knew what he was thinking right now. "I had fun tonight. Despite how awful Bat's Cave was."

"They were awful," he agrees readily. "But I had fun too. I like Gracie."

"I like Caleb." I do, even when he's antagonizing my best friend. "He's like a twelve-year-old in a man's body."

"Exactly. He can get pretty much any girl he wants."

"Probably not Gracie."

"We'll see." His quiet confidence is sexy.

It's also vaguely annoying, yet still sexy.

I shove his shoulder. "Don't say that. You make it sound like Gracie is easy."

"Nah. More like all that arguing is foreplay."

"Kind of like when we first hung out?" I raise a brow.

"We didn't argue too much."

"Somewhat. And I tried my hardest to push you. Out on the jungle gym." I smile, remembering that moment.

"When you took off your panties and shoved them at me?" he asks. I nod. "That was definitely foreplay."

"I was testing you," I stress, rolling my eyes, trying my best to keep the smile off my lips. But it's like I can't help it.

His hands slip from my hips to settle on my ass. They're big and warm and when he gives me a squeeze, pulling me in closer, I can feel how hard he is. "Testing me. Flirting with me. Whatever."

"You still have my panties?" I ask in a whisper.

He nods slowly.

I smile. "Where are they?"

"I'm not telling."

"I want them back."

"Nope." He shakes his head.

"Tony..." I draw his name out.

"You can't take back a gift," he protests.

"They're my underwear. They weren't a gift."

"I thought they were. You're the one who shoved them at me."

I really don't want the panties back, but I'm curious where he might be keeping them. I glance around the room, spotting Millicent the cat sleeping in a chair on top of a folded blanket, my gaze settling on the giant dresser against the wall. "Do you keep them stashed in there?" I nod toward the dresser.

"Like I said, I'm not telling." His lips thin into a straight line and he slowly shakes his head. "They're mine."

"You're very possessive," I say with a little pout.

"You have no idea," he drawls before he dips his head and presses his mouth to mine.

The kiss goes deep instantly. Open mouths and seeking tongues. I thrust my hands into his thick hair. He grips my ass tight, pushing me against the wall. Again he lifts me, and I wrap my legs around his waist, my thighs squeezing. He shifts closer, his denim covered erection obvious, and I blatantly rub my lower body against his, the delicious friction sending sparks all over my skin.

It's been a while since I've been with a guy. And I can't remember ever feeling so connected to a guy as I do with Tony.

"Are you trying to get off right now?" he murmurs against my mouth, sounding amused.

"What do you think?" I lift my hips, then drag them down. A little whimper escapes me as my pussy clenches in anticipation.

"I think you're unlike any girl I've ever been with," he says, awe tinging his voice as he leans in and kisses me yet again.

I don't think he's been with a ton of girls. That's my guess. He's only eighteen. I heard him mention a girl. Sophie? Did she break his heart? He's never mentioned her to me, and maybe it hurts too much to talk about her.

I hate that. I don't want him to have some girl in his past who wrecked him. Not in that way. I want to wreck him, but in the best way possible.

His hands slip beneath the hem of my tank, touching

bare skin. I suck in a breath, shivering when he slides those hands up, up, up. Until he's touching my bra. Just beneath my breasts. His fingers are featherlight, like a tease. Like magic. They're there, and then they're gone.

And now they're back.

I thrust my chest into his hands, wanting more. Curl my hand around his nape to deepen our kiss, indicating that I never want him to stop his exploration. He returns his hands to my breasts, his fingers streaking across the front of my bra, tracing the lace. Circling around my hard nipples.

"Feels so good," I murmur against his mouth, encouraging him.

He shifts his hands to my back, working the hooks on my bra. It springs free and within seconds, his fingers are beneath the bra, touching bare skin. His thumbs skim across my nipples, lightly pinching them. Driving me out of my mind.

The tank, the bra, it all feels like it's choking me. I pull my mouth from his and lift my arms above my head. He opens his eyes, staring at me, and I'm sure I look a mess.

"Take it off," I whisper and he reaches for the hem of my tank, this time pulling it up and over my breasts, along my arms, over my head, until I'm completely free of it.

He drops the tank and I rid myself of my bra, until I'm completely topless.

"I've dreamed of seeing you like this," he murmurs, reaching out to reverently touch me, his gaze locked on my chest. He runs the back of his hand against one breast, then the other. "After that night out on the jungle gym."

"I wanted to flash you so bad," I admit with a faint smile.

"You pretty much did," he says.

"Not all the way," I remind him.

"Just enough to fuel my imagination." His gaze returns to mine. "And trust me. Reality is better than my imagination."

A whispery sigh leaves me when he pinches my right nipple. He could do it harder. I wouldn't mind. "I'm so glad to hear it."

He cups my breasts, as if weighing them in his palms. His expression is indecisive, and I wonder what he's waiting for.

It suddenly feels like he's stalling.

"Everything okay?" I ask him after what feels like an eternity of silence.

He lifts his gaze to mine, and I see uncertainty there. It triggers something inside of me. Concern? Worry? Is he going to back out? Tell me he's not interested in this, in me?

Oh God. I try my best to be a strong, secure woman when it comes to my sexuality. Not much shames me or makes me embarrassed anymore, but I feel super vulnerable right now. Topless and exposed.

"Can I admit something to you?" he asks, his voice quiet.

I nod, swallowing past the sudden lump in my throat. "You can tell me anything."

"I—haven't done this much." He removes his hands from my chest and rests them on my shoulders briefly before he draws them down my arms.

"What exactly are you talking about?" Everywhere he touches me, sparks fly. My entire body is achingly aware of his. It's as if my every nerve and cell is chanting, *more, more, more*.

"Sex. I've messed around some. We messed around a few days ago. But—" He looks away and drops his hands, though his lower body still pins mine to the wall.

God, he's strong. And cute. Sexy.

Wait a minute.

Is he trying to tell me he hasn't had a lot of experience?

"You're doing fine," I whisper. "Better than fine. I'm encouraging you to keep going. If it's anything like last Saturday, we're on the right track."

His gaze returns to mine. "I've never had—actual sex before."

My mouth drops open. "What?"

"It's true."

"You told me you had moves." I'm teasing, but he looks so serious—and worried—I clamp my mouth shut before I say something that'll upset him.

"I do. I just—I don't know how to explain it. I guess I never got around to completely finishing the deed," he says, sounding miserable.

"What exactly have you done?" I cannot believe we're having this conversation right now.

"Everything else but." He cups my cheek. Tilts my head back so our gazes lock. "Don't make fun of me right now."

He sounds so worried. It makes my heart crack wide open, just for him.

"I would never make fun of you," I stress, slowly shaking my head.

I'm rattled though. He's saying he's a freaking virgin. Tony Sorrento, resident hottie on campus, a virgin!

Who knew?

Apparently no one. Definitely not me.

"What about Sophie? You never had sex with her?" I thought she was the great love of his life.

He frowns. "How do you know about Sophie?"

Well. This is embarrassing. I probably shouldn't have asked that. "I overheard you talking with Caleb earlier."

"Oh. Well. We got together last year. She was my first girlfriend. We messed around some, but I could never get her to have sex with me. She was too scared." He sighs. Shakes his head. "I don't want to talk about Sophie."

Maybe he's still in love with her. I can feel it in the way he closes himself off.

"Right. Not the time or place." I nudge my torso against his. At least his dick is still hard. That's a good sign. "Put me down, please."

He lowers me to the ground and I immediately toe off my low-rise Chucks before I start taking off my jeans. They're so tight, I basically peel them off my legs, and I get rid of them quick, a sigh of relief escaping me when they're off.

"What are you doing?" Tony asks.

"What does it look like?" I raise a brow.

"I thought you were going to leave."

I look at him. I mean, I *really* look at him, studying his face. He's worried. His face is set in a grimace, and his gaze is full of uncertainty.

This is silly. We're about to have sex—and it's his first time. It should be fun and carefree. Not traumatizing and worried you're going to get judged.

I can admit I'm a little thrown by his admission, but it's not enough to stop me. So I'll be Tony Sorrento's first. So what?

You'll be his first. That's a big deal. If he has a thing for Sophie? He'll have a bigger thing for you.

I shove that voice into the farthest corner of my head and tell it to shut up.

"Come here." I reach out my hand and he takes it so I can pull him toward me. He comes willingly, our bodies colliding, and he smiles down at me, his arms coming around my bare waist. "Do you have condoms?"

He nods, his fingers caressing my sides a total distraction. I tell myself to focus.

"Good. Then ravish me, my stoic, virginal duke," I tease.

He rolls his eyes, and then he does the craziest thing.

Without warning he reaches for me, picking me up and slinging my entire body over his shoulder. I can't help the shriek that escapes me, and I smack the solid wall that is his back as he takes me to the bed and dumps me unceremoniously on the mattress. I practically bounce when I hit the thing, and I push my hair out of my face, ready to give him shit, but the words get stuck in my throat when I see what he's doing.

He tugs the black T-shirt off, revealing a lean yet muscular chest. The boy has abs. A six pack, and I stare at them, tempted to lick all over his stomach and search those muscular ridges of flesh. His jeans gape a little at the waist, revealing nothing but a shadow beneath and anticipation curls within me.

Pretty sure Tony has the best bod out of any dude I've ever been with.

I lie back on the bed in just my panties and watch him, unable to fight the smile curling my lips. He smiles in return, reaching for the drawer on the bedside table and pulling it open, yanking out a box of condoms. He sets it on top of the table and I check the label.

"Twenty-four?" My brows shoot up. "Someone's hopeful."

"Uh huh." He reaches for the snap on his jeans and undoes it, getting rid of them in seconds. Not sure when he took off his shoes, but it doesn't matter.

He's standing before me in just his boxer briefs, and it's a glorious sight. Especially the way his cock strains against the black fabric.

"Want me to be honest?" he asks.

"Of course," I say with a nod.

"I'm worried the second I get inside you, I'll come." His gaze sweeps over my body. "You're so fucking beautiful."

My heart constricts at his confession and the compliment. "I can help with that. Get over here." I pat the empty space on the mattress beside me.

He joins me, crawling onto the bed. Crawling over me, until his face is in front of mine and our bodies are lined up perfectly. "Like this?" he whispers, just before he kisses me.

I wrap my arms around him and pull him down on top of me, needing the warmth. The weight. He's deliciously heavy and I wind my legs around his, rubbing the heel of my foot against the back of his hairy calf. I noticed he has a little bit of hair on his chest too, and there was a dark trail of it that led from the bottom of his navel to beneath his boxer briefs.

I want to follow that trail with my tongue. I want to do all sorts of things to him.

All of them deliciously dirty.

NINETEEN

MAYBE IT WAS A MISTAKE, being honest with Hayden. Yes, I've done a lot with other girls, even Sophie. Even Hayden. Pretty much everything you can think of sexually—except for that one thing. I've never really felt like a virgin before until this very moment, when I confessed I actually was.

Dumb, right? It's no big deal. I'm only eighteen. But then again, it's a huge deal, because I have no idea what it feels like to sink inside a woman and fuck her. To come inside her—come inside a condom, whatever. I've fingered girls. I've gone down on one. I've received a couple of blow jobs. I've been given hand jobs. I've grinded and dry humped a few too.

But yeah. Never the real deal. And here is Hayden, with far more sexual experience than me, and a confidence that I can't help but find incredibly attractive. She's unlike any girl I've ever been with before.

There's the difference. I need to stop thinking of her as a *girl*. She's a woman. She's a twenty-year-old woman who is the sexiest thing ever, and I can't wait to see what she's going to do to help me with my potential lack of control.

Shifting, I try to keep my weight off of her so I don't crush her into the mattress. But she doesn't seem to mind. She's wound herself all around me, and when our lips meet in a hungry kiss, she somehow uses her strength and rolls us on our sides so that we're facing each other, our mouths still fused. Our hands still busy. Her legs clamp around my hips and then she's moving us yet again, so now she's on top of me and I'm lying flat on my back.

I might've also gone willingly. No surprise.

She breaks the kiss and rises above me, resting her hands on my chest, her gaze warm as she studies me. "Last Saturday wasn't your first blow job, was it? I wasn't even giving you my best."

Damn. If that wasn't her best, I can't wait to see what she has in store for me tonight.

I slowly shake my head, reaching for her. She bats my hands away. "I want to touch you."

"Nope." Hayden circles her hips, rubbing herself against my cock. My eyes almost cross, it feels so good. "This is all about you right now."

Grinning, I cross my arms behind my head, as if I have all the time in the world. "Can't wait."

"Get ready for me to rock your world," she says with a laugh.

I laugh too. I love her confidence. The things she says, the way she acts. Hanging out with her and Gracie tonight offered me a glimpse of another side of Hayden. She loves her friend and is very protective of her. She knows how to have fun, dancing and moving to the awful music Bat's Cave was playing. She tolerated Caleb and his big mouth, which is huge. I think most people would've told him to fuck off like Gracie did, but Hayden never said a word to Caleb. Half the time she was laughing at everything he said.

I appreciate that. He's one of my oldest, closest friends. And I like Gracie too. We all get along. This is a good thing. I can envision us hanging out again. I can also see Hayden and I eventually becoming a couple, just like Diego and Jocelyn. Jake and Hannah. Eli and Ava...

I'm totally getting ahead of myself. Maybe it's not that I don't believe in relationships, more like I'm scared of them. Because guess what?

They're fucking scary. I've been burned before. I've witnessed my parents' messed up marriage. They would scare anyone.

But I shouldn't be thinking about any of that right now. I need to focus on Hayden, running her mouth down the length of my neck. She's kissing my collarbone. My chest. She's got her hand pressed against my dick, cupping it. Squeezing it. Her lips come closer and closer to one of my nipples and when she lightly bites it, I actually yelp.

She laughs as she tongues my flesh to soothe the sting.

As she shifts lower, I can't help but spear my hand in her hair, the silky strands clinging to my fingers. She grabs hold of my boxer briefs and tugs them down. I lift my hips to help and she pulls away, yanking them completely off. And when she returns, she rains kisses on the inside of one thigh, then the other. My eyes fall closed as I savor the moment, anticipation racing through me as I wait for her mouth to touch my dick.

She teases and torments and finally, finally her lips lightly touch my balls. She tongues the base of my cock, then runs it up the length of me, like I'm a fucking popsicle.

A jolt runs through me and I groan when her mouth wraps around the head, her lips tightening as she begins to suck. I crack open my eyes to find she's already watching me, and fuck me if that isn't hot. She releases my cock with an audible pop, her tongue swirling, catching drops of pre-come in the slit.

Fuuuuck.

"Feels good?" she asks, her voice sultry.

Damn, guess I said that out loud.

I nod, my "yeah" a rasp scraping my throat.

Thank fuck I didn't turn off the lamp so I can watch this show she's putting on for me.

Her fingers fist around the base of my cock and she continues to suck and lick. My eyes are glued to her every movement, noting the way she hums against my flesh, the vibration an added bonus. The slurping sounds she makes. She drags her tongue up and down the length of me before she wraps those lips around my cock once more, practically swallowing me whole. I bump the back of her throat and she gags a little, but she's a fucking champ because she keeps doing it.

Keeps sucking me down, her tongue in constant movement, her cheeks hollowing out as she sucks me deep.

I thrust my fingers into her hair again, holding her steady as I lift my hips and basically fuck her mouth. She lets me, keeping pace with my movements, her moans growing louder. Caleb's in the next room over but let that fucker hear.

How many times have I heard him with a girl since we've moved in together? Too many to mention.

Her hand grips me tightly as she continues sucking and licking me. I'm getting closer. There's that familiar tingle at the base of my spine. The rush of sensation gathering in my balls. As if she knows, her other hand cups them. Squeezes them. Massages them and another *fuck* drops from my lips as I arch into her mouth.

"I'm gonna come," I warn her, but she doesn't move.

She actually picks up the pace.

And then I am coming, shooting straight into her mouth. Pretty sure she swallowed, but she also pulls away, jacking me with her right hand as another stream of come shoots out of me, spilling all over her fingers. I'm shuddering, groaning loudly as she wrenches every last drop out of me.

Until I collapse on the bed, exhausted. Overcome.

She slides along my body until her face is in mine and I open my eyes to find her smiling at me.

"That was hot," she murmurs as she drops a kiss on my lips. I can taste myself, and she's right.

It was so fucking hot.

I kiss her deep until she pulls away, climbing off the bed completely. "Be right back," she calls as she makes her way to the connecting bathroom. I hear the tap turn on and assume she's washing her hands.

I lie there in a daze, reaching down to touch my dick. It's still semi-hard, sticky with come, and I can't help the chuckle that leaves me.

She just drained me dry and I still feel like I could come again at any second.

Hayden returns to the bedroom and lies down beside me, plastering her body to mine and draping her leg across my thighs. "Your dick is huge."

I bark out a laugh. "Are you trying to give me an ego boost?"

"I'm being honest." She drifts her fingers across my stomach, her touch making the muscles jump. "You have an amazing body."

"Thanks. I work out a lot." I close my eyes. Wrap my arms around her shoulders, savoring the moment. Satisfaction fills me and I could probably fall asleep right now, I'm so content.

"You going to show off your moves now?" she asks as her hand skims downward and she's cupping my junk.

My dick rises to the occasion. "You want me to?"

She laughs. "Duh."

"I might not be as skilled as you."

"It's not like I've sucked a ton of dicks, Tony," she says dryly.

"I never said you did." I open my eyes and gaze down at her. "Did I sound like an asshole just now?"

"No. I just—" She sighs and ducks her head. "Sometimes I wonder if people judge me for my attitude about sex."

"I'm not judging you," I say, stroking her shoulder with my fingers.

"I know you're not. You're benefiting from the experience." She sounds amused, and it fills me with relief. I don't want her thinking I look down on her for her sexual experience. I don't care who she's been with in the past. None of that matters because right now...

She's with me.

"I was afraid you'd judge me for my inexperience," I admit.

"There's nothing for me to judge yet. You haven't shown me your skills. They're supposed to be made up of things I've never seen," she says lightly.

I know she's throwing my words back at me, and I'm not sure how she can keep a straight face. I was a punk asshole when I said that to her a few weeks ago. "After what you did to me, I'm not sure if I can measure up."

"Enthusiasm makes up for any lack of experience. That's the first thing you should know," she says.

"Good advice." I give her shoulders a squeeze.

"And just for the record, I was really, really enthusiastic a few minutes ago," she says, making me laugh.

"Looks like I'll have to return the favor," I say with a sigh, acting like it's a burden.

It's definitely not.

I kiss her. We're all tongues and heated breath, and I break away, following the same path she took on me. I cover her throat in kisses. Suck on the spot where her shoulder meets her neck. Press my mouth across her collarbone, her chest, the gentle slope of her breasts. I spend more time there, licking and biting her soft flesh, drawing circles with my tongue around one nipple, then the other, back and forth.

When I suck a nipple deep into my mouth, she moans, her hands cupping the back of my head, holding me there, her legs restless, rubbing against me.

Hayden really likes having her nipples sucked. Noted.

I shift lower, my mouth on her trembling stomach. I dip my tongue in her belly button, making her giggle. Kiss the spot just beneath it. Somehow she got rid of her panties, and I can smell her musky, aroused scent. I slide my hand over the light tangle of pubic hair, cupping her. She's hot. I can feel the heat curl around my hand, my fingers.

She moans my name and lifts her hips, indicating she wants more. I give it to her, sinking two fingers between her lower lips, encountering nothing but wet, soft skin. I carefully stroke, searching, finding the nub of flesh at the top of her pussy and I press my thumb against it.

"You're a quick study," she says on a gasp and I smile, pleased.

Shifting, I remove my hand from her and rearrange myself so I'm face to pussy. She's got a landing strip of light brown hair covering it, but also revealing pretty much everything too, and I can't help but think it's incredibly sexy. I press my hands on the inside of her soft thighs and spread them apart slowly, revealing her completely to me.

Pink. Glistening. Beautiful.

I glance up to find she's watching me, her eyes wide, her teeth sunk into her lower lip so deep it looks painful. Her face is tense and I swear her chest barely moves. Like she's not even breathing.

I'm making her crazy, I realize. She wants my mouth on her so badly, she actually whimpers.

I lower my head slowly, brushing my lips against her as she lifts her hips.

We don't look away from each other.

Sneaking my tongue out, I lick. It's featherlight. A ghost of a touch. Her taste lingers on my tongue, making me want more and I lick again. Deeper this time.

"Oh God." She chokes out the two words and I map all that glistening flesh with my tongue, leaving no spot untouched. I'm everywhere, my nose buried against her as I thrust my tongue inside.

I search her folds, draw them between my lips and suck. I tongue fuck her again, then replace it with a finger. Another one. Until I'm sucking and licking and fucking her with bent fingers, trying to find that elusive G-spot. I might've done some Google searching in the last few days and studied some diagrams.

I want to learn how to please my woman, so sue me.

It's when I latch my lips around her clit that her entire body jolts, and I can feel her straining. Reaching for it.

"Don't stop," she breathes, and I keep doing what I was

already doing, not wanting to break the spell, desperate to keep up the same, steady pace. I would be so pissed at myself if I ruined this moment for her.

She made me come harder than I ever have in my life only a few minutes ago. I'd like to return the favor.

Hayden lifts her hips, mashing her pussy in my face and I lick. Sucking deeper, until I feel her shiver and shake against my mouth. She's coming, low moans falling from her lips, her hips gyrating, her fingers gripping my hair so hard, I'm worried she might pull it out of my scalp. It's kind of intense, her orgasm. My cock grows hard just feeling it and when I open my eyes to watch her, I grow even harder.

Fuck me, making a woman come with your mouth is hot.

"Oh God." She collapses on the mattress heavily, slinging her arm over her eyes, her chest rising and falling rapidly. I remain where I'm at, my mouth gentling, and I drop a couple of kisses on her still quivering flesh. She shivers, turning away from me slightly and a smile curves her lips.

"Sensitive," she murmurs.

I pull away completely, sliding up the bed so I'm right beside her. She curls into me, her back to my front, and I wrap my arms around her waist, holding her there. She slowly comes down, her breaths becoming even, her body relaxing against mine.

"How were my moves?" I finally ask.

She laughs. Wiggles her butt against my dick, which makes me twitch. "Excellent. I'd guess you've done this before."

Is it weird that we're talking about past experiences? Maybe. But I like how open we are with each other. "Never with you."

"True." She tilts her head forward and I take advantage, kissing her neck. "You knew exactly what you were doing."

"I followed your cues. You gave me some instruction."

"See, and that's the key. I don't know why so many guys can't get that right." She's quiet for a moment. "I make it sound like I'm talking about all these guys I've been with, when that's not the case. My friends and I are always comparing notes."

"I'm not judging you."

"I know. I just want to be open with you." She turns so she's facing me, and I study her face. Her cheeks are flushed a deep pink and her eyes are extra bright. She's gorgeous. "I'm big on being body and sex positive. Too many people cloak sex as this sort of shameful, secret act, when it's a purely natural function of the human body, you know?"

"So clinical," I tell her, brushing the hair away from her forehead.

She smiles. "There's more to it, I agree, but we shouldn't be ashamed of our body's desires."

I slowly thrust against her, letting her feel what she does to me. "My body still desires you," I say seriously.

A giggle escapes her and she winds her legs around mine. "Same."

Leaning down, I kiss her. "Is this going to ruin our friendship?"

She becomes quiet. "I think we've already gone too far," she finally murmurs.

"This was always beyond friendship for me," I tell her.

She's quiet even longer this time. To the point I start to regret what I just said. "Me too. I just—I didn't want to admit it. To you. To myself."

I touch her hair. Slip my hand between us to touch her between her legs. She's still so wet. Hot. "I want you."

Hayden nods. "I want you too."

"We do this, and I'm more than just your friend, Hayden." I begin to stroke her, and she sucks in a harsh breath.

"O-okay."

I roll her over so I'm on top and she opens her eyes when I don't move, her brows lowering. "What are you doing?"

"Looking at you." Savoring this moment. Studying every detail so I don't forget the night I had sex for the first time with the most beautiful woman I've ever met.

TWENTY

HAYDEN

TONY GRABS a condom from the new box and slips it on, me watching in quiet fascination the entire time. We kissed and touched. Rubbed against each other until it started getting into what I call the danger zone and I asked him to put on a condom. You know that point where he's rubbing his cock against you, and every once in a while, it kind of slips in. Like oops, look what I did?

Yeah, that's the danger zone. And while I'm on the pill, I'm not about to get an STD—I don't care if he claims he's a virgin, I totally believe him, but I'm not taking any chances. I'm all about double protection.

No babies for me. I saw that cute little baby earlier and those cute little babies who are her parents. No thank you. Sometimes I'm not even sure if I want to have children.

Tony got all serious a few minutes ago. Talking about how we're beyond friends. I agreed with him. It's always felt like that between us. I'm the one who pushed him away, who insisted we were friends and nothing more. I was fooling myself. Trying to convince myself we couldn't be anything else.

But he just proved me wrong. And I'm now lying here, watching him slip that condom on, my entire body tingling in anticipation of having him inside of me. I only just came what...fifteen minutes ago? My body is already raring to go.

This is how badly I want him.

He kisses me, and I drown in his taste. He presses his body on top of mine and I welcome it, wrapping my arms around him and holding him close. He's so hot, and so hard. Everywhere. Not an ounce of fat on his body, where I worry that I might be a little soft in a few places.

He doesn't notice. Or if he does, he doesn't mind. That's another thing I've learned. Women worry about their bodies when they get naked for a man for the first time, and men could give a shit. They're so eager with sex on the brain, they don't see the flaws. They only recognize the good stuff.

Tony has plenty of good stuff. Like his thick cock between us, nudging against my pussy. I spread my legs, and he settles in between them, lifting up so he can slide his hand in between us. He grabs hold of the base of his cock, guiding himself inside of me, and he slowly pushes inside.

"Oh fuck," he whispers harshly, and I lift my hips, sending him deeper. "Jesus."

I open my eyes to find his tightly closed as he's braced above me. I know it must feel good. He looks positively pained.

And he's not moving.

I lift my hips again, trying to give him a hint and he remains still, his eyes cracking open. "Afraid if I move, I'll come."

"You won't." I reach up and touch his cheek, my fingers streaking down the side of his stubble-covered face. "You already came once."

"And I feel close to coming again." He shifts his hips

forward, sending him deeper and I close my eyes, arching my body beneath his with a moan.

He's fully inside me now. I can feel him. Throbbing. Hot. He's large. Maybe the largest?

Okay, yes. He's definitely the biggest.

We start to move together, finding a rhythm. He breathes deep, trying to control himself, and while I appreciate him doing this, considering he is trying to make sure I find my pleasure too, I also want to see him lose control.

Become rattled. Wild. Overcome with need. He's always so calm. So composed. I want him to unleash on me. And I want to know that I'm the only one he loses control with.

I hook my legs around his hips and cling to him. Wrap my hand around his nape and pull him in for a kiss. His mouth is ravenous, the kiss becoming rougher, more out of control. He nips at my lower lip with his teeth. Thrusts his tongue against mine. Groans for every whimper that escapes me. He moves faster, his hips slapping against mine, our sweaty skin sticking together. He fucks and fucks, and I want to say so badly, "Look at how good you're doing!" but I don't.

He'd probably think that was condescending.

It's true though. He's practically an expert for this being his first time. It's as if he knows just where to touch me, and just how to move. There are no awkward shifts, no weird grabs. Maybe that's because we've taken the time to know each other, versus jumping into the sex thing headfirst.

Maybe there's something to the 'let's be friends and eventually turn into lovers' thing after all.

I realize when his entire body grows tense, his thrusts turning deeper that he's close. I squeeze my inner walls around him in a rhythmic motion. The startled groan that leaves him tells me he's just about to fall over the edge.

Within seconds, Tony comes with a ragged shout, holding himself over me, his body shaking. I hold him close, opening my eyes to watch him. His mouth hangs open, his eyes shut tight, high color on his cheeks, the tendons in his neck strained.

He's beautiful when he comes.

Without warning, he collapses on top of me, his lungs heaving, his breath hot against my cheek. "God damn, what did you do there at the end?"

"It's a special little trick," I tease, stroking his sweat coated back.

"Fuck. I tried to last as long as I could." He rubs his nose along my jaw, making me shiver. "Did you come?"

"No." And I'm not even mad about it.

He lifts away from me, frowning. "Really?"

"I already did," I say lightly.

"Yeah, but I was hoping you would come again."

"I wasn't so fixed on myself just now." I reach up to caress his cheek. "I was more focused on you."

"That's just wrong." He turns his head, dropping a kiss on my palm in the sweetest gesture. My heart literally pangs. "Let's go again."

"Again?" I raise my brows, surprised.

"I have twenty-three condoms left." He grins. "And plenty of lost time to make up for."

TONY WASN'T LYING. By the time I'm entering my apartment the next morning, I'm deliciously sore and almost deliriously exhausted. I stop short when I spot Gracie sitting on the couch, clutching a Starbucks to-go cup and scrolling through her phone.

"There you are," she says, her gaze still glued to her phone. "Good morning."

I shut the door and lean against it. "Why aren't you in class?"

She shrugs. "I skipped. Nothing much going on in there anyway. Plus, I have an A."

Gracie is one of those annoying people who can miss all the lectures and somehow ace the test. Or write the perfect paper. I'd kill for her ability to do that.

"I didn't think you'd be here." I collapse on the couch beside her.

"I made Robin drop me off. Last night after we talked." She glances over at me. "I ended it with him."

Thank God.

I try my best to keep my expression neutral. "Are you okay?"

She nods. Looks away. Sips from her cup. "It was the right thing to do."

"He was in the middle of cheating on you with another woman, so yeah. Definitely the right thing to do," I say drolly, wishing I had a Starbucks of my own.

"That was the problem. And the more I thought about it, the more I wondered if there had been other girls too. Would there continue to be girls? Probably. It doesn't matter if they're good or not—some women just want to get with a rock star," Gracie says with disgust.

"You've never been with a rock star before," I point out. "Until Robin."

"I never even had sex with him," she says on a sigh. "We messed around some, but nothing serious. Mostly kissing. He's the kind of guy who kisses you for approximately two minutes, then presses his hand on your head, trying to force you into a blow job."

"Ugh." I shake my head, our gazes meeting just before we burst into laughter.

We've both been with those types of guys. Only thinking of their pleasure, never about ours. I swear there's some sort of contest among the dudes on campus titled, "How Many Blow Jobs Can I Get?" All they can think about are their dicks.

"You spent the night with Tony?" she asks once our laughter has calmed down.

I nod. Smile dreamily.

"You don't have to say a word. I can tell by the look on your face that you had a good night with him," she says.

"I did. Oh God." I slap my hands over my face. "I think I have a crush."

"Isn't it a little beyond a crush by now?"

"I don't know. Is it? I really didn't want to do this with him. Well, I did. I always did, but then again, I knew it would be trouble. He's so sweet and thoughtful." Sexy, with a talented mouth and sure hands. Even a little rough. Once he got over the initial *this is my first-time* stage fright, he really got into it, making sure I was satisfied. And I was all for it, letting him use and abuse me.

Not that he literally did either of those things, but anyway.

"So he's good in bed?" Gracie lifts her brows.

I nod. Blush. Shrug.

"You have nothing to say about his skill set?" She sounds surprised.

I usually have *so* much to say. I blab all the details after my encounters with guys to Gracie. We like to discuss and dissect. Compare notes.

Right now, though, I want to keep what Tony and I shared last night to myself. It's mine to savor and think about.

The smile on her face is slow. Sly. "You must really like this guy."

"No. I don't know. I just want to keep it casual. That's been my plan since the beginning." I have to sit on my hands so I don't cover my face with them again. Why am I like this? And why is Tony affecting me this way?

I don't get it.

"You want to know what I've been doing this morning?" Gracie asks.

I'm so grateful for her subject change, I could almost weep with relief. "Tell me."

"Stalking Caleb on social media." She flips her phone in my direction, so I can see his Instagram profile. "Why am I doing this? Why do I care? Because he's cute? I cannot deny he's cute. And muscular. His shoulders are so broad. Did you see how easily he lifted me on those shoulders last night? His head was basically in my crotch, and I was bouncing up and down, screaming over another guy, and he never complained once."

"Probably has something to do with that 'his head is in your crotch' thing," I say, grabbing her phone so I can scan his photo grid. It's not much. He literally has ten photos posted and that's it. Mostly football pics. A graduation photo of him and his friends. I zoom in on it, staring at a fresh-faced Tony wearing a giant smile on his face, clad in a navy blue graduation gown.

He looks so cute, my heart skips a beat.

"Who's the girl?" Gracie asks, her face directly over my shoulder as we stare at the grad photo. Yep, there's a girl. There's a couple of them, but one is standing right next to

Caleb, gazing up at him as he smiles for the camera. "She's adorable. I hate her."

I tap the photo and she's tagged. "Her name is Baylee."

"Why didn't I check to see if it's tagged? I'm an idiot," Gracie groans. "Go to her profile."

I do exactly that. She's posted a lot. An endless stream of photos. She was a cheerleader. Cute and bubbly looking.

"Probably an ex-girlfriend," I finally say. There is no evidence of photos of them together, which tells me if they were together, she deleted or archived them all when they broke up.

"Why do I feel jealous? I have no reason to be jealous." Gracie scowls. "I don't even like him."

"They have no photos together alone, so maybe they weren't together." I hand her back her phone. "She's probably just a friend. You saw she was on the cheer team. She was at all their games. Cheerleaders are always close to the football team—or at least they try to be."

"Ugh. A cheerleader." Gracie's scowl deepens.

"Weren't you a cheerleader?" I ask.

She glares. "Yes. We're the worst."

I laugh. "You said you hated him."

"God, I do." She drops the phone on the couch beside her and drains her Starbucks cup. "So why can't I stop thinking about him?"

"Gracie." I knew this would happen. "You do this all the time."

"I do what?" she asks innocently.

"Move on to the next guy way too easily," I say gently. "Spend some time alone, without a guy. Or just be Caleb's friend and hang out with us. You don't need to rush into another relationship yet. You just ended things with Robin."

She ended things with the other guy too, only about a month ago. And then the other guy a month before that.

"Caleb's a player. He'd just want to fuck me and forget me."

"Exactly, so don't do that. Don't have sex with him," I stress.

"Is Tony a player?" Gracie asks.

"No." I shake my head. "Not really."

How much of a player could he be, considering he was a virgin?

Still hard for me to wrap my head around, if I'm being honest.

"He's so good looking," Gracie says on a sigh. "And he seems really into you."

"You think so?"

She nods. "He couldn't keep his eyes off you last night. I know you claim you just want to keep it casual with him, but I think he really likes you. And from the way you're so quiet, I'm guessing you might really like him too."

I do. Oh God, I do. This is a big mistake though. Huge. I shouldn't like him so much. I wanted to keep it friendly. He's the one who pushed for friends with benefits, and look at us now. That's what we've turned into.

But this isn't all his fault. I was a willing participant last night. I wanted it. I wanted him. I want more of him. We had sex twice. I had two orgasms and that lucky bastard had three. I'm worn out. Would love nothing more but to collapse in bed and sleep the day away.

I have class though. A test that I haven't studied for at all. I'm screwed, but I don't care. All I can think about his him. Tony. And when I might see him next.

This is bad. So, so bad.

"Hay? You all right?" Gracie nudges me in the shoulder.

I lift my head in a daze. "Did you say something to me?"

"I said I think you really like him too," she says. "Do you?"

I stare off into the distance. "I shouldn't."

"Well, there's *I shouldn't*, and then there's *I do*."

Ah Gracie, only logical when she talks about someone else's problems.

Then again, I guess I'm the same way too.

TWENTY-ONE

TONY

THE COLLEGE FOOTBALL season is exhausting.

It's mid-November and we're still playing. Just like when we were in high school and we made the playoffs, which was every year I was on the varsity team. The Bulldogs have made the playoffs too. The difference is in the travel. While in high school, the farthest we went for an away game was three hours one way. In college?

We were in freaking Minnesota last week. This week, we play Hawaii at home. Next year, we'll play in Hawaii.

Can't wait.

We're doing well, thanks to Ash's leadership on the field. I ran in a touchdown against Minnesota last week. I got a mention on ESPN. Eli was jealous as hell, though he also kept saying how cool it was. Jake called on Sunday to congratulate me.

It felt good. Everyone else usually gets the accolades. I'm the dude in the background getting the job done. Now I'm getting some attention, and not gonna lie...

It's awesome.

More girls are interested. They approach me on

campus. In class. After practice. And always after a game. I'm polite, but never too friendly. I have zero interest in them. I'm too busy thinking about that pretty blonde who's invaded my life.

Hayden and I have been seeing each other regularly. And if we don't actually see each other, we talk every day. The problem? I don't know what to call us. I don't refer to her as my girlfriend and she doesn't say I'm her boyfriend. Not that anyone's asked but...

I sort of want a label. Which is stupid and goes against everything I've said before about relationships. I still feel the same way about them. Mostly. They're for suckers. Someone always gets hurt. Long term rarely works. Everything between us is pretty great right now, but is that going to last?

Damn. I'm such a pessimist. I need to learn how to enjoy the here and now.

Though I see why people get sucked into this kind of thing. Why they believe it'll work. I get it now. Hayden makes everything so damn easy, and when I was with Sophie, yeah we had a good time, but at the end, it turned into a struggle. She didn't want to make time for me, and that would make me mad. More like it hurt my feelings. I look back on it now and we weren't the greatest match. Her family wanted her to focus on her dancing, and I get why. She was amazing. She didn't have time for me.

And that made me feel unwanted. Unloved. I've had enough experience with that with my parents. I didn't need my girlfriend to treat me like that too. So I gave up on her, on us, before things became even more complicated.

Hayden and I are both pretty busy, but we also make the time to see each other as best we can. As the fall semester winds down, her project load increases. She's got all sorts of group projects and presentations to give. While I'm practicing constantly and keeping up with my gen ed classes. Between all of that, we don't see each other as often as I'd like.

Though I'll say this, when we *are* together, it's fucking good. We hang out, we laugh, we watch movies, we go to dinner, we spend time with my friends, Gracie is usually included, and we always end up having mind-blowing sex.

Mind. Blowing.

It gets better between us every time. Like, every single time. So why wouldn't I ask her to be my girlfriend? I know she's anti-relationship. Supposedly, so am I. But I like this girl. A lot.

I don't know what to do.

We're all out to dinner after practice, at a nearby Mexican restaurant that has the best chips and salsa I've ever had. It's me, Caleb, Jackson, Eli and Diego, and we're downing baskets of chips as if we're all starving.

Which we sort of are.

I want to ask these idiots for relationship advice, but that also feels like I'm asking for trouble. And I don't know if I'm fully prepared for the shit they're about to give me.

That's our favorite thing to do. Give each other shit. It's always good-natured. Diego used to have a mean streak, but he's really changed, thanks to becoming a dad. He's a kinder person. I think Jos has something to do with that too. Besides him, Eli is the only other one who's in a long-term relationship, and I don't know if I can take him seriously. He's a good dude, but he also loves to talk. And sometimes, he says a bunch of nonsense.

Jackson and Caleb? What the hell do they know about relationships?

Nothing.

I take a huge gulp from my water glass and tell myself I don't need any advice. I'm winging it.

I got this.

"What's going on with the record deal?" Diego asks Jackson out of nowhere.

Jackson was the one who talked to the talent scout, not Bat's Cave. It was a woman, and she fell hard and fast for Jackson's performance, saying much of the same stuff that Hayden said about him that night. She got him a meeting with the record execs, and he flew down to Los Angeles and listened to their spiel. They took him to lunch, they gave him a tour of the office, they flexed on the bands and singers they've turned into household names, and at the end of the four-hour meeting, they made him an offer.

He turned it down.

They called him back, offering more money.

He turned down that deal too.

"They're going to make another offer," Jackson says, his lips curling into a sideways smirk. "My dad's lawyer is fully prepared to tell them no."

"Dude, why would you turn down all these deals if music is your passion?" Eli asks, shaking his head. "If that was my dream, I'd be all over that shit."

"When they know it's your dream, that's when they take advantage of you. I refuse to get caught up in some shit deal where I end up making mere pennies for every record sold," Jackson explains, sounding perfectly logical. His father is some big business mogul and full of good advice, though I still have no clue what he does exactly. "This offer isn't my ticket out of nowhere. I love making music. I love performing, but I refuse to cave to the first deal offered."

"This isn't the first deal," Eli reminds him. "It's your third."

"If the money is right, I'll accept it," Jackson says. "My father always said, if the terms aren't to your liking, walk away. If they want you bad enough, they'll chase after you."

"You might end up having a bunch of teenaged girls chasing you every night and that's it," Caleb says, making us all laugh.

"If that's the case, so be it. The right offer will eventually come along," Jackson says with a faint smile. "I know it."

I wish I had half his confidence when it comes to life. I feel like I'm winging it most of the time.

"I can't even believe you were sneaking around and performing on the down low," Diego says. "You had us all fooled."

"Why tell you when you'd all give me shit?" Jackson looks at every one of us, and we all duck our heads, save for Caleb. "Except for you, my number one fan."

Caleb grins. "If you hit number one on the charts and sing a duet with Ariana Grande, I will gladly suck your dick after you introduce me to her."

We all throw chips in his direction and he holds up his hands, batting them away. "You know she'd jump on this." He points at himself.

"Like I'd let that happen if I was singing with her. She'd be jumping on me," Jackson says, tapping his chest with his thumb.

We all can't help but agree with that.

The server comes and takes our orders. Caleb tries to get a beer, but she asks to see his ID and he says never mind. Once she's gone, we all start talking about Jackson again, and his potential record deal. Something about it fills us all with possibilities, and it's kind of fun to dream along with him.

"You could tour with The Weeknd," Diego suggests.

"We don't make the same kind of music," Jackson says.

"He's just saying that because of the Super Bowl." I point at Jackson. "You could end up performing there someday."

"That would be cool," Jackson says with a nod.

"And I'll be playing in it. Leading my team to the win!" Eli throws his hands up in the air and makes a crowd roaring noise.

We all roll our eyes, but secretly wish for that too.

Well, not me. I'm practical. I know college will be the end of my football career. And I think Caleb feels the same way. He doesn't put a ton of effort into it. And Jackson? He has bigger things to accomplish, like his music career.

"Why didn't you ever tell me you were performing at Strummers?" I ask Jackson when the other three start talking about video games.

We became closer in the summer. We both come from rich fathers with high expectations. Mine was rarely in my life, while Jackson lives with his dad, but he's never around. And because he's never around, he's constantly giving Jackson money, alcohol and weed to make up for his absence.

It's kind of fucked-up. I don't know who's worse. My dad or his.

We bonded over that, and that's why we started having a bad attitude about practice. We'd smoke a little weed, drink some Jack Daniels, and say fuck it to practice. Jackson had something else to occupy his time, but I didn't.

Football—and my friends on the team—were it. Glad I realized that before I really messed everything up.

"I don't know. I thought you'd give me shit," Jackson says with a shrug.

"I get it. We all have a dream. Eli wants to be the next Drew Callahan." I wave my hand in Eli's direction. "Diego has high hopes too, but he also wants to raise his daughter and have a family with Jocelyn. That's his focus right now. Caleb wants to fuck his way through the entire campus."

Jackson laughs.

"And you want to be a successful musician," I add.

Jackson's face grows sober. "But what about you, man?"

I frown. "What about me?"

"What's your dream?"

His words linger with me throughout dinner. I eat, I joke, I think about asking them about my relationship with Hayden, but in the end, I say nothing. I can't get Jackson's words out of my head.

What's your dream?

I don't have a damn clue. I'm only eighteen, so isn't that okay? Do I have to know what I want to do with the rest of my life? Is it really that important that I make that decision right now?

My phone buzzes with a text, just as we're wrapping up dinner, and I quickly check who it is, thinking it's Hayden. But it's not.

It's my dad.

You're coming here for Thanksgiving, right?

I read those words over and over, trying to push past the lead ball that suddenly sits in my stomach. I don't want to go to his house for Thanksgiving, which is—shit—next week. I asked Mom about the holiday and she said she was going to Mexico with her newest boyfriend. She mentioned I was more than welcome to join them, but I said no. Which she knew would be my answer, so she got away with that scot-free.

Didn't cross my mind that my father would want me

sitting at his table for Thanksgiving. After I visited there for the weekend, we've kind of kept in contact, but after a while, we stopped texting each other. I've been too busy with football, school and Hayden to make the time to see him again. If he really wanted to see me, he could come here.

But, of course, he doesn't.

My phone buzzes again, another text from my dad.

Dad: **????**

Me: **Hadn't planned on it.**

Dad: **Helena and I both really want you here. We're a family now. It doesn't feel complete without you.**

I roll my eyes. What a bunch of horseshit.

Dad: **She also mentioned you have a girl-friend. Maybe you should bring her with you.**

My entire body goes stiff. What the hell? How does Helena know?

Me: **I have no idea what you're talking about.**

He would flip his fucking lid if he knew I was dating Hayden Channing.

Dad: **Come on. You can admit it. Helena has mentioned her to me multiple times. I can't wait to meet her.**

Is this some sort of game she's playing? Does my father not know who I'm with? I can't even call Hayden my girl-friend. Not officially.

Me: **I'll try and come, but I can't bring her. We're not that serious.**

Dad: **Don't worry. I won't embarrass you in front of her. Helena says she's adorable.**

This is so freaking crazy. How did he find out about

Hayden? Though from the way he's texting, I would say he doesn't know my girlfriend is Hayden...

This is more like—how did Helena find out? And what the hell is she up to?

We exit the restaurant, me absently making my way to my car and Caleb walking beside me. I'm so in my head, Caleb is talking a mile a minute and I don't pay attention to what he's saying. All I can think about is Helena telling my dad about my girlfriend and how adorable she is. When Helena has to know what's going on. She fucking has to. Is she coming at me as some sort of veiled threat?

"Hey." Caleb snaps his fingers in front of my face, snapping me out of my thoughts. "Are Hayden and Gracie coming over tonight?"

"I don't think so." I shrug, picking up my pace when I spot my car. "I haven't talked to Hayden about it."

"Okay, cool. Maybe you shouldn't. Though it's no big deal when they're at our place, I'm thinking tonight isn't a good night." Caleb is acting all nonchalant, when I know deep down, he's got a total thing for Gracie. Not that he'd ever admit it, and even if he did, he'd claim it was purely sexual and he just wants to fuck her. And maybe that's true.

But doubtful.

I warned him to leave her alone. Hayden informed me that Gracie is attracted to him, but trying to wean herself off toxic men. We both agreed Caleb is toxic—for Gracie. So we discourage the two of them spending time together as much as possible, without being obvious about it.

Of course, it feels like every other day they're somehow together.

"I'll text her when I get home," I say absently as I unlock the doors and climb into the driver's seat.

"You should text her now," Caleb says. "Make sure they're not coming over."

He's up to something, but I'm too preoccupied to worry about it.

"I have to call my stepmom first," I tell him grimly, starting the car.

"The chick who wants to fuck you?" Caleb laughs. "That ought to be interesting."

I say nothing. My father gave me her number a while ago, saying if I couldn't get a hold of him, to try Helena since she's always on her phone. I'm sure that was a total slam, and I sort of brushed off having her number, but now I realize it's coming in handy.

I hide away in my room as soon as we arrive home, pulling my phone out and looking up Helena's number. I don't text her. I don't want any evidence that my father could find, so I hit the call button and the phone starts ringing.

She picks up on the third ring, greeting me with a breathless hello.

"What are you doing?" I don't beat around the bush. I want her to know I'm pissed.

"Who is this?" she asks just as sharply.

"You know who it is." I pause for only a moment. "Why are you telling my dad I have a girlfriend and you want me to bring her home for Thanksgiving?"

"Because you *do* have a girlfriend, and your father deserves to know that you don't listen to him whatsoever." She sighs, sounding bored. "The golden child isn't so golden after all."

She's confusing the hell out of me. "What are you talking about?"

"All I ever hear is how great you are. How you're going

to take over the business someday, and I'm going to have to answer to you. Who the fuck are you, anyway? Just some snot-nosed college kid who never sees his dad, but fully expects him to pay his way for everything," she says, her voice low, like a hiss. "I'm the one who's stood by his side for the last five years. I'm the one who helps him with everything, offers up my opinions, reads over legal paperwork, and puts up with his constant bullshit. But do I get any credit? No, I'm just the baby mama who's only good for hosting his parties, arm candy and spreading my legs."

Her hostility renders me silent. This is clearly a problem between her and my dad, and somehow, I'm getting dragged into it. "I never asked to be the heir to his company."

"While I have. Countless times, but he always brushes me off. Or he flat out laughs at me. I've proven myself to that man time and again, and he has zero faith in my abilities. So I thought he should know who his son is fucking around with," she says.

"How the hell do you know what I'm doing? Are you keeping tabs on me?" I can only imagine this crazy bitch hiring someone to follow me. Watch over me.

That's fucking insane.

"I don't have to waste money on hiring a private investigator when I have a friend who keeps me up-to-date on your love life." She laughs.

Shit. The woman who's dating Hayden's dad. Lauri? I think that's her name. They're close friends.

So Hayden is talking to Lauri about us? When she knows her father doesn't want me seeing her either? That's messed up.

"I'm not coming for Thanksgiving," I tell Helena.

"If you don't come, I'm telling your father you're with

Hayden Channing, and that you're spilling all the family secrets to her while you two are cozied up in bed together late at night. He'd believe me too, because Brian Channing just underbid another one of your father's offers and got the deal a few days ago. He's furious, and positive there's a spy at the company who's giving up all of our secrets. He finds out you're with Hayden? He'll think it's you. I'll turn him against you forever." She sounds triumphant.

I almost don't care if she does turn him against me. "And if I do show up?"

"You tell him you have zero interest in the business and you think I'm the one who should eventually take it over," she says.

"He'll never listen to me." When does he ever?

"Better you try and convince him than me tell him you're with Hayden, don't you think?" She sounds like she's enjoying this.

"This is really fucked-up," I tell her, clutching the phone so tight my hand aches. "You do realize this, right? You're basically trying to blackmail me."

"You're the idiot who can't keep his dick out of the one girl he's not supposed to fuck," she says with a laugh. "You have no one to blame but yourself."

She ends the call and I throw the phone on my bed, fuming.

Fuck Helena. She's a backstabbing bitch. Like I'd tell my father she could run the business. I don't even know her. She's just greedy and wants that money all to herself and their twins. She hates that I exist.

I collapse on the bed, running my hands through my hair. I don't know how I'm going to fix this. Will my dad believe me when I tell him I'm not telling Hayden anything? I've barely talked to my dad since the last time I saw him, so how could I spill any company secrets? And Hayden and I aren't talking about our parents. Not anymore. We talk about everything *but* our parents. She'll tell me something about Palmer on occasion, but that's it.

Helena's got me, though. I am seeing Hayden, when my father told me I shouldn't. And Hayden's father told her the same damn thing. So could Hayden be blabbing to her father's girlfriend that we're together? Who then opens her big mouth and tells Helena?

Such bullshit.

My mind is racing with too many overwhelming possibilities. Is Hayden trying to fuck with me to help her dad? Maybe she is. Maybe that's part of the plan. To get close to me, and find out all my dad's secrets? But how is that even possible when I'm not that close to my father? I know nothing.

Absolutely nothing.

So that theory is out. The relief that hits me is strong. I don't want to think of Hayden as scheming against me. That would tear me up. I like her. I care about her.

I could fall in love with her.

My father would never approve. He's a logical person—unless he's angry. Then logic is tossed out the window and all he can focus on is his rage. I know nothing about my father's business dealings. So therefore, I have nothing to tell Hayden, and she has no information to give to her father. We're not the ones who are being shady here.

Someone else is.

And I'm thinking it's Helena and Lauri.

TWENTY-TWO

HAYDEN

"DID you text Tony and let him know we were coming over?" Gracie asks as we approach the condo's front door.

I shake my head. "It's a surprise. I'm living on the edge."

"You sure that's a good idea?" Ever since she caught Robin with that other girl, she's not big on surprises.

I can't blame her.

"He's with his friends. They're hanging out. It's a typical Thursday night. He told me they were going to dinner after practice, and his car is in the parking lot. I know he's here." I march right up to that door and start knocking. "I'm not worried about another girl being in there," I tell Gracie as I look at her from over my shoulder.

She shakes her head. "I wish I had your confidence."

Her confidence has somehow left her completely, and I don't understand why. All because of Robin? If that's the case, why give that little asshole so much power? I don't get it.

But I'm full of all sorts of confidence, thanks to being with Tony this last month. Yes, we're busy. Yes, we have to make time for each other, but oh, when we do? It's magical.

And I'm not just talking about the sex.

We have fun together. He makes me laugh. He makes me think. He's smart. Full of wise words for being so young. Sometimes I think he's wiser than me, though I would never tell him that. He's good to his friends. And I even like his friends. All of them. I feel like we're part of the gang when we come over to hang out.

Gracie and I come over as often as we can.

The door swings open and it's Diego standing there, a smile stretching his mouth when he sees us. "Hey. Come in." The door swings open wider.

We walk inside and I glance around to see only Jackson and Eli in the living room. The TV is on, and for once in their lives, they're not playing video games.

Thursday Night Football is on instead.

"Where's Caleb?" I ask, so Gracie doesn't have to.

"Uh, he left." An uneasy look flashes across Diego's handsome face, but then it's gone. "He went to see a friend."

Uh oh. I bet it's a female friend.

I don't acknowledge what he just said. "And Tony?"

"He's in his room. Hold on." Diego turns toward the stairwell and cups his hands around his mouth. "Tony! Get your ass down here."

Seconds later, I hear the bedroom door swing open and Tony's thunderous footsteps come down the stairs. He stops midway when he spots me.

"Hayden."

I smile. Wave. "Hi."

He doesn't move for a few seconds, and I second-guess myself. Maybe this was a mistake, showing up unannounced.

But then he makes his way down the rest of the stairs and comes straight for me, pulling me into his arms and pressing a soft kiss to my forehead. "I didn't know you were coming over."

"Surprise." I give him a squeeze before I pull away. "Brought Gracie with me too."

"Hey G." He nods in her direction and she smiles. Then goes over to the couch and plops onto it, sitting between Eli and Jackson. Though she's more noticeably closer to Jackson.

Hmm.

Tony turns to me once more, running his hand up and down my arm, making me shiver. "Just thought you'd drop by, huh?"

I nod. "I hope you don't mind."

"I don't mind at all. Your timing is perfect, actually. There's, uh, something I want to discuss with you." He glances around before he returns his gaze to mine. "But not out here. I'd rather do it in private."

Worry immediately fills me and I shove it away. "Oh." I look over at Gracie, who's chattering away to Jackson. He's watching the TV, nodding along with everything she says. "I don't want to leave her alone with the rest of the guys just yet."

"We do all the time," Tony says with a frown.

"Because Caleb is always here." I wave my hand around. "As you can see, he's gone."

"Where'd he go?"

"Diego mentioned a friend."

Tony rolls his eyes. "Great. Probably a girl. He usually tries to keep that behavior under wraps when Gracie's around."

We don't get those two, but we're also part of the problem, since we encourage them to leave each other alone. We probably make them want to spend more time together.

"Let's sit and watch the game for a little bit," I suggest with a smile. "And then maybe we can talk?"

"Sure," he says with a nod, his expression solemn.

We settle into the giant overstuffed chair with matching ottoman, the two of us cozied up next to each other. I love sitting with him like this. My head on his chest, his arm wrapped around my shoulders. Usually he strokes my back or plays with my hair, but not tonight. He's too busy watching the game, his jaw tense, his gaze fixed. He looks upset, and I refuse to be one of those chicks who constantly asks her man what's wrong.

But it's like I can't help myself.

"Is everything okay?" I ask him quietly when there's a commercial break.

He nods, his gaze still on the TV. "Sure."

I don't believe him.

I think back on the last few days. Weeks, even. And I can't recall a single thing that I did that would irritate him enough that he'd feel the need to talk to me about it. Why am I even thinking it has anything to do with me? Maybe something's going on elsewhere in his life. Maybe his dad. Or his mom. They always stress him out.

I know my parents always stress me out.

Gracie flirts with Jackson throughout the game, and he's receptive, flirting with her right back. I think of Ellie. Ava's friend who crushes on Jackson hard. I've heard enough about her to know Jackson treats her like a friend and that's it. The girl throws herself at him and he's not interested.

Ouch. Poor thing.

But I know Gracie isn't interested in him either, though he's right up her alley. Musician. Sexy. An air of mystery about him. I watch them chat, how flirtatious he is with her.

How he touches her on the arm frequently and she laughs at everything he says.

Shit.

The door swings open near the end of halftime, Caleb walking in with a familiar face.

That girl from the photos. The one Gracie was jealous of.

Baylee.

Double shit.

"Look who I found," Caleb says excitedly and the guys greet her halfheartedly, despite her enthusiastic wave and smile. It's immediately replaced by a frown when she realizes none of the guys care.

Double ouch.

"Hey. I'm Hayden," I tell her with a wave, ignoring Gracie as she glares at me. I don't have it in me to be rude toward this girl. I also don't bother saying I'm with Tony. With the way we're snuggled up together, it's fairly obvious.

"I'm Baylee," she says, her smile grateful. I'm sure she appreciates the acknowledgment. Why are the guys being such asshats?

She's pretty. Brown hair that's curled to perfection, sparkling brown eyes. She's got a cute style, her long legs clad in faded mom jeans and a cropped white tank with an oversized black zippered hoodie covering her, though it hangs open. Very on-trend.

Gracie sends me daggers with her eyes before she rises to her feet, making her way to Caleb and Baylee. He's frozen in place when he spots her, his expression saying, *uh oh, busted.* I almost feel sorry for him.

Almost.

"Hi," Gracie says, her attention for Baylee and no one else. "It's *so* nice to meet you. I'm Gracie."

"Hi," Baylee says cheerily, "Baylee."

They shake hands.

Caleb looks ready to hurl.

"Is this your latest conquest?" Gracie asks him.

His cheeks turn blazing red.

"We're old friends," Baylee explains, her smile fading. Probably thanks to the obvious snark in Gracie's voice.

"Old friends who fuck on occasion?" Gracie asks her, her gaze still on Caleb.

"G," he warns, and she shakes her head.

"No, fuck you, Caleb. Bringing a girl over here." She stabs him in the chest with her index finger a couple of times before she turns and marches over to the couch. She grabs hold of Jackson's hand and jerks him onto his feet. "Come on. We're going out."

"Wait a minute, what?" Jackson asks, sounding sleepy. He runs a hand through his longish hair, sending an apologetic look in Caleb's direction. As if he knows what's going on. "I'm beat. Can't we just stay here tonight?"

"Let's go to the spare room then," Gracie says with determination, glancing over at Caleb to make sure he's watching.

Of course, he is.

Gracie drags Jackson up the stairs, and seconds later, we hear the door slam shut.

Not a one of us speaks for a moment, the only sound the game coming from the TV.

"What the fuck was that?" Caleb finally says, running both hands through his hair and clutching the back of his head as he glares at the empty stairwell. "Did she really just take him up to Diego's room so she can fuck him?"

"I doubt—" Diego starts, but Caleb interrupts him.

"Yeah, I think she did." He starts pacing the living room,

Baylee stepping out of his way, looking uncomfortable. I feel sorry for her. She just got dragged into the middle of this. "What the hell? Who does she think she is? And with Jackson? I should've known."

"Caleb, seriously," Baylee says. "What's your problem?"

"Women," he spits out. "That's my problem."

He stalks off into the kitchen, Baylee chasing after him.

Tony sits up, and I do as well. Diego and Eli both shrug and return their attention to the game.

I guess they don't care about the drama unfolding right before them.

"Should I go talk to Caleb?" Tony asks.

"I don't know. Would he listen? And why were you guys so cold to Baylee just now?" I ask, curious.

"Old history. Baylee's best friend our senior year was this girl we all can't stand." His voice lowers, his gaze briefly going to Diego. "Cami Lockhart. She's a total bitch who really screwed with Diego and Jocelyn's relationship. Got in the middle of Eli and Ava's too."

"That's not Baylee's fault though," I point out, feeling sorry for her.

"I know, you're right. It's just—hard to forget all that, you know? Still feels fresh." Tony sighs. "I'm loyal to my friends. I know what Cami did to Diego, and it was messed up, and I can never forgive her. Baylee's guilty by association."

Reaching out, I touch his face, the stubble prickling my palm. "I love how much you care about your friends."

I sound like a complete sap, but screw it. I don't care.

He smiles, but it doesn't quite reach his eyes. "You want to go check on Gracie?"

"What if they're—doing something?" I wrinkle my nose.

He chuckles. "They could be, but I don't know. Jackson

probably wouldn't touch her, if he knows how much she means to Caleb."

"Does she really mean something to Caleb?" I ask, my eyebrows shooting up.

"I think so, though he'd never admit it. Did you see the way he was just acting?" Without warning Tony jumps to his feet, holding out his hand so he can pull me up. "Let's go to my room."

The nerves come back, twisting my stomach into tight knots as we walk up the stairs and head for his room. He wants to talk to me. And I have no clue what it's about. He's acting perfectly normal, but I can tell he's preoccupied. Something's bugging him.

Looks like I'm about to find out.

He shuts the door and locks us inside as usual, and then he's reaching for me. Pulling me into his arms. Kissing me ferociously. We fall onto the bed, our bodies and our tongues tangled. His hands are in my hair and mine are beneath his T-shirt, touching his abs—one of my favorite parts of him.

What am I saying? I like all parts of him.

"We need to talk," he pants against my lips at one point.

I push him off me, hating how easily his kisses, his touch made me forget he wanted to discuss something with me. "What is it?"

I also hate how breathless I sound. I clear my throat and turn away from him, righting my clothes, sitting up and smoothing my hair out of my face. I want to appear composed if he's about to drop a bomb on me.

Though I don't know why I'm automatically thinking the worst. Maybe because nothing good comes from someone telling you, "We need to talk"?

And that's the truth.

A sigh escapes him and he sits up as well, his thigh pressing against mine. If he wanted to break up with me, he wouldn't be sitting so close.

Wait a minute. We're not together, so there's nothing to "break up." I'm clearly being ridiculous.

"I got a text from my father tonight." The words sound bitter and I frown.

"When was the last time you two talked?" They never talk. Or at least, he never talks about his father with me.

"God knows. He's too busy and I don't care." More bitterness. "He invited me to Thanksgiving at their house. Told me to bring my girlfriend."

My frown deepens. "What?"

"No name was ever mentioned. And I denied having a girlfriend." That hurts. More than I'd ever admit. "Then he said Helena talks about my girlfriend all the time. Called her adorable."

"What?" I'm repeating myself; I can't help it. "I don't talk to Helena. Ever. How would she know about us?"

"Like I said, your name wasn't brought up, but I knew who she was referring to." He takes a deep breath. "So I called Helena and confronted her about it."

Damn, he has balls. I like it. "What did she say?"

"She's pissed at me over my dad's business and how I'm going to inherit it when she believes she deserves to." He waves a hand, dismissing it. "But what really got me is she knows about you and I because of Lauri."

His words hang between us, heavy and accusing. "They're friends."

"I know."

"I've never told Lauri about us. Ever."

"Come on, Hayden." He blows out an irritated breath. "Just be real with me."

Anger stiffens my spine. "I am being real with you. Are you accusing me of lying?" If he is, that is some straight up bullshit.

"Of course not." He runs his fingers through his hair, shoving it out of his face. "I'm sorry. No, I don't think you're lying. But how the hell does she know about us?"

"I don't know." I stand and start pacing the room. "What does it matter anyway? So our parents don't approve of us together, so what? They can't tell us what to do. We're not some modern-day Romeo and Juliet. This is just some quick college fling, right?"

He watches me, his dark eyes never leaving me as I walk back and forth, back and forth. "It's more than that and you know it."

I come to a stop, glaring at him. "I didn't tell Lauri about us. I rarely talk to Lauri." Realization dawns, slowly but surely, and I touch my mouth with trembling fingers, my brain going into overdrive. "Oh no."

"Oh no what?"

My gaze meets his once more. "I've told Palmer. Palmer knows pretty much everything about us."

"You've told your sister about us?"

"Of course I have! We're close. We share everything." I glance around the room, my vision hazy. "What if she's told Lauri everything?"

"Why would she?"

"They're close, I think. Lauri sucks up to her. She always wants Palmer on her good side." I start pacing once more. "Should I call my sister?"

"Yeah. Do it. I want to figure this out. Helena is telling me if I don't show up for Thanksgiving and talk to my dad about her potentially taking over the business someday, she's going to tell him that I'm sharing business secrets with you and helping your dad steal deals from mine."

"That doesn't even make sense," Hayden says, shaking her head. "You don't even talk to your dad that much. What business secrets do you know to sabotage him?"

"That's what I was thinking." He scowls. "She's fucking with me. I shouldn't let her threats scare me because they're pretty weak."

"They totally are." I pull my phone out of my pocket and call Palmer. She answers quickly. "Where are you?" I ask her.

"In my room."

"Anyone else in there with you?"

"No, I'm watching Euphoria for the twentieth time," she says, sounding irritated. "What's up?"

"Is Lauri asking you questions about me?"

"No, we don't really talk about you," she says. "Why?"

"She knows stuff about me and Tony. And she's telling Helena, Tony's stepmom," I explain. "Be honest with me, Palmer. Has she ever asked you about my relationship with Tony, or have you told her anything?"

"No, I swear, Hay. I haven't said anything. You told me you wanted to keep it quiet, and I have. I definitely didn't tell Daddy," she says.

"Thank God," I say dryly. "Okay, keep it that way. I've gotta go."

"Bye."

"I heard what she said," Tony says when I end the call. "And I'm thinking Lauri has some sort of spyware on your sister's phone."

My mouth drops open. "Why would she do that?"

"Uh, to spy on you?" He cracks a smile, and seeing it fills me with relief. I don't want him thinking I have anything to do with this. Because I don't. "Or she might even have spyware on your phone. On everyone's phone, for all we know." He's scrolling on his phone, looking up spyware. "It's pretty easy. You can monitor someone's phone remotely, and they'd never know."

"But why? I don't get it. What can she gain from this?"

"Anything? Everything. She might monitor your dad's phone too, and know all of his secrets," Tony points out.

My father cheated on my mother. I wouldn't put it past him that he'd cheat on Lauri, and I'm pretty sure she's sneaking around with someone else behind his back. Even though my father is her ticket to the good life. Without him, she has nothing. If I was afraid of losing it all, maybe I'd do the same thing.

"Should I talk to Lauri?" I ask. "Confront her about it? She'd deny it."

"Of course she would."

"Get a new phone then? With a new number?" That would get rid of the problem, at least for me.

Though I'd have to tell Palmer she can't talk to me for a while.

"We can check if your phone is being monitored. Let's do that first, and see if Lauri is spying on you," Tony suggests.

My heart sinks as I settle on the bed beside him, leaning my head on his shoulder. "I'm so sorry this happened. It's all my fault."

"No, it's not."

"But it's happening because of me. Because of Lauri."

"And Helena. For whatever reason, those two are working together," Tony says as he slips his arm around my shoulders and holds me close. "It's okay. We'll figure this out."

I glance up at him to find he's already watching me. "I never thought something like this would happen between us. Spies and espionage."

He chuckles. Leans in and kisses me, his lips moving against mine sweetly at first, until it turns heated. "You're exaggerating," he murmurs.

"Maybe. Maybe not," I say, circling my arms around his neck. "Let's have sex before you unhack my phone."

"I guess unhacking the phone can wait," he says.

Right before he kisses me.

TWENTY-THREE

TONY

SEX WITH HAYDEN is a complete distraction, but I want it. Need it. Feels like I always need it with Hayden. I crave her touch. Her taste. The way she moves and stretches beneath me. How her breath catches when I suck her nipples deep into my mouth. Or how she goes extra wild when I go down on her, my fingers inside her pussy, my lips latched around her clit.

I make her come like that every single time, and when she shudders and shakes beneath me, losing complete control, I feel like a superstar. Like I just caught a game winning touchdown.

Other emotions are swirling within me. The complete relief that Hayden isn't spilling our secrets to her dad's girl-friend is downright overwhelming. Not that I ever really thought she was saying anything to Lauri, but there was that tiny, niggling chance she might've. I've known from the start she's not a huge fan of Lauri's, so it never made sense Hayden would tell her anything about us. Palmer could've, but I believe her little sister too. Her loyalty lies with Hayden, not Lauri.

I guess my worry over Hayden is a result of witnessing my parents' messed up marriage, and how distrusting they became of each other, especially near the end. They were always accusing each other of something. Cheating. Lying. Of course, I'd grow up skeptical. But I need to realize I'm not my parents.

I'm just me. And Hayden is just Hayden. I can't lump her in with everyone else who's done me wrong.

The spyware thing on her phone is mind-blowing. Haven't confirmed it yet, but it's the only theory that makes sense. I've never given that stuff much thought before. Guess my dad could keep tabs on me like that if he wanted to, but I don't think he cares enough.

On any other night, that would bother me. Sit with me and remind me that, yet again, the important people in my life abandon me, and it sucks.

But not tonight. Not when I have a willing, gorgeous woman in my arms, kissing me as if her life depended on it. Hayden cares. She never brings up the 'friends with benefits' thing anymore. We haven't come out and defined it, but we're together. We're a couple. She's my girlfriend, just like Helena told my father. If she got anything right in this giant mess she's created, it's that.

I push all thoughts of our families out of my mind and refocus on Hayden. Kissing her. Touching her. Savoring her. I slip my hand beneath her shirt, my fingers seeking the lacy edge of her bra. I cup her breast, her nipple pebbling beneath my palm and I tug at the hem of her shirt with my other hand, yanking it up.

Breaking the kiss, I shift lower, running my mouth across her cleavage. Shoving the bra up, freeing her breasts. I lick and suck her nipples, and she squirms beneath me, her hands in my hair as she holds me to her chest.

We shed our clothes quickly, eager to get naked. Hands everywhere, hers curve around the base of my cock, mine diving into the sticky hot wetness between her thighs. We touch and stroke, working each other into a frenzy.

I feel more eager than usual to plunge inside her tonight. Maybe it was all the stress from my dad and Helena. My worry about Hayden. Hell, even witnessing the dramatic blow-up between Caleb and Gracie threw me a little. A little theatrical, but it was a day of reckoning, and I'm so fucking grateful that my night is ending with this girl in my arms.

We roll over so she's on top of me, and she grinds her pussy against my cock, making me groan. She's nothing but wet, welcoming heat and I'm desperate to be inside her.

Desperate.

A shift of my hips and I slide inside with ease. She goes still and I open my eyes to find her staring at me.

"You didn't put on a condom," she whispers.

That's why it feels so fucking good. I lift my hips some more, sending myself deeper, and I close my eyes against the sensations spreading through me. "Want me to get one?"

She rocks against me, lifting up, sliding down my length. She shudders, her pussy clenching tight and, oh fuck, I could come quick if she keeps that up.

"No," she gasps when she does it again. "I'm on the pill."

"You're the only girl I've been inside," I remind her and she leans in, smiling against my mouth before she kisses me.

"I don't know why, but I seriously love that," she murmurs.

She's been using the word love rather freely, though it doesn't bother me. I'm not scared of a relationship with

Hayden. I'm realizing what Sophie and I shared was kid stuff. I cared about her. I still do. I don't wish her harm. But what we had was a sweet relationship that wasn't meant to move beyond high school.

Maybe I feel so much stronger about Hayden because she's my first, but there's just something about her. She's a challenge. She's fun. She's intelligent. She has a plan for her life and she's going to do it. She's a spoiled rich girl and she knows it, but she wants more. She wants to teach and help children. She wants to change lives.

Wonder if she knows she's changed mine?

"You feel good," she whispers, burying her face against my neck and kissing me there while she rides me nice and steady.

I grab hold of her hips as she rises up, guiding her movements. I open my eyes, not about to miss this show. Her hair hangs around her face as she smiles down at me, her breasts swaying, her hands braced on my chest. We move together, back and forth, and I grip her hips tighter, holding her still as I take over.

A cry escapes her when I begin to thrust deep. I do it again and again, driving myself inside her, a selfish bastard as I chase after my orgasm. It builds and builds, my stomach muscles clenching tight, my balls drawing close to my body as I fuck her relentlessly. She keeps up the pace, matching my every thrust, until she fumbles, her torso stretching upwards, her muscles going tense.

"Tony," she chokes out, her expression changing, crumpling, her mouth hanging open, her eyes sliding closed when it hits.

She's overcome by her orgasm and I watch, in a trance as it rushes through her. She's shaking. Trembling. Her hands curl into my chest, scratching my skin, but I don't even feel it.

I'm too caught up in her. Too caught up in us.

Somehow, I never stop. I'm still moving. Thrusting. And when I come, a hoarse shout leaves me. Loud enough for everyone in the condo to hear, but I don't care. I'm coming. It feels like I can't stop coming. And when it's finally over, I sink into the mattress, my body languid, as if my bones turned to liquid.

She collapses on top of me, her hands moving across my chest in lazy circles, her breaths ragged. I can feel her heart racing and mine is keeping the same beat.

I rest my hand on her back and slowly stroke. Up and down. Back and forth. I skim my short nails across her skin and she shivers, a soft huff of laughter breathes across my pec.

"What got into you?" she asks after a few more beats of silence. "That was..."

"Amazing?" I kiss the top of her head. "And you're confused. I got into you."

"Right," she says dryly, lifting her head so she can mock glare at me. "Seriously. That was..."

"Amazing," I repeat softly. I lean in and she lifts up at the same time, our mouths meeting in a light kiss. "Guess I should get pissed more often."

"Were you really pissed?"

"Yeah. Sort of."

She settles her head on my chest once more. I can feel myself softening, but we're still connected. "At me?"

"No." I shake my head. Squeeze her tight. "At Helena. At Lauri. Why are they interfering in our lives?"

"Because they can," she says bitterly. "They've got nothing else better to do."

"Helena is determined to make my father's company hers. She doesn't want me to have anything to do with it," I say, my thoughts drifting—unfortunately—to Helena. And her motives.

"Why? Is she really that passionate about it?"

"More like she's passionate about his money." That's the only thing I can think of.

"And what about you?" Hayden asks.

I don't say anything for a moment and she glances up, our gazes connecting. "What about me?"

"What do you want? Your father's company? Do you want to run it someday?"

I make a face. "I don't even fully understand what he does. The only reason I'm majoring in business is because it's the most general major I could find that could cover a lot of things. He took it as me aspiring to join him at the helm one day."

"But that's not what you want." Hayden says.

"I don't know what I want. I'm only eighteen. Right now, I'm happy where I'm at. Going to school, playing football and being with you. Isn't that enough? Why do I have to make a decision right now?" I sound like a miserable whiner, and I clamp my lips shut, annoyed with myself.

"You're right. You shouldn't have to. You need to tell your stepmom to back the fuck off." Hayden shifts upwards so her face is in my mine, dropping a lingering kiss on my lips. With the change in position, I slip completely out of her, come leaking and most likely creating a wet spot. I guess that's an extra benefit to condoms—no wet spots.

So fucking stupid, what Helena's doing. "She threatened me, remember?"

"Will you really be that upset if your father believes her

lies and cuts you off? Will it really make a difference in your life?" Hayden asks.

"No," I say slowly, realizing that she's right. "Our relationship is already pretty weak."

"Is it the money you're worried about?"

"I come into a trust that no one else can revoke or touch when I'm twenty-one. It's mine. Most of it is money from my mother's side of the family," I explain.

"So money isn't a motivator either." She kisses me again, and I cup the back of her head, keeping her there so I can kiss her some more. "She has nothing over you."

"You're right," I murmur against her lips, just before I tease them with my tongue. A thought hits me and I pull away so I can look into her eyes. "What about you?"

"What about me?"

"If Lauri tells your dad you're with me? Will he be pissed?"

Her eyes darken, and I know the answer before she says it. "Probably. But we can make it work."

"Can we? Do we want to?" I'm tense. I almost don't want to hear her answer.

But then again, I'm hanging on her every breath, waiting for every word that'll come out of her mouth next.

"Yes. I want it to work," she says carefully. "What about you?"

I grin. "I thought you said relationships were for pussies."

Her smile matches mine. "I did, but maybe that's what we are. A couple of pussies."

"You think so?"

"I know my pussy likes you," she says, laughing.

I grip her hard and flip her over so she's the one lying on her back. "I know I really like your pussy too."

I can't believe we're having this conversation about her pussy right now. But it's making me laugh. She makes me smile just thinking about her.

Damn, I've got it bad for this girl.

"So are you my boyfriend now?" she asks in a sing-song voice.

"Is that what you want?" I gently thrust against her, my erection already returning and raring to go. Not a surprise. He makes frequent appearances where Hayden is concerned.

She nods. Smiles. "I told myself I wouldn't do this."

"Same." I nod, thinking of our past discussions.

"I thought people like us were suckers." She strokes my shoulder. My chest.

"We are." I kiss her, my mouth lingering on hers. "Suckers for each other."

Truer words were never spoken.

TWENTY-FOUR
HAYDEN

IT'S the day after the night Tony and I agreed we're officially a couple and I'm walking on campus, enjoying the
warm sun combined with the cold wind, grateful for the
thick hoodie I'm wearing that wards off the chill. I feel
like I'm in la la land. I don't know how else to describe it,
but it's as if I'm in a Disney movie and there are birds
chirping and squirrels running across the campus lawn,
their gazes, their chatter only for me. Everyone I pass, I
smile at them as if I'm Snow White or Cinderella, the
prettiest girl about to go meet up with her Prince
Charming.

I always related most to Cinderella when I was little.
Not because of the wicked stepmother and stepsisters or the
fact that they treated Cinderella so poorly. More because
she was blonde—like me—and I had a thing for that
gorgeous blue gown she wore to the ball.

In my eyes, that chick had it all. She got hers in the end
—thanks to no one else but herself.

I murmur a hello to a professor I had last year as we
walk past each other, my mouth stretched in a too familiar

grin. The professor nods, walking faster and I stifle a giggle. She probably thinks I'm crazed. I feel a little crazed.

Is this what being in love is like? I've never experienced it before. Not really. There are crushes and falling hard for that cute boy who asked you to prom your junior year—actual experience. There's the first high school boyfriend who took your virginity and swore his undying love afterward, and you agreed. Then you broke up a month later and moved on to another guy within a couple of months.

Is that love? I'm not saying those feelings aren't real or intense, and they're based in love, but is it true, deep, I cannot live without this person love?

Not what I experienced, no.

With Tony, I can see myself living without him. But it doesn't look very fun. More like it looks pretty lonely and hollow, and I'd be a moping mess if he broke up with me right now. I'm not sure what we have is love, but it's close. We're getting close.

If we keep going down this path, we're definitely going to be saying I love you to each other by next year. And next year isn't that far away.

I head toward the building where my next class is when I feel my phone ring in the back pocket of my jeans. I whip my phone out, not paying attention to whose name is flashing on the screen because I assume it's either Tony or Gracie. They're the only two people who call me on a regular basis.

"You're seeing Sorrento's son when I told you to stay away from that asshole?"

I come to an abrupt stop, absorbing the words just said to me. "Hello to you too, Father."

"Don't be coy with me, Hayden. Lauri told me what's going on. That you're with that boy when I specifically told you to avoid him," he growls. "What the fuck are you thinking?"

"What the fuck are you thinking, calling me out of the blue and chewing me out like this?" I retort as I resume walking. A little brisker this time, anger fueling my steps.

"Don't you talk to me like that, young lady," he says, and I can't help it.

I laugh.

"Don't pretend you care about what I'm doing unless it can somehow affect you and your bank account," I tell him, and he goes quiet.

Scary quiet.

"You don't think I care about what you're doing?"

"You never call me unless it's something like this," I say, my voice softening. I need to remember I'm dealing with a ticking time bomb when he's mad like this. I don't want him to explode. It takes a lot to make my father angry, and while I know I crossed a line by saying what I just did, I couldn't help it.

I'm a grown woman who can do and see whoever she wants.

And funny how this call comes the day after Tony talked to Helena. Looks like the friends are comparing notes and stirring up trouble.

"Sorrento and I are business rivals," my father explains. "Can you imagine what will happen when companies we're trying to do business with find out that our children are dating?"

"Think of it as more of an opportunity. Hey, I know what you two should do—you should merge your companies. Instead of being two fighting rivals, come together and become a complete powerhouse," I suggest.

He scoffs. "That's the most ridiculous thing I've ever heard."

"I don't think it sounds like a bad idea at all," I say, pausing outside the building where my class is. "I'm guessing you two have more in common than you think."

"Sorrento is an underhanded bastard who will rob and steal to get the deal," my father says.

I laugh. "You're a poet."

He sighs. I can tell his anger has diffused somewhat. Go me. "You're exasperating."

"It's your favorite quality of mine," I tease. He chuckles. I turn serious. "Who told you Tony and I are seeing each other?"

I don't bother trying to hide it, though I'm not fully admitting it either. What's the point? I know Tony's father doesn't know it's me, that Helena is trying to hold that over Tony's head. But fuck that. We're adults. We can see who we want. Helena has no business trying to threaten Tony.

"Lauri," he admits. "She said Helena told her. Which is another issue I have. I don't like that those two are still friends."

"You can't tell Lauri who she can and cannot talk to. She's not your child," I remind him.

"Looks like I can't do that either."

"Because I'm not a child. I'm a grown woman."

"Don't remind me."

"I have class in two minutes, Daddy. I have to go," I tell him, glancing around as people rush past me, either exiting or entering the building.

More like seven minutes till class, but he doesn't need to know that.

"So that's all you have to say? You're not going to deny that you're seeing that kid?" he asks.

A sigh escapes me and I lean against the wall. "What does it matter? I have no clue what you do at work, and Tony doesn't know what his dad does either. We're not trading business secrets. We could care less. We're just hanging out and having fun together."

"That's code for you two are a serious couple and you care about him," my father says. "Be honest with me, Hayden. You don't need to gloss over this situation."

Huh. Guess he has me figured out more than I thought.

"It's not that serious," I say, raising my voice when he tries to talk over me. He goes quiet. "Tony and I, we have an understanding. Like I said, we're having fun, but we both know it's probably going nowhere."

"Whatever you say." His tone is sharp, and I can tell I've irritated him. "I'll let you go. We'll talk later." The call ends.

An irritated sigh escapes me and I glance up to find Gracie standing there, so close, I know she heard every single word I just said to my father.

Oh, and Caleb is standing right beside her. Watching me. His eyes dark with unmistakable disgust.

Shit. Shit, damn *fuck.*

I try to play it off with a smile and a wave. "Hey guys. I thought you two were mad at each other?"

"We talked," Gracie says, her expression pleading. "And we worked it out."

"Friendship still intact then?" I say lightly.

"Definitely," Caleb says with a glower aimed at me. He turns to Gracie. "I need to go. See ya later."

He walks away without another word.

Gracie approaches me, her expression worried. "Who were you just telling that you and Tony have an understanding?"

A sigh escapes me as we enter the building. We have

this class together. "My father. Our families figured out last night we're seeing each other."

"Oh. And that's still a problem?"

"For whatever reason, yes. I wish they'd stay out of our business," I say bitterly.

"Yet you told him it's probably going nowhere," Gracie says. "With Tony."

It's the worst thing ever when someone repeats your words back to you and you realize just how awful they sound. I lean against the wall right outside our classroom, and study the floor, running over everything I said before my father hung up on me. It was bad. All bad. "Caleb heard it, huh?"

"Yeah."

I lift my head. "You think he'll go tell Tony?"

She nods. "Probably. Want me to do damage control for you?"

"Is it really that bad?" I ask weakly.

"Hay, you said you two had an understanding and you knew it was going nowhere," she reminds me.

"I said probably going nowhere. And I didn't mean it. We pretty much declared ourselves boyfriend and girlfriend last night," I say, shaking my head. "If Caleb tells him what he heard me say, he's going to be devastated."

Or pissed.

We enter the classroom and sit in our usual seats. The class is about half-full, and the professor is always running late, so I decide to change the subject. I need to think about something else.

"What happened with you and Jackson last night?"

Gracie's cheeks turn pink and she waves a dismissive hand. "Absolutely nothing. I am embarrassed to say I tried to make a move."

"Oh God."

"I know." Gracie nods. "And he turned me down in the sweetest way. He said he didn't want to ruin his friendship with Caleb since it's still so new, and that's why he couldn't do anything with me. Though he did say I was beautiful, and he was tempted. He might've just been saying that though."

"At least he has some standards," I say.

"Right? God, he's just—*painfully* attractive. He smells really good too. And he says nice things. Kind things. Unlike some people I know." Gracie scowls. She's referring to Caleb.

I say nothing. What can I say? Besides, I'm too busy mulling over what Caleb heard, and what exactly he might tell Tony.

I could try and beat Caleb to the punch. I should pull my phone out right now and text Tony. Let him know what happened, and what they overheard. How I was trying to blow off my dad and pretend what Tony and I have isn't a big deal.

But it is a big deal. It's a huge deal. I care about him. I don't want things to end because of a misunderstanding. Because Caleb said that I said, blah blah blah.

That's so high school.

No, it's worse. It's so middle school, and we're above that. We're more mature than that.

Right?

I grab my phone and open it. Click on Tony's name and contemplate what I might say.

At the same exact moment, the professor sweeps in, announcing there's a surprise quiz, and I put my phone away, telling myself it's okay. I can wait.

I can wait.

TWENTY-FIVE

TONY

FEELS like it always happens like this. Life is just cruising along, everything feels good, you're all right with the world, the world is right with you, and then it's like BAM.

A slap to the face.

A punch to the gut.

And your life changes.

Caleb found me on campus. In the library. I stopped by here for the hour break I have between classes, going over a chapter I skimmed yesterday that we might have a test on today. I've been distracted lately, and my grades are slipping. Nothing serious, but all I want to do is play football or spend time with Hayden. School has taken the backburner, when I need to watch out. I have to maintain a certain GPA to play on the team and I'm not about to risk it.

"There you are," Caleb says when he finds me, practically skidding to a stop in front of the table I'm sitting at. "I've been looking everywhere for you."

He's breathless. His chest is heaving, as if he's been running.

"Are you okay?" I ask.

He settles into the chair across from me, his expression stern. "I overheard something."

Dread slithers over me, pooling in my gut. "From who?"

"Hayden."

I thought this was team related. Not girl related.

The dread grows, spreading through my blood. "What are you talking about?"

"I don't know who she was talking to, but I was walking Gracie to class." I start to say something, but Caleb holds his hand out, stopping me. "Don't give me shit. I'll tell you about that later. Anyway, we ran into Hayden. She was on the phone."

"Okay," I say slowly, hating where this is going.

"And she said something like, 'Tony and I have an understanding. We're going nowhere.'" My friend's expression is pained. "I hate being the bearer of bad news, but I thought you should know before she goes to you and tries to make it seem like she didn't say that. I heard those words come out of her mouth, Tony. She said it. Wish I knew who to."

I nod, taking in his words, running them over and over again in my mind. The dread is still there, but I'm not angry. Not yet. More like I'm viewing this revelation as a puzzle, and I'm trying to figure it out.

Why would she say that? And to who? After everything we discussed last night, I thought we were on solid ground. As solid as we've ever been. I was feeling good. I'm halfway to being in love, while she's on the road to nowhere.

Maybe she was playing me last night, but why? She's always been upfront, right from the get-go. She doesn't believe in relationships. She thinks they're pointless, and I do too.

I especially do right now.

"This could be nothing," I tell him after a few moments of tense silence.

"It could be everything," Caleb says. "I'm not trying to sabotage your relationship, bro. You have to know that. I just don't—I don't want you thinking that everything's perfect, while she's telling other people you two have an under-standing." He does air quotes with his fingers around the last word.

That is something I've never seen Caleb do before in his life.

"I hate seeing you guys go through it," he continues, sounding sad. "Diego and Jocelyn? What a mess. Jake and Hannah, when they were having their troubles? Awful. Now you and Hayden?"

"It could be nothing," I stress again, my mind still replaying what Caleb said.

"Right. Keep telling yourself that," Caleb says, his voice ringing with doubt.

Damn, he's right. I sound like an idiot. I don't want to be the idiot who thinks everything's okay when it's not. I've already done that once.

"You and Sophie?" Caleb says, his voice gentle. I lift my head, my gaze meeting his. "She broke you. You put on this act like nothing affects you and you don't say shit, but I saw it. We all did. She broke your heart and you pushed it aside like no big deal. You never even talked about it with us."

"What was there to say?" I shrug, not wanting to think about Sophie.

Definitely don't want to talk about her either.

"If you don't talk about shit, you just let it build up and fester inside of you. How healthy is that?"

"What do you know about healthy relationships?" I throw at him.

"My parents. They've been together over twenty years. They love each other," he explains. "My dad has never done my mom wrong, and she's never done him wrong either. They love and support each other."

"Then why are you so messed up? Out with a different girl every night, when you've got one standing right in front of you, wanting to be with you. Shit, you've got two," I say, thinking of Baylee and Gracie.

A flicker of emotion shines in Caleb's eyes, but otherwise, nothing. "I'm not ready to tie myself down yet. That's nice and all, a forever kind of relationship, but I'm young. And wired differently than the rest of you. I won't settle down until I'm forty."

"Forty." I snort. "Please."

"My problems are not the issue right now," Caleb says. He points at me. "Yours are. What are you going to do about Hayden?"

"I don't know," I say truthfully. Maybe I should let her approach me first. She'll tell me she's not interested in me anymore, and she's ready to move on. Just like they all do.

My parents. My first girlfriend. Now Hayden. They're all the same. They leave me. The only people I can count on are my friends and my teammates. That's it.

They're all that matters.

Maybe I'm thinking unfairly and I need to give Hayden a chance to explain, but I can't help it. People leave me. People shit all over me. As I've gotten older, I prefer beating them to the punch versus letting them punch me with their rejection.

It's easier that way. Does that make me fucked up? Probably.

But it's like I can't help myself.

"Don't give her the upper hand," Caleb says. "That's

what you did to Sophie. You never said a goddamn word so, of course, she ended it. When you knew she was getting ready to leave, you never protested, you never begged her to stay, nothing."

"She wasn't going to stay," I say dryly. "Her mind was already made up. She wanted to go to that school. Her parents were encouraging her. It was an opportunity she couldn't pass up. I wasn't going to stand in her way."

"Do you know what she told Hannah before she left?" Caleb asks me. He slaps a hand over his mouth the second the words left him. "I wasn't supposed to say that."

"Now you have to tell me." I sit up straighter, curiosity filling me. I want to know. I deserve to know.

Caleb sighs and hangs his head, speaking to the table. "She would've tried a long-distance relationship with you. She really wanted to. She was in love with you, but once she told you about the other school, and how she was leaving, she said it was like you shut down completely."

It's true. I did shut down. It's what I usually do when they leave. What's the point in acting like I care when they clearly don't?

"If you'd shown even a glimmer of caring, she would've jumped on it. You two could've had a relationship. Long distance, which sucks, but she was totally willing. She loved your sulky ass, and you let her go," Caleb says.

"She didn't love me," I start, but Caleb shakes his head, and I go silent.

"She did. She told Hannah that again and again," he says.

"Right and Hannah told you?" Most of the time, Hannah thought we all sucked, and she was right. We did.

Well, I didn't. I told Jake to go for her. I'm not like these assholes. I don't need to brag and shout and show off. I just do what I need to do and keep going.

"Jake told me. He was worried about you. We all were."

I send Caleb a scathing look, hating how fucking logical he sounds when, normally, Caleb is anything but. That's my role. "When did you suddenly get so wise?"

Caleb laughs. "I'm not wise. Not even close. I just listen. I'm open to what people have to say. I'm not ready to cut them off and ice them out when I think they don't care anymore. It goes both ways, Tony. I know you've got some issues, and I think they're all tied in to your shitty parents. You want to feel wanted, but the people in your life want to feel wanted by you too."

I remain silent, staring at him.

"Your friends feel the same way. We care about you. Don't ice me out when I'm saying something to you that you don't want to hear," he continues, his voice soft.

A sigh escapes me. "What do I do about Hayden?"

And why am I asking Caleb, of all people?

"Talk to her. Call her out."

That's something I don't really like to do. "Confront her?"

"Yeah," Caleb nods enthusiastically. "See if she denies it. If she does, she's a fuckin' snake in the grass."

"She won't deny it." I know she won't, not when she had witnesses.

Plus, I don't think Hayden would lie to me.

"Then yeah, confront her, and fight a little. Show her that you care. Don't let her walk all over you and then walk *out* on you. Fight for her. Like Diego fought for Jocelyn," Caleb says.

"That's a different situation." I lean back in my chair, remembering how fucking painful all of that was, and it only just happened. I never want to experience something like that. Witnessing Diego and Jocelyn's struggle back to each other was difficult. I can't imagine being the one doing all the struggling. Both of them went through so much.

Love trumps all though. They fought for each other because they loved each other. They each thought the other was worth the fight, and at different times too. Jocelyn fought for Diego when he had no fight in him, and then Diego brought it and fought hard for Jos and their baby when she'd given up.

Relationships aren't even. Someone is always working a little harder than the other, and that's in everything. Family. Friends. Romantically.

And that's the thing. Caleb is...holy shit, I can't believe I'm thinking this, but...Caleb is *right*. I've never had to struggle for anything. I have all the money I could want. A house, a car, I'm in school, I'm starting on the football team, I do my thing. When people walk out on me, I sweep it under the rug and proceed with my life like it never happened. Even recently, spending time with my dad again, I forgot about all the shit he did to me in the past. I let it go, I got mad at him all over again, and I gave up on continuing a relationship with him. He might've moved on from me, but I moved on from him as well. Two wrongs don't make a right, isn't that the old saying?

I let Mom get away with all her shit too. Maybe if I would've said something, she'd stuck around more. It's not all up to me since I'm the kid, but I could say something now. Call her on her shit.

Not that I want to. I don't like confrontation.

There's my issue. I don't want to confront Hayden because I'm not one to yell and carry on. I saw enough of that between my parents before they divorced. While they divorced. After they divorced.

It fucking sucks.

"I don't want to fight with her," I admit, my voice low. "I dealt with enough fighting in my life growing up. My parents went at each other nonstop."

"I remember," Caleb says. "They'd fight at games. They'd fight at school. We all saw it."

Humiliating. I'd sort of blocked out that shit, and I can see why. "They were the worst."

"Don't let their terrible relationship control you, bro. Fighting sucks. Arguing sucks. My parents do it all the time," he says.

"Wait a minute." Caleb meets my gaze. "They argue *all* the time?"

"Well, not all the time, but they argue a lot. Over small stuff. Big stuff. Mom says it keeps the passion alive between them. They have a yelling match in the kitchen, one of them gives in and the next thing I know, they're kissing on each other." Caleb laughs, shaking his head. "They call it communicating, and I guess it's the way they communicate. Having an argument with someone you care about doesn't have to be a big, life ending thing."

He shrugs. Like what he keeps on saying isn't a big deal. But it's a huge deal.

"What the fuck, Caleb? Where has this version of you been all our lives?" I stare at him in bewilderment. He's making so much sense, it's kind of freaking me out.

"None of you assholes take me seriously. You think I'm some dumb bro who doesn't give a shit about anything but girls," he says.

"That's how you act."

"I'm deep, motherfucker. Not as deep as Jackson Rivers, but I've got layers," he says, sounding defensive.

I start to laugh. And it's like I can't stop. I should be freaked out and worried about my relationship with Hayden. Those shitty words she said to whoever. But I sort of don't care right now. I'm too blown away by my friend and what he revealed.

Like about Sophie.

My laughter dies, and memories come at me, one after another.

"I fucked everything up with Sophie, huh?" I say as I stare off into the distance. Regret hits me, and it's bittersweet. I slowly shake my head.

"You did," he agrees without hesitation. "You should reach out to her sometime. Tell her you're sorry for how it ended. She'd probably like to hear from you."

"How do you know?"

"I comment on her Instagram posts. She's doing well. I didn't cut her off like you did," Caleb says.

I unfollowed her everywhere. Didn't want the painful reminder.

"Don't do the same thing to Hayden. Me giving you this information, I know what you'd normally do. You'd slowly withdraw, but try and tell everyone it's okay. You're okay. You'd pull away from Hayden. Claim you were busy all the time. Act distant when you are together, which will eventually become a rare occurrence. Hold on to all that crap and let it grow and build. Until you can't take it anymore and you tell her you want out. She'll agree because you've been such an ass, she wants out too. And then it's over."

The way Caleb just mapped everything out...is painfully accurate. Reminds me of what I did to Sophie. Though she's the one who broke up with me first.

I glance at my phone to check the time. I have twenty minutes till class starts and I didn't study for shit. Not like I can concentrate. It's a full day of classes, and then practice. I won't be finished till late tonight, and we have a game Saturday. A big one. We're on our way to playing in a bowl game, which is exciting. A big deal. I want to relish in that. Enjoy it. This could be my only chance. Asher Davis is an excellent QB, and he could be one of the best I've ever played with, beyond Jake.

Maybe Eli can step up, but it'll take time. I'm on top now. I'm with an elite team. The local news can't stop talking about us. Sports networks are making predictions. It's an exciting time, yet I'm having to deal with relationship bullshit.

It's so damn tempting to end things with Hayden. Not bother discussing it. Just be done, cut it off, sweep it under the rug, and move on.

But it'll hurt. More than it did with Sophie. It'll be like cutting off a limb. I don't want the ghost of my relationship with Hayden to haunt me for the rest of my days. I want to fight.

I need to fight for her.

For us.

TWENTY-SIX

HAYDEN

LATE FRIDAY AFTERNOON and I'm sitting in my apartment on the couch, trying to write yet another paper that's due Monday and thinking about Tony. I still haven't talked to him since Caleb and Gracie happened upon my saying stupid shit to my father. Not really. Oh, we've texted a few times. Things that really meant nothing and one voicemail from him, explaining that he was busy, he missed me, and hoped that he could see me tonight.

Tonight as in *tonight*.

The football team leaves early tomorrow morning to play an away game against San Jose State. That's only a couple of hours from here, and they didn't feel the need to leave this afternoon to practice on San Jose's field in the morning. Makes sense.

I'm tempted to convince Gracie to go with me to the game so we can show our support, but I'm also really stressed out over what Caleb heard me say, and worried Tony might tell me to go to hell. He's a fair and reasonable person, but I know he shuts people out if he thinks they've fucked with him.

I know Caleb must've gone to Tony and told him what he heard me say. Gracie all but confirmed it, but she's being mysterious. Said that Caleb handled "everything perfectly."

What the hell does that even mean?

Here's where I share a little fact about myself: I'm an avoider. My mother used to say that about me all the time. When I was little, if I broke something, I hid it. In the sixth grade, my report card was mailed home and I stashed it in my closet for weeks. I didn't want my parents to see my shitty grades—my math and science grades were so bad. I had a C and D, respectively. I got caught when my mom overheard me telling my friend on the phone that "no, my parents hadn't seen my report card yet because I got it out of the mail before they could."

Busted.

So, of course, I don't want to mention what happened to Tony. I'd rather pretend I never said it at all, and if Caleb and Gracie wouldn't have walked up at that exact moment, I could've done exactly that. My father and Tony won't compare notes over that conversation. I could've gotten away with it.

Unfortunately, that's not how it panned out.

It's not like it's any big deal, what I said. I didn't mean any of it. I told my dad those things to placate him. If anyone would understand, it's Tony. I'm sure he did the same thing to his father and his wicked stepmother. In fact, I know he did. I'm being dumb right now.

So dumb.

What happened to Hayden Channing, independent woman who takes care of herself? Who doesn't need anyone? Who owns her sexuality? Her relationships? Her life? I tell myself I'm a badass, and sometimes I believe it.

Right now is not one of those times.

I hear the front door unlock and glance up just in time to watch Gracie open it and walk into our apartment, stopping short when she sees me.

"I didn't think you'd be home yet," she says.

"Here I am," I say, trying to inject some enthusiasm into my voice, but failing miserably.

Gracie shuts and locks the door, and then joins me on the couch, her expression solemn as she studies me. "Are you all right?"

A sigh escapes me and I snap my laptop shut, settling it on the coffee table in front of us. "Not really." I pause. "Why did you let Caleb tell Tony what he heard me say?"

Gracie's mouth pops open. "I can't control him. Even if I told him not to do it, he would anyway. Tony's one of his best friends."

I look away, my stomach churning. I haven't eaten anything all day, and I know if I do try to eat something, I'd probably want to puke it right back up.

God, I'm a complete mess.

"Are you—mad at me about this?" Gracie asks when I haven't said anything. "Because if you're mad at anyone, it should be yourself."

I turn to her with a roll of my eyes. "Come on, G. I'm not mad at you. I know it's my fault. And I was talking to my dad, remember? I'll say anything to appease him. He was giving me so much shit over dating Tony."

"Why? I don't get it."

I explain the business rival angle, Helena and Lauri's friendship, and how their men don't approve—again because of the business rivalry. How they're bored, rich housewives and I believe they get a little thrill out of messing around with mine and Tony's relationship.

"That's straight out of reality TV, overblown drama," Gracie says when I'm finished.

"Right? Plus, it's dumb," I say in agreement. "Who cares if Tony and I are seeing each other?"

"Well, clearly your dads do." Gracie's face brightens. "I do like your suggestion of the two of them merging together, though."

"I thought it was a great idea. My father did not." Another sigh leaves me and I lean my head back on the couch, staring at the ceiling. "I still haven't really talked to Tony since I ran into you guys yesterday."

"Don't you think you should do that?" Gracie asks gently.

"Of course. I just don't know what to say. He left me a voicemail saying he wanted to see me tonight."

"You should get together with him. They have an important playoff game tomorrow," she says.

"You want to go with me to the game tomorrow? If Tony hasn't told me to fuck off, I sort of want to go," I say.

"Are you going to see your family while you're over there?" she asks.

I didn't even think of that, I'm so focused on Tony. "I don't want to."

"So it'll be a quick drive over, watch the game, drive home kind of thing?"

I glance over at her. "Yeah. It will. Does that work for you?"

Gracie nods, looking pleased. "I didn't want to stay the night or get caught up in your family's drama."

I grab a throw pillow that's nearby and bop her gently in the face with hit. She laughs. "You've met my family."

"Your dad and your sister. I don't think I met his girlfriend."

"Lucky you," I mutter, annoyed all over again at the meddling those women decided to do in my life.

I'm twenty years old. I don't need two grown women trying to maneuver my relationship for me—or sabotage it. I can do it on my own, thank you very much.

And they weren't trying to help me, ever. They were trying to *break us up.*

I mean, seriously. What the hell?

"Text your boy," Gracie encourages. "Ask him to come over."

"Really? Aren't you staying here tonight?"

She slowly shakes her head. "I'm going to a sorority party. Remember Baylee?"

Wait a minute...

"Yes," I say slowly. "What are you scheming?"

"Nothing," Gracie says with a laugh. "I ran into her on campus yesterday. We hung out. Grabbed a coffee. Talked a lot. I like her."

"You do not," I say immediately, making her laugh harder.

"I do! She's nice. We don't really talk about Caleb, because I feel like that's something we both are trying to avoid."

"That's awkward."

"Not really. I feel like I have a lot in common with her. She's only eighteen like the rest of them, and after spending so much time with her, I feel almost—protective of her. I don't know. It's weird." Gracie's expression turns thoughtful for a moment, and then she dismisses it with a giant smile. "Anyway, she pledged a sorority, told me they were having a party and asked me to come! She said I could bring a guest, and I would totally bring you, but looks like you're otherwise occupied."

"I would so go but yeah, Tony." I smile weakly, hoping everything will work out tonight. "I think it's weird you're friends with the girl Caleb tried to hook up with a couple of nights ago."

"Caleb admitted to me they hooked up off and on a lot in high school," Gracie confesses.

Now it's my turn for my mouth to drop open. "Gracie, what the hell are you doing?"

"It's nothing! I want to be her friend." She grins. "Keep your friends close, and your enemies closer?"

"I didn't think you were interested in Caleb that way," I remind her.

"I don't know how I feel about Caleb. Or any man, for that matter. They're all ridiculous." She waves a dismissive hand. "Did you know Jackson's performing tonight at Strummers? He's the lead act."

"Get out." I remember how much I enjoyed his performance last time. "Maybe Tony and I can go in support."

"Caleb said he's going to try—and he invited me to go with him." She rolls her eyes. "I declined."

I'm proud of her. "Did it feel good, telling him no?"

"It felt *amazing*." She leaps to her feet. "I'm going to take a quick shower and get ready."

"It's still so early."

"I want to look extra fire tonight," Gracie says, her smile turning wicked. "I'm in a mood to pick up boys."

"Oh God." I laugh nervously, though deep down, I envy her mood. I wish I felt as carefree as Gracie seems.

But I have to put on my big girl panties and take care of a few things first.

A FEW HOURS later my doorbell rings. Gracie is long gone, having left early to go to Strummers and watch Jackson with everyone else before she went to the sorority party. I texted Tony, asking him to come over and he agreed readily, which I found reassuring. But I'm also trying to find any sign as positive right now, so maybe I'm overcompensating.

When I open the door to find him standing there, wearing that leather jacket he had on the last time we went to Strummers, along with a black T-shirt and jeans, my mouth goes dry.

He is too handsome for words, swear to God.

"Hey." He smiles. His dark eyes are warm as he takes me in and I stand there for a moment, soaking up his attention.

I startle a little when he says, "You going to let me in?"

A nervous titter leaves me and I step aside, opening the door wider for him to walk in. He enters the apartment and I shut and lock the door, then lean against it, enjoying the view. Trying to calm my racing heart. Buying time as I try and figure out what to say next.

"You're being weird," he says.

"Caleb told you what he heard me say," I blurt as Tony speaks at the same time.

We stare at each other for a moment, and my heart rate kicks up another notch.

"He did tell me," he says quietly. "He let me know later that you were talking to your father?"

I nod, my body still plastered to the door. I'm afraid if I step away from it, I'll crumple to the ground. "Lauri told him about us."

His expression tightens. "Of course she did. She's been comparing notes with Helena."

"And so I was trying to play it off, you know? Like what we have is no big deal."

"Right." He nods. "I get it. I probably would've done the same. I sort of did, when I was texting my dad."

"Exactly." Relief trickles through me, but not enough for me to walk away from this door. "I said some shitty stuff, and I'm grateful Caleb went to you and told you."

Tony frowns. "Why are you grateful?"

"That you have friends who care about you enough to tell you the truth, even though they know it might hurt you." I swallow hard. "I know you don't have many people in your life who you trust, Tony. Your family lets you down. Your ex let you down. Your circle is small, and I get why. You only let a few people in your inner circle, because you don't want to get hurt."

He nods, not saying anything else.

Another swallow, this one a little more difficult since my throat is like sandpaper. "You let me in, and now I'm terrified that I ruined everything."

He's still quiet, and oh God, it's so unnerving. It's how he copes, the silence, and I get it. It makes people say a lot when he doesn't have to say anything at all, and I'm guessing that, sometimes, those who are blabbing say things they don't mean.

And ruin everything.

I refuse to say a bunch of nonsense. I can play his silence game too.

So that's what I do. I go quiet, waiting for his response.

"I get why you said what you did," he murmurs. "When Caleb first told me, I was ready to shut down, and shut you out. It's easier to think the worst of someone, rather than try and figure out exactly why they did or said something."

"Yeah," I rasp, at a loss of what to say.

"That's my usual mode. That's what I do. I shut people out when I think they're going to leave me. Caleb called me out on it. Told me I sabotaged my relationship with Sophie last year because I knew she was going to choose going to another school over me, a school that meant everything to her and her future dancing career, so of course she's going to choose it. Even though I was being completely unfair, and I fucking knew it, I did it anyway. I shut her out, and gave her no choice but to break up with me, because," he explains, his expression pained. "I'm over her, I swear to God I am, but it also hurts, knowing how I fucked that up, and at the time, I didn't even see it."

My heart slows and softens for him. I hate seeing him in so much pain, and his face is wracked with it. "We all have our coping methods."

"Yeah, well mine also sabotage my relationships. I end them before they can hurt me, thinking I come out of it unscathed. But that's not true. I still end up miserable." He glances down for a moment, as if he can't face me. "And that's what I wanted to do with you. End it before you did any more damage to me," he admits.

"Do you—still feel that way?" I ask hesitantly, petrified of his answer.

Lifting his head, he comes to me, his approach slow. Methodical. Until he's standing directly in front of me, his body lightly pressed against mine, his warm, minty breath wafting across my face. That minty smell fills me with hope. Tells me he cared about his breath and planned on kissing me.

I sort of want to laugh at myself, but I don't.

"No," he says, his gaze locking with mine when I tilt my head up to look at him. "I don't. It doesn't matter what our parents say. Let Helena alienate me from my father. Let her take over the business and leave me out of it. I don't give a fuck."

I want to reach out and touch him so badly, but I keep my hands braced against the door. "I told my father he should get together with yours and merge their businesses. Become a powerhouse together."

Tony cracks a smile, and my heart starts racing again. For a different reason this time. "I love it."

"He didn't think it was a good idea."

"I'm sure he didn't." He reaches for me. Tugs on the ends of my hair, skims his fingers down the length of my arm. I shiver at his touch, my lids lowering and I tilt my face up in an unspoken gesture.

Kiss me.

He doesn't answer in the way I want, but he doesn't stop touching me either, so that's promising.

"I'm sorry for what I said," I whisper. "I'm sorry you had to hear it from someone else."

"I forgive you," he says, pressing his body more firmly against mine. "Caleb gave me good advice."

I blink up at him. "Excuse me? Caleb?"

He nods. Chuckles. "Can you believe it? He was so fucking logical, it was almost scary."

Giving in, I rest my hands on his warm chest, the T-shirt fabric soft beneath my fingertips. "I can't believe it."

"I couldn't either, but it's true. He helped me see the light." His expression turns serious. "He told me I should fight for you. Argue with you for a little bit. Show you that I care."

"I thought you didn't like to argue." It was one of things we agreed on, during a late-night talk while wrapped up in each other in his bed.

"I don't. But he reminded me the best things are always

worth fighting for." He cups my cheek. Tilts my head back and leans in.

And presses his lips to mine.

I melt against him, our mouths opening, tongues tangling. Our lips connect. Break apart. Connect again. The sound amplified in the quiet stillness of my apartment. He wraps his arm around my waist, hauling my lower body against his and I can feel his erection.

It's so good, I almost want to cry. And I never want to cry.

Like, ever.

"I like you," I murmur against his lips at one point during the endless kiss we're sharing. "I like you a lot."

I can feel his full lips curve into a smile. "I like you too."

"Can I admit something?" I run my hands up his chest, circling my arms around his neck, so I can bury my fingers in his hair.

"You can tell me anything," he says.

"I was scared I was going to lose you," I confess, tightening my hold on him. "And I couldn't imagine what tomorrow would be like, if I couldn't talk to you. See you. Touch you."

"Guess you don't have to worry about that," he says before he kisses me deep. "You're stuck with me."

"I'm not complaining," I say with a laugh, our mouths fusing.

At the same exact time, my stomach growls. Loudly.

"Sounds like your stomach is complaining," Tony says against my lips.

I still haven't really eaten anything. And now that my nerves are gone, my stomach is ready to be fed. "I'm starving."

He lifts his head away from mine. "Let's go grab something."

"Are you sure?"

"Yeah." He smiles. "Let's go to that taco truck near Strummers."

Oh, I know where he's going with this. "Do you think he's performed yet?"

Tony tilts his head. "How'd you know Jackson's performing tonight?"

"Gracie told me. She headed over there a while ago," I admit.

"Caleb's there too, with everyone else."

I grab hold of his T-shirt, giving it a gentle shake. "Let's go."

"You sure?"

"Yes. Oh my God, it'll be so much fun, and it definitely won't suck." I laugh, thinking of Robin and Bat's Cave.

"All right, let's go then."

I grab my phone, leaving my purse behind so I don't have to take it into the bar. I slip on a jacket and when we climb into Tony's car, I'm hit with the delicious scent of rich leather.

"Did you wear that jacket in anticipation of going to watch Jackson?" I ask him.

"Maybe," he says sheepishly. "It's the closest thing I've got to a rocker look."

"I love it."

Someday, I just know I'm going to blurt out, "I love you," to Tony. And I'm okay with it.

Perfectly okay.

TWENTY-SEVEN

TONY

THE CLUB IS PACKED. There's another shitty band on the stage, the jangle of guitars and nonsense being spit into a mic filling the room, and I grimace as we make our way through the throng of teenaged girls everywhere. I'm holding Hayden's hand, leading her into the crowd that surrounds the small stage, when I spot my friends, standing head and shoulders taller than pretty much anyone else in the building.

Much like last time, there aren't a lot of guys here tonight.

As we approach, I see the shocked expressions on my friends' faces, save for Caleb and Gracie, who've both experienced this chaos before. Diego, Jocelyn, Eli and Ava all appear in a daze. Like they can't believe this is happening.

Exactly how I felt when we were here last time. Actually, it was worse because we had no idea Jackson was going to perform. That was even more shocking.

"You guys made it!" Caleb roars when he spots us, his grin taking up half his face. He looks pleased. "And just in time. These assholes are going to wrap it up soon."

I give Caleb a bro shake and he does the same. He then hugs Hayden, who laughs nervously.

"Thanks for giving Tony such good advice," she tells him.

Caleb is still grinning. "Any time. I'm glad to see you two are together."

"Told ya," Gracie says, slugging Caleb in the forearm. "You owe me."

"Tell me you didn't bet on it," Hayden says.

Gracie's expression turns innocent. "We didn't bet on it."

She's lying, I can tell. Hayden can too.

The lead singer shouts into the microphone, "Thank you everyone, and good night!" and the stage lights go down. The girls start hopping up and down, screaming their heads off.

"They're all yelling for Jackson?" Eli turns to look at us, his eyes wide. "Right? They don't give a shit about the band that just finished."

"Yep," Hayden says. "It's all for Jackson."

Eli whistles low. "Damn. I think I made a mistake, pursuing football. I should've taken the rock-star angle like he did. He'll get pussy for fucking days! Oops, sorry Ellie."

I didn't see Ellie at first, but there she is, standing with Ava. Glaring at Eli.

Yeah. Oops.

We all talk. About Jackson's performance the last time we were here, both Gracie and Hayden going on about how good it was. How great he sounded. We talk about the potential of his performance that's happening in mere minutes, and Eli tells us Jackson has yet another deal on the table.

"He hasn't refused this one yet. His father's team of

lawyers is looking it over. I'm thinking he might take it," Eli says.

"What about school?" Ellie asks. "And football?"

"Fuck all that if he can land a million-dollar contract and tour the world," Caleb says with a laugh. "If I were him, I'd go for it. Maybe this is his dream, not football."

"He likes both," Eli says. And since he's the one who's closest to Jackson—besides Ellie—then I'll take his word for it. "And you can't tell me he doesn't love this constant adoration he's getting. There's nothing but girls here."

"They're young," I say, glancing around. "Mostly still in high school."

"*We're* still in high school," Ava says, waving a hand between herself and Ellie.

"Yeah. You're proving my point," I tease her.

She sticks her tongue out at me. "Hey, my brother will be home next week."

"He mentioned that. We talked some a few nights ago," I say. I plan on seeing Jake as much as I can during this Thanksgiving break.

"You should come over for Thanksgiving," Ava suggests. "Mom mentioned it to me earlier when I told her I was going to see you tonight. She asked what you were doing."

I think of my dad's invitation, and how I really don't want to go. This is the perfect excuse. "I'd love to go."

"You should come too," Ava says, turning toward Hayden. "I'm sure my mom would love to meet the girl who stole Tony's heart."

Hayden blushes, and now I can't imagine showing up to the Callahan's house without her. She doesn't even realize the power she has over me, does she? "Are you sure?"

"The crowd around the table grows every year, I swear. My parents love it though. This is their favorite holiday."

Ava smiles as she scans our group of friends circled around her. "You should all come if you can make it. At the very least, stop by for dessert."

They all agree they'd love to stop by, and I study each of their faces, overwhelmed with the affection I feel for all of them. It may sound corny, and I feel like a sentimental asshole who would never admit any of this out loud. My friends would give me endless shit, but...

These people I'm with right now? They're my family. Jake and Hannah are too. I don't want to spend the holiday with my father and Helena. It would be a tension-filled dinner with my dad lecturing on and on while Helena shoots daggers at me with her eyes and tends to those crying toddlers who are my half-sisters.

Still can't quite wrap my head around that, but whatever.

"Do you really think it would be okay if I came with you to the Callahan's for Thanksgiving dinner?" Hayden asks me.

I nod, slipping my arm around her shoulders and hauling her in close to my side. "Definitely. Coach and his wife are cool. They seem to really enjoy having a ton of people over on Thanksgiving."

"I'm supposed to go to my dad's for the holiday, but I really don't want to." Hayden makes a face and I lean down, dropping a kiss on her lips.

"Spend it with me. And my friends. *Our* friends," I amend.

She smiles. Tugs on the front of my T-shirt. "Okay."

Maybe it was a mistake, coming to watch Jackson, even though I was all for it earlier. If I could, I'd suggest we leave now. I can't wait to get this girl alone. Get her naked in a bed. Mine. Hers. Whatever. I just want to be with her.

But this works too. With our friends in the middle of a smelly hot bar, waiting for our friend to walk on stage and perform for his screaming fans.

We all chat while we wait for Jackson to appear. The anticipation is ramping up in the room. You can feel the crowd growing more and more anxious, girls shouting his name at random times. Ellie looks mind-blown. I don't know if she's ever been at one of his performances like this before, and I bet she's overwhelmed.

She's not the only fan of Jackson's anymore. He has a whole slew of them.

Finally, the lights go out. The screaming increases. Caleb is screaming too, chanting Jackson's name over everyone else. We're laughing. Eli is losing his mind. Ava, Ellie and Jocelyn are hopping up and down, clutching each other's hands. Hayden rearranges herself so she's standing directly in front of me, just like last time, and I wrap my arms around her, holding her close.

Finally, the lights go up and there's Jackson. Sitting on his throne once again, a single beam of silvery light focused only on him. He's clutching his guitar, his hair in his face, clad in a white T-shirt and jeans. Layers of chains hang from his neck. Rings glint off his fingers.

The girls go wild.

"JACKSON, YOU'RE SO FUCKING SEXY!"

That's from Caleb.

"Good evening. My name is Jackson Rivers."

And then he begins to play.

It's an unfamiliar song. It starts out slow and soft, before it starts to build. I'm sure it's his own creation, and I don't remember it from last time, so I'm guessing it's new. It gets a little faster, and when he switches to the chorus, the entire stage is lit, showing a full band behind him.

The screams are deafening.

Only for you, I'd hesitate
Only for you, I'd stand and wait
It's only you that can change my mind
And only you would leave me behind

It's a bittersweet love song. I know it. But for who? Maybe his fans. I glance over at Ellie, who looks ready to swoon.

She probably thinks it's for her.

When he finishes, the girls are screaming so loud, my ears start to buzz. Jackson smiles at the crowd, and when he spots us, his grin grows. He waves, and the girls in front of us think he's waving to them. They lose their goddamn minds and lunge for the stage, but a beefy security guard stops them, holding them back.

"He even has security," Eli shouts at us, sounding envious. "Holy shit."

"This is insane," Hayden says with a laugh.

"Good song though," I tell her, giving her a squeeze, thinking how right those words are.

Hayden is the only girl I'd do anything for. And when I say anything, I mean *anything*.

I tuck her in close, resting my chin on top of her head as Jackson launches into the next song. Another original, one that's familiar, and Hayden starts to move to the beat. I glance over to catch Caleb helping Gracie onto his shoulders and she beams at Jackson, singing along with the chorus when it starts. Ava's on top of Eli's shoulders already, and Ellie and Jocelyn are dancing around Diego.

Being surrounded by my closest friends, both new and old, my girl in my arms, this is the best feeling in the whole damn world. Bar none.

My heart is full.

TWENTY-EIGHT

HAYDEN

JANUARY

"OH MY GOD!" I start running toward Tony the moment I spot him out on the field. He stops when he hears me, aiming a smile my way as he throws his arms out, waiting for me. I slam into him, his strong arms coming around me, my face pressed against his chest as I breathe in his sweaty, familiar scent.

The Bulldogs just won the Las Vegas Bowl.

When I pull away from him to look at his face, he's grinning. His helmet is long gone, and his hair is a sweaty mess, dark clumps of it clinging to his forehead. His uniform is filthy. They played hard tonight. Tony caught a touchdown in the third quarter. He also had possession of the ball a lot, gaining plenty of yardage. His stats are stellar. He's most likely going to start next season, his coaches informed him a few weeks ago.

And he's only a freshman.

"I'm so proud of you," I murmur as I stare into his eyes.

I'm overwhelmed with pride and happiness. This is a good night. One of the best nights.

And we've had a lot of them lately.

"Thanks." He dips his head, his mouth barely touching mine. "Love you."

"I love you too," I say before he really kisses me.

Right there, out on the field, in front of everyone. Guess I don't mind public displays of affection anymore.

We said our first "I love you" to each other over Christmas. It felt right. From the start, being with Tony has always felt right. Who cares about our fathers' hatred for each other? What does it matter that I'm two years older than him? That shouldn't even be an issue. All I care about is Tony. And he only cares about me.

That's the most important thing of all.

Ash Davis is nearby, holding his fiancée Autumn as he talks to someone from the NFL Network. He asked her to marry him at Christmas, and of course, she said yes. He's sure to get drafted. It's a big deal, winning this bowl. Being on this team. Tony has told me more than once while they were in the playoffs that he couldn't believe his luck.

But I know the truth. It's not all luck. The team is just that good, and Tony is a huge contributor to their overall talent and skill.

"My mom is here. She flew in this morning to watch the game," Tony says when we finally end our kiss. "I just saw her on the field. She told me she's proud of me."

I can hear the emotion crackle in his voice and I hug him tight, overwhelmed. They've been trying to piece their relationship back together, thanks to Tony reaching out to her on Thanksgiving. He told her he was grateful she was his mom, and he wished they could spend more time together, and she agreed. They've been working on that, and it's been a beautiful thing to witness.

We even spent Christmas with her, and we had a lot of fun. His mom went all out. The house was beautifully decorated, with a massive Christmas tree in the living room, filling the entire space with the delicious scent of fresh pine. It snowed the few days we spent there, and Tony took me all over his hometown, showing me where he went to school, where they used to hang out and party.

He even took me to the Callahan's house, which was kind of a trip. We were supposed to visit them for Thanksgiving, but I ended up going to my dad's after all. I really only went to spend time with Palmer. Not one of the Channing family's most memorable holiday moments, that's for sure.

When Tony and I showed up at the Callahan house, I realized quick every single Callahan is beautiful. Like, no joke. Plus, they were the most down to earth people I've ever met, and Drew Callahan has ten times more money than my dad, who's a pretentious asshole.

Oh shit. Speaking of pretentious assholes...

I see Anthony Sorrento Senior approaching us, Helena holding onto his arm as she manages the field in her sky high stilettos. I almost roll my eyes at the sight of them, but I restrain myself.

Barely.

"Tony," his father says smoothly.

We both turn to look at them. I can barely hold back the sneer that forms on my face when my gaze lands on Helena. We haven't spoken since the Thanksgiving incident. Tony didn't spend the holiday with them. He told Helena via text to go fuck herself.

Proud moment right there. He didn't back down even

an inch when it came to her. And Tony is the nicest guy I've ever met. Just don't come for him, like Helena did.

She never brought up anything to Tony's father either. Her threats were all empty. Pointless. We know what she was trying to gain, but her method was weak. I'm guessing this marriage won't last long. Knowing Tony's father and his past, I'd say it was doomed to fail from the start.

But maybe that's just me being a pessimist. People can change, right? I mean...

Look at Tony and me.

"Hey, Dad," Tony says weakly, his expression hopeful. My heart aches, only because I know that despite everything, deep down Tony just wants his father's approval.

"You played well tonight," Anthony says as he glances around the giant stadium before his gaze returns to Tony's. "Congratulations on the win."

Tony grins, his arm tightening around my shoulders as he tugs me closer. "Thank you. I didn't know you were coming to the game."

"I was able to get some time away from work. It's not every day your only son plays in a bowl game in Las Vegas," his father says, sounding boastful.

I chance a glance in Helena's direction. She looks positively miserable.

I don't feel bad for her at all.

"Great job tonight, Tony," Helena adds, and I can tell somehow Anthony made her say that.

"Thanks," Tony says coolly, his gaze barely meeting hers before he smiles down at me. "It's been a good season."

"The best season," Anthony says. "We were hoping the two of you might have time to go to dinner with us?"

I stiffen under Tony's arm. That sounds like absolute torture.

"Ah, yeah. I appreciate the offer, but I can't. I need to head back to the locker room here soon," Tony says, pulling away from me slightly as he quickly glances over his shoulder. "They're having a party for us later, just for the team. Back at the hotel. Wish I could go to dinner with you guys though."

He sounds so sincere, I almost believe him.

"That's too bad. Maybe some other time. We're leaving tomorrow," Anthony says.

"So are we," Tony says, smiling down at me. I love that he treats us like a package deal, even in front of his dad.

"You should come to our house and visit again," Anthony suggests. "Spend some time with your sisters. They're growing so fast."

Helena smiles, but it doesn't quite reach her eyes. I wonder if she's unhappy with her life. If there's anyone to blame for that, it's only herself.

"Maybe I will, once everything calms down," Tony says. "I'm glad you came."

"I'm glad I came too, son," Anthony says, his voice sincere, his eyes glowing with pride. "Thank you for the invite."

"I didn't think you'd be able to make it," Tony says truthfully. "I just sent it on the off chance..."

"Of course I wanted to be here. I might not show it enough, but I care about everything you do. I love you, son." He grabs hold of Tony and they embrace. I watch them, a tiny smile curving my lips, emotion making my chest tight. I love witnessing this. Both his mother and his father came to this game tonight. They showed up for him.

And that's all Tony has ever wanted. Support from his parents.

My gaze goes to Helena, who's tapping away on her

phone. I step closer to her, lowering my voice. "Texting your boyfriend?"

Her head jerks up, her eyes wide. "What do you mean?" she asks, the slightest tremble in her voice.

"Hmm, I don't know. I remember being in the bathroom at the country club that one night a few months ago. Overheard a few things you and Lauri talked about." I shrug. Might've mentioned those things to Lauri too, when I spent Christmas Eve with them.

Definitely not my most memorable Christmas with Dad and Palmer, since everyone was so tense, including me. But we'll get through this. If that means Lauri won't be in our lives anymore eventually, I'm definitely not going to complain.

"Like what?" Helena asks warily, taking a few steps away from the men who are still quietly talking to each other. I go with her, a faint smile on my face.

I'm probably enjoying this way too much.

"Gossipy shit you should be worried about your husband hearing, that's for sure" I say, not mincing any words. "Like how hot you are for your new stepson."

Her gaze shifts to the men for the briefest moment before returning to mine. "That was nothing."

"I wonder if your husband would think it's nothing if I mentioned it to him." I make like I'm going to walk over there and she grabs my arm, stopping me.

"I don't like threats, Hayden," she spits out, her eyes narrowing.

"Neither do I," I tell her pleasantly, jerking my arm out of her loose hold. "And don't touch me ever again."

A cajoling smile appears on her beautiful face. Too bad all that beauty hides a black soul underneath. "It was no big deal. I was just making conversation with my friend, you know? You don't need to tell anyone about that conversation."

What's funny is I haven't told anyone. I sort of forgot about it—until Helena made her threats toward Tony. And still I never mentioned it to him.

"As long as you leave Tony and I alone, it can remain our little secret," I whisper with a pleasant smile. "Don't ever forget that."

"How am I supposed to trust you?" she asks, her voice full of doubt.

"I feel the same exact way about you." She's such a chicken. She's never going to carry out her threat against Tony. I'm confident about that. "Be careful when you gossip in bathrooms. Someone might be in a stall and hear everything."

I walk away from her with a flounce, approaching Tony, who watches me with a gleam in his eyes.

"We're going to take off then so you can get to your party," Anthony says to the both of us. Helena is sulking just behind him. "Have fun. Enjoy your night. You deserve it."

"Thanks, Dad," Tony calls as they turn and start to walk away. Helena glances over her shoulder, her gaze meeting mine, and I offer her a little wave.

She scowls and looks away, shifting closer to her husband as they leave the field.

"What exactly did you say to her?" Tony asks me.

My smile is mysterious. "Nothing much. Did you want to meet at the hotel later? After your party?"

"After? Uh, I don't know if you realized it, but you're going to the party with me," he corrects.

"I thought it was just for the team." I frown.

"You're definitely invited. I can't celebrate tonight's win

without you. Hell, my dad probably could've gone too, but I didn't want Helena there. I kind of hate her." Tony chuckles. "You know you want to go. They'll have free food and booze."

"Of course I'll go. It sounds amazing," I tell him, excited to celebrate their win. I rise up as he bends his head down, our lips meeting for a brief kiss. "Can't wait."

"Maybe I can stay in your room tonight?" he asks. The team has to share rooms when they travel for away games to cut down costs, and he's rooming with Caleb. Diego and Eli are together, and Jackson is rooming with another teammate, I can't remember his name.

I still can't believe Jackson remained on the team. He's been wined and dined by multiple record companies the last couple of months, but he hasn't committed to any of them yet. He claims he's not sure if it's even something he wants to do. And he doesn't want a bunch of executives in suits trying to stifle his creativity—a direct quote.

I get where he's coming from, but everyone else thinks he's crazy. They believe he should jump on the money and chase the fame.

"Are you allowed to stay in another room?" I ask Tony.

"I don't know. I sort of don't care. You're staying at the same hotel, so what's the big deal," Tony says with a shrug. He glances around before he pulls me in for another too brief kiss. "I want to be with you later. Just the two of us."

I'm not going to protest.

I want to be with him too.

"OH MY GOD," I say with a moan, arching beneath him just before he rolls off of me and climbs off the bed. I lie in the middle of the mattress in an exhausted, barely breathing heap of satisfaction while Tony's in the bathroom.

I stretch before tugging the comforter over me, and close my eyes. Life is good. Way too good. And I don't even have that foreboding feeling like I used to have, when I worried that the rug was going to be pulled out from beneath my feet and all the good would turn to bad.

A lot of that is thanks to Tony.

Minutes later and he's climbing back into bed, pulling me into his arms. I go willingly, settling my head against his chest where I can hear the steady beat of his heart. He gives me a squeeze and I run my hand back and forth across his ridged stomach, smiling when I feel his muscles contract beneath my fingertips.

"That was amazing," I whisper. I didn't expect us to have sex tonight, but I'm not complaining. I figured he'd be exhausted from the game, the excitement afterward from winning, the party that went on for hours. It's so late, almost three in the morning, and I can barely keep my eyelids open.

I'm not the one who played an intense football game either.

"Yeah, it was," he agrees. I lift my head, dropping a kiss on his firm jaw.

"You were a little unhinged," I whisper. We've become more and more comfortable with each other sexually. As in, we're getting a little more experimental.

It's been fun.

He glances down at me, amusement dancing in his dark eyes. "You were the one smashing your pussy on my face."

"I know. It felt good." I shrug, owning it.

"You were a little out of control too."

"You make me excited."

"Oh, I know," he says dryly and I smack his shoulder. He laughs. "It was good." A pause. "It's always good."

"So good," I say on a sigh.

We remain quiet. The curtains are still parted, showcasing a gorgeous view of the Las Vegas city lights, and I think about how I should close those curtains soon because when the sun comes up, it's going to be brutal.

But I don't move. It's like I can't. Tony doesn't move either. We're too content. Too tired.

"Sophie sent me a congratulations text," he admits, his voice whisper-soft.

I stir against him. "Really?" Hearing her name used to fill me with intense jealousy, I'm not going to lie, but I started reminding myself that I have Tony now, not her. And then I realize what he did to her, how he shut her out and she broke up with him because she felt like she had no other choice. Now I just feel sorry for her. That she didn't get to keep him. Enjoy him more, like I do.

But that's okay. He's mine now. I love him.

And he loves me.

"Yeah. She saw me on our local news. I think her parents saw it, actually. She told me she's happy for me," he says as he rakes his fingers through my hair.

"That was nice of her."

"I thought so too. I just wanted you to know. Didn't want to keep it from you." He stays quiet only for a moment. "My mom says I'm on a karmic voyage of discovery, how I'm reconnecting with people and finding closure with some of them."

My hand goes still on his stomach. "That's...interesting."

He chuckles, the sound rumbling in his chest, against

my ear. "Right? She's become very spiritual lately. Reading all sorts of self-help books."

"She gave me that set of affirmation coasters for Christmas," I remind him.

"Exactly. Burning candles and collecting crystals. You should see her Buddha collection. She has a lot of them," he says. "We're not even Buddhists. She says she likes the vibe they bring to the house and yard. Looking at them gives her peace."

"Whatever helps bring her peace. I won't judge." My eyes fall closed, finding my own peace with this gorgeous, thoughtful, smart man lying beside me.

"I told her the same thing." He drops a kiss on my forehead. "Thank you."

My eyes pop open. "For what?"

"For giving me a chance. For sticking by my side. For tolerating my bullshit."

"Um, right back at you," I tell him, my hand starting to drift once more. "I'm ridiculous sometimes."

"So am I," he says, sucking in a breath when my hand settles gently over his burgeoning erection.

The guy never stops. It's one of my favorite traits of his.

"I love you," I murmur as I begin to stroke him.

"You're just saying that so we'll do it again," he accuses, and I can hear the laughter in his voice.

"Is it working?" I ask innocently.

"Always," he murmurs.

Just before he kisses me.

EPILOGUE

TONY

I'M WALKING by the library, minding my own business when I hear a low whistle sound somewhere to my left. I glance over at the cluster of picnic tables nearby and spot my girlfriend sitting at one of them, her best friend right next to her. The both of them trying to act like they don't see me, looking everywhere else but in my direction.

Of course I know Hayden's the one who whistled at me. She's been doing it a lot lately. She's kind of weird sometimes, but I love her.

Pausing, I lower the shades on my face, so I can peer over my sunglasses at the two of them. Gracie barely looks my way before nudging Hayden in the ribs. My girl smiles at me and waves. "Hey sexy."

Chuckling, I approach them, stopping beside the bench they're sitting on. They both scoot over, allowing me some room, and I settle in right beside Hayden, reaching for her. Kissing her. "I'm done," I murmur against her lips.

"Yay!" She throws her arms up in the air before wrapping them around my neck, giving me another, longer kiss.

"Ew," Gracie says, making a face. We both glare at her. She laughs. "You guys are gross."

"You're just jealous of our love," Hayden says teasingly, and I tighten my arms around her waist. I refuse to let go of her.

It's like I can't.

"You know I'm not jealous. I'm actually really happy for you guys," Gracie says with a wistful sigh.

It's the end of the spring semester. I just took my last final. I'm officially done with my freshman year. And it's been better than I could've ever expected. I went into this school year a little nervous, not expecting much, and crossing my fingers I'd pass my classes.

Instead, I started on a championship winning football team, I made the Dean's list for the fall semester and will most likely do the same for the spring, and I've fallen in love. I've even reformed a tentative relationship with my parents. A good one too, especially with my mother.

Didn't give her back Millicent though, even when she asked. Millicent is my cat now. Mom got herself a teacup yorkie instead. She named him Mr. Nutters.

Whatever.

"Are we celebrating the end of the semester tonight?" Hayden asks me.

I can think of the many ways I want to celebrate with just Hayden tonight, but I know that's not what she's referring to. "We're having a barbecue at our place. Everyone's invited." I say this specifically to Gracie.

She makes a face. "Including Caleb?"

"Gracie. He lives there," I deadpan.

She rolls her eyes. "I was hoping he was excluded from the festivities."

"Will Jackson be there?" Hayden asks, her eyes lighting

up. She has a slight thing for him, but I don't mind. He still hasn't signed with a record company yet. He's playing hard to get, and hopefully it's working for him. He recently produced a couple of his own singles thanks to his dad's money, and one of them got major airplay.

He's turning into kind of a big deal. We're going to be able to say we knew him when, I'm pretty sure of it.

"Yes, your secret boyfriend will be there." I bop her nose with my index finger and she laughs. "He says he has an announcement."

"Oooh, I wonder what his announcement will be." She frowns. "He hasn't mentioned anything to me yet."

She's kidding. We like to joke that Jackson is Hayden's side boyfriend. He has no idea we make this joke either. Jackson doesn't talk much to Hayden. He doesn't talk much to any of us lately. He's been too busy. Once football was finished, he was off, taking only a couple of classes on campus and some online, while the rest of the time, he's in the studio making music.

I don't know if he'll be on the football team this next year. As of right now, his name is still on the roster. But things could change. He's pursuing his passion and he's throwing his entire self into it. He can't do that if he's playing football *and* doing the music thing. Eventually he's going to have to choose.

Can't wait to see where his path takes him.

"Jake will be there tonight," I tell Hayden.

"Oh, that's so great." She met him at Christmas, and she got along great with him and Hannah. Of course she did.

Hayden gets along with pretty much everyone. Except my stepmother. But no one likes her. I don't even think my father likes Helena much anymore. Which is probably for the best. I don't trust her. My father shouldn't either.

"Yeah, I'm excited to spend time with Jake. We all are," I say, pushing all thoughts of my dad and his wife firmly out of my mind. Why focus on the bad stuff, when there is so much good happening right now?

"What time do you want us coming over?" Gracie asks me.

"Around six? Food will be on the grill by then. There will be beer."

"I'm making white wine spritzers," Hayden adds.

"Ooh, delicious," Gracie says with a smile. "Can't drink too much though, since I'm driving over."

"You can stay the night," I suggest.

"And risk having to listen to Caleb fuck his latest conquest all night long?" Gracie firmly shakes her head. "No thank you."

Those two are still going at it. They're either friendly, or at war. It's exhausting.

I think they enjoy it.

"I'll stay the night," Hayden murmurs to me and I kiss her again. Unable to resist, as usual.

"That was always the plan." I squeeze her close, my ass going numb considering it's half hanging off the bench seat. "I'm out of here." I rise to my feet.

"So are we," Hayden says, and they both stand as well. "We were just waiting for you to get out of class."

"Really?"

Gracie nods. "We do that a lot for you."

Hayden nudges her, making Gracie laugh. "We were done with finals yesterday, remember?" Hayden asks me.

Yeah, I remembered. Sort of.

Okay, maybe I forgot a little.

I go to my girlfriend and wrap her up in my arms, kissing her soundly. "You're the best."

"Don't ever forget it," she says, smiling up at me.

Oh, I won't.

THERE ARE SO many people crowded in our condo and our tiny backyard, it's kind of blowing my mind. Even better? They're all people I know and care about.

"You know how to throw a bash," Jake says as he stands beside me, watching me turn chicken on the grill. "I'm fucking starving."

"There's food inside," I tell my friend and he grins at me.

"And miss watching a future barbecue master work his magic at the grill? No way." Jake takes a sip from the beer bottle he's clutching.

Jake and Hannah showed up at the condo before everyone else, allowing us the time to catch up with them. Caleb and I asked Jake all sorts of questions about football and the team at USC, to the point that Jake said he couldn't say anymore because he felt like he was revealing trade secrets. We laughed, acting like he's joking with us, but I think he was kind of serious.

Hannah suddenly approaches us, a plate full of chips and salsa, vegetables and dip and crackers and cheese in her hands. "Here you go," she delivers to Jake with a kiss.

"Thanks, babe," he says, immediately digging in.

"No wonder you didn't care about going inside to get food. You had someone taking care of you," I say to him once Hannah is gone.

He grins, munching on a baby carrot. "She's good to me. Like, it's better than ever between us."

"I'm glad you two are still together." I flip the pieces of chicken yet again, that satisfying sizzle music to my ears.

"We ran into Sophie a couple of weeks ago," he says conversationally.

I don't even visibly react. It's no big deal. Thinking about her doesn't make me feel like shit anymore. It doesn't make me feel anything at all beyond a fondness for her. Nostalgia more than anything else.

That was a different time. And I was a different person then.

"She looks good," he continues. "She was checking out the USC campus. They have a great dance program there, and I guess she made it in for the next semester. We saw her at a restaurant that's not too far from school."

"Cool." I nod. Slather barbecue sauce on a couple pieces of chicken before I turn the flame down to low. "I'm glad she's doing well."

"She said the same thing about you." When I glance over at Jake, I see he's watching me. "Yeah, we talked about you. I'm glad you found Hayden, man. I liked Sophie, but I think Hayden's better for you."

"I think so too," I say with a smile, pleased that Jake likes her. "She likes you and Hannah too."

"You guys should come down to Los Angeles and hang out with us for the weekend over the summer," he suggests.

"I'd love to. I'll check with Hayden, though I'm sure she'd be down."

"Down for what?" Caleb magically appears, a beer in hand and a girl under his arm. And it's not just any girl either.

It's Baylee. Shit.

"Hey, Baylee," I say to her, and Jake does the same, the both of us completely unenthusiastic.

It's not that we don't like Baylee, I just hate what Caleb is doing to her. The back and forth has gotta get old. You'd think Baylee would put her foot down and say enough is enough.

But I guess not.

"I told Tony he should bring Hayden and visit Hannah and I later this summer," Jake says.

Caleb nods. "That sounds fuckin' awesome. I'd love to hang out with you guys. Go to the beach, pick up some babes."

He says this in front of Baylee and she doesn't even blink.

"Sounds fun," she says, glancing up at Caleb with stars in her eyes.

Oh man.

We keep up the conversation, talking about—of course —football, and Baylee eventually leaves us by ourselves. The moment she's gone, Caleb frowns, draining his beer bottle before he says, "I need to break it off with that chick once and for all."

"Yeah, you do," Jake agrees mildly. "You're just stringing her along."

"How would you know? You haven't even been here," Caleb says defensively.

"You did the same thing to her in high school. I don't think much has changed," Jake points out.

"True." Caleb looks miserable. "I'm a dick."

"At least you can admit it," I say, Jake and I laughing.

I eventually take the chicken off the grill and throw a couple of burgers and hot dogs on. I take the plate of chicken into the kitchen, where Hayden is holding court with the rest of the women, making her wine spritzers for them as they all chat and laugh. Hannah, Gracie, Ava, Ellie,

Jocelyn and Baylee. Diego is in the living room with his baby girl, Gigi, and Eli. They're in some sort of competition with each other, trying to get Gigi to walk to them first.

"Ooh that smells wonderful," Jocelyn says when she spots me. "I'm starving."

"Everyone is, I think." I set the platter on the counter and the girls grab paper plates, ready to fork it up. "Save some for us."

The women laugh, ignoring me completely.

I hear the front door slam and I glance up to find Jackson ambling into the kitchen without a care in the world. He recently cut his hair, and while it's still long on top—his blond locks hanging in his face always make the girls go wild—it's shorter on the sides. Despite the shorter hair, he's got the rocker vibe going on strong, with the torn jeans and the faded black T-shirt. Chains around his neck and rings on his fingers. An unfamiliar girl under each arm.

Damn. What is with these guys tonight?

"I've got good news," Jackson says with a grin, his gaze sweeping over the women who are all staring at him, their appetites forgotten. "Hey, ladies."

"Hey, Jackson," they all say like the fangirls they are. The only one who looks pissed is Ellie. She's glaring at the girls. Glaring at Jackson.

Ouch.

"What's up? Is this your big announcement?" I ask him.

"Yeah. Where's everyone else?" Jackson asks me as he approaches me. "This is Lydia and Linda by the way. They're twins."

"No, we're not," one of them says, playfully swatting at his chest.

"Oh. My bad." He grins at me. "They just look exactly

alike. And their names sound the same. I can't tell them apart."

I roll my eyes. I wonder if he's banged them both. Together. At the same time.

Probably.

"They're outside," I answer Jackson, jerking my thumb toward the sliding glass door that leads to the tiny yard. "Want me to get everyone inside?"

"I'll do it." Jackson makes his way to the door, the girls still firmly under his arms, as he shouts for our friends to come in.

Within minutes we're all crammed into the kitchen, Jackson remaining close to the slider, the girls flanking him, smiling up at him adoringly. "I've got news. I know I said I wanted to hang out with you all this summer, but you're all going to have to miss me instead, because I'm going on tour!"

We all start cheering for him, offering our congratulations. Jackson takes it all in, a smile on his face, looking pleased. There are all sorts of questions and he answers them, and the gist of it is this: he hired a management team in the spring, and they were able to book some gigs for him up and down the West Coast. Small venues mostly. Some outside, at festivals and fairs. He doesn't care where they're at, as long as he can perform live. It's his favorite thing to do, he says.

"What about football?" Diego asks him.

"We'll see where this tour takes me," Jackson says with a shrug. "I have gigs scheduled through July, so I still have time to return for practice if that's the choice I make."

If he blows up any bigger, he'll leave us. I'll miss him. He's become an integral part of our friend group. Eli will flounder without him, especially with Ava going away to college.

"And no, I haven't signed a record deal yet. I'm still waiting for the right offer to come along," Jackson adds with a shit eating grin. "Now where's the food? I'm fucking hungry."

Lydia and Linda are in a race to prepare him a plate and I watch it all unfold with amusement.

Until I smell something burning.

"Ah shit."

I run outside to the grill, flipping the lid open to find my burgers are black circles of coal and the hot dogs are shriveled and burned to a crisp. "Damn it," I mutter, scraping everything up with my spatula and dumping it all on a paper plate so I can throw it away. Thank God I bought extra.

I toss the burned meat and put new burgers and dogs on the barbecue, telling myself I can't leave. It's hot as balls out here though, and I'm sweating within minutes.

"Here you go, hottie."

I glance over to see Hayden standing beside me, looking sexy in a red tank and denim shorts, a chilled glass of wine in her hand. She hands it to me. "Try my spritzer."

I do as she says, and damn, that's delicious. "Refreshing," I tell her after a couple of gulps. I resume grill duty, not about to let shit get burned again. "Thank you."

"Exciting about Jackson, right?"

"Definitely," I say, my gaze never straying from the grill.

"We should go watch him if he performs somewhere close."

"For sure."

"Did you see Ellie though? She looked pissed that he

brought those girls with him." I glance over at Hayden just in time to see her roll her eyes.

"She probably is pissed." Ellie and Hayden have become friends, which is nice to see. Ellie could learn a thing or two from my ball buster. Girl needs to get a spine and Hayden is just the woman to teach her how.

"I know. We've talked about him. She realizes she's a complete sucker for anything he does, and I told her she needs to learn to stand up for herself." Hayden glances over her shoulder inside the condo. "Honestly, I think she should move on."

"She probably should," I agree.

"And then there's Caleb." She sighs loudly. Grabs my glass from where I left it and takes a big gulp. "What is up with him and Baylee?"

"They did this in high school too. It's annoying." I flip my burgers. Turn the hot dogs.

"You're so sexy at the barbecue." Hayden sidles up to me, slipping her arm around my waist. "I'm glad we're not in the middle of a bunch of drama."

"I hate drama," I tell her seriously. "You should know this by now."

"Oh, I do, Mr. Calm, Cool and Collected." I bend down to drop a kiss on her upturned lips. "I guess we'll let all of our friends indulge in the drama and we'll just watch out for them."

"That's all we can do," I tell her, kissing her again before I gently shove her away and swat her on the ass. "Now get out of here. You're distracting me. I already burned the first round of burgers and hot dogs."

She laughs, doing a little shimmy as she heads for the sliding glass door. "Love you," she calls, waving her fingers at me.

"I love you too," I murmur to myself, watching her go, my gaze lingering on her shiny blonde hair.

Damn. How'd I get so lucky?

JACKSON RIVERS' story is next in The Sophomore, coming June 17th! Keep reading for a sneak peek!

THE SOPHOMORE EXCERPT
CHAPTER ONE

Ellie

The text notification shows up every night at approximately the same time. I wait up for it, anticipation racing through my veins as usual. Anything to do with him has me on the edge of my seat, which is ridiculous.

He doesn't feel the same way about me. It's clear. It's been clear for a while. My friends tell me I'm wasting my time on him, but I can't help it. I care about him.

Too much.

I lie in bed with the lights off, my phone in my hand as I scroll TikTok. I work mostly nights during the summer anyway, so I'm usually up till the early morning hours. He knows this. He's currently traveling the west coast and has a hard time sleeping too.

Jackson: **You around?**

I smile, my heart rate kicking up. I decide to make him wait until the two minute repeat notification pops up, and then I'll answer him. Not like he's sitting around waiting for my reply. i get this image of him living this glamorous, bohemian life. Traveling in a tour bus his dad actually bought for him, writing lyrics and having spontaneous jam sessions with his newfound band members.

What I don't try and think about are the groupies who he could be getting with on a nightly basis. The girls go crazy for him. His social media has blown up since he's gone on tour, and most of his followers—and fans—are women. I'm scared he'll find so much success, he won't come back here.

Worse, I'm scared I'll never really see him again.

This is why I live for the nightly text conversations. Just like we used to have when we were in high school. Back then, I thought they meant so much more to me than they did to him, and that secretly devastated me. Especially when we'd be together at a party or whatever, and sometimes he'd act like I didn't exist.

He's a terrible human sometimes, I swear. But there's something about him that's so appealing. He's charming. A natural charisma you can't help but be drawn to. Oh, and then there's his face. and the way he looks at me when he sings his songs.

As if he's singing them to me.

According to my best friend Ava, I let him take advantage of my kindness. She's probably right. I'm a nice person. Too nice. Tony Sorrento's girlfriend Hayden has been giving me lessons lately in standing up for myself and learning how to not take any shit. I love her. She's my mentor. I hope to be just like her when I grow up.

I mean, she's only around three years older than me, but still. She's strong and smart and she doesn't back down from anything. While I'm quiet and shy and sometimes a little scared of trying something new. Ava doesn't take any crap either. She stands up for what she believes in no matter what. I'm going to miss her. She's going away to college. Her boyfriend isn't too happy about it either, but we can't convince her to stick around. If we try that, it'll push her to leave even more. She's kind of stubborn.

I wish I was more like her. And Hayden too.

Jackson's text pops up again and I tap it, contemplating my reply. I decide to keep it simple.

Me: **Hey! What's up?**

The gray bubble pops up, surprising me. Maybe he was waiting for me to respond.

Jackson: **Nothing much. Tired. Homesick.**

Me: Getting tired of traveling already?

He's been gone over a month. He said he'd come back at the end of July so he could be back at school in time for football practice, which is about three weeks before classes start. He claims he's going to be on the team again this season, but I don't know. How is he going to do that? His entire life is changing, and he's currently split in two directions. He's going to have to make a choice soon, and I'm thinking he'll give up football.

Jackson: **Yeah. I miss sleeping in my own bed.**

I wish for once he'd say he misses me. He misses my smiling face. Something, anything like that would send me over the moon.

Of course, it would also send my expectations soaring sky high and I'd end up sorely disappointed when I found out yet again that Jackson isn't interested in me like that. I'm a friend in his eyes.

That's. It.

Shoving all negative thoughts aside, I focus on our conversation.

Me: **Where did you perform tonight?**

Jackson: **At an outdoor music festival on the outskirts of Seattle. It was so fuckin cool, E. We went to the place where Kurt Cobain killed himself.**

Me: **Uh, that's gruesome.**

Jackson: **He's my fuckin idol, you know this. Anything that has to do with him, I want to see. Fuck, I want to absorb whatever I can. Seattle is an amazing city.**

I've never been there. I haven't been many places, really. I didn't even bother applying to colleges anywhere else. I chose Fresno State because it's close, and thank God I got in. I'm not adventurous. Not even close.

Me: **I can see you living in Seattle.**

Jackson: **I would've come up here in a heart-beat if it was the 90s. But it's not. The music scene is cool here, but not like back then. Those were the good days.**

Me: **I think you were meant for another time.**

Jackson: **I think you're right.**

We talk a little more about his travels. Where he's going next. When he's coming home. He says record executives are chasing after him, trying to get him to sign deals. But he's not ready to tie himself down with anything. He claims he's not sure if this is what he really wants.

Me: **You're going to have to make a choice sometime.**

Jackson: **I'll keep up the dual life as long as I can. I'm only nineteen. I want to go party with my friends too, you know? This is starting to feel like a grind. Like a job.**

Me: **Are you performing at Strummers when you come back home?**

Jackson: **Yeah. I have a performance lined up for July 31st. Didn't I tell you? Though I'm coming home on the 27th so I can have a little time to relax. I can't wait.**

My heart cracks wide open. He'll be home in less than three weeks. I can't wait to see him.

Me: **It'll be nice to have you back.**

Jackson: **Can't wait to see you.**

He sends me a heart emoji.

Don't read too much into that. Don't do it. Don't.

Me: **I'm sure you have plenty of female company.**

Jackson: **They're not you though.**

He doesn't deny he's with other girls, which I'm sure he is. Can't focus on that though. That's a downward spiral I don't want to go down right now.

Me: **I'm glad we're friends.**

There. What can he say to that? We are friends. And that's all we're gonna be. That's all he'll allow.

He doesn't respond and I keep scrolling TikTok, my eyelids growing heavier and heavier. I'm tired. It's already past two. I need to go to sleep. I work at eleven tomorrow, so I won't get to sleep in as much as I usually do when I close.

Jackson: **Sometimes I wonder why we're not more than that, E. Why are you always so good to me? I don't deserve you.**

I stare at what he wrote, reading it again and again. He's right. He doesn't deserve me. And he doesn't mean it when he says he wonders why we're not more than that.

Me: **Because we both know it would never work.**

Jackson: **Right. I'd mess it up.**

Me: **You would. Oh, and you're right.**

Jackson: **What about?**

Me: **You don't deserve me.**

Me: **You never really have.**

Want more? Preorder The Sophomore, coming to Kindle Unlimited June 17th!

WANT A FREE BOOK? SIGN UP!

Dear Readers,

I hope you enjoyed **THE FRESHMAN!** If you haven't already, please sign up for my newsletter so you can stay up to date on my latest book news. Plus, you'll get a **FREE** book by me, just for signing up! Click below:

Monica Murphy's Newsletter

Are you on Facebook? You should join my reader group! That's where you find out all the good book news FIRST! Click below to hang out with us:

Monica Murphy's Reader Group

ACKNOWLEDGMENTS

Starting a new series is scary, but it's a little easier with the **College Years** series, thanks to so many familiar faces from the Callahans series. I knew as I wrote the **Callahans** books that I would need to write books for their friends and well, here we finally are. I hope you love Tony and Hayden and the rest of the gang as much as I do.

Thank you always to my publicist Nina and the rest of the gang at Valentine PR. Y'all are the absolute BEST. To my editor Becky for her careful insight and telling me where I messed up. This story is better thanks to you. Also to Sarah for the excellent proofreading and to my scariest beta reader Brittany U who breaks it all down every time. Hang Le, thank you for the beautiful cover.

To my daughter, for all of the stories throughout her high school years. For being so open with me, always. Who's graduating high school and going to college so YAY hopefully she'll still tell me all of her funny and sometimes even heartbreaking stories. She's a font of inspiration.

Finally, to the readers. Thank you for reading my books, and for picking this one up. I hope you enjoyed it.

It would mean the world to me if you could take a few minutes and leave an honest review for **The Freshman**.

Thank you.

ALSO BY MONICA MURPHY

Standalone

Things I Wanted To Say (but never did)

College Years

The Freshman

The Sophomore

The Junior

The Senior

Dating Series

Save The Date

Fake Date

Holidate

Hate to Date You

Rate A Date

Wedding Date

Coming 10/19!

Blind Date

The Callahans

Close to Me

Falling For Her

Addicted To Him

Meant To Be

Coming 2/10/21!

Making Her Mine

Forever Yours Series

You Promised Me Forever

Thinking About You

Nothing Without You

Damaged Hearts Series

Her Defiant Heart

His Wasted Heart

Damaged Hearts

Friends Series

Just Friends

More Than Friends

Forever

The Never Duet

Never Tear Us Apart

Never Let You Go

The Rules Series

Fair Game

In The Dark

Slow Play

Safe Bet

The Fowler Sisters Series

Owning Violet

Stealing Rose

Taming Lily

Reverie Series

His Reverie

Her Destiny

Billionaire Bachelors Club Series

Crave

Torn

Savor

Intoxicated

ABOUT THE AUTHOR

Monica Murphy is a New York Times, USA Today and international bestselling author. Her books have been translated in almost a dozen languages and has sold over two million copies worldwide. Both a traditionally published and independently published author, she writes young adult and new adult romance, as well as contemporary romance and women's fiction. She's also known as USA Today bestselling author Karen Erickson.

facebook.com/MonicaMurphyAuthor

instagram.com/monicamurphyauthor

bookbub.com/profile/monica-murphy

goodreads.com/monicamurphyauthor